A Curious Collection

STORIES AND POEMS

Robert J. Dockery

Author of

A Lesson in Love

A CURIOUS COLLECTION

An Imprint of Hafroke Books
COPYRIGHT © 2020 by Robert J. Dockery
All rights reserved.
Printed in the United States of America
Hafroke Books of Tarpon Springs, Florida
None of the names, persons, events, or situations depicted in the stories are real, or based on real persons. Liberties are taken with the geography and locale descriptions.
Some of the individual works have been previously published in various media.
Paperback ISBN: 978-0-578-66709-6
e-book ISBN: 978-0-578-66712-6
Library of Congress Cataloging-in-Publication Data
Author: Robert J. Dockery
A Curious Collection / Robert J. Dockery
First Edition, 2020
Cover design by Kathleen M. Vorperian

This book is dedicated to my wife, Sheila, our four daughters Anne and Mary (who are no longer with us), Kathleen and Elizabeth, their spouses, and to my grandson, Daniel, and my granddaughter, Adrianna. It is also dedicated to the family and friends who over the years have been good and faithful companions and soul mates.

Table of Contents

"The only things worth learning are the things you learn after you know it all."

- ***Harry S. Truman***

Author's Note

The works presented in this collection were written during the period roughly 1998 to 2019. They represent a variety of moods and genre. Most reflect life before the explosion of electronic communication and digital media platforms. Where each falls in the table of contents is not related to when it was written. Some were written with a particular magazine or journal in mind. A few have been published previously in various print media. The ones chosen have been chosen because I like them. I trust you will like reading them. None is particularly long, and most of the stories can be read in five to ten minutes.

Acknowledgements

I would be remiss if I did not point out that this collection of writings is assembled, edited and published only because of the encouragement and assistance of Doctor David C. Edmonds, a wonderful friend, and accomplished educator and author of over thirteen novels and documentary books, including: Yankee Autumn in Acadiana, Lily of Peru, The Girl in the Glyphs, The Heretic of Grenada, and Flamenco in the Time of Moonshine and Mobsters. I thank him for all that he has done.

I also thank my daughter Elizabeth Bugliarello-Wondrich, John Robert Davison, Joan Jennings, Lor Pearson, Joan Tobey, and my daughter Kathleen Vorperian, for their willingness to assist in reading, commenting, and editing. Their help was tremendous.

Kathleen Vorperian created the artistic cover design utilizing her amazing digital skills and suggested the title.

Rebecca Emlinger Roberts, a well-known essayist, has given me her thoughts on poetry and essays which helped in choosing works to be included in this collection; though, she would not necessarily agree with all of my selections.

Members of the Tarpon Springs Florida library writers group have, from time to time over the years, given critiques of some of the selected works. Such critiques have always resulted in better results, and to them I am also indebted.

Cops and Robbers

The idea of a holdup comes to me while I wait in line with my friend Chunky Bert at Fatso's Emporium, a little fast food restaurant that doesn't even have a safe. With all its Formica and chrome and the linoleum floor, Fatso's is in a time warp—a place where my grandpa would feel at home. Its owner is as clueless about protecting the money he takes in as he is about how old and crappy the place looks.

I decided to enlist my friend Chunky as my accomplice. "Got a great idea, Chunky, a plan to get us some walking around money."

"Ain't into robbin' banks yet. I'm waitin' until next year when I'm eighteen."

"I'm serious, Chunky."

"So am I. Robbing a bank is easier than bein' a workin' slob all your life like your dad."

"I am not talking bank heists."

Chunky bobs his head from side to side like he wants me to know he's thinking about my idea. He says, "I'm starvin' to death. If I don't get somethin' to eat pretty soon, I'll die. Let's get us some food first. Then you can tell me about it."

Three evenings a week, a kid from my high school stands behind the counter with that weird grin of his, taking orders and working the cash drawer. His real name is Arnold, but he started bragging once about how he was bigger than the real Arnold. Chunky started calling him, Mister Sausage.

Robbing the place is so simple. Me and Chunky will walk in with toy guns. I have one from when we played cops and robbers, an old silver cowboy pistol I got from my Gramps a long time ago. I think he got it from his dad. It looks like a real gun but only shoots off caps. I don't have any caps to shoot in it. Gramps said you used to buy them in rolls. Each time you pulled the trigger; the hammer came down on a cap and made a bunch of noise.

I tell Chunky my plan. "We'll come in and tell Arnold we want the cash."

We know from talking to Arnold that they hide the extra cash under the counter near the register. A half-hour before the place closes, the owner stops by the joint and takes most of the cash to the night depository at the Bank. He hides the cash drawer in the old wooden desk in his office.

The old lady in the line in front of us turns around. She stares daggers at me. At first, I think she must have overheard me talking. I'm thinking maybe I should tell her we were only joking. She turns back around to give Arnold her order. I relax.

Even though we've known each other since the first grade, when it's my turn Arnold doesn't even say, "Hi. Gino." He just looks at me and hollers into the stupid, dorky microphone he wears, "One special with a large orange brain freezer." Then he laughs at his own dumb joke like it was the first time he ever called my slushy order a brain freezer. All the while, he's punching at the little screen in front of him, so he doesn't even need to holler my order. I hand him a ten. He pops open his cash drawer to give me change.

I wait for Chunky to get his order. The two of us slide into a booth away from the other three customers. The place should have gone bust eons ago with so few customers. He takes a gigantic bite out of his burger and, with his mouth full and still chewing, says, "Every time you have an idea, I'm the one gets in trouble."

"Not this time. It's foolproof."

"Where have I heard that?"

"At least listen to the plan."

He chews and chews. "Okay, let's hear it," he finally says.

I tell him the details of my idea about holding up the place with toy guns. "You still have the plastic automatic your dad gave you a long time ago, the one used to have the orange barrel until you painted it black?"

"It's around the house, somewhere. I can always bring a real one that isn't loaded. Dad has an arsenal. He won't miss one gun if I borrow it for an evening."

"Don't do that. If you can't find the one you had when we used to play cops and robbers, I can bring an extra toy gun for you to use. I don't want it to feel like a real robbery."

Chunky takes another huge bite and washes it down with gulps of soda. He says, "You think Mister Sausage will go along?"

"Of course he will," I say. "Even split three ways, he'll get a nice bit of change to jingle in his pockets. Anyhow he's always complaining he has the shorts."

After a long exaggerated sigh, Chunky says, "It's almost quittin' time. Let's hang out here until we can talk to Mister Sausage in private."

We play games on our phones until all the customers and the owner have left. Arnold joins us.

He reacts well to my plan. "I'd call the plan brill. Totally awesome," he says, stamping his feet and clapping his hands. He's such a dork.

"I can count you in then?" I ask, not sure whether his reaction is only suck up or true glee at the opportunity to be part of my plan.

"I'm all in. I'll swipe some of my dad's pantyhose."

Chunky pulls a face and says, "Your dad wears pantyhose?"

"It's not like what you're thinkin', Chunky. He wears them for jogging, so he don't chafe. Professional runners do it too."

"Thanks, Mister Sausage, but I prefer to bring my mom's. You'd probably forget to wash them after your dad wore them."

"I meant for me to wear."

"You're behind the counter like always. You don't need to disguise yourself."

Arnold nodded. His dense brain is like a bowling ball—goes where you roll it. But he got the idea. "Yeah. Of course. I totally understand," he says. "What was I thinking? Tell me the plan one more time."

"We'll play the bad guys. We walk in. All you have to do is give us the money and tell the cops that two tough-looking robbers with guns held you up. We'll arrive near closing, so there won't be many people." I look around the place. "Like tonight. We just need a few to testify that you didn't steal the money yourself and to say you got, you know, robbed. There'll be lots of cash. You give us the money, we wave our toy guns around to scare the customers. Be here and gone before the owner comes in for his daily collection."

"You don't got to scare nobody."

"Yes, we do. If we don't act like real robbers, your boss might suspect it was an inside job with some of your friends acting as your co-conspirators."

"That's what I'm doin'."

"It's pretend. We're playing cops and robbers. They call it a caper like in the old movies–not a real robbery."

Chunky rolls his eyes. Arnold claps and says, "A caper. I like that."

Arnold gives each of us a refill on our slushies and a bag of French fries. He takes the rest of the left-over food scraps to the dumpster. Through the window, we see a couple of homeless people obviously waiting for him. Arnold doesn't just toss the stuff in the dumpster. Instead, he carefully picks out some items and hands them to the man and woman who have been waiting. He talks to them for a couple minutes and then comes back in to shut the place down. Me and Chunky show our appreciation for the fries and the slushies. We put the chairs up on the tables, so Arnold can do a quick go-around with the old, smelly mop they use on the floor.

I'm driving my 1969 Volkswagen Beetle. We stuff our co-conspirator in the back seat, so he won't have to walk the two miles home. He spends the whole trip thanking us for including him in the caper. Even though he was nice to the homeless couple, he's still a dork.

We drop Arnold off and head for my house. I turn to Chunky and say, "We're obliged to give ten percent to the Church. My dad does that. Mom too. It's only right to do that. Besides, it's not a bad thing. We will be doing it for the Church."

"How about one percent," Chunky says.

"Has to be ten. That's why they call it a tithe. The word means ten and not one. If it were one, the word would probably be, like, uno. You never hear anyone talking about an uno going to the Church."

"Okay. Done. Be sure to remind Mister Sausage, so he doesn't complain that we're skimmin' his cut of the loot. People get killed for that."

"I doubt that Arnold will kill us, but we best tell him."

"The math is simpler too. That'll make it 30% for each of us and 10% to Saint Andrew's. When you confess the robbery, don't forget to tell Father Grady that we're givin' the tithe. Maybe it will go easier for us."

"Wait a darn minute, Chunk. I'm not so sure that what we will be doing is a sin. If it's not a real robbery, then it's not a real sin."

He says, "Of course it is. You sound like Mister Sausage. We're takin' somethin' don't belong to us. That's a sin. Don't matter how we steal it."

I know that Chunky is wrong but not quite sure why, so I don't get into an argument with him about the morality of what we got planned. It is what it is.

Mom is already in bed when we arrive at my house. My father is away traveling for his company. Me and Chunky raid the refrigerator for cold beers. We settle ourselves in my dad's den for some TV baseball, but I can't find the control sticks.

"Guess we have to talk about the caper," Chunky says.

"Guess so."

"Mister Sausage works Monday, Tuesday, and Wednesday, so it has to be one of those nights."

"Let's go in each of those nights around the time we will be doing the actual caper and case the joint. They talk about how important it is to do that on all the TV crime shows."

"Good thinkin'. That'll give us an idea of the best night."

"As Arnold said, the idea is brilliant. And since it is my idea, I suppose that I'm brilliant too."

Chunky sneers. "Yeah. Right. I want another beer."

On Monday I go with Chunky to the Emporium. We are both kind of short on funds, so we only have slushies. Two tables out of the twelve have customers. All of them look as though they are escapees from the old folk's home down the street.

"Perfect," Chunky announces. "Too bad we ain't doin' it tonight."

"Not so quick," I say. "We got to do this right. We come back tomorrow and Wednesday too."

The next two nights, we find pretty much the same situation. None of the few customers in the place on either night appear to present a threat to two desperados waving guns. Like on Monday, they were all really ancient and way older than my dad. The younger customers mostly come in earlier.

Thursday, we tell Arnold that we'll pull off the caper on the following Monday. He agrees to try and make sure he's working that night. He also agrees to tell us if something comes up at the last minute, and he can't make it.

All weekend I run the plan over and over in my mind, thinking through every detail. On Monday, an hour before closing time, we arrive at the Emporium. Chunky decides to drive his dad's air-conditioned pickup because he thinks it's more appropriate than my VW for the caper.

We pull into the parking lot, empty except for one other pickup. We can see through the windows that Fatsos has no customers. We don't see the owner's car. So far. So good. Before we get out of the car into the warm, humid evening, we pull the stocking masks over our faces and slide the guns out of our pockets.

"No cops around," Chunky says.

"You sound like you got a bad cold Chunk."

"I'm using my deep voice. That's so we sound older than we are. You need to do it too. It helps if you put your chin against your chest."

"Then I can't see. You better do the talking. I'll grunt and wave my gun at the customers."

"Who owns the pickup?"

"Don't know. I think it's a guy who lives in that white house down the street."

"So, no customers."

"I know that. I mean, if any customers come in while we're doing the caper."

Me and Chunky walk into Fatsos. Chunky goes in first. His shoulders swing from side to side. The fingers of his free hand spear the air. He holds his gun sideways. He obviously thinks he looks tough, like the gang bangers we saw on one of the cop shows.

Chunky stops so unexpectedly that I bump into him; my fake gun goes flying into a corner and bounces off the floor. I run to retrieve it before anyone can see what I'd dropped. Out of the corner of my eye, I see what made Chunky stop short. A girl stands at the cash register. No Arnold anywhere.

The girl seems not to notice the guns or our disguises. She just stands there, staring at us.

"Where's Arnold?" I ask.

"He had to take off tonight."

"This is a holdup," Chunky says.

"I know. Arnold told me to expect you. There's only me and Tina back in the kitchen. I'm doing the drive-up and the walk-ins. Not much going on this time of night. Manager said we're closing early."

"Where's the manager?" I ask.

"He's gone home. Came in early tonight. Took the cash too, so there's only what's in the register. Tina's in charge." She glances at her watch. "You should've come in a half-hour ago. We close in a couple minutes."

Chunky slams his hand on the counter and says, "It's only 9:30. You close at 10:00." He sounds angry.

"Not my fault," She says. "The manager decided to close early. No customers. And anyhow, Tina has to get home. Her baby's got something wrong with him. I should've locked the doors already, but I was waiting for you guys."

I can't believe what I'm hearing. Arnold has spilled the beans on our caper and to a girl no less. What a dork. We didn't plan on our inside man taking the night off or telling some girl. The two of us must have looked scared because the girl says, "Don't worry. I told Tina about you guys coming in to hold up the place."

"Great," Chunky says and waves his gun around the empty room as if trying to intimidate a crowd of customers. "She probably called the cops the minute we came in."

"She did not. She has to get home. If she called the cops, they'd have her here 'till morning questioning her. Besides, what does she care about you taking what little is in the cash register?"

Chunky, still seeming super angry at the situation, says, "You didn't have to tell her."

"Sure did. Tina keeps a machete in back. If she came out here swinging that big old thing, no telling who might get hurt."

Chunky sits down at one of the tables. "What's your name?" he asks.

"Caitlin Moody. I recognize you from school. But I didn't put the names with the faces until you came in tonight."

Chunky says, "Tell Tina I want a free burger and a slushy for not robbin' you guys. Same for Gino."

"I'm not hungry, Chunky."

"It's okay," Caitlin says.

I didn't notice Father Grady, a small man with a heavy black beard that gave him a pirate look, come into the restaurant.

"A little early for Halloween boys," he says with a wide smile. He giggles.

Chunky springs out of his chair. He points the gun at Father Grady. "This is a stickup, Father. Don't move, or I'll mow you down."

Father Grady starts laughing. Then Caitlin laughs. A masked man pointing a gun is definitely not funny, but I start laughing too. Because of the stocking distorting his features, I can't tell if Chunky looks as angry as he sounds.

Thinking the gun is a harmless toy, I don't worry–until the gun goes off. The recoil flips the gun up, so that it points at the ceiling. Chunky doesn't hold onto it, and the gun drops with a clatter onto the floor. The force of the bullet hitting Father Grady in the shoulder makes him flinch to the left as if he wants to look around and see what's going on behind him. He stands wide eyed for a moment. His knees buckle.

Chunky, completely surprised by the gun's recoil, falls backward and lands on his butt. His jaw goes slack, and his eyes get wide. He grabs for the gun. My ears are ringing.

I hollered, "Chunk, what did you do?"

"It was an accident," he shouts. "I didn't mean it."

For an instant, I think Chunky is going to shoot me and Caitlin. He shoves his gun at me. I take it. He jumps to his feet and rips off his stocking mask. I see the desperation on his face. Tina comes out, waving her machete with one hand and waving her cell phone with the other.

Chunky runs out of the restaurant. I watch him through the glass. He sprints to his dad's truck and drives away with tires squealing.

I lean against the counter. My knees feel like they won't hold me up. I feel sick. My ears are still ringing.

Tina stuffs the phone in her apron pocket and lays the machete on a table. She kneels over Father Grady. For a moment, she studies his wound. "Caitlin, grab me a bunch of towels. We need to stop the bleeding." She turns to me and shouts, "You two assholes are really in trouble now. You move, and I cut you in half."

The police swarm in a few minutes later with guns all pointing in my direction. They shout different commands. I can't make out what any of them are saying. I can't blame them for being angry, with me holding a pistol in each hand and still having on my stupid stocking mask. I start to raise my hands but forget to drop the guns first. Last thing I remember hearing before waking up in the hospital is more gunshots and Caitlin screaming.

Shadowland

Every aspect of nature has something to say about who we are and the life we lead. We find ourselves on a sunlit planet with mountains, lakes and streams, valleys and plains, an atmosphere that creates weather and seasons and, living in all of these, flora and fauna. This is our environment—our womb, as well as our crucible.

Sitting in the shade of my porch on this wintry Florida day, I see a backyard teeming with life, from the tiniest of insects to the wild turkey that chanced to venture here—visiting from the nearby Brooker Creek Nature Preserve. A squirrel hides in the shadow of the laurel oak. Trees and shrubs and flowering plants dot the landscape. Beyond shrub and tree, fish and dolphin and shorebirds and all sorts of other creatures inhabit my bayou. And were it not for the brilliance of the sun, I could observe a galaxy of stars. All of these speak to me, though some—like the endless variations of light and dark, shadow and shade—only in a whisper.

We concoct comparisons with our environment and its elements—analogies, similes, and metaphors—to help us understand ourselves and others. Perhaps we do this because we are inseparable from what we see all about us. We are, after all, of the fauna. When we make such comparisons, we are commenting in a manner that illustrates our community with what we experience in nature. We are like our natural surroundings but different from them. In our comparisons, we position ourselves as something more than a product of the primordial ooze. In nature, there is neither good nor bad. These distinctions arise only when we humans step into the picture. We decide what is good and what is not good, what is right and what is wrong. We make value judgments.

Weather is the environmental feature that most regularly invades my consciousness. Consider, for example, temperature. I often think about how folks can be rude by giving someone the cold shoulder. That reference to chilly weather is obvious, as is the thought of a teenager worried about being cool. A young woman might see a popular boy as being hot but be disappointed if she gets to know him and decides he is cold. These observations are useful; however, there is another way to think of weather that can provide insight into human behavior. Discussion of climate change shows us how numerous people can see the same situation and behave quite differently toward it.

Some scientists tell us that our crucible is warming. It seems our situation may be somewhat analogous to sitting in a large pot and being boiled. There are those of us who take the matter seriously and strive to reduce the greenhouse gasses that attack the atmosphere. Others, who may have never read even one scientific journal or learned article, reduce the argument to partisan politics and mindlessly rail against findings that do not support their view—seeing them as tools of a political elite.

Still, others accept the findings and yet do nothing to improve the situation. These are the lukewarm thinkers, the ones who complain about hot summers but for all their talk cannot bring themselves to give up their gas guzzlers or set their thermostat a bit lower in the wintertime. Lukewarm toward all aspects of being, they are never enthusiastic or excited over important matters affecting their lives and their future. Liking but never loving, believing but never acting on those beliefs, sensing the malaise while content to ride it out and see what becomes of their world.

For now, let us set aside such weighty matters and dwell on more pleasant elements of our existence. I will tell you that my friends say I have a sunny disposition. I tend to be windy if trying too hard to explain simple concepts. When I'm cleaning, I come into a room that looks like a cyclone hit it and move through it like a tornado, leaving it clean and fresh as a spring breeze.

Sometimes the trees or the animals catch our attention and give rise to comparisons that help us consider the complexities of our personality and the personalities of those around us. A person might be sly as a fox or strong as an ox, a tree of a man. My friend, Eduardo, who works at the local bodega, acts like a sheep, easily led, easily persuaded. Perhaps he is that way because he never applied for citizenship and must live in the shadows. Nevertheless, I prefer strong willed and fearless people who are lion-hearted.

And so it goes. Beginners of low talent are bush leaguers. Devious people are snakes in the grass. I know a few of these. Usually, there is something fishy about them that you notice right away.

Am I peevishly invested in this tiny planet that sits in a milky way of a billion stars? If not, I certainly ought to be. I am its fauna, fauna given the ability to contemplate such things. This Earth is my home. It needs to be kept clean and tidy.

At this point, a listener may judge these comparisons to be tired clichés. Well, I'm sorry, but that person simply can't see the forest for the trees. (How many trees make a forest?) Clichés don't start as clichés. They only become so because they are the truth, so well stated that people won't let go of them. My listener fails to understand that—within the context of these observations—my reductive comparisons carry a fair amount of complexity. Earth scientists spend their time reducing the intricacies of nature to models from which they can derive theories. Their reductive comparisons make it possible to look more deeply into a natural phenomenon.

We seldom give much thought to what is under the earth's surface. That gets our attention only when volcanic magma from deep inside spews forth in a fiery spectacle. When I hear of a volcano erupting, I think of those unfortunates struggling with a borderline personality disorder that gives sway to fits of anger.

So, we see ourselves and those around us reflected in nature as well as seeing nature in us and in our evaluation of friends and associates. However, these are, again, relatively superficial comparisons. I need to look further to discover something in nature that provides an opportunity for deeper reflection. Eduardo's having to live in the shadows has got me thinking. For more profound analysis, I can look to a derivative of flora and fauna, namely, the shadows they cast both upon the landscape and upon various portions of their forms.

Except maybe in some fantasy world, shadows are not themselves objects but are dictated by the shape and movement of the objects which cast them. Bobbing and dancing on windy days, shadows that nature creates could reasonably think themselves free to move about, not connected or controlled in any manner with or by the objects creating them. As the puppet might look in a mirror and fail to observe the strings attached to its limbs, so we might see ourselves, ignoring for that moment all the rules and regulations, the fears, inhibitions, mores, the anxieties that restrict our ability to be truly free to think and do as we wish.

Not only are the shadows dependent on objects for their shape and size, their shape and size are also dictated by the sun. In daylight, shadows are captive of our sun as it appears to move across the sky, determining moment to moment how shadows behave. And after dark, the sun lights a moon that sits incongruously in the void of space, creating nighttime shadows.

Am I the unfortunate puppet, which not only failed to notice the strings but is ignorant of the puppeteer? Or am I, in truth, also the puppeteer?

In the early morning, the east side of a tree is lighted, and the west side is in shadow. If limbs on the east side are sparse, the tree appears ugly, though the west side may be full and lush and green. That same tree in the early evening, with the setting sun hiding the poor side in shadow, appears to be something quite different.

At what time of day do we present ourselves to the world? Do our prejudices cast shadows that cause us to reject simple truths and, in turn, cause us to make decisions that hurt our neighbors? Or do we present ourselves as a beautiful tree seen from the sunny side, treating everyone fairly and giving each what is due?

And how about in the evening. I look to the west. The world is in shadow against the failing light. Gazing westward, I see everything in silhouette, bathed in a soft–often multi-colored–glow.

Can I seek to shed the dark thoughts and moods into which I often fall by contemplating the beauty of the twilight and the light just beyond the twilight's glow? The dying day causes me to conjure thoughts of endings and the ultimate ending–death. Yet there is a beauty here in the colorful setting of the sun, awash in a complexity of colors and moods. There too is the thought that just beyond the twilight's glow lies a day to be lived, to be enjoyed even as I regret its passing.

I sit here in my old wicker chair—like me, unraveling in places—and, as the unmoving shadows creep into a new beginning, I think of what message these ever changing patterns are sending. My artist's eye tells me that the colors I observe are merely avatars for a continuum of tones, from dark to light. The structure of all that I can contemplate depends on the shadows, for only the shadows can define the light. You say only the light can define the shadows—a different perspective to be sure. Take your pick while the colors play upon your psyche, defining your mood.

One might say of an aging singer that he is a mere shadow of his former self, or observe that a politician casts a long shadow. Another message is there in the shadows, a message much more profound than any such direct comparisons. The shadows we meet in literature and our dreams are often dangerous and evil, cloaking improprieties or hiding a man in ambush lurking. During the daylight hours, shadows are usually seen as good—inviting, providing shade from the sun's heat. At night they are often seen as evil or dangerous. Which of us has not rested on a sunny day in the welcoming shade of a tree? But we speak of shadows, not shade. That is a value judgment.

When I mention here the thought of a value judgment, what do I intend to communicate? From flora and fauna, we can derive elements of truth as well as falsity, the real as well as the unreal. Where lies reality, and where lies merely the perception of reality? Are we so certain that we know which the ventriloquist is and which the dummy?

The midday sun creates shadows that are short compared to those I see in the morning and in the evening. In the evening, they stretch across my yard and over the fence and onto the property of my next-door neighbor. If he took the time to note their daily passing, I'm sure he would try to stop them from encroaching. He says he hates the long shadows. The law of nature to which he ascribes is survival of the fittest. But after he lost his grandparents along with many of the relatives of their generation at Bergen-Belsen—the Anne Frank camp—I would be wrong to blame him. So, I excuse his sometimes surly disposition. Yes. I am making a value judgment. Shade or shadow. You choose.

Shadows sway when the wind disturbs the tree canopy. But despite their steady and ineluctable progress across my yard, I cannot see their forward movement. Yes. Yes. Of course, I can see them move as the wind blows through the tree canopy and clouds pass overhead and animals dart about. I speak here of a specific sort of forward movement, of the passage of time, of progress, of diligent effort, of dedication to ideals, as well as to the task at hand.

No matter how I focus on the lengthening shadows, they move without moving. Let me just concentrate on one bit of shadow that is about to invade the flagstone walk leading down to the water. I will be able to see its progress because there is a definite line it must cross before the day is done and the sun slips below the rooftops to my west.

I recall incongruously that in his poem, "Say Not the Struggle Nought Availeth," Arthur Hugh Clough wrote, "And not by eastern windows only,/when daylight comes in the light,/in front, the sun climbs slow, how slowly,/but westward look the land is bright."

A raptor glides into my view, soaring over the bayou, most likely eyeing the small birds that come and go to and from my bird feeder. The little ones seem unafraid, or perhaps unaware, of the winged menace lurking above. The hawk glides in circles. What a majestic creature!

I glance back at the flagstones. Nature has played one of its many tricks on me, totally capturing my attention when I ought to have been studying the progress of shadows. In the short time I spent admiring the birds; shade has crept over the walk. The little bit of shadow I had focused on is nowhere to be seen, swallowed up by larger shadow mass, in a sense overtaken by something larger than itself. This is the sun's work, not of the trees that line the eastern boundary of my property. Is there a lesson here for me? Are there forces acting on me that will overtake whatever I attempt? Am I the little bit of shadow that must have been cast by a few leaves growing by themselves on an errant branch?

The ever-moving sun we know does not move around the Earth. We move. That is an altogether different relationship. The sun stands still in relation to us. So the shadows it creates are not its doing. The shadows move, but we do not see them moving. The earth rotates around the sun—always spinning, but we don't feel it spin. Nature is replete with apparent contradictions—so much like the way we lead our own lives—the more to confuse and frustrate us.

Not only in literature can we find comparisons of light and shadow to our own existence. Visual artists who study the flow of light prefer to paint a landscape in the early morning or the late afternoon. Shadows make a landscape come alive by giving depth to objects that appear flat in midday. Might I strive to bring a new dimension to my otherwise flat and uninteresting existence? At the very least, I can resolve to rise early, to paint outdoors, and catch the new day heralded by sunlight reflecting golden off high thunderheads. Perhaps one day I can do more.

That is for tomorrow. Right now, I see the lengthening shadows have overtaken even my neighbor's yard and are themselves being overtaken by the nighttime that creeps in from the east to lie upon the land and begin to define it differently.

The inviting shade of my favorite tree has become one of the dangerous and fearsome shadows encountered in nightmares. The shade of death abides in my little world. The shade is now a phantom, a spirit, a ghost, an ephemeral element signaling what may be the end of my worldly existence, another contradiction with which I need contend. How must I value the inviting shade of my beloved trees when shade can transform itself by mere dint of meaning to mark my end? Borrowing liberally from Shakespeare's sonnets, I might state boldly that death will not claim me for his own, his shade. Would I be wrong?

On such matters, I must not dwell. The distinction is, as I have noted, a value judgment. The reality of a frightening dream can be more real than the reality of our waking hours. Perhaps life is the dream, and what we perceive as truth is the nightmare.

I look up. Stars dot the heavens, forming a milky brew with light from a far distant past. Sitting here on my sagging wicker, I am at once traveling in time to each of those distant sources of light. My eyelids grow heavy. The contemplation of time travel will need to be put off to disturb my reverie another day.

The Osprey And The Mullet

~ — ~

The Osprey—also known as the fish hawk—is a bird of prey with long talons used to catch fish that the bird sees in the water as it circles, alert for its prey. It often nests near water and often carries its catch up into one of the nearby trees. The following verse is an ode to this marvelous bird.

The puckish mullet beats the running sea
With fins of silver-green.
An osprey lay with outstretched wings upon the humid air,
Lurking high above the water's flow
With world and time suspended in the sea below
Waiting for the mullet to venture toward the sky.
Hungry eyes locate the meal displayed upon the sea.
And the osprey dives in nature's testimony
To the hunter and its prey.
Then bird and fish fly away to a towering pine
Along the water's edge
Where the bird sings its elegy to the fish.

Odyssey In Appalachia

John Delaney sat in the new 1921 Packard driven by Mister Trent, his neighbor from Watertown, New York. "We'll be arriving in Allentown in a few minutes," Mister Trent said. "We have to turn off there. Mother Trent and I would like you to come with us to Brooklyn."

"I appreciate the offer," John replied, "but I got to head on down to Logan and take care of my Aunt Bessie. I told you about how Uncle Mike got blown up when the powder house exploded and about how the mine owner kicked Bessie out of her house. She ain't got a pension."

"You can send her money orders from New York after you get a job."

"Since Mom died, I'm her only kin. She needs me with her."

"Trouble's brewing in West Virginia, John. There's talk of miners forming an army to march against the owners."

"I don't know about any army. All I want is to find a job and look after Bessie."

Mister Trent stopped the car. John grabbed his bag, stepped onto the road. He watched until the car was only a distant plume of dust. He felt very much alone.

John walked until a mud-spattered motor bus pulled to a stop ahead of him. The driver hollered. "Where you headed, young fellow?"

"West Virginia."

"We're headed to Charleston. We have an empty seat. You can ride with us."

Much obliged, sir," John replied and climbed aboard. He looked at the passengers attired a lot like him in white shirts, rumpled jackets, and caps. Each man wore a red armband. Though most of the windows were open, the bus stank of sweat and tobacco. He slid into an empty aisle seat.

The man sitting next to him by the window said, "Name's Michael Wilson. We're union men fed up with the treatment of miners in West Virginia. We've decided it's time to stand and fight."

"Mister Trent talked about an army. Is it like in the War?"

"Might come to that. What about you, young man?"

"Country's had enough of wars. I was fixin' to get work in the mines. My Aunt Bessie Fuller lives in Logan. Things are rough for her." John took off his cap, rolled it up, and shoved it into his coat pocket.

Wilson nodded and smiled, "What's your name, son?"

"John Delaney."

"Well, John Delaney. You stick with us, and we'll see you get work."

"I will, sir, but I don't aim to be fightin' a war."

Wilson patted John on the shoulder. "And all we ask is that folks stand with us. Can you do that?"

John nodded.

"Good. Now get some sleep. We have a long ride ahead of us."

Awaking to the smell of motor fuel and the sound of men nosily filing off the bus, John took a minute to recall where he was. When he stepped off the bus, he felt a cool night breeze. He looked up into a cloudless sky. Men were relieving themselves on the grass. A few walked toward the nearby woods with newspapers in hand.

A slim figure strode up to John and held out a red bandana. "This is for you, Delaney."

John looked at the bandana but made no move to take it. "You're a girl."

"So, they tell me."

"Who are you?"

"Flo Dooley from Brownstown."

She's pretty, he thought. He couldn't think of anything to say.

"I'll tie it for you."

John held out his arm.

Flo Dooley twirled the bandana into a rope and tied it on John's arm. She stepped back and tilted her head as if studying her handiwork. "Now you're one of us," she announced before turning and striding toward the bus, joining the men who drifted in groups of twos and threes back to the road.

John dreamed of Flo Dooley in a long red dress with her black hair blowing in the breeze and didn't wake until they were pulling into the state capitol. When the bus stopped, he pushed his cramped body from the seat, grabbed his duffel from the overhead, and stepped into the aisle. Flo Dooley tugged at his sleeve. "Leave your things here," she said. "We'll be gettin' back on after we hear some speechifyin' from Mister Keeny. He's my cousin. Stick with the men that has the red. Stay clear of the Baldwin and Felts men. They're the mine guards."

"How do I tell them from regular folks?"

"They're the mean lookin' ones. Two of 'em killed Mister Hatfield on the steps of the courthouse. That happened in McDowell County. Down on the Tug. Hereabouts is a mite more tolerant. But don't take no comfort in that. Even here, they'll find any excuse to arrest you."

"I'll be careful," John assured Flo, who quickly disappeared into a sea of men with red armbands. John estimated the crowd to be near a thousand though he learned later that it numbered no more than about four hundred.

A familiar voice shouted, "Delaney!"

He looked about and spotted Michael Wilson. "Come on over here, Delaney. I want you to meet a real fine gentleman." Wilson stood off to one side of the crowd in the company of a man in a pressed white shirt with collar and necktie.

"Delaney, this here gentleman is Mister Frank Keeny. He'll make you a member of the United Mine Workers. We'll worry about dues when you get your first job."

Keeny shook John's hand and shoved a clipboard and a pen at him. "Sign next to the x, son."

He scratched his name on the paper, wrote in "Logan, West Virginia" as his address, and handed it back to Keeny.

"Now, you're one of us," Keeny said.

Michael Wilson put a hand on John's shoulder. "Go and join your union brothers. We'll be hearing from Mother Jones in a couple minutes." The words made John see the other miners as his family. He wasn't alone any more.

John tried to recall exactly what Flo Dooley was wearing that might help him find her among the hundreds of men standing in front of the Capitol Building. He needn't have worried. She found him. "Come with me, Delaney," she said. "You look like a lost puppy." She wrapped an arm around him and steered him toward the front of the crowd.

Mother Jones was telling the assemblage that she could get President Harding to help the miners. John listened. He wanted to understand the desperation that could drive workers to armed warfare.

Flo laughed and said, "I bet you'd rather be somewheres else right now?"

"Reckon I ought to stay and listen."

"I was really askin' whether you like bein' with me."

John felt the blood rise in his cheeks. His ears felt hot.

Flo pulled him away from the crowd. "Where we goin'?" he asked.

"You and me, we're gonna set ourselves down by the river and be a listenin' to the birds and havin' us a good old time."

"That's better than pretendin' to be a soldier if there ain't a war to fight."

Flo stepped in front of John. She poked a finger into his chest. "There is a war. That's what I been tryin' to explain to you." She turned away. "Why am I talkin' to you anyhow? You're only a boy."

"I ain't a boy. I'm near on seventeen. Been workin' regular since I was thirteen. Maybe I can't bring myself to shootin' anybody, but I know how to use my fists."

"So you're a tough guy. And you're pretty too. With that little mustache, you look like Douglas Fairbanks." Flo leaned into John, planted a kiss on his lips, and immediately backed away. "We need to collect our things and head for my hometown, Marmet."

"You told me you're from Brownstown."

"They call it Marmet now to please some damn mine owner.

"We get there, first thing you're gonna do is take a bath and wash your clothes. You smell somethin' foul. I got lye soap, and the river ain't so cold that we'll catch the grip."

Near Marmet, John laid his jacket and his bag on the river bank, kicked off his shoes, and jumped into the Kanawha River. Flo followed him. After a few minutes roughhousing, she said, "I'm gettin' out and findin' that bar of lye soap. You take off them trousers and that filthy shirt."

John stripped to his shorts and threw his shirt and trousers on the river bank.

Flo tossed him the bar of laundry soap. Neither spoke again until John climbed out of the river. Flo had wrung his clothes and put them to dry on tree branches. They sat next to each other on the river bank talking for a while, John in his shorts and Flo in her wet clothes. "Cousin Frank is wantin' me to go to college," Flo said. "When this business is over, I aim to do exactly that."

Flo looked at the sky and turned to John, "Guess we best be gettin' on. You put on your britches. I'm a-goin' in the bushes and wring out mine."

John grabbed his shirt and trousers from the tree branches, pulled them on, and slid the red bandanna back on his arm. He turned and looked at Flo higher up on the river bank, partially hidden by the brush, dressed only in a camisole, wringing out the wet from her shirt and trousers. At that moment he fell in love.

Flo came out of the bushes with her wet clothes clinging to her body. They walked for about ten minutes when Flo pulled him to a stop. "See that fellow, the one with the pistols, wide-brimmed fedora, leanin' against the fender of that Tin Lizzie?"

"He a friend of yours?"

"He's a Baldwin and Felts man. He's wearin' a badge. That's so he don't go to jail when he shoots us."

"He ain't fixin' to shoot us."

"Might gonna do exactly that. Would you shoot him to protect me?"

"Of course."

Flo poked him in the chest. "See. You ain't no different than any of us."

"I care about you, Flo. But I ain't ever fired a pistol. All I want's a chance to work and help Bessie get on."

Flo grabbed John by the arm and held him close.

He patted her arm. "If we leave that detective alone, he'll leave us alone. Ignore him."

"He's a starin' at us funny."

"No, he ain't."

"I got a gun."

John looked at Flo. "You what?"

Flo patted her bag. "If he starts a shootin', I got a pistol in my duffle."

"Keep it there."

They continued down the road. "Look at the beauty of this place, Flo," John said with a note of wonder in his voice. "Watertown's got no mountains like these. We got a river too, but even that's different."

Flo held his arm tighter and pulled him closer to her.

"Exactly where do your kin live around here?" John asked.

"They're all gone now."

"So we sleepin' outdoors?"

"We can sleep at my girlfriend's place."

"I got money," John said. He tapped his chest, where a money pouch hung.

Flo said, "Can you afford fifty cents a night."

John nodded.

"Ain't any problem then."

Flo led John down a narrow dirt road. "We go along here a ways, and then there's a cross street. My friend lives there."

The detective they had passed earlier overtook them in his car, pulled alongside, and kept pace with them. John ignored him, but Flo yelled, "Git on along and stop pesterin' us." She waved her hand as if shooing flies.

The Baldwin-Felts detective turned into their path and angled his car across the road.

Flo pulled hard on John's arm. "He's makin' trouble. If he goes for his gun, I'm a-gonna fill him full of lead."

"No," John said. "He's the law. You shoot him, and you'll hang."

"Won't nobody know. You see anyone around?"

"You stay calm. He's havin' his fun scarin' us."

John pulled Flo across the road to the opposite lane. The detective grinned and backed the car across the road to block their passage on that side. He took off his hat and set it on the seat next to him. John and Flo stopped a few feet from the grinning man in his shiny Tin Lizzie, his glistening black hair slicked-down.

"I saw you two in town with those miners," he said.

Flo shouted. "You just wait. Your time's a-comin'."

"You threatening me?"

"We don't want trouble," John said.

"You say, but might be you are scouts. Word is that the miners are heading this way next couple days."

"We don't want trouble," John said again.

"Why are you wearing that red armband?"

John had forgotten the bandana wrapped around his arm. "They made us put them on."

Flo pulled away from John. She shouted. "Damn you, John Delaney. You said you're one of us. Now you're tellin' this murderer you ain't."

The Baldwin-Felts man opened the door of his car and stepped onto the running board. He stood there for a moment—one hand on the car and one hand resting on his gun belt—looking down on John and Flo. He hopped off the running board onto the road, raising a little cloud of dust.

John took a step back. Flo didn't move. With a tilt of his head, the detective looked directly at Flo. "You're both standing there in wet clothes. What have you been up to?"

"Took a bath," John replied quickly, hoping to silence any further word from Flo.

Without taking his eyes off Flo, the detective said, "Wasn't talking to you, boy. I was directing my inquiry to the lady."

"Go bugger yourself," Flo said.

The detective laughed. "I guess you're no lady."

"We don't want trouble," John said again.

"I bet you two have been trying to blow something up. Empty those bags."

John watched Flo slide the old cloth bag off her shoulder and let it drop slowly to the ground. He tossed his bag at the feet of the detective. In a slow and measured cadence, he said, "Empty it yourself."

The detective took his attention from Flo and looked at John; anger was clouding his features. With one practiced motion, he pushed back his coat and drew his pistols. He fired at John while he was turning to look at Flo. An expression of astonishment flashed across his face. Both shots missed.

Flo fired two quick shots. The Baldwin-Felts man appeared to be settling his backside onto the running board. In an instant, John was on top of him, pinning down his arms. He struggled for a moment before he sagged to the dusty road.

John's whole body trembled. He stared at the lifeless form which moments ago had been a feared mine guard. He looked at Flo. "We got to turn ourselves into the law."

Flo gave him a withering stare.

"We should at least find out who he is."

"Damn you, Delaney. We'll remember him as long as we live. He'll haunt us. We ain't givin' that ghost no name. And I sure hope you can drive because you're drivin' back to Charleston. Grab his coat and hat. You two look kind of the same, except for the greasy hair."

John couldn't stop his limbs from shaking even while he dragged the man off the road and into the brush. Flo seemed unfazed, giving him orders about how many paces he needed to be from the road before he started scratching out a shallow grave. They buried the man and his pistols in a small clearing near two large trees.

John reversed the Ford onto the highway and headed back in the direction they had come. On the trip to Charleston, no one seemed to give them notice.

They parked the car on a quiet side street. John tossed the borrowed coat and hat onto a heap of garbage. They found the bus in the same spot near the capitol and under the watchful eye of an old man with a red armband who glanced at them and nodded. They tossed their bags on a seat. No one was aboard.

"The law will be lookin' for me," John said. "I can't stay in West Virginia. I'd like you to come with me when I leave, Flo."

"We'll talk about that later. Right now, we got to find Cousin Frank."

They found Frank Keeny sitting at a small table set up on the sidewalk. Men standing on either side of Keeny smiled at Flo. They made no attempt to stop her when she walked up to him from behind and whispered in his ear. He turned and looked at John, who had hung back to let Flo approach the Union leader alone. Keeny said something to one of the men standing next to him. The man took Flo by the hand and walked over to John. "My name is Goose," the man said. "We have a lot to do."

Flo tried to tell him about what happened in Marmet. Goose cut her off. "I don't need to know any details of the incident. I do need to know where the body is buried. We must get it far away from there before the lot of us head south."

Flo drew a map for Goose and told him how they piled up twigs and stones. He studied the map for a moment and said, "Show me the car."

John and Flo led Goose to the car and returned with him to the bus.

Goose told them to stay inside until one of Keeny's men came for them. "You two need to get out of West Virginia. We have a car leaving for Ohio tonight. Be ready when they come for you. In the meantime, don't talk to anyone."

"How do we know," John asked, "that they ain't the law comin' to fetch us to jail?"

"I'll have my man doing something different–maybe sporting a pocket-handkerchief or a straw hat, something out of place. You see someone like that–go with him."

Goose left them at the bus where some of the men had already returned and appeared to be settling in for the night. "I need to pee," Flo said. "I'll be back." She stepped off the bus. John watched her until she was out of sight.

A short while later, John spied a man standing near the bus in a grey suit with an incongruous white handkerchief dangling from his breast pocket. The man with the handkerchief waved at him. He led John to a nearby car and opened the back door. John tossed his bag onto the seat and climbed in. A second man sat behind the wheel.

"Flo's not back yet," John said. "We need to wait."

"We'll pick her up directly," the driver said.

As they sped north, John became convinced that Flo had stayed behind. The two men answered John's barrage of questions about Flo's whereabouts with evasions like, "She'll likely be along shortly," and "Don't you worry. She's all right."

John thought back through the past three days. He had started out in Watertown bent on a simple personal mission–going to Logan and getting a job to help his Aunt Bessie. He knew nothing of Frank Keeny or the problems in the West Virginia mines. But from his Aunt Bessie's experience, he'd had all the information he needed to see a larger picture. He just hadn't put it together.

With the miles rolling by, he thought about the dedication he saw in the leaders of the UMWA and their willingness to risk their lives to help people like his uncle and his aunt, treated shamefully by the mine owners. He thought of the mine guard who had goaded him and Flo into a gunfight. Never in his young life had he experienced anything like the events in Charleston and Marmet.

He leaned forward and said, “I want to go back.”

The man driving pulled the car onto the shoulder of the road and stopped. “Our instructions are to take you with us.”

“That’s only because I told Flo I wanted to leave. I’ve thought on it. I want to stay.”

“We have our instructions.”

“Flo ain’t runnin’, is she?”

Both the men in the front seat shook their heads.

“Well, neither am I.”

The driver said, “You’ve been seen cozy with Mister Keeny and his cousin. You came to town with Mike Wilson. He was arrested a couple hours ago.”

“Aunt Bessie needs me. And there’s more goin’ on here. Flo ain’t runnin’, and I ain’t runnin’.” The two men glanced at each other. Both nodded. The driver made a U-turn and headed south.

The Miser's Tower

~—~

He is in a golden tower where the world
He knows, and fears cannot reach him.
It is very near at hand; though,
Out his window
And just below and down the hill.

The songbirds try to pick him up and carry him
Out of the tower to a different place.
When their voices make a different sound,
He cannot follow and is bound there
With their songs repeating in his ears.

His secure day in the tower begins when he awakes
And hears the stream of life singing over stones,
The world glistening in the water in a golden droplet
Which has within it all his clever bones.

Wind blows through the open tower window
As he feels upon the air a trace of what will be,
Blue and yellow winds blowing green daisies
On the lea below in his tower's shadow.

When he lies down and looks above him
He can see the sky which nature made
To seal the world but mostly him
From terrors which abound in outer space.

He can taste the time of day in,
The blossoms in the fields and in the rotting hay.
No food grows in fallow fields, and children starve
For want of food to eat.

Crowds of people mill about his lodging.
They shout and push and make an awful cry
For bread or milk to feed their babies.
His ears hear none of that in his private Hades.

He walks upon a floor of stone and does not leave
A footprint by which he can be known.
Even you who walk upon the beach make
At least a print for a moment, until the tide
Comes in and washes it away.

The miser's tower is a fine protected place,
But it cannot keep the spirits out, and he feels
A dread that when the darkness falls, the cold
Will invade his earthen walls, and the ghosts
Who rise against him will sweep him far away.

Bumper Skiing

My friend, Tommy Murphy, and I waited for the inevitable confrontation we knew was coming. We stood on the sidewalk in front of Pop's ice cream store. The store was closed. Pop ordinarily stayed open until ten, but that night he had closed early–most likely because of the weather. If we knew the store would be closed, we probably would have gone back to the parish hall. Too late for that now.

"Almost ten. Won't be long now," Tommy said, as he looked at his wristwatch, the one his dad bought for him–his lucky charm. He told me how he had a dream about the watch. In the dream, his dad was talking about how dangerous the world is and told him he wouldn't ever get hurt while he was wearing it. That dream was last November, two days after his father was killed in an accident at the Mill. Tommy and his dad were really close. His dad had played football in college and was always coaching Tommy on the mechanics of each position and how to spot certain plays.

Tommy didn't wear the watch while he was playing football, but he rubbed it before workouts and every game, like it might be a lucky rabbit's foot. He was having a good season and said that he owed it all to his dad and to the watch. Important as it was, Tommy had almost lost it a couple days ago because of the bad clasp on the band. I kept telling him that he would lose the watch if he didn't get the band fixed. Adhesive tape wasn't the same as fixing it.

"Maybe we'll be lucky," I said as I stood with Tommy in front of the store, me puffing on a cigarette and arrogantly defying the snow blowing around us and trying to keep warm in my light poplin jacket. Pop was most likely home and warm in his bed. We two eighth-graders, having less sense than an old man, stood on the cold, snowy street corner, waiting and hoping for an unpleasant encounter that would make us more with it. At least that's what I was hoping. Don't know about Tommy, except that he seemed preoccupied with something. Things hadn't been the same at home since his dad died.

The needle on the big thermometer over the door of the butcher shop across the street told us it was 29 degrees. It always read warmer even though it was on the north side of the triangular building at the corner where my street linked up with the intersection of Griffin and Cleveland streets. Everybody around there called it the five points.

The temperature had been dropping since dawn. The storm had started around four o'clock that afternoon as sleet and freezing rain. The white stuff started as flurries. By dark, the roads were covered with snow, hiding a dangerous sheet of ice on the pavement underneath.

Not many cars were on the road at that time of night in the hazardous driving conditions—a few tire tracks here and there. The snowplows and salt spreaders would not be by until the morning. Our neighborhood was far from downtown and had only one main road. Things were different when the mayor's brother lived on my street, but that was then, and this was now.

I was proud of my friendship with Tommy, the most popular kid in my class, maybe even in the whole school. We'd been buddies since third grade. I was the bookworm. Tommy was the athlete. Playing sports was his life. He didn't care much for studying. His so-so grades suggested that. He was really smart but never studied.

The elementary school didn't have a football team. Tommy played quarterback the past two years on the church team. He played baseball in the summer with the college kids on the team sponsored by Hennessey's Bar and Grille.

Everyone expected him to quarterback the high school team next year. He was planning on attending the summer camp run by the coach. Unofficially, he would be getting coached, but it was just a summer camp and not a football training camp. I knew he was going to the camp for free.

Tommy had his heart set on playing in the pros someday. He already was looking at Notre Dame. Figured he was a shoo-in there because the high school was run by lay brothers who taught at the university.

Tommy pushed back the top of the driving gloves he was wearing to look at his watch again. The gloves had belonged to his dad. They were real leather.

"Hope they get out a little early," Tommy said. "Cold as a witch's ass. This waiting is getting to me."

"Probably will–all this white stuff."

Tommy and I had been at the Canteen at the parish hall, you know, the weekly dance. We left early for a smoke and some fresh air. One other kid, Jeffy Bourke, left with us, but he had complained of the cold and went home almost as soon as we were outside. Tommy didn't usually smoke. I did. That night, probably because of the cold, he asked me for a cigarette. Normally we would have hung around the cemetery next to the church hall. There were snowdrifts in front of the gate where the swirling wind had piled it, and the latch was frozen solid. The gate wouldn't open.

Despite the sparse attendance, at the Canteen they had managed to elect the officers for the following year. Everybody knew it would be Tommy elected to represent the freshmen class and Eddie Mueller as the guy in charge of the Canteen. Tommy had said he needed some air. I told him it was freezing. He said he had to think and couldn't think in the hall. "Too hot," he said. "Canteen will be over in a few minutes, anyhow.

"Be by the cemetery," he announced as he buttoned his jacket and headed out.

Tommy and I had on our dress shoes. We hadn't expected all the snow that fell while we were in the dance. Amazing how much snow can accumulate in two and a half hours, and the wind was blowing it into drifts. The storm was not predicted to be more than a flurry. Otherwise, they would have called off the Canteen. The high school kids at the Canteen would come looking for Tommy. To be sure they didn't think he was a chicken, he went back in and told them he would meet them at Pop's.

We watched a car come by, its wipers laboring to brush away the snow. On the pavement, the dry flakes almost immediately blew into the track behind it as it slipped and slid going up my street. The snow lay as a glistening blanket of yellow-white under the glow of the street lamp at the end of the block.

The cars trying to navigate the sharp turn created a zig-zag of lines on the roadway. Some of the designs looked like great big eggs or maybe footballs.

Even though my hands were hurting from the cold, I made a snowball to toss at a car going up the hill. I figured the driver would never stop to chase us. He would have had to back down to the intersection to get another run up the hill, or he wouldn't make it to Lorain Street. I was right. He kept going, ignoring my snowball that fell harmlessly on his trunk and disappeared in a powdery fluff.

"Not many girls I knew there tonight," Tommy said. "Made the Canteen sort of dull."

"A real bitch. Huh?"

"Not so bad. Met some new girls. Sophomores. Maybe a date for the prom next year. Got to plan ahead."

I bent down to make another snowball, packing the powdery flakes with the heat from my hands, what was left of the heat. I planned to bounce it off the roof of the next car that came along.

The custom was to take the pants off the boy elected the freshman president–They never elected a girl.–and toss it high somewhere where he would have to climb to collect it or go home half-naked in his underwear. A favorite place was a tree in the cemetery.

Neither Tommy nor I thought that would happen. We knew there would be some other indignity just as bad but different because of the cold and the snow.

The two of us likely could have fought them off enough to discourage anything silly from happening to us. Tommy was already six feet and close to 200 pounds. But that never happened. You were expected to be a good sport and suffer the embarrassment with minimal resistance. It was a ritual, one of life's passages that you told your grandkids about, maybe with some embellishments. We could have retreated to my house, a few doors from Pop's, but that would have branded Tommy a chicken and me his accomplice in chickenry.

"Here they come," Tommy said and pointed toward the parish hall a short block from where we stood freezing half to death. A small but noisy group came out of the hall and advanced toward us led by Eddie

Mueller and little Cappy Jones, two juniors from Ignatius.

Cappy disappeared behind a car, moving slowly toward us. The car turned onto Cleveland Street, its tires spinning to gain some traction on the slick pavement. He let go of the rear bumper and slid along the icy roadway, gliding easily to the curb and stopping almost directly in front of us. It was a cool maneuver.

"Trying to hide, huh?" Cappy said, looking at Tommy and ignoring me for the moment.

Tommy didn't reply. He just kept pretending to puff on the cigarette he had borrowed from me and had not lighted. He stared at the kid nearly half his size, though three years older.

"Wait 'til you see what we got for you and your little friend," Cappy said. "We are going to test your manhood. You know what that is." He snickered and turned to see if the little mob had caught up and gathered around. The little guy was the leader of a group of three or four kids from the neighborhood that were always in trouble with the cops.

Convinced his special buddies were all there, Cappy continued. "You're in for it now." He laughed like the guy on the used car commercial–all fake. Eddie should have been the leader of the hazing party, but he had deferred to the stronger personality.

Tommy took a long, pretend drag on his cigarette and flicked it at Cappy, who had to jump back to avoid it hitting him. He lost his footing and fell into the snow. The group from the Canteen, now numbering about 15, broke out in raucous laughter. I mentally scored one for Tommy but was worried about what might come next, fueled by the little guy's violent temper and willingness to fight anyone anywhere.

The snowball that I had been holding in my hands somehow ended up flying at Cappy as he struggled to stand on the icy sidewalk in his leather-soled cordovans. When the snowball hit him, he fell backward to land on his backside. The little group ate it up. Peals of laughter and raucous comments pierced the crisp stillness of the wintry night.

"That's it," Cappy shouted and got to his feet, helped by his cronies "Both of you are in for it now," he said while his friends pushed to the front of the group and stood next to him, menacing looks on all their faces.

I no longer felt cold. My mind was occupied with which of Cappy's mean friends might fight me. I wondered if any of my friends or Tommy's would stand up for us in a fight.

In the silence that followed his pronouncement, I pulled out a pack of coffin nails from my jacket pocket and tapped out the tip of another cigarette, pulled it out the rest of the way with my mouth, and stuffed the pack back into my pocket. With the cigarette hanging what I hoped was casually from my lips, I felt tough enough to take on the world. I lit the cigarette and took a couple puffs. Amazingly, while I was doing all of this, nobody moved. They all stared at me. "Let's get on with this," I said through clenched teeth.

Cappy stepped toward me, grabbed the cigarette from my mouth, and threw it into the snow. A real fight seemed inevitable until one of the girls shouted. "No fights. Somebody will call the cops. They'll cancel the Canteen forever." Others in the group shouted in agreement. A chant of "No fights, no fights," started.

"Okay. Okay" he said. "We'll do the manhood test. Tommy has to hitch a bumper ride to the top of the hill. If he doesn't make it, you girls can see how small he really is when we take his pants."

There were shouts of support for the test. Most everybody knew that Tommy had never been willing to bumper ski, even though people called him a coward. It was not that. He just didn't like to do stupid and dangerous things. He couldn't play sports if he injured himself doing something crazy.

Finally taking charge, Eddie said. "Right. No ride. No clothes. We take everything off." Eddie turned to me. "That includes you, punk." The declaration was met with wild cheers and jeers and a new chant of "Take them off. Take them off."

"The situation had deteriorated into something I had never expected. They never took anything off, but the pants, never the underwear or anything else, even on warm nights.

If he failed, the girls would see us bare-assed naked. I could never live it down. I would rather come into my house bloodied by a fight than naked. Every girl I went out with from that night on would remind me of what happened.

"That's dumb and dangerous," Tommy said. He glared at Cappy. "Even you couldn't hold on all the way to the top without falling off."

"Yeah. I remember that time. I wasn't going to Lorain. Just wanted to show you how it's done."

Cappy grabbed the bumper of a Caddy that had stopped for the stop sign before heading up the hill to Lorain Street. He crouched down, so the driver couldn't see him. People cheered as the big car, equipped with chains that bit into the ice, continued slowly to Lorain and made the turn without even stopping for traffic on the through street. He dropped off and stood with hands raised in triumph. Even I felt like cheering.

Cappy started down the hill toward us, slipping and sliding on his leather soles, almost as if he had on skis. About that time, a Chevy sedan drove through the intersection. Tommy ran after it and grabbed onto the bumper. The car began to fishtail and slow as it approached the steepest part of the street. Tommy holding onto the car didn't help. The car stopped about halfway up the hill. Tommy should have let go as the car began to slide backward on the icy road.

He tried to get out of the way when it was clear the driver no longer had any control of the car. Tommy couldn't get his footing and fell. The driver, by this time, wasn't even trying to make it up the hill and had reversed for another try. The Chevy ran over Tommy's leg and then slid into the curb, to trap him between the fender and the curb.

Chaos ensued. Everyone was rushing up the hill and shouting. One girl screamed, "Oh no! He's dead!" She started to cry. Someone yelled, "Mrs. P, call the police."

The car's horn was blowing. Mrs. Pitchkawitch was out on her porch in her pajamas. She shouted, "I'll call the police."

Tommy lay face down in the snow, his legs partway under the car, his body wedged between the rear wheel and the curb. Everyone was making suggestions on what to do. Eddie wanted to drag him out. The driver insisted they wait for the cops. The police arrived in a couple minutes. About five minutes later, the ambulance arrived.

I told the cop that Tommy wanted to bumper ski and grabbed hold of the Chevy. When he inquired about the crowd, I told him that we had been coming from the parish dance and were going up to Lorain for sodas and ice cream. People overhearing my explanation nodded in agreement. Everybody he talked to parroted my story. Cappy and his cronies were nowhere in sight. The cop seemed satisfied, not at all suspicious. Nobody said anything about hazing or a fight or anything like that.

The ambulance took Tommy away. The kids headed in all directions, anxious to get home to tell their family and friends about what they had witnessed.

On the way down the hill to my house, I saw one of Tommy's gloves lying in the snow. I bent to grab it. That's when I saw his watch. The clasp had broken. The watch was stopped at twenty minutes after ten, the exact time his dad was killed.

Time To Travel

Normally I don't stop at garage sales, but when I spotted a crazy looking contraption sitting on the driveway of a very large home, I had to stop and take a look. What a mistake!

Soon as I pulled over and got out of my van, the guy running the sale hustled over to me. The man was short, no more than five-two with a long white beard and big ears. Wore bib overalls, old high-top tennis shoes. His bright red necktie struck me as a bit incongruous, even in that neighborhood of mansions.

He had other customers. A young gal pawed through a pile of clothing heaped on a long trestle table. Three older ladies wandered around other tables loaded with clothing, old lamps, rusting small appliances, and knickknacks of all description, nothing that seemed to fit the neighborhood. An unattended metal cash box with a few bills and some change sat on a table.

"What you interested in purchasing?" he asked.

He spoke English, but the way he pronounced the words had me straining to understand him. He waved a finger at the sign on my van. "I see you're in the water purification business."

"Yep. Invented a new way to take impurities out of water."

"Invented. So you must have a patent."

"It's all in my head. More of an art than a science as they say."

The man took me by the arm and steered me toward the tables. I got the idea that he'd never held a garage sale. He didn't know he was supposed to sit around half asleep and wait for somebody to offer him a ridiculously low price for his junk or his family heirlooms—as the case might be. It was all the same to the average garage sale addict.

I cast my gaze over the various sale items. I pretended to see the contraption for the first time. I pointed at it. "What's that gizmo over there?"

"That. That's a time machine."

"You don't say. Time machine, huh? Does it work?"

"It brought me here, didn't it?"

The reply got a chuckle out of me. Maybe the little guy was a salesman, after all. "I suppose so. I mean, if you say so. Can you give me a demo, you know, take me for a spin?"

"I would surely like to give you one. But, you see, it has a small problem."

I knew there had to be a catch. I said, "It's a fake. It's from a movie set. You got it from some property company.

"All right. How much you askin' for the thing?"

He scratched his chin and looked askance. "I'm thinking $700. It's worth a whole lot more than that. One of a kind."

"Mind if I sit in it?" I asked.

"No can do. You push the wrong button, and you're out of here like that." He snapped his fingers.

I stroked my chin and strolled around the so-called time machine, pretending to be considering the price and waiting for him to start bidding against himself.

The thing was basically a giant steel ball about six feet in diameter with a big window in the front. Three little hot dog-shaped feet sticking out of the bottom prevented it from rolling down the driveway.

Through the open door, I could see two comfortable looking seats and what appeared to be a control panel with gauges and a row of colored buttons. A single short pedal stuck out of the floor. The person who designed it didn't have much imagination. I could have cobbled together a much more convincing time machine. Must never have seen the Jules Verne movie.

I jumped in surprise when the little guy slapped his hand on the machine. He said, "It works fine in forward, but it has no reverse, so it's only good for going ahead in time. That's why I'm letting it go so cheap."

I couldn't help but chuckle at his sales efforts. "Come on. Take me for a spin."

The little guy looked at the pavement and shook his head. "I could, but then we will both be sometime else and have no way to get back."

He paused, looked up right into my eyes. "This time machine is you," he said with a real sense of honesty in his voice. "I can go a little lower on the price if you're really interested. Can't give it away, you understand, but I can bargain."

I said, "I don't know. No reverse gear. What kind of mileage it get?"

He laughed. "Runs on a new type of atomic power. Go for years without needing any upkeep. Besides it just sits where you put it. It's a time machine, not a Maserati.

"As you can see, it seats two. You can take your girlfriend or your wife—or not. If you're having debt problems, or you just want to rob a bank and make a clean getaway, it's perfect for you."

The idea of getting away for good was very appealing. I'd only recently started the new business that was struggling in a bad economy. My wife of five years had left me for her yoga instructor. I was behind on my under-water mortgage. The thought of new surroundings was the reason I half took the weirdly dressed little man seriously. "Wouldn't actually need reverse then, would I?"

He cackled and shook his head.

He'd told me he was ready to bargain, so I figured I'd have some fun with him. I looked him right in the eye and said, "From our conversation, I guess that you came from the future while the reverse gear was still working." That got a nod from him. "And I suppose you can tell me a future time you think I'd like."

"Certainly. In fact I can set the machine to such a time. No need to worry about getting stuck sometime really bad, like in the middle of a war."

"You'll need to show me how it works."

"Of course. How about if we take a ride for, say, a minute into the future? You look at your watch. We show you how to crank up the machine. We go. You look at your watch again. Would that convince you?"

This guy was good, a real salesman. He was determined to have me part with my hard-earned money for a movie prop. What the heck. At the right price, I could use it as a lawn ornament.

He hopped in and slid over. I'm six-five, so I had to kind of wedge myself into the seat next to him. "Close the door," he said. "It won't work with the door open."

I closed the door. He flipped up a lid exposing a small keypad and quickly typed something. He turned to me and said, "This is the brains of the device. I'll set it to a good future time, so all you have to do is push this green button here on the control panel. Make sure you are depressing the foot pedal when you hit the button, or you could end up sometime else.

"Look at your watch," he said.

He pushed a red button and hollered, "Blast off." A low beeping began. I looked out the window. Was it my imagination, or were the ladies moving more quickly? I glanced at my watch. It appeared to be ticking away normally.

My pilot was grinning so wide that he put me in mind of a deranged elf. "Okay. We're here. It's a minute later. You impressed or what?"

"Of course, it is. We didn't go anywhere. We just sat here for a minute. We never went forward in time."

"How about if I throw in a free repair kit and service manual?"

Mention of a service manual got me thinking the contraption might actually do something more than just beep. Yet I still wasn't done bargaining. I shook my head and said, "Still too much."

"And a set of steak knives?"

"Okay. But you got to do better on the price."

He put on that extra-wide grin of his, spit in his palm, and offered his hand to me. "You drive a hard bargain. Let's make the price two-fifty. It's my final offer."

It was my turn to laugh. I spit in my own palm and reached out to shake his hand. "What's your name," I asked.

"Tombo. My name is Tombo. No, H."

"Well, Tom. One thing I can say to you is that you are one hell of a salesman. You just sold a time machine that doesn't work."

"Oh. But it does work, only not like you may imagine."

"Yeah. Right."

"Give me your address, so I can deliver it. Won't fit in that van of yours. You can pay me when I drop it off at your house."

He pointed at the sky as if he had just gotten a bright idea. "In fact, maybe you can help me load it up right now into my pickup. I will follow you to your home."

"No need for that. I can pay you now and come back for it. Don't want you to lose any sales. Besides, you leave, and these ladies will rob you blind, deaf, and dumb."

"You have to have faith in human nature," he said and scurried to a red pickup truck parked at the curb. He backed the truck up the driveway, jumped out and pulled the pin holding the gate, letting it drop open with a loud clang. Eying his very spare frame, I asked, "How we gonna do this, Tom?"

"I will show you." he said, and flipped out two small ear-like handles. "You grab hold of these and lift. I lift from the other side. On the count of three, we both heave it into the truck."

Expecting the alleged time machine to be heavier than it was, I overdid the old heave-ho and hoisted it onto the truck bed in one quick motion. I lifted so fast that Tom lost his grip and bounced off the truck and went flying backward onto the grass.

I expected him to be hurt, but Tom popped to his feet and dusted at the grass stains on his overalls. "They are going to like you," he said.

"Who's gonna like me?"

He hesitated a moment before he said, "The ladies there."

I turned to find the women staring at the two of us as if waiting for an encore. Tom bowed a low curtsey. The gals clapped.

With the red pickup following close behind, I drove the three miles to my house, parked at the curb, and motioned Tom to go on into the driveway. He backed the truck almost to the garage doors, leaving just enough space to drop the gate.

"Nice place you have here," he said.

"Can the compliments, Tom. You made the sale already. But thanks, anyhow."

The wind suddenly picked up. A bolt of lightning struck nearby, and the ensuing thunderclap introduced a note of urgency into our unloading project. I raised the garage doors and unhooked the truck gate. "Stand back," I said. "The thing's light as a feather, whatever the heck it is." With one hand against the side and one on the handle, I easily swung the machine onto the garage floor.

Tom glanced at the clouds rolling in and said, "I must go. Don't want those women robbing me blind, deaf, and dumb, now do I?"

"Hey, Tom. Can you set the time, so that I can make a few short trips to show off to my neighbors before I disappear forever into the future?"

When I heard myself saying the words, I almost couldn't believe what my ears were telling me. I didn't really expect the contraption was anything more than a movie prop. Yet, a guy can't be too careful.

"Be happy to do that for you. I didn't get your name."

"Call me, Slugger."

He nodded. "I will set the time machine for successive two-minute increments without using the pedal. To go all the way, press the green button and step on the pedal at the same time."

"Like stepping on the accelerator, giving it the gas."

Again he nodded. "Remember. For short trips: red button and no pedal. For the longer trip to the very nice time I picked out for you: green button and press pedal. You don't need to press the pedal for the short trips because what's a few minutes here and there."

"Exactly how far are you sending me."

"Not far. Guarantee you will enjoy it." Tom opened the door and slid into the seat. He poked at buttons, twisted knobs, and typed on the keyboard. He emerged and stated very matter-of-factly, "All set up for you, Slugger. Now remember. You press the green button and step on the pedal only to leave for good. No reverse. No turning back. No changing your mind. Got it?"

"Got it." I could hardly get out the words without laughing. Tom seemed to enjoy playing the part of a real time traveler. Believe you me. It was funny to see him pretending to set the controls, all the time with that earnest grin spread across his face.

"Thanks," I said. We shook hands. No spitting this time. I stood in my garage and watched Tom drive away, thinking what a sport he was and hoping his sale wouldn't be spoiled by the storm.

The moment I shoved my hand into my pocket and felt my wallet, I realized that I hadn't paid him. My first reaction was to chase him. Feeling the first few drops of rain, I decided to wait until the storm passed before I went back and gave him his money.

I couldn't wait to show the time machine to my snooty neighbor,

Louie Blasedale III. He was always braggin' about his new cars. And I could have some fun with my girlfriend, Sally, you know, pretend that we're going on a time trip. She'd appreciate that.

I shut the garage door against the rain and wind and took a seat in my new acquisition. I touched the red button, but nothing happened. I reached out and pulled the door shut and pressed it again. The loud beeping startled me. Nothin' changed. I glanced at my watch. It ticked along as if I was just a dumb hick sitting in his garage on a rainy Saturday afternoon in a fake time bubble. I figured that if I were really traveling into the future, the hands of my watch would be moving faster. So the thing didn't work. I was a fool to think it might. The beeping kept on for two minutes. At least I got some sound effects out of it.

My watch and my stomach both told me it was lunchtime. Took me about a half-hour to go in the house, make a baloney sandwich, and wash it down with a beer.

The rain stopped well before I reached Tom's. His garage sale hadn't been washed out. However, the scene greeting me on my arrival in front of his house came as a surprise. People were carting off the last of the sale items from the tables, nearly empty of the heaps of merchandise they contained less than a scant hour earlier. Neither Tom nor his red pickup was anywhere in sight. The table with the used clothing lay on its side.

With a quick, nervous glance or two, the looters ignored me. My first reaction was to tell them all to leave. I hesitated because it wasn't my problem. Tom had left without asking me for his money. Maybe he was in a giving mood.

My repeated knocking on the front door drew no response until a man clutching two table lamps shouted, "Nobody's home." He shoved the two lamps into the back seat of his Chevy and drove away. I went all around the house, peering through windows. The house was vacant and bare–no furniture, no appliances, no nothing.

Approaching one of the neighbors, a middle-aged woman in jeans poking at a flower bed with a little trowel, I asked, "Do you know what happened to Tombo?"

She stopped but didn't look up. "Tombo. Don't know anyone by that name. He live around here?"

"The guy runnin' the garage sale."

"Oh. Him. He came by early this morning in a box truck. Unloaded the truck. Set up the tables. Left for a while. Came back in the red pickup."

"He doesn't live here?"

"House been empty for months. Real nice couple used to live there. The husband died. Kids took the mother in. Cleaned out the old homestead and put the place up for sale. Typical kids. No feelings."

"Have you seen him around?"

She shook her head. "Suppose I ought to have called the authorities, but he seemed, you know, to belong. Figured he must be the new owner. He do something wrong?"

I responded with, "Don't know yet." She gave me a sideways glance and went back to poking in the garden.

I thanked the woman for the information and drove back home. On the way, I tried to figure what had happened since I first stopped at the sale. All I could think of was that now I was in possession of a large steel ball that had a windshield and that beeped after I pressed a red button. Big deal. Maybe. Stolen. Maybe. I drove back home, trying to think about what I should do with my new possession. Can't call it a purchase because I didn't pay for it.

Under the seat, I located a bag of odd-shaped implements, a greasy manual with lots of diagrams, and the promised steak knife set. Gazing up at the cloudless blue sky left behind by the scudding clouds, my thoughts turned to thoughts of what a future time, maybe like a hundred years hence, would be like. How would I fit in? Tom had said not far, yet I had no idea of what that might mean.

Louie Blasedale III, came sauntering up the driveway. "Whatcha got there, Slugger," he asked.

"New vehicle. I figure that it gets about a hundred years to the gallon."

"You mean miles. Where're the wheels?"

"Doesn't use them. It hovers. It's a hovercraft. I'd show you, but I want to keep it off the street until I get the tags."

"Understood," he said and ran his hand over the smooth surface. "A real nice unit. Be buying one myself soon. Not a cheap compact like yours, though. Been looking at the full-sized models."

He grunted a couple times–in approval or disdain, I didn't know which—turned his back to me and walked away.

That night I slept fitfully. I worried that the machine was stolen from the federal government. I was afraid to turn on the television for fear the news might report that Area 51 misplaced one of their time machines they had in for repairs to the reverse gear. Of course, they can't call it a time machine. The talk would be about NASA losing a weather balloon or part of a low-orbit satellite.

Would the FBI come knocking? Or worse, might it be Homeland Security. Might I be snatched up in the night, maybe taken to a secret government facility where they water-boarded people? Preposterous? Why else would the little guy I got it from disappear?

And who dressed him. I couldn't imagine any wife happy with his ridiculous get-up. Rich people can be eccentric, but there's a limit even for them.

In the morning, I noticed that my wristwatch was three minutes slow compared to the clock on my cell phone. That got me thinking. Had I really gone three minutes into the future, or was my old watch just running slow again. Did I miss three minutes of real time by jumping three minutes into the future? I read somewhere that Einstein thought going forward in time, your watch will speed up because you are going faster than the people you are leaving behind. He may have been wrong.

Still, in my pajamas, I hurried down to the garage and squeezed myself into my new machine. Each time I pressed the red button, the beeping started. When it stopped, I pushed it again and again until I had made ten two-minute time trips. I hustled outside to find that the morning had brightened. Based on the time shown on my cell phone clock, my wristwatch was about twenty-three minutes slow. Time had passed more quickly outside the machine than inside it. Wasn't that just the opposite of Einstein's theories? Who cares? All I know is that the thing works.

My elation at my good fortune was tempered by the realization that any effort to commercialize the machine surely will result in Homeland Security confiscating it. All that morning and into the wee hours, I overworked my brain, trying to think of what to do. Tombo's idea of robbing a bank and scooting off into the future began to seem more and more the thing to do.

Being an honest man, I decided to clean out only my own bank accounts and head into the future with enough money to get me a new start in the clean water business. If I went far enough into the future, my money would have antique value. That might offset inflation. Wish it had occurred to me to ask Tombo for exactly what year he set the machine, but I didn't believe him then. To help steer clear of Homeland Security, I eventually decided to keep only a small part in cash and with the rest buy gold and diamonds, even some platinum bars.

During the next six weeks, I slowly withdrew my savings, sold the van, and asked Sally if she wanted to take a trip with me to a far-away place and never come back.

After thinking about it for all of ten seconds, she smiled and said, "Totally."

On the day of my departure, I loaded the machine with a case of Glenfiddich, a change of clothing, and my stash. Sally brought along her makeup kit and an extra pair of fancy sunglasses with little decorative birds on each side.

"Here we go on the adventure of our lifetimes. I hope this craft is well made."

"Exactly where are we going," Sally asked.

"To the future," I replied.

Sally smiled wanly and planted a wet kiss on the end of my nose.

We squished ourselves into the time machine, with Sally all the while trying to pry out of me our intended destination. I took a deep breath and pressed the red button.

Sally waited about a minute before she began a hysterical laugh. "You are the joker," she said once her funny bone stopped tickling.

"I did it wrong. Just hold on a second."

On my second try, I pressed the green button but forgot to press down on the foot pedal. At first, nothing seemed to happen except the beeping. About the time I figured the whole thing was a complete failure, the machine began to shake and buck so violently that I thought it might tip over.

Through the windshield, my garage quickly disappeared to be replaced with an open field. Images came and went so quickly that eventually, I couldn't distinguish anything more than vague shapes. All I could think of was that indeed time and space were linked like they say in the Sci-Fi movies. I was going into the future traveling faster than the speed of light, yet I was not moving relative to my surroundings but rather relative to the passage of time. The machine continued to buck and shake. What was happening? Was the machine bending space and time? I wished I'd paid more attention to my brother, the physicist.

Sally screamed. She kicked at the door. I grabbed hold of her and hugged her as much to comfort me as to comfort her. We went on like that for nearly five minutes until the shaking and the bucking smoothed out, and the images changed more slowly.

The beeping stopped. The scene outside was chaotic. We sat in an open field between what appeared to be opposing armies. Large armored vehicles that reminded me of tanks shot at each other. Their projectiles soared over us to land with loud, bright explosions.

Sally reached out and pushed the green button. The war vanished in a blur. The time machine started shaking and beeping. Wreckage and bodies lay all about us. The armies had destroyed each other.

The next time, I pressed the green button and remembered to press the foot pedal. In what seemed like only a few seconds, the shaking and beeping stopped. We found ourselves inside a large cage-like enclosure with heavy bars. The cage sat in a clearing with dense woods on three sides and a large gray, windowless building on the fourth side.

Tombo stood outside the enclosure, the necktie and bib overalls replaced by a long robe. I swung open the door. "Took you long enough to get here," he said.

I asked him, "What's goin' on?"

"I am a hunter. I go out and find exhibits for Yesterday World."

"For what?"

"I work for Yesterday World. It's a theme park. Sort of a life-sized, moving diorama where people with different skills from different times go about their daily work in special enclosures we build for them. I get paid a bounty for every catch. Your woman is a pleasant surprise. I get a bonus for her."

"Send us back, you little twerp."

"No can do, Slugger."

"But I don't do anything folks might want to look at me doin' all day."

"You will be making your special water purification systems. We need them desperately. Water pollution is a real problem."

I shouted, "You conniving rat."

Tombo shrugged. "To make the park interesting, we try to get people with different skills from different time periods. For example, we have stonemasons building an ancient cathedral with vaulted ceilings. I was sent out with my crew to capture somebody in your time that knew about water purification. Do you realize that your approach is novel even now?"

"How'd you choose me?"

"Found you in the phone book of local businesses. Figured out your routine. I would have been disappointed if you passed up my yard sale. Clever of me, don't you think?"

"You lied to me. You little jackass."

"Did not. You came freely, your choice. Has to be like that."

"Well, then, you misrepresented yourself. That's not fair."

Tom shrugged again and said, "We feed our specimens well and care for you. Of course we cannot have your likes roaming about. You need to be confined. Not to worry. You will do just fine." A wide grin spread slowly across his face.

"Now, the two of you, please step out of the machine and walk into that smaller transport cage on your right, so that we can take you to your new home at Yesterday World."

"Screw you," I shouted and pulled the door shut. I pushed down hard on the green button, I purposely didn't step on the foot pedal. The machine beeped. I watched the grin disappear to be replaced by a look of pure horror. The machine shook violently. Tom's image blurred.

When the machine stopped shaking and beeping, we were still in the cage. Tom was gone. I pressed the green button again and again until the cage disappeared completely. I kept pressing it, traveling in increments of time. I stopped when Sally said, "It's all gone, the cages, the big gray building. Everything's gone."

I looked about. We were alone.

I reached under the seat and fished out the service manual. It took me about an hour to figure out how to get reverse gear working again and to set the time destination. It was obvious that Tombo had purposely disabled it. I suppose he never thought we would go forward in time the way we did to get away from him.

I dialed in a past time destination. I didn't care. I only wanted to get out of there far enough to know Tombo would not suddenly re-appear. A couple hours later Sally and I were talkin' to some really nice folks in the year 2119 who took us for members of some sort of religious sect because of our outdated clothes. They didn't believe we were time travelers. That was pure fiction. And they'd never heard of Yesterday World.

Dangerous Dalliance

A pretty girl sashayed into the soda shop. She fixed me in a pouting gaze.

"Four bucks," the counter guy said.

I grabbed my chocolate cone and shoved five dollars at him. I turned around. She was gone.

"Her name's Caitlyn," he said. "Year ago, she choked right here on a gummy right where you're standing. If a male customer's here when she comes in, we never see him again. Bad for business."

I took a lick of my cone, gave a short guffaw to be polite, and hurried into the street.

Caitlyn leaned against a mailbox.

"Love chocolate," she said. She winked and slid her fingers between mine. "I live around the corner—at the end of the alley."

Until we turned the corner and headed down the alley with the late afternoon sun behind us, I didn't notice that only my shadow bobbed on the concrete.

To Come About

One September day, I invited my dear friend Craig to take a ride with me in my open cockpit runabout. At the time, Craig and his wife were visiting at our weekend retreat near Cooperstown, NY. With the bitter cold that each winter invades upstate New York fast approaching, I was anxious to take the boat to its winter home on the western shore of Lake Otsego. The boatyard was the boat's home when the lake froze over so thick they could drive big trucks on it, fishing shanties might be seen on the ice, and the little houseboats in which a few hearty souls lived year-round put out bubblers hoping to keep the water from freezing around them and damaging the hulls.

Craig and I had been friends since we were in our twenties. We both went to college and later to law school. Neither of us wanted to be litigators, so rather than go to work for a law firm, we became corporate attorneys. We agreed that we were going to throw huge parties the year we reached the big six-O. We planned to make enough money by then to retire early and travel together and just enjoy life.

My Cooperstown retreat was an ancient farmhouse actually located in the nearby town of Cherry Valley. The central part of the home probably was built before George Washington became our first president. The house later became a modified Greek revival style with three windows on the second floor and a central entry door flanked by two windows in the gable end that faced the street. No stately columns—a poor man's version. By the time we bought it, alterations and additions had made it nondescript. The building fascinated Craig. He managed to figure out exactly how walls had been moved, and the interior shifted around and made drawings of how he thought the interior looked during its Greek revival period.

With five big bedrooms, the farmhouse was way large enough to have all our various children come with us. Nevertheless, they had been left at home, so we might have some adult-centered time to ourselves. While both Craig and I dearly loved our teenage kids, they quickly insisted on becoming the center of every activity, making futile any attempt at mature discourse. Anyhow, they were old enough to take care of themselves.

I never considered Craig much of a sailor. He turned down my invitation to go sailing on the little sunfish with the dagger board that you could pull up, so you didn't get stuck in the shallows. I think maybe he didn't like to be on the water in a small craft, even on our not so big Lake Otsego, the one James Fenimore Cooper wrote about in his Leatherstocking Tales, the one his characters called, Lake Glimmerglass, headwaters of what farther south becomes the mighty Susquehanna.

That morning, the fog was so thick at the farmhouse in Cherry Valley that it was impossible to see much beyond the front porch. I knew that on the lake it would be even worse. Thinking back, it might have been the fog that made Craig feel comfortable enough to join me. People sometimes speak of fog as being a blanket. Maybe for Craig, it was like a security blanket.

We drove with our wives to what Craig called the yacht club. It was in reality a country club with a clubhouse for parties and sometimes just a casual drink with friends, tennis courts, and slips for small boats. Nine miles long and a mile and a half at its widest, the lake wasn't big enough for anything that might be reasonably called a yacht. But Craig insisted on referring to it as a yacht club—probably more to annoy me than truly believing it. In retrospect, maybe he was simply trying to make me feel good. I ought not to have taken it so negatively.

Arriving at the club, we donned life jackets and headed for the dock. The wives stayed behind in the warmth of the car. While I started the outboard motor, Craig collected leaves and twigs blown into the boat by the previous day's storm that had the windows of the old farmhouse rattling and the chimney howling like a ghostly presence. It was a raw morning. I wore the heavy woolen sweater I'd bought in Ireland, the one like the Irish fishermen wear, and the one, my Irish sister-in-law, refers to as my ironwork sweater because of its bold weave.

The vintage Boston Whaler I kept on the lake had plenty of seating, yet as we backed away from the mooring, both of us stood. I stood because I wanted a better view of the water surface as we slowly made way through the mist. To give Craig a more interesting ride, I planned to sail south past the Otsego Hotel and the City marina and then hug the opposite shoreline, turning west only when we were abreast of the boatyard. I figured that I would know we were on the same latitude and be able to turn at just the right time to make the last half mile or so a straight shot across the lake.

Craig said, "Man, this fog is thick. I can't see much of anything."

"Be sure to wave," I said. "The girls will expect it." I knew they would watch until we were out of sight. Then they'd sit and chat awhile before they began the short drive to the boatyard to meet us with a Thermos of hot coffee. Craig turned and gave a half-hearted wave in the general direction of the car parked on the high ground above us in the parking lot.

Normally I would leave the boat docked until the fog lifted. But that morning, Craig and his wife had to drive home right after breakfast. We planned to leave a bit later—once we packed some things away and drained the water pipes. We kept the place heated all winter, but I usually drained the pipes as an added precaution against the bitter winter chills. We would be coming up again to the house for Christmas, and I didn't look forward to plumbing problems.

The Christmas season was a special time in Cooperstown. The nearby Farmer's Museum and the Fenimore House were always busy and cheerfully decorated for the holidays. Craig and his wife had joined us one year between Christmas and New Year's.

Nothing so bright or cheerful as the Fenimore House in its holiday grandeur was in sight that dreary late summer morning as I steered the Whaler out into the lake, only the cold and the heavy fog. I knew that there was a good chance we would be the only boat on the lake at that time of day and so late in the season and didn't expect to run into any watercraft that might be hidden in the misty shroud. To be certain, though, I asked Craig to sound the horn. Each time he pressed the button, he smiled. The horn blast seemed to drift out onto the lake and then come slowly back at us through the mist. It was more a haunting sound than a true echo and rose goosebumps.

A car horn answered his third blast. Craig turned toward shore, raised up on his toes, extended his arm, and gave a long and hearty wave. He laughed and made short toots, each of which was answered by a short reply beep.

After the fifth short blast, I said, "That's probably enough. If there is anybody out there, they will be thoroughly confused by this time."

He put a hand on his ample stomach and bent in an exaggerated bow as if he had just finished a virtuoso performance. He straightened and blew kisses to the wives who probably could not see him unless they had decided to walk down to the shore, but then who might have beeped? All the while, Craig clung to the windshield. He had a thick frame that belied his six-foot height. People took him to be a former football player, but I think his bulk was due more to eating well than to regular exercise.

His short burst of juvenile behavior over, Craig reverted to his usual dour demeanor. It was his mask. It was his way of trying to make sure he was in control, letting people know that he might be on the verge of a scold or reprimand should they displease him.

Standing there with one hand on the windshield and one on his hip, unsmiling, staring off into the whiteness, he seemed completely relaxed and at peace with himself and with the world. Yet I had the feeling he was alert, waiting for something to happen, waiting for something unexpected to emerge from the fog, and challenge our progress. He was like that, always looking for the next challenge, always wanting to test his intellect and his resolve.

While I was content to stroll through life, Craig needed to be hard-charging. Since he planned so well, he seldom ever looked back much less ever retraced his steps. In nautical terms, I often had to come about on a new heading–to go back and get things right because I hadn't spent enough time figuring out where I was going in the first place. Yet with all of his drive, Craig never seemed discouraged. He was an optimist. When I talked with him about something that had not gone well, some concern or bother I was obsessing over, he'd say, "There's always tomorrow."

His company's board of directors had elected Craig their President. Because it was a foreign-based company, he had to move overseas. It would be a long time before he might be able to come again to the farmhouse. The visit had been two full days, but it seemed way too short and was ending all too soon.

Sometimes simply sharing a quiet moment with a friend is enough. Neither of you needs to be doing anything special. All of my problems with family and job seemed to be absorbed into the vapor that I could feel—cold against my cheeks as if someone was flicking beads of water at me. The only sounds were the monotonous chugging of the outboard and the water lapping at the hull.

For me, the event was magical. I didn't want it to end. I throttled down, below 1100 RPMs. Our wake all but disappeared. We were making the trip without a GPS, relying on my familiarity with the lake and the boat's compass to tell us the heading.

When I looked at my friend, I thought him pensive and wondered what was going through his mind. His life was about to change dramatically. He was about to take on the responsibility of running a large company with employees and vendors and customers depending on him. In addition to that, the thought of uprooting and moving far away from relatives and lifelong acquaintances had to be nothing short of traumatic for a family-oriented man.

In the moment, neither of us said much. We exchanged a few offhand comments about the lake and the beautiful rolling hills in that part of New York State, though we saw little of them through the mist. After a particularly long silence, Craig asked me if I knew how to get to the boatyard dock. "We'll have to see," was my answer.

"But you can't see it in this mess," he replied. I told him that I was sure I would know to turn and didn't need to see.

"Bet you overshoot," he said.

"Bet I don't. I've tooled around this part of the lake a million times. Know it like the back of my hand. And don't you go telling me about boating just because you're a member of that snooty club."

He chuckled and said, "Fog makes things seem different."

"Only if it's in your mind, Craig."

"Whatever you say, but you're going to overshoot. Just make sure we don't run into anything. I don't trust this life jacket."

"Got it covered, Craig. No sweat."

"I haven't learned to swim yet."

"I know. Now relax and enjoy the scenery."

"One thing more."

"What's that?"

"We're already past the boatyard. You'll be needing to come about."

Looking aft, I saw that I had already passed the little Kingfisher Tower. Craig was right. Mentally in another place and time, I had become completely absorbed in the moment and had forgotten even where we were headed.

~—~

Craig never had the opportunity to celebrate his 60th birthday. They found him in his office, slumped over the desk, his head cradled in his folded arms as though he thought what killed him was only a passing pain or ache that would go away if he could just rest a moment.

I did not attend the funeral service at the local church, which we had gone to on so many Sundays and then strolled into town to have breakfast together at the restaurant that was always crowded and where we had to wait for a table. You could have made it, I tell myself with more than a little guilt. I should have been there in person to give my support to the main people in his life, his wife, and his children.

I missed the opportunity to tell them face-to-face, at a time when it would have meant the most to them, of the role he had played in my life. He had been a help when I needed him to be. He had been an inspiration. I missed him then and still do. I ought to have told them about his quirky sense of humor that I so much enjoyed when we were alone but that I didn't see him exhibit at home. I spoke to them later. It somehow wasn't the same. We still keep in touch.

I picture him now in some far off place that I know to be way beyond the universe. I can't tell you exactly where because I can't see anything but Craig standing in a dense fog, staring ahead—expectant, confident. Through the fog, he spots headlights as the girls swing into the parking lot at the boatyard. He turns and looks at me, smiles, and speaks. I can't actually hear the words, but I know what they are. They are always the same. "You overshot. You'll be needing to come about."

Much of my life is still run that way, winging it with only a foggy view of what lies ahead and not being concerned enough to prepare more carefully. With the memory of Craig as my pilot, eventually, I may come to do better. There is always tomorrow.

Dragonfly

Dragonfly was written to honor dear friends. It is the name they gave to the family's summer place on a quiet lake in way upstate New York, near the Canadian border.

On the loon-reflecting lake
Calling sky to Earth enshrined
Lies a silky shore
By the gods above bestowed
With mighty trees, their limbs unfold,
Embrace the solitude of old.

Times when locals roamed the shore
And glided in their birch bark boats,
Glimmering pool beneath them flowed.

Dragonfly, our lakefront home,
Looks upon a tranquil scene.
Locals in their bark canoe
Long ago have drifted by.

Birch and oak and pine
Sentinels on the shore
Remain to mark, ring-by-ring
The passing years.

We upon the porch of Dragonfly
Watching afterglow subside
See saplings spring and know
They in time will rake the passing clouds
As their forebears do, keeping watch
Over Dragonfly when we have gone away.

The Standard Patient

Eppillus Faucet waited alone in an examining room at the Sixth Galactic Medical School Surgery in Georgetown, Guyana, waiting for his third standard patient to arrive. He wiped a bead of sweat from his brow and glanced at the old fashioned wall clock that disguised a modern time display. Earlier in the day, he had been questioned by the Medical Examining Committee. The committee soon would choose the winner of the last available off-world medical license, his only means of escape.

Earth's foremost astrophysicist estimated that the planet had no more than five years before the Armageddon. Some experts argued that the huge meteor hurtling ineluctably through space on a collision path with Earth, not only would destroy a vast area of the planet, but also might even knock the planet out of orbit with more disastrous results.

That morning had been difficult for Eppillus. When he took his seat in front of the long examiner's table, the examining committee chairwoman scowled at him. "Medical intern Faucet, how many hearts does an adult groth have, and where are they located?"

He marveled at his good fortune for having started with such an easy question, a gift graciously bestowed by providence. He had treated many young groth. They all had two hearts. "Two," he answered and realized immediately, by the examiner's expression, that he had answered wrongly.

The chairwoman frowned. "Do you wish to reconsider your answer?"

He looked to his right and then to his left as if to draw support from his fellows. Except for him and the examiners, the room lay quite empty. Eppillus sat alone on an uncomfortable wooden stool in a hall that could accommodate two thousand people. A feeling of complete isolation overwhelmed him.

He imagined the other interns standing in the gallery above the examiners' table, looking down at him squirming on the stool in a vain attempt to get comfortable. They would be laughing. The laughing never bothered him because he knew they envied his family's high social standing. He was better than them, even though he often struggled with his courses.

"Intern Faucet, your silence tells me that you are unsure."

She looked down at her view screen. "I will give you a hint. I asked about an adult groth, not a child or a youngling. An adult, Intern Faucet."

He blurted out, "Of course. Yes. Yes. Of course. Older groth seldom travel off their home planet. I had been thinking of my groth patients who are all younger. In the older groth, one of the hearts takes over the job of pumping blood. The second heart withers until it becomes simply a thick point in the arterial wall."

"And the locations?"

"The locations. Well, the hearts are located in the thoracic region as with humans, but higher up."

The examiner shook her head and shot him a look of exasperation. "Intern Faucet, you do not impress me with your knowledge of the physiology of our off-world sisters. How can you expect to be given an off-world commission if you are not able to know something as simple as this?"

The examiners pressed on with questions about obscure diseases and afflictions seen only in creatures from the most distant cultures.

Eppillus' discomfort grew with each question. "Tell me what a mariner living on Getriclon might be suffering from if she complained of sharp pains in her extremities?" And then. "How many nerves might I expect to find in the spinal cord of a calornian?"

His answers became more and more hesitant, more and more tentative. In his mind, the laughter of the gallery grew until he thought that he could actually feel its vibrations. He tried to breathe evenly and deeply and to keep his sweaty hands still. With each new question, he nervously massaged his thighs, and the gulps of air he took couldn't seem to find their way to his lungs.

Three hours later, in a formal tone, the chairwoman announced, "Intern Faucet; that ends our questioning." For an instant, her face softened. "You passed this part of your examination. However, you have incorrectly diagnosed not one, but two standard patients. You will have one only more opportunity to remedy that this afternoon with your final patient."

Eppillus pushed the chairwoman's words from his mind. In a few minutes, his third standard patient was due to come through the door to the examining room. The individual would pretend to have many physical problems about which there would be complaints: pains, aches, dizziness, difficulty breathing, body parts not working as they ought. It might be human or groth or any of the other intelligent life forms that inhabited the nine worlds.

As the examiner reminded him, he had already improperly diagnosed two standard patients. He knew that he had to get it right.

Only folks with special skills or talents needed on other worlds were allowed to emigrate. Eppillus realized that without his medical skills and knowledge, he was hopelessly devoid of anything else, like athletic prowess, which might qualify him for an off-world assignment.

At four feet eight inches tall, Eppillus was too short for any real sport. He was good at curling, but they had never allowed anyone to leave Earth because they were good at curling. People had been allowed to travel if they were talented in some of the more popular sports, football being the most coveted. A footballer could name his world.

Eppillus understood that he would never be a footballer and that if he could not correctly diagnosis all of the ailments his third standard patient would be faking, he had to give up his dream of leaving a possibly doomed Earth. When the meteor hit, he would be staring at the sky and wondering how it felt to be dead.

Again he looked at the wall clock, which told him it was eight and eleven moments in the 18 by 40 duration. "Local time," he said, and the time changed to 6:40PM. He got up, opened the door, and looked out into an empty hallway. Ordinarily, the place would be bustling with physicians, nurses, orderlies, and patients. He walked out to the lobby to find it as empty as the hall, except for a guard at the reception desk.

The guard turned to him and said, "Hello, sir, I didn't know anyone was still about."

"Been waiting over an hour for a patient. Anyone ask for me?"

"And that would be?"

"I'm intern Faucet. I am expecting a patient who is apparently running late."

"I've been here since nine by two durs. Nobody's come in askin' for ya.

"Hey. Ya know, Doc since yer already here, ya could do me a big favor. The main door don't lock until nineteen by naught, so if ya could jest hang out here 'till then in case someone comes in. I'd sure appreciate it."

"Excuse me?"

"Only one's gonna come in this time of day'll be yer patient. Don't know why yer botherin'. We'll all be dead when the big rock hits."

"It might not be so bad. Scientists are wrong sometimes. Anyhow, it's a long way off. You never know what will happen in the meantime."

"Why wait. I'm goin' across campus to the women's dorm. Maybe hook up with one of those new interns."

"What about your job?"

The guard sniffed. "Stations are all down. Don't need to make my usual rounds. Anyhow, I wanna watch the game later. They got a giant holoscreen over there."

"You can pull it up on the frescoscreen right here."

"No can do, Doctor Plumber."

"Faucet."

"They shut everything off 'cause of the changeover to the new building. Today's the last day fer this old place. When they sell off the furniture and transfer all the supplies, whole building gonna be ripped down. Yep. Everything shut off."

"I thought it closed next week. My examining room works."

"That's different, Doctor Faucet, completely self-contained. Uses backup power, like the OR and the emergency lights."

"Okay. Off with you, then," Eppillus said to the guard who already was sauntering out of the lobby.

Bastard'll probably never come back. Guess I'm stuck. Someone needs to be at reception to receive my patient.

No one had thought to tell him that everybody was leaving early to attend the party celebrating the new building. Not the first time that he had been forgotten. His birth mother left him on a door stoop of a family that subsequently adopted him.

Abandoned like garbage, he had succeeded beyond anything even his wild imagination could conjure. A minimum of effort and the help of his influential adoptive family had brought him to the threshold of a new and exciting career.

Calling up a training video on the monitor at the reception station, Eppillus awaited the arrival of his patient. He had missed the phone call informing him that the expected patient would not be coming until after the move to new facilities.

He quickly became absorbed in a video describing what happens to a Biquad if the wrong kinds of food are placed in the feeding pouch.

"Are you the doctor?"

He looked up. A tall and beautiful female stood in front of the desk. He judged her to be all of six feet, heel to head.

Eppillus recognized her immediately as a bigun. That wasn't their scientific name. He never could quite reproduce the guttural grunts and clicks that sounded like two bamboo shoots being rubbed together, so he simply relied on the name that the general public called the creatures.

With his arms, he propelled his short frame out of the chair and onto the floor. He stood on his toes, pressing his fingertips against the desktop to steady himself. The woman's scent, fresh-cut gardenias, tickled his nostrils, and he breathed deeply, filling his mind with the fragrance.

He closed his eyes for a moment, letting the aroma carry him to the home of his youth, where his adoptive mother kept one of the last private gardens to be allowed by the authorities. They suffered her indulgence in gratitude for her achievements in bringing a diplomatic end to World War III.

The biguns were a civilization much like humans, living mostly on the far world, Galaxticon. They often mated with humans and produced healthy offspring. There were differences. The bigun heart is located on the right side. The large intestine includes more extensive tubing with several turns not found in humans. Some scientists theorized that they actually colonized the earth and that Earth people were descendants of the bigun.

Galaxticon women were known throughout the worlds for strong features and striking beauty typically enduring into old age. The woman standing in front of him with her dark eyes, smooth brown skin, and long black hair was the most beautiful creature he'd ever seen. Her tight-fitting business suit showed off her every line.

To get a better look, he walked around to the other side of the reception desk. Nature endowed her with large glands and a slim waist above hips that struck him as more than adequate for childbearing.

Trying to sound authoritative by lowering his usually squeaky voice, he said, "Do you know that you are over a half-hour late? I have been waiting for you all afternoon. I don't have all day, you know."

Biguns were known for being polite and solicitous. The woman smiled and said in a pleasant voice, "I am truly sorry that my presence offends you. My driver went off to find a physician in the new hospital building, but I am afraid to pass out while I waited, so I came here." She paused. He made no reply. She said, "I really hope you can help me. I do not feel at all well."

Eppillus, feeling his superiority established, gave a backhand wave of dismissal to the person he thought to be his expected standard patient. "That's quite all right. Please follow me."

In the examining room, he activated the holographic video recorder. He then asked, "Have you been a patient here."

"Never. I see the sign and think you might be able to treat me. I suffer from a belly ache since this morning, and my lower back aches."

"Possible pregnancy or urinary tract infection," he mumbled to himself. "A scan would tell me." From the desk, he picked up a tablet which he pretended to examine for a moment. He pressed a button on the screen. "Name, please."

"Tritxxkt."

He looked up at her. "No. No. Your federation name and occupation." He returned the tablet to the desk.

"Sorry. Yes. My name is Aeron Mansel, Secretary-General of the Federation of Inhabited Worlds."

Eppillus clacked his tongue. He knew that the standard patients sometimes assumed roles to put more pressure on the interns.

He said, "Ms. Aeron, I will need you to undress. I'm sorry that we haven't any gowns that you can put on. The celebrations and all. The staff already left."

She nodded and said, "The celebrations. Yes. I am planning to attend."

Relishing what he took to be another part of the usual standard patient ruse, he said, "Maybe we can get you out of here in time for you to do just that. You can lay your things there." He pointed to the chair in which he had been sitting. Then he patted the examining table. "When you're done, please sit here."

With his heart pounding against his ribs, he looked away while she took off her suit and blouse and shoes until she stood in her bra and bikini pants. Her hands made slow, circular motions across her stomach.

Aeron Mansel slid her backside easily onto the high table and placed her folded hands in her lap. She gazed at them for a moment and then looked down at Eppillus and smiled. "I am ready," she said.

Eppillus turned and felt his face redden and his throat tighten. He was barely able to say, "Ah, Ms. Aeron, what is your Earth age?"

"I am 45 Earth years since I birthed."

"Age 45 years," he repeated, putting one hand on his hip and rotating his head to look with a certain degree of professional pride at his image posing on the four frescoscreened walls.

"Please lie down on your back, Ms. Aeron."

She flopped awkwardly on her side and then rolled over onto her back, seeming to be in much distress.

"Have you felt nauseous?"

"Yes. Yes, she said. "I feel that way. My stomach experiences the water sickness with waves coming and going, and the little birds flying round and round in my gut."

Suddenly Eppillus found himself enjoying the diagnostic session. His entire career depended on getting the correct diagnosis, and things had not gone well for him up to that point. Even the political clout of his family couldn't get him an off-world commission if he flubbed this one. Yet he felt extreme confidence for the first time since his examination boards began.

His mind wandered. He thought. Somehow this woman will know what is at stake for me and make certain I get it right. I've heard some of my female colleagues talk about how such feelings are a sure sign of love. Why not? Adjusting for overall longevity, I'm around her age. How could I help but be attracted to her, and why not her to me?

Bigun custom held that a female would consider for marriage only eligible males of proper age who performed an extraordinary service for her. The biguns had a saying, "Everything is possible under the six moons of Galaxticon." But Eppillus could not imagine anything special he might do for this beautiful woman.

Pushing the unprofessional thoughts from his mind, he bent closer to her. Beads of sweat lay on her forehead. He glanced at the room thermometer on the frescoscreen. The room was cold. Perhaps she was nervous. He took a napkin from the dispenser and patted her forehead and cheeks. He saw beads of sweat upon her chest.

He pressed lightly against her stomach with his index finger just above the naval.

The muscles are taut. A sign of good coaching. Obviously, she purposely tightened them to indicate a symptom.

Peritonitis. This is going to be too easy.

"Try to relax," he said. "I am going to press again. It might hurt." Recalling that the biguns had a reputation for their stoicism, he said, "Don't be afraid to tell me if it does."

She smiled and nodded. "I understand, Doctor. Please do what you must."

With his gaze fixed on her face, he laid the heel of his hand on her belly and dug his fingers into her flesh. He saw a minor twitch near her eyes. When he released his fingers, he saw her features distort and heard the low gasp that escaped through her clenched teeth.

He again laid the heel of his hand on her stomach. She grabbed his arm and shouted, "Please, not again. It is very painful."

From deep in his brain, a thought began to find its way to the surface. Something is terribly wrong.

In a halting voice, Eppillus said, "I am going to, to ask you some questions. Please answer as honestly as you can." The woman nodded. "Are you my, my standard patient?"

"I do not understand."

"You told me that you are, the secretary-general of the federation of inhabited worlds. Is it the truth?"

"Yes. Yes. Why are you asking me these questions? What have you discovered?"

He didn't tell her that she hovered near death. The bigun physiology being in many ways quite different from humans, his patient lay in grave and immediate danger.

"Please lie very still." He took off his lab coat and placed it over her, tucking it under her chin. "I will be back in a few minutes."

Eppillus left the examining room and ran to the reception desk. He pressed the intercom to summon the guard. Nothing happened. He punched the button on the outside communicator. Nothing. He punched the emergency button. Nothing. Only then did he realize that the board, usually a dazzling display of colored lights, was dark. He had neglected to charge his own phone for days. It too was dark. Every means of communication from the surgery had been shut down, and his personal phone was useless.

He was alone with one of the most important individuals in the known universe. He ran down the main hall looking in vain for one of the cleaning people to summon help. He found no one.

He ran to the glass entrance doors and peered out. The street was deserted in both directions.

I could prop the door open, go looking for her chauffeur. What if I didn't find the chauffeur? What if somebody shut the door, and I can't get back in?

A grim realization settled upon Eppillus. He would have to treat the patient himself, even though that would kill any chance of his ever going off-world or even becoming a practicing physician on Earth. An intern who treated a patient without supervision committed an unforgivable breach of ethics. To compound the breach, he would have to break into the pharmacy and steal drugs.

What if I fail? What if she dies? I will live out my days in a prison colony on a faraway world.

He raced back toward the examining room, muttering to himself, "I can do it. I can do it. I'm not some over privileged rich boy pretending at this." On the way, he took sheets and towels and a pillow from a supply closet.

Back in the examining room, he asked, "How are we doing?"

"I'm sorry. I vomit while you are out. I feel very, very sick." Sidestepping the mess on the floor, he came to her and wiped her mouth with a towel and put the pillow under her head.

Eppillus asked, "Have you a personal communication device?"

"It is in my car. My battery is dead. I forgot to recharge it this morning. My busy schedule and all–you doctors know about busy schedules. I find them an intrusion. I pretty much rely on my secretary and my driver."

"That's all right. I'm going to wheel you into another room where we have the equipment to deal with your complaint. We'll get you fixed up. Don't worry. You're in capable hands. I've done this a dozen times." He felt it prudent not to add that the dozen times had been on a holograph. There would be time for that later, time to admit also that he was not even a doctor yet.

In the operating room, Eppillus moved his patient to a table and exchanged his lab coat for sheets, carefully draping them. He took a warming blanket from a cabinet and placed it over her legs and then secured her to the table.

He needed to stand on his toes and reach up in order to pull a large instrument along a track above the table and center it over her abdomen. Eppillus dragged in a chair to stand on, so he could study the holobox located on the side of the instrument. He puzzled over the images for several minutes. He finally saw that the appendix had ruptured into the peritoneal cavity. For a race as ancient as the bigun, natural selection should have done away with the appendix. It seemed such a useless organ.

He stepped off the chair, took a deep breath, and let it out slowly before he said, "You are very ill. You require emergency surgery. For reasons too complicated to go into now, you and I are the only ones in the building. Because all systems are shut down, I cannot call for assistance. I myself could go outside to get help. I might not return in time."

He took another deep breath. "I'm not yet a doctor. I'm just an intern who has completed his studies and is sitting for final exams. I've never used these instruments on a living person. I need your agreement before I can continue. Of course, you have a right to wait for a second opinion."

"It appears you are my only reasonable option. Please proceed, Doctor."

He started to tell her again that he was not a doctor, but the words stuck in his throat. He had more important things to consider. He quickly checked and found that the necessary equipment would run on emergency power long enough to complete the operation.

Neither the frescoscreen nor the holographic room camera in the OR was operational. Whatever happened, the two of them would be the only witnesses. Years of hard and fast protocol shouted for him to abandon the effort and seek help.

No one can fault me if I simply slip on out of here and bring back a real doctor. Even if she dies, I will have acted according to protocol. I'll get my actual standard patient to diagnose. Life will go on.

When he looked into Aeron Mansel's eyes, she stared up at him. In her face he saw a quiet confidence that he had never seen—a confidence in him.

"I'm going to put you to sleep for a while," he said. "When you awake, you will be fine. I won't leave your side."

Aeron nodded. "You are a wonderful man with a healing spirit."

He administered the anesthesia. Aeron smiled and reached out to him. He took her hand and cupped it between his palms.

~—~

Four months later, Doctor Eppillus Faucet, newly appointed medical director for Galaxticon world, waited in the Main Transport Terminal for a special boarding call. Next to him sat Aeron Mansel, Secretary-General of the Federation of Inhabited Worlds—his bride. When he heard the voice on the loudspeaker calling for Eppillus and Aeron Faucet, he turned to her and smiled.

Culloden

Prince Charles Stuart wished to wrest the English Throne from the House of Hanover. In early 1746 the Scottish Highlander army of Prince Charles met the army of King George II on a field called Culloden's Moor, near Inverness, Scotland. The better equipped and trained English troops led by the Duke of Cumberland fighting for King George II defeated the army of Prince Charles and ended the Jacobite rebellions. The Highlanders, armed mostly with swords, were defeated after a bloody hand to hand battle. The following verse is dedicated to their valiant efforts.

The happy cry of death
He cries this day,
Heard on April wind
Hastening through the meadow.
Wildflowers sing to him
As he, running,
Treads them underfoot.
Musket done and claymore raised,
On to Satan's portals
There to triumph, now he shouts.
The glens respond in echo
Astonished in reply.
Cool of even prayer,
Ashen sky above

Welcome warriors fallen
In cause so hopeless cast.
Ponder this the gallant men,
Expired clansmen by their side.
When the clouds at which they stare
Fade at last from view
Only grassy mounds of sod will
Pay them all their due.

A Different Sort

From the moment I came into the world, I had a bad feeling about the whole business. I'm one of what is supposed to become a new breed, a genetically engineered human, engineered from the ground up, so to speak, from the instant of conception.

New-breeds are designed to learn in the womb during an extended 18 month gestation period. I had an extensive vocabulary at birth. I turned to the doctor who delivered me and said, "You forking idiot. That hurt." Since I hadn't spoken before, I said it all sort of gurgly but was he surprised that I tried to form words instead of just crying my lungs out. His jaw dropped, so he looked for an instant like some forking hick watching a circus act for the first time. He was old school–never delivered anyone like me–and didn't realize that I needed no slap on the ass to get myself going. I wondered why none of the other docs were around. Specialization maybe?

Okay. Okay. So I got the obscenity wrong. Hearing what people are saying is not the easiest thing to do when you're floating in soup.

Mom said something like, "Jacob, you shouldn't talk that way to the doctor. He's only trying to help." The words were bubbly because there was still stuff in my ears, but I think that was the gist.

One of my other doctors ought to have told him about me. If I'd been stronger, I would've punched his lights out right there, the little schmuck.

Looking back, I know mom realized from the start of the program that the future with her new bouncing baby boy contained some real problems. I can't imagine somebody like her actually thinking that she could raise me. I took a good look at mom when the nurse set me down on a little crib after giving me her idea of a bath. Mom seemed so short. I took a good look at the doctor. He stood about the same height. Between them, they didn't have more than about 10 or 11 feet.

I wasn't really sure at the time, but I kind of felt that I might be a little big for my age—no other infants to compare. I knew I was too long for the tiny bassinettes they had in the nursery. It took about a millisecond for the nurse to figure that one out.

Mom is a dress size six at most. I'm not so sure about that, but you get the idea. During the second phase of her pregnancy, she spent the whole time in bed with the doctors attending her round the clock, and having me nearly killed her. She required tubes in and out of every natural orifice and some new ones they made, and she existed on a diet of mush for nearly a year. A normal birth was out of the question after 18 months, so I came out by Caesarian Section.

My mother expected a big baby based on the size of her bump, but 21pounds and 22 inches were a lot more than either she or the doctors planned. To put it mildly, I was a shock to everyone except, I later found, to my siblings, who had no adult frame of reference. They took things in stride. No sweat. Just a really, really big baby brother. Something to brag about.

Had I not been an experiment, they would have squashed my head and dumped me in the trash. Unlike the old days when people gave a damn about each other and life had some sanctity, when I birthed, more than half the pregnancies in the country were being terminated for population control. I was too valuable—like the first man. They ought to have named me Adam.

Mom and I stayed in the hospital for the rest of a week. I spent my first night sleeping next to mom. I'd felt happier in my primordial goop. The real world, while fascinating, can be scary for a kid a few hours old with knowledge of all sorts of bad things that can happen.

Around a month after mom and the scientists started me on my career as a person, mom got mugged. The bastard nearly killed me in the process. I can still feel that punch as if it was yesterday. Had I been out of the womb at the time, I'm sure I would have laid into the dumb bastard, maybe busted a few of his ribs.

Even in the womb, sounds of the real world assailed my ears like a band warming up before the big performance—discordant. Everything sounded so loud too—the sheets when mom moved in her sleep; the crunching of shoes when the people walked past our room; even the sound of mom's heart which I ought to have been used to by then.

Mom's thoughts didn't bother me. I got used to them a long time ago. I had the ability to turn off my telepathic powers. Let me rephrase that. I'm always aware of what people around me are thinking. In order to keep my sanity, I turn down the volume until they're no more than a faint hum.

Whatever the scientists had done with my genes, I had some important abilities that nobody else had. My ability to grasp new concepts was enhanced. Math and physics and chemistry were no problem. I learned these as fast as one can turn a page. And the telepathic gig. Now that was an ability the scientists didn't even know I possessed. Wasn't about to tell them either.

I finally got to sleep that first day. I slept right through until the morning. Most likely, the sun streaming through the window woke me. Our room happened to be on the east side of the building with no shades or curtains.

I tried to pull away from mom. She hugged me closer to her and spoke to me in a whisper. "Jacob, you make me the happiest person in the whole wide world. Your brothers and sisters made me happy when they came along. They were special. But you, you are especially special. That makes me feel important in a way that I can't explain. Do you know that you will not likely ever have a virus or that microbes will never make you sick?"

I responded. "At least that's what the scientists tell us. I hope it's true."

"Oh, it is, Jacob. It really is. They are all very smart men."

"Yeah, mom. I remember you and the others talking about that. One thing you did not talk about was why I am so big compared to the other newborns I saw yesterday. Will I get much bigger?"

She turned away and seemed to be looking out the window. I waited for her to answer. She turned back to me and said, "Jacob, you will grow bigger."

"How much bigger? Bigger than you?"

"We have no idea how big you will be when you grow up. Your head seems huge now. Your body will catch up eventually."

"Why will I be bigger?"

"The doctors didn't know how to engineer you for a long and perfect life and still make you small like your father and me."

"We're naturally genetically this way because the world is running out of the capacity to feed us. Little people eat less. Big people eat more. It's called natural selection, survival of the fittest, a Darwinian thing I do believe."

Even though I had no idea what she was talking about, I nodded. I never heard anybody discussing such things while I floated around in mom's belly, even my teachers.

I stayed in the room with mom mostly the whole time. I was too important and too big to be kept in the nursery. They only took me there to poke and probe me.

When it came time for us to leave the hospital, they wheeled me out in a chair and belted me into a special seat that replaced the one like mom was sitting on in front. It surprised me to see mom driving. I thought at least we would take an Uber or maybe a taxi.

We'd barely turned out of the hospital parking lot when I said, "Mom. Please put more of those cushions under me, so I can see out better. I'm mostly looking at the sky. About all, I'll be able to see from down here are clouds."

So much to see. Being in the womb, it's impossible to do more than imagine how things will be on the outside. After the first six months or so in the womb, I developed telepathic powers and could tap into what mom thought. As good as that is, it's not the same as seeing things with your own eyes.

"Jacob, darling. You are going to take some getting used to. Your brothers and your sisters were more like four and five before they were as advanced as you are right now—and you only born such a little while ago. Your thinking is scarily adult. Your vocabulary is amazing. I would love to be inside that brain of yours. Maybe that is why you are so big. Your head is at least a couple inches bigger than average. You must have grown more than three inches since you were born. The doctors told us that your growth will quickly slow, but still, I mean three inches in such a short time?"

I felt sorry for mom. But then I hadn't seen our house yet or the rest of my family. The emotion and circumstances wouldn't come together. While I was gestating, my father talked about cold fish. I first thought he was talking about things that swim in the water. Eventually, I got the idea that when a person is a cold fish, it means they never connect their emotions with the thinking part of their brain. Maybe my brain is screwed up? I knew the concept of emotion, yet never could figure what it is. I felt nothing toward mom. Knew that wasn't right. I didn't know how to fix it. I had heard the doctors talking about autism. Couldn't be that. I was supposed to be perfect. Autism is some kind of disease that I'd need to learn more about

Mom pulled the car to the curb. She grabbed loose cushions from the back seat and put them under me. That raised me up, and I could see everything we passed. Everything I looked at seemed small. I got a weird feeling like I was a giant and would need to step carefully so as not to crush all the little people like mom and the hospital staff. Of course, they were all way taller and bigger than me, yet I felt really big. I think maybe my brain was charging forward already and knew what the world would look like when I did get taller. Could I have been looking through other people's eyes, even though in the womb I was blind? Whatever the fork it was, the sensation was disquieting.

Some of the experts tell us that infants learn best during their first six months. For me, my education began at around six weeks, but that was after I was conceived, not after my birthday. Teachers were brought in to talk to me. By my tenth month, I realized that my lips were moving in an effort to answer the strictly rhetorical questions put to me by the teachers. They covered a lot of ground in a very short time. I have near-total recall of all the material as well as what I overheard eavesdropping and also what I gleaned from my mom's mind, as well as everyone else around me after the telepathic abilities kicked in.

A lot was left out of my pre-birth education. The fact that I am so big, for one. I developed a mental picture of our family homestead without anything except the hospital's oversized rooms and doors to give me a hint about the actual size of it. Too bad mom didn't hold a scale up to the front door, so I might have gotten some idea of the height and girth of things compared to my size.

"We're almost there, Jacob," mom chimed in a bright and cheerful tone. "We live in this block."

She turned into a long paved pathway. It led to a dwelling located in a small clearing cut from a copse that belied the residential nature of the surrounding neighborhood. Standing by the front door—the rest of my family, all looking pretty much alike: my father, my sister, my brothers.

To say that the sight of the family shocked me is to belittle the sense I felt on seeing my siblings for the first time. A little more than a month old, I already stood as tall as one of them, the one-year-old, my older sister, Sara. Of course, I couldn't yet stand by myself. I would learn how to do that soon enough—but just the size difference. It amazed me. My gaze shifted to the background, to the house, to the place where mom intended to raise me. The homestead seemed suddenly very tiny indeed.

What I thought at the time was that neither my mom nor my dad knew that the national government had planned to take me away from them a few months after I was born. The plan was to give me a brief period of natural home life and, thereafter, put me through all sorts of tests. They would then quietly do away with me at some future date.

I'd discovered this in the womb when I read the thoughts of people in a nearby room at the hospital. It had come to the point in this country where killing any child less than seven years old was considered to be a legal abortion. They chose seven years because that was considered to be the age of reason. What good was a person that was not old enough to reason, anyhow? Since such young kids couldn't reason, they couldn't be disciplined under the threat of being killed if they didn't behave. So, all sorts of youngsters were aborted under the new and broader meaning of the word because their parents either didn't want to or couldn't discipline them.

Those terminally stupid—and did I also say, evil—bureaucratic types were in for a surprise if they tried to abort me. The dumb shits were going to get some aborting done on them. My strength and movement were equal to that of most adults—little people adults.

No way am I about to let anyone know all the powers I have at my disposal. I already know that my physical strength will soon be beyond most adults—not just little people adults either. That will be the most difficult thing to hide, much more difficult than my mental acuity. I'll need to walk the fine line between appearing to be their great success and not appearing to have such powers that they will lock me up so tight I won't be able to save myself when the abort date rolls around, whenever that might be. I'll need to find that out ASAP.

Too, I hope I stop growing before I get so big that the government guys and girls decide I'm a threat simply because of my size. I need to pretend I'm kind of weak but developing, and not too smart but learning kind of fast.

During the next six months, the bureaucrats left me alone. I really grew during that time. When I was born, the doc measured me at 22 inches long. I think he cheated because my legs were like a pretzel. My bet is that he was guessing. Anyhow, let's call it an even 24 inches. Funny, when you are very small, they don't measure your height but your length. But screw that, I was about two feet tall at birth. I had a growth spurt right afterward. I have been averaging about a quarter inch a day. I'm now nearly six feet tall.

I loved to watch television. So much to learn from it. The universe fascinated me. Even I could not grasp the enormity of it all, planets and stars and galaxies, untold billions, each different than the next.

Sitting by an open window and inhaling all the scents that wafted on the breezes became a particularly rewarding pastime for me. I learned to identify dozens of different odors and fragrances. Mom helped me figure out the source of many of these.

Mom has been going broke feeding me. She said that I eat like a horse. My guess is that I eat more like an elephant. The National Bureau of Birth has been giving mom a subsidy. Like most government programs, it is way too little to make up for my appetite, yet it is too much when you figure that there is no reason for the government to be giving us anything. It was Mom's choice to have me engineered. She volunteered. So why should the financial burden be on the public taxpayer?

They read Freud to me while I was still inside. What an asshole that guy was. But he did get a few things right. I understand that this is my superego phase–I think. So here we are in the superego phase, with me worrying about taxpayers. I heard mom complain enough about taxes to know just about none of them are fair. Folks like mom pay more than their fair share. The fat cats–not sure exactly who they are–cats must be like people somehow and pay the government. I got to look into that a little more, try to understand it. I'm probably taking it too literally.

Forget about it. All this stuff is not my worry. Leave it to the adults. My problem is that those scientist types are sure to try and do away with me just as soon as they see me as no longer useful. Can't complain to mom. She would probably never believe me and, worse, maybe even tell them about my complaints. I figured that if she did—gonzo, forget about me growing old.

It might have been better if those government types had not been so talkative at the hospital. Then I could bask in ignorance like so much of the population, ignorant of the way perfectly good children are killed every day because they are considered more trouble than they are worth. I suppose that it won't be long before that principle applies to everyone at every age.

Time is coming right up that mom will have to let the bureaucrats see how big I am. That will be interesting. I look more like my big brother Mordechai. He's almost 14. We look a lot alike, except that he already has a beard, and I have apparently not entered that stage they call puberty when hair starts to sprout all over. That's good for me. If I had a beard, the docs might be afraid of me. But with this child's smooth skin, they will see me only as a very large child.

A couple days later, right after breakfast, on my six month anniversary, mom told me that we were going for a car ride. It was my first time out of the house since I came home from the hospital.

The weather had turned cold. Snow from our first fall of the season lay all about, even blanketing the driveway and the road in front of our house. Mom had bought me cold-weather clothing that I objected to wearing when she first showed it to me. But the minute I hit the frigid air, I appreciated her concern. Knowing about snow from vicarious womb experience isn't the same as walking in it or picking it up and letting the powder sift through your fingers. The snow reminded me not to be too cocky about all my powers. I lacked lots of simple life experiences other people took for granted. Hubris (The docs loved that word.) would be my downfall. I needed to fight it, develop my sense of humor, and grow some humility.

She hugged me and said, "We are going on a trip, a kind of extended vacation. Your growth has been slowing. In the last few days, you haven't grown at all, least not enough for me to measure with my tape measure. You've been eating less too. Time for us to be going."

"Where we going?"

"I've been planning this for a very long time, even before you were born. But I've been playing dumb, so not even you would think I was anything else but a gullible member of the great body of the unwashed. That is what the National Bureau of Birth thinks too, the whole butt-headed lot of them."

I didn't recall reading mom's mind about any trips. She must have been so preoccupied with being a mom that she never thought about a vacation so soon.

"Where we going?"

"We are going far away. Nobody will look for us because they will think we both have been killed in a terrible explosion and fire. Your father is looking at that aspect of my plan. He's going to nearly vaporize some poor woman and her kid."

"Dad shouldn't kill anybody just for me. That is definitely not right."

"He will kill nobody. It is a woman and her child who were hit by a car last week in a hit and run. Dad came upon the remains on a back road. He checked. No next of kin. Homeless mother. Perfect situation. We've been waiting for something like this. It's all good. The woman has nobody. No one will miss her. They will find some of our DNA and think themselves clever for figuring out how to determine the woman and her child are you and me. To be sure, the scull will be missing. They will not even try to find it. There will be no tracks.

"In a year, the way you are maturing, nobody will recognize you. Maybe be a little tall, but I can tell folks that you play basketball."

"Basketball? Don't recall learning anything about that. Baseball and football, yeah. Guess you need to be tall to play basketball, huh."

"No matter. We will be teaching you ethics and not sports. Those dickheads at the bureau created you to be the perfect bland human in every way."

"But that's a good thing, right?"

"No. That is a bad thing. The bureaucrats do not want engineered people to be ethical. They want to be starting with a perfectly unethical person."

"That would be me."

"Correct. Their idea of the truly perfect human is someone who has no ethical compass, no morals, someone who the national government can manipulate any way they want. What they planned was to study you, figure out if you had developed an ethical compass. What they want to have is a person that they can have do anything without moral qualms. They planned on providing you with their moral code. They tell you what's right and what's wrong."

"I'm capable of thinking for myself. For example, I would never knowingly let anything happen to you or my siblings."

"Those people only wanted you to study. If you were a moral person, they figured on aborting you before you could do any harm. They never wanted you to grow into manhood. If you show any morality, any empathy, you are no use to them. You are a machine to them. Nothing more. It would scare them to death if they thought you did. That's why we have to pretend you're dead. Otherwise, they would turn the country, the planet, upside down looking for you."

"They can't turn the world upside down, can they?"

"No. It's only an expression. Hyperbole. You remember learning about that."

"I get it. Those bastards. It is a lot worse than I knew. I see past insincere people. I understand things like killing are evil. I already was hatching a plan to make the world better."

"Those are emotions, feelings bred of anger. Anger by itself is not enough. Anger by itself is bad. With your powers and the ethical standards we will teach you, the national government as it is now constituted, led mostly by evil sycophants, won't stand a chance against you."

She was right, of course. Already, I had figured to be their worst nightmare for wanting to abort me, be a pain in their collective asses and then split and live a quiet life. Mom had just shown me that I ought to aim a lot higher. Being elected President seemed a worthy challenge.

Being born with an incomplete moral compass and telepathic powers–not autistic like I first thought–I know exactly how most people think about all sorts of things. They believe, for example, that abortion after birth is plain and simple murder–and the same for many assisted suicides that, more often than not, are simply confused or lonely people. What happens to folks to cause them to accept such terrible actions?

I knew who I was from almost the start. I heard doctors talking about how some non-engineered children have pre-birth memories, so maybe that part of me wasn't so special. My first memory is of waking up and trying to make sense of who or what I was.

I also knew the situation about aborting both young and old. Yeah, they talked about end of life termination as abortion. Strange how those things become acceptable. So long as something like abortion was illegal, people pretty much used it as a last resort. Folks figured that if the government and their preacher speaks against it, well, then it must be a bad thing to do. But when the government says, "Hey, it's okay to kill," then individuals can more readily ignore their conscience or their clergy and just go ahead and leave the regrets for later—when the deed is done and there's no going back. No end to what a little engineered unborn can learn from eavesdropping on the conversation around him.

I turned to mom. "I'm ready to go to war."

"Don't rush things, Jacob. You have plenty of time."

I didn't say it, but with my telepathic powers, it will be a cinch to find the right people. And I won't even need to meet them personally to recruit them. I can do that by remote control, so to speak.

"You need to gain experience, Jacob. You feel pretty big shot right now, but you still have so much to learn. My brother lives in the mountains as a hermit. He doesn't know we are coming. But he will accept us when he hears our story. Soon as the authorities interview him for the second time about our disappearance, we'll join him. That's when your real education begins."

I knew then that I was, in fact, the second Adam. My prospects were unlimited. I would rule the planet. A sighted man in a blind world, that was me. My prospects truly were unlimited.

~—~

What I didn't know at the time is that the scientists had engineered into me a kill switch that would automatically terminate me on my tenth birthday.

The Mind's Eye

Jackie Brown, recently hired as a security guard at The Willows Condominiums, was driving around on patrol during a rainstorm when he saw a tall, husky figure in the middle of the road. The figure–that he took to be a man because of the size–wore a hooded garment and had his back to Jackie's patrol car. With arms outstretched and feet wide apart, the man hopped from one foot to the other, blocking the narrow lane. Jackie stopped the car.

Despite the effort of the car's wiper blades to clear the torrential downpour from the windshield, shapes in the darkness beyond writhed and twisted. Even the tree trunks seemed to move. Speaking to himself–as Jackie often did when he was alone–he said, "Damn! Is my mind playing tricks? I need to get this one right. What a crazy situation."

He ran a finger down the wide scar that started below his right eye and extended to his chin. He pressed the heel of his hand against his forehead. He tried to will his migraine to end, imagining cruel creatures inside his head pounding on his skull. Jackie hunched his shoulders up to his ears.

Jackie had been hired for the security job on the recommendation of his cousin, Moe. He chose not to disclose to his prospective employer that on his last security job in Cleveland, he'd accidentally killed his partner. It'd been on a stormy October night just like the one in which he sat staring at the hopping man: rain, wind, strange shadows.

He rolled down the window and shouted. "Hey, pal. Can I help you?" The hopping man ignored him.

The wipers slapped back and forth. "This weird damn storm. So much lightning. Usually, not much of that this time of year. Too damn cold."

Jackie again shouted, "You okay?" No reaction. "You sick?" Still no reaction. "Too much celebrating?" The figure in the glare of his headlights appeared to shrug but kept hopping and made no reply. Suddenly the figure disappeared from view.

Jackie's radio crackled. He closed the window to keep out the pelting rain. Against a backdrop of thunder, he heard, "You there?" It was his cousin, Moe.

He and Moe grew up together. Moe's folks dropped him off at the local firehouse and disappeared. Jackie's maiden aunt raised both boys. Jackie's parents were serving life sentences for the murder of a drug dealer. His schoolmates teased him without mercy about his scar and his jailbird parents. When he fought back, he got blamed.

"Can't talk now, Moe. Got some crazy guy in the road. Call you back in a minute."

"Crazy like me? Maybe he's playin' a joke on you."

"Maybe. But he could be real trouble too. You never know about some folks."

Jackie had been like a brother to the younger Moe, looking after him, making sure he got enough to eat, fighting his battles at school, making Moe feel part of a family.

The figure reappeared. Jackie let the car roll toward the man in the hoodie and stopped about six feet away. Again he opened the window and yelled. "Hey. I'm talking to you, dude. Mind letting me know what you're doing out here? It's sixty-four degrees out."

Jackie's psychiatrist had told him that guilt and remorse and shame for killing an innocent person might be one reason for his headaches. The doctor said that a man ashamed of what he's done sometimes twists reality. If reality is too difficult to endure, people create fantasy.

Jackie understood that the person hopping side-to-side in the rain, in the middle of the night, blocking traffic could be a product of his mind. But he sure looked real, mighty suspicious too. Jackie felt compelled to discover what kind of threat the man posed and to deal with it.

On his cell phone, he pressed the speed dial for the local police. Jackie had already called seven times that night, alerting the police to various items that seemed to be dangerous, including a suspicious-looking old lady walking a dog. "Ben. That you?"

"It's me, Jackie."

"What's it this time, Jackie?"

"A guy in the road. He's hopping. He's on West Oak near Hibiscus."

"Doing what?"

"Hopping. You know, like side-to-side. From one foot to the other."

"What's he look like?"

"Tall. Big guy. In a black hoodie, dark trousers."

"I'll send a car 'round to check. You sit tight. You in your vehicle?"

"Yeah."

"Stay there."

A bolt of lightning slashed across the sky. The lightning lit up the world in front of him. It struck a tree on the side of the road near the hopping man. He felt the hair on his arms stand straight out.

Jackie shut his eyes for a moment, trying to adjust them to the darkness. He opened them and studied the tree where the lightning struck. An instant later, the free end of a downed electric wire began to jump and spark.

Again Jackie pressed the speed dial for the police. "Ben. That you?"

"It's me, Jackie."

"We got a car on the way. Lots goin' on tonight. We'll get to you."

"It's something else, Ben."

"What is it now, Jackie?"

"Lightning struck a tree on West Oak Street. Live electrical wire whipping all over the place."

"Stay in your vehicle. Keep away from that wire. Your man involved?"

Jackie leaned toward the windshield and squinted into the dark. Shadows rippled with the swirling wind. "He's gone, Ben. Must've took off when the tree limb dropped."

"Sit tight."

Had the man in the hoodie been real or only a shadow given substance by his mind? He angled his vehicle across the road. Out his side window, he watched the wire jump and spit.

A police car rounded the corner and came slowly toward the downed line. The policeman pulled up beside his car. "Go on and get yourself a cup of coffee. We got this."

Jackie gave the policeman a salute and headed for a nearby all-night diner.

He leaned against the diner's counter, his trembling hands around a hot coffee cup. He wondered why he was always the guy weird things happened to. He touched the scar on his face, trying to remember what he had done to make his mother angry enough to brand him with her hot iron. The coffee felt good going down. As the caffeine-laden brew took effect, his headache eased off.

He keyed his radio. "Hey, Moe. You hear about the electric wire down on Oak?"

"Sure. On my scanner. Heard the fire trucks too. How's it goin' with you? You get that guy outta the road?"

"He's gone."

Moe laughed a screech-owl laugh that turned into a giggle. "You get all the fun."

"Yeah. Right. I'm going over and patrol in the Palms section. Love ya, bro."

Moe grunted.

Tears welled in Jackie's eyes.

Jackie was glad to be working with his boyhood chum. Remembering happy times, he smiled. Moe was the consummate practical joker. He often went to considerable effort and expense to pull off a joke. They were always funny after the fact and never hurt anyone. One Christmas Moe put on a Santa outfit, climbed up on Jackie's roof, and tossed a brightly wrapped box down the chimney. Then he started calling for help as if he was stuck in the chimney.

Through the front window of the restaurant, Jackie stared at the rain splashing on puddles in the parking lot. Coffee in hand, he pushed open the door and stepped out into the storm.

No sooner had Jackie turned the corner on Palm Street when he saw the hooded man in the road again, hands stretched and feet wide apart. If not for the hopping, it was like the figure might have been hung on a cross. The religious significance had escaped Jackie on his first encounter with the man.

As Jackie tried to come abreast of him, the man did a hippity-hoppity slide to his right. Jackie honked. The man didn't move out of the way. Jackie honked again, this time longer, pushing as hard as he could against the steering wheel. No reaction.

"I've about had it with you," he shouted.

He glanced at the world beyond his windshield. The man still hung as if being crucified on a jittery cross. Jackie choked back a wave of nausea.

After watching the hopping man for a few more minutes, Jackie couldn't wait any longer. "This guy is a nut case. I don't care what the cops say. I need to deal with him. If he gets away, no telling what he might do."

Jackie flung open the door and advanced toward the hooded figure. The man appeared to melt into the shadows and reappeared moments later farther down the road. Jackie shouted. "Stop. I'm putting you under arrest."

Above the sound of the storm, he heard an owl whinny.

Standing in the chilly rain, Jackie was in no mood for insult. He ran toward the figure, slipped on the wet pavement, and fell hard on his knee. Excruciating pain shot down his leg. He got up and hobbled toward the hooded man. Jackie reached out to grab him. He ran. Jackie chased him, hobbling through back yards and yelling, "Stop. Stop. You're under arrest."

Near a muddy mangrove thicket, Jackie lost his quarry. He leaned over with his hands on his knees to catch his breath. Something pushed against his butt, propelling him forward. He landed full face in the mud. Jackie struggled to his feet. Mud covered the front of his uniform jacket. With his scarred face raised to the lead-gray sky, he closed his eyes tight against the downpour.

Muck slid down the front of his grass-stained jacket and dropped to his shoes already thoroughly soaked. He felt a compulsion to brush the front of his jacket. That served only to spread the filth that he felt was oozing into every pore.

The pain in his head and leg engulfed him, encircling his limbs like a vile, black fog. It pried open memories like a mental jar opener.

The face of his former partner flashed across the screen of his mind. He tried without success to push down the images that swirled in his head. The unrelenting pain tore at his psyche.

Fear and shame and regret bubbled up from deep in his chest and stuck in his throat. He screamed at the top of his voice, railing against the wind and the rain and the specters that danced among the trees. "Go away. Leave me alone," he shouted.

A rustling sound in the woods pulled him immediately alert. "Come out," he hollered. "I've had enough nonsense from you for one night."

Jackie squished slowly and deliberately through the muddy grass toward a clump of low brush and the trees beyond. His fingers reached for the hammer strap on his holster.

From behind a nearby tree, the hooded man popped. Hands and feet outstretched, he lunged at Jackie. Jackie raised an arm to fend him off. He drew his weapon. He fired. Again and again, he fired until his magazine was empty.

On the ground in front of Jackie Brown lay a scarecrow-like figure constructed of black clothing stuffed with hay and stretched on a wooden frame to resemble a man. For a long moment, Jackie stared at the contraption. Hearing a groan, he looked up.

His friend Moe stood upright against the tree that he had backpedaled toward as the bullets hit him. Jackie stared in disbelief at his friend. The thought seeped into Jackie's confused mind that Moe had played an elaborate trick on him, a horribly tragic practical joke.

Moe's eyes widened. His jaw dropped. A look of surprise spread across his face. His head fell forward. His body crumpled to the base of the tree and was still. A screech owl trilled.

The rain stopped. The cool glow from the moon, visible through a break in the clouds, bathed Moe's body in light. Moe's spirit rode the moonbeam higher and higher. In a soft voice, almost a whisper, Jackie said, "I can't let him make the trip alone."

He pressed the gun barrel against the soft flesh under his chin.

The Sundial

Today lots of young people have never seen a sundial, an ancient timekeeping device that depends on the shadow cast by a rigid, vertical "sail" stood upright on a horizontal clock face. As the sun moves across the sky, the sail shadow moves to show the time of day. They are now mostly seen as occasional garden ornaments. "I count only sunny days," is a motto seen on many decorative sundials. The following is my elaboration on that introduction.

I count only sunny days and not
When pain, or grief, or misspent ways
Are threatening clouds that hold
The sun from smiling down on me.

And hours do not there, seriatim,
Make their frantic daily flight
Even though the sun, unmoving, glides
From night to day and back to night.

Before the sun can cast its glow
Upon the earth to make us feel,
The clouds take charge and block
The days from being counted on my face.

A wisp of cloud or two does not bother me,
For as it passes in its place
The brightness glows, so when you look
My time is there for you to see.

Your time does not need the sun.
If my face in gloom resides
A day slips past and is forever gone,
Never to be lived by me again.

A day so lost in best forgotten
For tomorrow may be the only one
To let you live your fantasy and
My sail to mark the hours, one by one.

Cloudy days do not permit
My countenance to tell the time of day.
So cloudy days I always seem to miss,
And that seems just as well, I guess.

I leave behind the gloomy days.
They pass. Since none of us,
No matter how we try,
Can think a spinning top
From spinning round and round.

Do not count the gloomy days.
Do not even note their passing!
I seek brightness for the asking,
So upon my face, the hours there to mark.
I do not count them, nor should you.
Weave the fabric of your life from strands
Of golden light which are made
From sunny days that even I can count.

Breaking Up

Hot remorse bears upon her senses.
She walks on burning feet through
Prickly, lost-love pebbles of despair.
Heat weakens her resolve to blow
The images away and pull her cloak about her
And bend her shoulder to the wind.

Pain beats against her heart's desire:
Needles and pins wounding her,
Drowning wonder-coated feelings
Bred on warm and sunny days.

Shame drips from off her longing
Dropping to her feet
Making puddles through which her self esteem
Must splash.

Her breath is labored in the heavy
Memory of him.
Bits of song-filled nights
Sitting by the Television
Hit against her face and sting,
Making tears to pool
Where her eyes gazed
Happily upon romance.

She hears a voice she knows quite well
Call her to turn and trace again her steps.
She falters in resolve
For a moment, then resumes.
She knows it is the wind that speaks to her,
That she must not go back to him.

The Radioman

~—~

Gus, the man in the following poem, was a feisty little Italian who endured the uncertainty of 50 missions over hostile territory and lived to tell his story. The Radioman is a tilt of the hat to all the airmen who served during WWII including the more than 200,000 airmen on all sides of the conflict who lost their lives.

My friend, Gus almost never talked about
The Big War, except sometimes to his children.
So I was surprised when he opened up
To me one hot Florida afternoon,
Giving me a very complete
Account of his scariest bombing run.
It was coming back from Ploesti, Rumania.
His captain had to drop out of formation
When the plane was badly damaged.
For some added protection
They joined a slow-moving Liberator for a while
Until it was attacked by fighters
And crashed in the sea.
At that point the navigator decided they were lost.
And started to cry.
Gus cursed the man's inattention
When Gus asked for a position fix

The Allied coastal stations would not respond.
He had been given yesterday's password.
Eventually, most likely because of a steady stream
Of his very American choice of words for the
People he knew were listening,
They allowed him to triangulate his position.
Since that day, we've talked often
Of his wartime experiences as a
Radioman on a B17 bomber.
In WW II.
He flew fifty missions, fifty bombing runs,
Never a milk run, never ferrying planes.
Considered charmed to have survived,
He became very much in demand
As a crew member after around 40 missions,
A lucky rabbit's foot.
He saved a badly injured crewman's life.
He never avoided an assigned mission.
Those times changed him forever,
Making him fiercely independent for one.
It made him just as fiercely loyal.
He was awarded
The Distinguished Flying Cross,
An award not given to many enlisted airmen
In his theatre of operations.
He was never told specifically why.
Did he ever feel bad dropping bombs?
"I had to do it," he once told me.
"It was a war. I was very young."
"I was more focused on the radio
And getting back alive
Then what the bombs were doing."

Signs Of Trouble

For half an hour, I painted like a man possessed, slapping on great gobs of pigment, blending, and scrubbing. The colors soared from my brush. Never had I felt so free, so alive.

I've been ignored long enough, living from hand to mouth, camped out in my studio, selling my work for the price of a meal. No more. When I finish this canvas, the whole universe will take notice.

For the first time, I was painting with the colors I'd taken from Carrion World following an unfortunate and bloody struggle that left the paint master lying dead. The horrible scene played back a hundred times in my head and troubled my sleep. Modgar, the brutal Tyranthian, habituates those nightmares. In them, he discovers the secret of the paints and comes to take them from me.

On my canvas, the specially blended pigments melted into each other as if by magic. I stepped back, drenched in sweat.

"That's it for now, Helen," I said to my figure model. I'd met her when she tried to hustle me for a handout.

"Take a break."

Helen stepped off the stage and plopped into my overstuffed chair. She'd been born on Earth. Her family immigrated to the Empty Quarter with a bunch of colonials—a planet called Noctiluca 25—out towards the edge of the Milky Way. Out there, you lived hardscrabble. The day she turned 18, Helen left home. Thumbed her way back to Earth, where she made a living on the streets.

I looked at her curled up in the chair, naked except for the blanket draped over her. She was truly an inspiration, yet there was more going on. I never felt so inspired by any flesh and blood model, except Helen, with whom I found myself falling in love.

Modgar, the infamous Tyranthian convicted for the murder of over 300 people and sentenced to life on Carrion World, sent me the chair as a gift. He did the upholstering himself. Used swamp boar hide.

The studio I kept spartan. Its furnishings included the chair, my easel, a workbench where I kept paints and brushes, a mattress on the floor, a small cook stove, and a cold water sink connected directly to a hand-cranked well.

I studied the painting. I'd barely laid in the outlines of my model's perfect figure. Yet I already knew it would be my finest work, my masterpiece, my Mona Lisa, my Starry Night, my Guernica. No more begging on street corners.

In ancient times, the building where I painted served as a one-room schoolhouse. It sat on the crest of a barren hill far from any town. The structure had been preserved for hundreds of years as a museum until the beginning of the First War. It eventually fell into disrepair. A government on an all-out war footing can't afford museums.

With its great big fireplace, lots of space, high ceilings, and north-facing eyebrow windows, the place could not have been designed better for an artist. I'd fixed it up a little and tried to insulate, but with money scarce and my talents at construction meager, well, you know. I needed one of the G10 multipurpose air furnaces, the ones with atomic batteries, but they cost a bundle. No way that a starving artist can ever afford one of those, even used.

The harsh winter wind whistled through cracks in the siding and rattled the window panes. Nature sang its tune. I don't know why Helen wasn't freezing.

She stood up and came around in front of the canvas. "I like it already, Danny."

"Just wait and see. This will be the most fantastic work of art ever created."

"You look tired, Danny."

"I'm exhausted. Put on some boots and some clothes," I said. "Let's go outside. I need fresh air." She put on neither boots nor clothes but did agree to step outside.

When we stepped out, I saw five-foot snowdrifts across the road, downed power lines, and the top knocked off the cell tower on the hill.

"Feel the air, Helen. It's like tiger claws scratching at the soul, tearing it open. Feel it. Embrace it."

I unzipped my parka, spread my arms, and faced into the wind. Helen pulled the blanket more tightly about her. "I'm freezin' Danny. Let's go back inside."

"The wind is alive. I sense it in the tips of my fingers. The forest is alive. I'm alive."

"If you stay out here, you ain't gonna be alive long. You can freeze to death. I'm goin' in."

Reluctantly I followed Helen back into the warmth of the studio. Flaming tongues of fire licked greedily at the logs piled on the andirons in the huge fireplace. Despite the fire, when I approached my canvas, I felt a chill, like an Arctic storm raged inside my studio, turning everything to ice. Outside in the wind and snow, I felt warm. In the warmth of the studio, standing next to my painting, I felt cold.

"Helen, do you feel the chill?"'

"Not now. I'm toasty warm here with the fire goin' and this blanket over me." She settled back into the chair and pulled the blanket more tightly about her.

"It's cold near the painting."

"Quit actin' goofy, Danny."

I immediately dipped my brush and splashed a blue stripe across the edge of the canvas. My hand darted back to the yellow. I scrubbed and blended and mixed, and soon Helen stood in a green meadow.

"These paints are special, Helen." I put down my brush. I wanted to share with her my elation, the pure joy that I experienced painting with my new colors.

"How so, Danny?"

"You remember I told you they're formulated with DNA?"

"Not really. They may be made with dog poop for all I know."

"No. No. With DNA. With the very essence of life."

"Yeah?"

"Yeah. Let me explain. Since this painting will make us both famous, you should know."

"Famous? I like that. Let's hear it."

"Well. All of life everywhere in the universe is pretty much the same in the basics. Since the paint has DNA, it's controlled, so to speak. DNA is the manager. DNA tells a cell what it's supposed to do and how to do it. The DNA in my new colors tells them what to do. That's about the best explanation I know."

"Cool. Where'd you get 'em?"

"Carrion."

"The little planet with the prison colony?"

"That's the place. Except for Paradise Island, the whole planet's overrun with thieves, murders, rapists, God knows what else. Only the worst criminals, people who commit the most horrendous crimes, go there: torturers, serial killers, Congressmen, corporate executives."

"I heard it sucks."

"It sucks all right—asshole of the universe, worse than New Jersey, a world with polluted air, parasite-infected water, and poisonous reptiles. It's worse than ever now. The Subaridites—they used to run the place—pulled out after their contract expired. Federation wouldn't negotiate a new one. The cheap bastards. Inmates took over when they left."

"What were you doin' there."

"Worked the front desk on the island. You know, 'Welcome to paradise ladies and gentlemen. We hope you enjoy your stay.' Good pay. Easy work. Gave me plenty of time to paint. Lots of young girls: eager models, inmates from the colony. The girls kept the visitors entertained."

"Until they drop dead from pleasure."

"Yeah. Well. I didn't remind them of that part."

"Seems fittin' they located such an awful place on a planet the likes of Carrion. Yuck. How'd you stand it?"

"I left right after the Subaridites pulled out. The local guards couldn't handle it. Most of them threw in with the inmates. Everything went to hell super-fast. Inmates threatened to take over the transporter station. Some of them tried to swim over to the island. Wasn't safe anymore. I got afraid I might be stranded there. Been the past year workin' my way back to Earth. One damn cargo ship after another."

I picked up my brush and dipped it into a bottle of paint. Helen took off the blanket and resumed her pose. One hand, she laid seductively on her hip. She tucked the other hand behind her head, elbow pointing at the ceiling to lift her breasts, giving the pose a feeling of movement.

My strokes quickly blocked in the rest of her body and set about creating the perfect background. Quiet greens, dramatic yellows, exotic reds, sky-lit blues. My hand went to the right colors without me having to give it any thought. The paints drew me to them and decided how they wanted to be placed on the canvas. My breathing labored like I just finished a marathon. Legs wobbly, weak. I felt I was losing control. I needed to stop again.

"Never seen anybody work so quick," Helen said. "That brush is outta control. At one point, it looked like the brush flew away, with your hand tryin' to catch up."

"That's silly, Helen. You guzzled too much Tequila." She laughed. Her breasts bobbed; for an instant, I thought I caught a glimpse of the same movement in the figure on the canvas.

"Tell me more about the painting, Danny. You weren't makin' much sense last night after you finished off that bottle of moonshine. You kept talkin' about capturin' true personality. Is it like that Dorian Gray guy I read about? His portrait made him get old or somethin'."

"No. Nothing like that guy. The DNA in my paints is from Subaridites. The DNA strands are mixed in a special soup that encapsulates it: something like what happens in a living cell."

"And that's special, why?"

"It's like I'm painting with their blood. That's the best analogy I can think of."

"Paintin' with blood. That I can appreciate. You're finally tellin' me something I can understand."

"When people talk about living color, well, I got living color. DNA is living."

"That's somethin', Danny. Ain't really livin' though, is it?

"Not sure. I think it is. The DNA I got from Carrion is not the same as from humans. That wouldn't do anything. The Subaridite people are the ones that get inside your head. They're telepaths. Guys jump into your brain, make you do things you may not want to do.

"I don't get it."

"We'll, I noticed signs painted everywhere. The inmates seemed to be controlled by them more than you would think from just any ordinary signs."

"You wanna paint signs now?"

"No. No. When I first got there, I worked a few revolutions with the paint master. That's where I found out the sign paints were manufactured with a formula that includes DNA from live Subaridites."

"So, big friggin deal."

"I think the paint actually acted in some way to keep all the bad people under control. It's almost like the signs were actual Subaridite guards standing there using their mind-altering techniques. Everybody obeyed. Don't forget. They're a band of cutthroats on that planet. Must take a lot to keep them under control."

"That's crazy, Danny."

"Maybe. Yet it happened. I know what I saw. I figured if I could get hold of some of that paint, I could paint in secret messages that told people my paintings are masterpieces, then they would see them as masterpieces. You know. Sort of like those signs on Carrion."

"You don't need that."

"So long as I don't get discouraged, my paintings will reflect my confidence. But there's more to it than the paint. The paint can take you only so far. After that, it depends on the artist."

"I see your stuff around here. You're the best, Danny."

"Then why can't I sell, Helen? If I'm so damned good? Why? I need that extra push the new colors will give me."

She glanced about the studio at my paintings lining the wall. She looked at me and shrugged.

"Come on, Helen. Get up there again. I need to paint. Don't ask so many questions."

I resumed painting, more excited than before about my progress. The work was taking shape. Helen seemed sexier in the painting than in real life. Somehow I had managed to make her irresistible. I roughed in the eyes. The figure suddenly looked straight at me, daring me to take her in my arms. I looked again at Helen. It wasn't her that spoke to me, but the image I created of her, an image far from complete.

Abruptly I put down my brush and strode to the fireplace. The fire seemed alive. I felt an urge to incorporate it into the painting. The painting would be changed, so that Helen would be standing in the flames, not in a green meadow.

I grabbed the poker and smacked the logs, sending sparks flying in all directions. With poker in hand, I stood close to the fire until my body seemed to be burning. The heat seared my closed eyelids. I stretched out my arms and held them there. I stepped even closer to the flames leaping up from the logs.

"Maybe I'll catch on fire and be consumed like those idiots on Paradise Island who pay millions to enjoy their last days."

"Come away from the fire, Danny. You're too close. One of those sparks might land on you."

With the poker raised above my head, I swung round to face Helen, who stood toe to toe with me. For an instant, I was on Carrion. It wasn't Helen standing in front of me but a Subaridite guard who discovered me with the paint. I resisted the urge to bring the poker down on his head and flee as fast as my legs would carry me out beyond the stars, out to the nothingness beyond the universe where God lives.

Helen shouted, "Danny. Put the poker down. You're scarin' me."

Helen's words brought me back to reality. I threw the poker onto the hearth. The tip hit a log and splashed sparks in all directions. I shuddered at the thought of what I had almost done.

I raced to my easel and took up my brush. Helen hadn't moved. The light from the fireplace silhouetted her body, reflecting just enough glow off the white studio walls to cast her figure in soft, flickering light. The flames moved from side to side with the draft. Outside, the storm played about the chimney top. The fire danced the Tango to the rhythm of the wind.

"Stay right there, Helen," I said.

She assumed her pose in front of the fireplace. "I don't know what's goin' on with you, Danny. But that's okay. It's a lot warmer here than on the stage. Temperature must've dropped since the sun went down."

My hands trembled. Events unfolded simply by me willing them. I thought of changing the background of the painting with my model posing in the fire. Then, magically, Helen came and stood by the fire.

I pressed my hands against my chest to stop the trembling and contain the feeling that my heart would beat its way out of my chest. I took a deep breath.

Again I painted, splashing and blending, scratching and scrubbing. I became wholly absorbed, body, and soul by my work. My brush flew from paint to canvas and back again. The colors jumped and slid and cart-wheeled.

"I'm gettin' tired, Danny. How 'bout a break?"

I'd been working for nearly an hour, in a daze, unaware of the passage of time. I'd scarcely looked at Helen. My hand knew what to do without me even being attached to it. The fire still roared with fiendish energy. Helen must have added logs and poked it up. I hadn't noticed, so immersed was I in my work.

"Let's make it quick."

I put down my brush, did a finger flex exercise.

"I don't want to stop long."

I looked up at the high windows. Snow no longer fell. A new moon bathed the studio in soft light. Except for the moon glow and the leaping flames animating the shadows, I had been working in darkness. I strode to the fireplace and sat on the floor next to Helen.

Helen didn't go back to the chair. She rubbed her arms and did deep knee bends. As I looked at her moving so seductively, my mind spun round and round with the evilest of thoughts. I again found myself on Carrion World. I felt as if I was looking out through the eyes of the murderous Modgar. I reached out and grabbed Helen's leg. She tumbled into my arms.

"Hey, Danny. That hurt."

Pushing her to the floor, I straddled her, grabbed her wrists, pinned her arms. She didn't resist. I'd knocked her unconscious.

That's all right. I don't need her anymore. I have my painting.

I picked Helen up and dropped her onto the mattress. I went back to my canvas. The instant I looked at it, my head filled with voices, loud voices, men's voices, women's voices, voices screaming at me from all directions. "You have done a bad thing! You are a bad person! Go! Help Helen, you ignorant pig! Redeem yourself!"

I covered my ears and dropped to my knees. "Go away!" I shouted to the voices. "Leave me alone." They wouldn't stop.

I went over and knelt beside Helen. After a while, she opened her eyes. I offered her water. She took a sip and let her head fall back onto the mattress. "You're way too rough, Danny. You nearly killed me."

The recent events caused me to think back to the time on Carrion World when I decided to take the paints. It hadn't happened quite as I told Helen. The Subaridite paint master had just finished mixing the colors when he got the word to evacuate immediately. He left me alone with the open cauldrons, full of paint, and ready to be poured into individual bottles.

I returned home. Later I came back with the infamous murderer, Modgar, from the Tyranthian world and one of his equally unsavory friends. I brought them along to help me carry the paints.

Modgar, similar to other Tyranthians, had a hairy coat over his entire body, not unlike that of a bear, and stubby arms ending in huge four-digit hands, one opposing digit. Tyranthians are incredibly strong creatures and quite antisocial. They kill slowly and have their way with the hapless victim, sometimes ending the encounter by eating them alive. Their favorite pastime is bragging to each other of their brutality; the more brutal, the greater the social standing. Their one weakness is that they are unusually vain and may spend hours in front of a mirror admiring themselves.

In my naiveté, I did not fear Modgar because I saved him from certain death when I found him being accosted by a particularly large swamp boar. Swamp boars are afraid of humans yet will attack Tyranthians because they move slowly and are paralyzed by its venomous bite.

According to the strange code followed by criminals such as him, Modgar owed me a favor in return. Apparently, he felt that helping me get the paint was not enough to even the score. The chair, his additional gift, arrived at my studio before I did. My landlord stored it for me until I got back.

I intended simply to help myself to the paints and carry them away with the aid of Modgar and his companion. The paint master unexpectedly returned to retrieve his personal belongings and to dump the paint he had mixed.

Alone, I would have abandoned my plan and allowed the paints to be discarded, but I could not control the situation. In a particularly bloody struggle, Modgar's associate and the paint master killed each other. Blood spattered on every wall of the mixing room. I was drenched in it. Specks of blood floated on the surface of the paints. At the time, I paid it little attention, scooping enough of each color to fill the large earthen jugs I brought along. What remained in the cauldrons, I spilled into the sewer.

Helen interrupted my musings. "Who the hell you think you are anyhow, a big shot hologram star?"

"I'm sorry, Helen. I don't know what happened. For a moment, I was possessed by evil. It's like in my picture there's a fight going on between good and evil. I'm being affected by it. The struggle is making me bad one minute and good the next."

She stared blankly at me for a moment. "It's not your fault, Danny. Look at your hands. They're covered with that stuff." I scratched at my paint-stained fingers.

She patted my arm. "Stay with me, Danny. I'm afraid."

For a full fifteen minutes, I remained next to Helen. Neither of us spoke. Eventually, I felt the painting calling me back to her, like a Harpy on some far off rocky shore.

If Tyranthian DNA is mixed with the paints, what may that mean to my greatest work? The donor, a brutal beast, raped and butchered a dozen women. Could that be causing the evil thoughts that rage in my head?

I left Helen and went back to admire my canvas. The flames moved as if the figure stood in the fire and not in front of it. I looked about. My studio walls were on fire. For an instant, I panicked. The hair stood out from my flesh on tiny bumps. Yet I knew that so long as I painted, the blaze would not consume.

In my painting, Helen stood in profile. A few minutes earlier, she had been looking full face, smiling. No matter. Whoever looked upon it would see something different. Is that not the essence of genius: to paint a picture the viewer never tires of looking at, a painting that, over time, discloses new and exciting details?

Of course, I knew nothing changed. Disguised in the dancing flame, I had written the words, "All who gaze hereon I say will see me different day by day. And tell all with whom you deal the picture here is nonpareil." My masterpiece was complete. I was not.

A frightful compulsion gripped me. I shoved the workbench to the back of the studio and began to paint on the wall. My mind blanked out. I had no idea what I wanted to create. I needed to keep working, trying to cover the blaze that defiantly pranced about. Only when I realized that my paints were getting low did I stop.

The picture that emerged on the wall following two hours of frantic effort surprised me. I'd painted Modgar, the Tyranthian, sitting in the swamp boar's hide sofa, a broad toothy smile on his hairy face.

"I thought you'd never finish," Helen said.

She had built up the fire, making the studio comfortably warm. My easel stood empty; my new painting leaned against the far wall. I didn't recall moving it. No matter.

"What's that a picture of, Danny?"

I told her the complete story of how I got the paints. When I finished, her jaw dropped open. "Yikes! That is friggin weird! Never heard anything like that. Not even on Noctiluca 25."

"He's the Tyranthian I told you about. It's not finished. I need more paint."

Out into the freezing dawn, I went to fetch more paint. The landscape spoke to me of a world over which I reigned as King. The ice, the snow, blue-gray and silent, called me. "I can't come now," I shouted. I have work to do. Later. Later I will come and rule over you."

I carried jugs of paint back into the studio from my storage shed. The effort took multiple trips.

Thinking to personalize my work, I cut my arm and dripped blood into the paint bottles. I didn't really expect that to do anything, yet one never knew.

When I awoke from a short sleep, Helen had bacon and eggs cooking in my old black-iron fry pan. The smells must have awakened me. She'd put on one of my old paint-spattered shirts yet still looked incredibly beautiful. While we ate, dawn gradually found its way into the far corners of the studio. I felt refreshed and ready to again tackle my latest project: the picture of Modgar on the wall.

My strokes were steadier than on the previous night. I worked more deliberately, more slowly. About forty-five minutes later, I stepped back to study what I had accomplished. Despite the warmth of the studio, I experienced the same chill felt the prior evening.

This time the voices demanded nothing of me. "Beware. Modgar is coming to kill you," one voice said. "He sent you the chair to completely even the score." A new voice joined in. "I am free to do away with you."

I shouted. "It wasn't me. It was the Tyranthians. I only wanted the paints. I didn't want anyone hurt."

"What's wrong, Danny? You look as if you've seen a ghost."

"I'm hearing voices, Helen. Coming right out of the wall."

"That's crazy, Danny. You're workin' too hard. You got no sleep last night. Every time I got up to tend the fire, you were paintin' like the devil been chasing you. I asked if you needed anything. You didn't answer."

"He's coming for me."

I grabbed the holoscope cap I used for bird watching and raced outside. Snow still covered the road.

I dug in the drifts until I located the ladder I recalled seeing there before the snowstorm. I wrestled the ladder out of the snow piled high against the studio wall, extended it to the full thirty-foot length, and climbed to the top from where I scanned the smooth expanse of white between the studio and the road, nearly a mile downhill.

At first, I thought the dark movement might be a bear. I pulled down the lens. The movement came into sharp focus. I was staring at a squat furry creature walking upright on snowshoes: a Tyranthian.

Beyond the furry creature, down on the highway, a vehicle stood on the freshly plowed road. Three figures, whom I recognized as Subaridites by their long necks and large, round heads, alighted from it. From their wild gesticulations, I concluded the conversation must be an argument. One pointed at the Tyranthian laboriously, making its way over the soft snow. The other two looked up. One of them pointed higher up, right at me.

At that moment I heard a voice. "Lock your doors and bar your windows. The man climbing toward you is a notorious criminal. We cannot follow him onto private property until your local authorities give permission."

I looked again at the climber having difficulty with the loose, powdery drifts. From a distance, all Tyranthians looked pretty much the same to me, but it had to be Modgar. I looked back to the men on the road. They were nowhere in sight.

Scrambling too hurriedly down the ladder, I lost my footing. The snow broke my fall and prevented serious injury, but when I tried to walk, my ankle would carry no weight. I hopped back to the studio.

"Now what?" Helen scolded.

"I'm hurt."

"Oh, Danny, Danny. What happened?"

"Fell off the ladder."

"The ladder?"

"No time to explain. You remember that Tyranthian I told you about?"

"The one you painted on the wall last night?"

"The same. He's on his way up here to kill us."

"No jokes, now, Danny. This ain't the time."

"Lock the door. Pull the workbench in front of it. We need to keep him out until help arrives." When Helen didn't respond, I shouted, "Now! We need to do it now!"

Without another word, she locked the door and, with some considerable effort and little help from me, pushed the workbench in front of it. She slid the chair against the bench.

I looked at the painting of Modgar I'd created. The likeness was exactly as I remembered him. Why had I ever given him my address? What a stupid move just to get a dumb chair.

I hopped over to the wall and grabbed a brush. I slashed at his likeness. Tried to obliterate it. The more I painted, the sharper the image became. I had no control over what appeared on the wall under my efforts. My ankle ached. My head ached. I dipped my brush in paint but couldn't raise my arm to continue and collapsed onto the floor, the brush still in my hand.

Wham! Bang! The door stove in with splinters flying. The heavy bench and the chair slid across the floor. Modgar stood in the doorway. He looked at me, then at Helen.

"Welcome, Modgar, my old and dear friend," I said.

He growled. "You are not my friend, Mister Danny Kilbane. You took the paint that can make me a king. You never told me it was magic paint. Instead of sharing with me, you took it all for yourself."

"I would have. All you had to do was ask. You can take it now."

"Later. Right now, I see something that interests me even more than slowly squeezing the life out of you."

I watched Modgar slip off his snowshoes and lean them against the wall by the door, never taking his eyes off Helen.

"Hello there, sweet thing," he said.

He's in no hurry. He doesn't know the Subaridite troopers are hot on his trail. Once they get authorization, they can be up here in minutes on their flying sleds. They may even be hovering right now.

Helen picked up the old black-iron fry pan and threw it at Modgar, hitting him in the head. Modgar staggered back but did not fall. He let out a howl that might have been heard down on the road. Helen retreated to a corner of the studio near the fireplace. She picked up a log and threw it at Modgar. He batted it away and laughed. While Helen occupied him with her well-aimed log throws, I reached up and quickly scribbled a message on the painting in a language Modgar could read.

When Helen ran out of logs, he looked in my direction. "This will be fun, Danny Kilbane." He snorted. "Two for one."

Hoping that Tyranthians are afraid of open flames, I scooted on all fours across the floor to the hearth and banged on the logs with the poker.

I turned back to see what Modgar might be about. He had moved the picture of Helen leaning against the far wall and set it next to the image of him I'd painted.

He sat with his back to us on the floor, his legs crossed, not speaking, not moving. I finally got up the nerve to scoot closer to him, keeping the poker at the ready.

With brows knotted and a crooked but thoughtful grin on his hairy face, he stared intently at the painting of Helen posing by the fireplace. He looked from the painting of Helen and back to his own portrait again and again. His gaze eventually fixed on the message I had scribbled on the painting in the desperate hope of protecting the wholly innocent Helen from his wrath.

"You love the girl by the fire. You will sit quietly for an hour, contemplating that."

He sat in silence in the identical position until the Troopers arrived. He was arrested without incident.

A Fitting End

It felt good to be relaxing in a golf shirt and shorts. Never thought I'd say that about waiting in a dentist's office for painful root canal work. Hey, you got to roll with the punches, take life in stride. Yesterday my divorce was finalized. I felt so elated that I'd probably be happy standing in a bed of hot coals with my shoes off. I'd called for a two o'clock tee time. Catch a quick nine holes, then, if I got lucky, dinner with Charlene, a hot girl I'd met on a blind date a couple weeks ago.

I picked up a magazine that had been lying face down on the lamp table next to my chair. I stared absently at the back cover for a moment, kind of reading it but not really reading it. Then the words sunk in.

The advertisement seemed too good to pass up. Being a salesman myself, I can recognize a great sales pitch. Right there on the back of the magazine: "Shoes: $100 a pair. Guaranteed for ten years. No questions asked. You walk in any time wearing the old shoes and walk out with a new pair on your feet. You can trust Walter D. Shoemaker, Inc. 1103 Jordan Lane."

I figured there must be a catch. There always is. Yet a smart person never lets a bargain like that get away from them. It was something I definitely needed to check out.

I asked the receptionist if I might take the advertisement. She said, "Sure, take the whole thing if you want. Our patients are always bringing us their old issues."

I didn't want the whole thing, so I ripped off the back cover of the magazine, folded it a couple times, and shoved it into my pocket. That simple act set in motion an unfortunate chain of events. Too bad, there are no Mulligans in life like there are in golf. I sure could have used one that day.

Why hadn't I looked at the front or even read one of the stories inside? Don't know. If I'd done either, I might have noticed the date. If I noticed the date, my whole week would've been a lot different. That's for sure. You know, golf every day, probably a nice meal out with Charlene.

But I didn't notice the date, probably because my mind was focused on the relaxing two-week vacation in front of me. With my late tee time, no sweat to swing by and check out the shoe offer.

Later, when the dentist finished with the root canal work that hurt like hell while he was doing it but not so bad after he got done, I set my GPS for the address of Walter Shoemaker, Inc. It turned out to be on the south side, near the railroad yards.

It's not the best area of town. Used to be mixed business, industrial. Most of the businesses moved out years ago. Squatters occupy a lot of the buildings: crack houses and dilapidated homes, graffiti everywhere. The location certainly kept the overhead low. Maybe that's why they offered such a great bargain on their shoes.

I turned into a narrow street strewn with chunks of macadam and dotted with the potholes they came from. The roadway sat between brick structures that looked to be more than ready for gentrification.

A guy, looking like he hadn't shaved or changed his clothes in a week, sat against one of the buildings. He gave me the eye. Creepy. Probably homeless. Went right along with the general feel of the neighborhood. A brown bag didn't do much to conceal the outline of a bottle he held in his lap, one fist tightly wrapped around the neck.

For the next couple of minutes, I drove slowly and tried, without much success, to avoid the holes in the roadway, hoping my car's alignment wasn't suffering from the experience.

The annoying voice of my GPS announced, "Arriving at destination on right." On one side was a boarded-up gas station. On the other, one of the ubiquitous buildings along the road that must have been a shop or warehouse at some time in the distant past, its windows long since blocked over with what I have to call sloppy masonry work.

The place had no signage, so I wasn't even sure I'd found the right address. I thought, well, I'm here, so I might as well stop. An arrow directed me to park behind the building. I pulled into a spot next to a high wooden fence. Only one other car was in the lot.

Fishing my cell phone out of its belt caddy, I punched up Charlene's number. I figured that I'd ask her out to dinner and maybe a late movie afterward. Who knows, maybe this is my lucky day. Two tries and no bars showing on my phone. I stuffed it back into the caddy. The damn shoe store was located in a dead zone. My hot date would have to wait, but not to worry. I looked at my watch. Plenty of opportunity to call after I got my new shoes. I headed around to the front door.

With a squeak and a groan, the ornate wooden door opened immediately onto a small, windowless room with three old chairs lined up along one wall. On the outward rush of cold air, I caught a disagreeable musty odor. Smelled leather too, like if you go into a leather goods shop.

A strange-looking contraption in the far corner reminded me of the pedicure station at my ex-wife's hair salon. A pair of metallic boots stood on the footrest. They looked like something out of an old alien movie, the ancient ones that you see on late-night TV where the aliens are all dressed up like the tin man in The Wizard of OZ.

A moment later, a short, elderly man with a head of sparse white hair appeared through a door across from the contraption. He had on a pair of wrinkled trousers at least a couple of inches too long for him. The wide cuffs nearly hid his wingtips and dragged the floor at his heels. His shirt was tucked in on one side. On the other, it hung loose as though I had surprised him while he sat on the toilet, and he had to rush out to greet me. Man, oh, man. If I ever showed up at a customer's business looking like him, I'd never make a sale. I'd starve to death. Yet something about the guy struck me as charming, like a kindly grandfather on the verge of losing his memory, you know, some cracks showing around the edges.

He smiled and said in a low, soft voice, "Good afternoon, young man. My name is, Walter. We've been expecting you."

"Good afternoon to you, too."

I fished the advertisement out of my pocket and waved it at him, wondering if I ought to ask him how he knew I was coming. I figured he probably said the same thing to all his customers.

Walter suffered from a spine curvature that thrust his head forward, making him seem perpetually off-balance and giving him a mousey look. I shoved the advertisement at him. He took the crumpled page from me and studied it before he said, "Where'd you find it?"

"I was at the dentist's office this morning and discovered it in one of the magazines in his waiting room."

He coughed and cleared his throat a couple times. "We have a situation here."

"What do you mean?"

"I ran this ad nine years ago. We charge a little more today."

"You're not going to do a bait-and-switch on me now, are you, old-timer? Because if you are, I'll turn around and walk right out of here. There's no mention of any time limit in the ad."

Walter paused and stared at me. He said, "No. No, you're correct. My fault. I ought to have included an expiration date. I'll honor the price." As if to reinforce his words, he tapped the page with the backs of his boney fingers.

"And yes, we will also honor the usual ten-year guarantee. That hasn't changed. We still give that. Why you can walk across the country and back, and we'll be walking right along with you. Think of how many pairs of ordinary shoes you'd wear out doing that."

"I suppose a bunch. How do you make any money?"

He chuckled and patted the seat of the contraption. "Please take off your shoes and socks and sit here in our fitting chair. When you're comfortable, put your feet into the two sizing boots attached to the bench." I followed his instructions. "Just slide them right in. That's right. Very good."

Once I got my feet completely into the sizing boots, I felt something tighten around them. Kind of like if they take your blood pressure and pump up that cuff around your arm. While I sat there, the pressure evened out until my feet were locked in the vise-like grip of the sizing shoes. I couldn't even wiggle my toes. The metal boots were attached tightly to the footrest. It felt like my feet had been encased in cement from the ankles down.

"You'll feel a little pressure as the computer sizes your feet. That's normal. Just sit back and relax while I get some information from you."

"Never saw anything like this before. You have quite the setup."

Walther chuckled again. "I may be getting old, but our operation here is way ahead of everyone else in the business. Using our special computerized manufacturing process, we can make a pair of shoes for you in less than an hour. Better than any hand sewn pair. And we guarantee a perfect fit every time."

He handed me a thin stack of glossy, dog-eared catalog pages. "Pick out the style you want. We have a fairly limited selection, but then you can imagine why that is."

I couldn't imagine why that should be. Seemed to me he ought to have lots of styles to choose from. Maybe he was going out of business, and my guarantee would go flying out the door right along with him. "How long you been in business here?" I asked.

He gazed at the ceiling as if my question awakened a memory long lost. "I started the business at this location near on seventy-five years ago."

"Wow. You must have been a little kid when you started."

He laughed a squeaky little laugh that came out of his mouth more as a wheeze, ending with a brief coughing fit. He looked about the room. "My father started the business. It is getting a bit run down," he said. "I apologize for that. You know, with the recession and all, business has been a mite slow of late. I haven't felt good about spending a lot of money on remodeling. That'll need to wait until the economy turns around." He swept his hands out in a broad gesture as if urging me to see the waiting room as a metaphor for all that was wrong with the economy and not simply a result of a failing business and Walter's advancing years.

The wallpaper peeled in one corner, and the rug was worn to the backing in spots. The fabric on the chairs had seen better days. The space stood in desperate need of a freshening up with a new paint job and some pictures that didn't look that they came from the Dollar store.

"Can't afford to advertise any more either. Most folks rather go to one of those giant discount shoe stores out on the highway. People don't want to pay for real quality anymore. Nope. Not too many customers these days. In fact, you're my first customer in over a month."

When I heard that, I started to think of how I could gracefully get out of buying shoes from the old guy. I didn't want to upset him, but the ten-year guarantee was starting to look a bit shaky.

I was thinking, old Walt must be over ninety. There is no way he will even be alive in ten years—even on a paleo diet, much less still in business. He looks like he's on his last legs right now. Poor guy. Hope I don't end my days like him. I got to resolve to do more selling and not loaf so much.

In a rush of charitable beneficence, I chose a pair of brown ankle-length walking boots with a little strap in the back to help put them on. Walter had been cordial and agreed to honor a nine-year-old promise. He took the time to get me set up in his fitting machine. And he obviously needed the business.

He handed me a couple cans of soda and three Sports Illustrated swimsuit issues. Fire still smoldered in that old belly of his. Without another word, Walter shuffled across the room and went out through the door he had come in from, leaving the door open behind him.

From my vantage point in the chair, I observed him open a large bound book and move his hand slowly down the page. About halfway down, he punched the page with his index finger and said to no one in particular, "The man has exquisite taste. Got the material I need in stock. Won't be any time at all."

Walter took a seat at a workbench, sitting partially with his back to me. He sat in front of a screen set so high on the wall that he had to push his crooked spine against the slats of the chair in order to look up at it.

On the screen, a three-dimensional image of my feet appeared. I watched the image change. A second line that defined a sort of sock appeared on the feet. In the image revolving on the screen, the outlines of the shoes I had chosen from the catalog took shape. All the while, Walter mumbled to himself. From the words here and there that I could make out, I concluded that he carried on a running recitation of what happened on the screen. "Feet. . .mmm. . .good, good. Yes, the sizing. . .mmm. . . .

That went on for a few minutes. Walter half turned to me. The way his face contorted sent a shock from my head right down to my toes locked into the fitting machine boots. His eyes rolled back into his head. He slid off his chair and fell with a thud onto the floor.

For a moment, my mind struggled to comprehend what had happened. I sat dumb, staring at Walter, expecting him to get up. I popped out of the chair and tried to take a step, but my feet were stuck in the fitting boots. I had all I could do to not fall forward and break both ankles. "Walter! Walter!" I shouted. "What's wrong?"

I reached down to pull the fitting boots off, but they were locked tight around my feet and ankles. Even if I couldn't free my feet from the boots, I figured there had to be a way to pry the boots themselves loose. To get some leverage, I grabbed for a nearby floor lamp but found that it stood about a foot out of my reach. Holding the armrests of the fitting chair, I tried to hop it closer to the lamp. Walter had it bolted in place.

Again I looked at Walter sprawled on the floor next to his chair. The image on the screen revolved and tumbled, top view, bottom view, front, side, back, over and over. The image of my new shoes turned a light brown color. Thick crepe-like, black soles grew across the bottom of the shoes. The strap in the back appeared. Laces threaded through the grommets.

Then I remembered my cell phone and pulled it out of the caddy. When I flipped the phone open, bumps rose on my flesh. "No bars. Damn! Of course, this old wreck of a building is in a dead zone." I dialed 911 and hollered the address again and again until I finally gave up and shoved the phone back into the caddy. I'd try later.

Maybe they're just about ready to put a new cell tower on line in this neighborhood. Or maybe sunspots will change the cell phone reception. Who knows? Anything's possible. Maybe that homeless guy I saw on the street will walk in here looking for a handout. If he does, I'll give him every cent I have.

I closed my eyes and took deep breaths. First I looked for a release button. No luck. I figured that since I couldn't phone for help, I'd just have to deal with the situation myself. Bending over, I reached down and tried to work the boots free. With a hand on the front of the boot and a hand at the back, first one and then the other, I wiggled and shoved and pulled, trying to get the boots loose from the chair. Perspiration soaked my clothes.

When the desperate nature of my predicament finally filtered into my consciousness, I shouted, "Help! Help! Somebody help me!" I hollered at the top of my lungs, loud as I could, until my voice was hoarse.

Eventually, I stopped shouting and took more deep breaths to calm the panic that gripped me. I needed to focus my efforts on pulling the metal boots off my feet, first one, and then the other.

The minutes passed. A fly buzzed around Walter's head. No matter how hard I tried, the metal wouldn't budge.

I heard a clink, and out of a chute next to Walter's computer popped a pair of shoes just like the ones on the screen. My shoes, ready for me to slip on and walk out. So far, so good, but to get them on my feet, I had to get out of the damn fitting chair.

Taking a different approach, I was able to get my pen down into the little space formed by my ankle bone and the boot top. Maybe I can loosen the material inside and eventually pull at least one foot free. That will give me a shot at getting to the floor lamp. I can use that to knock Walter's telephone off his desk and pull it over to me.

Unfortunately for me, the stuff inside the boot proved to be hard enough to resist my every effort. All I managed to do was crack my pen and chafe my skin.

I'd heard of trapped people cutting off their arms, but I'd never heard of anyone cutting off their feet to get free. I didn't want to go around the rest of my life with no feet. How did they stop the bleeding? They must have had a knife or something to saw with. I could use my pen to cut the skin and then just break the bones. That frees me. A tourniquet will stop the bleeding long enough for the EMT's to get to me.

No. No. I knew I could never cut my feet off. Anyhow, I faint when I get my flu shot. With all the blood, I'd pass out and bleed to death. My heart raced. "Don't panic," I said aloud to myself. "Somebody will come through that door any minute now."

My mind started to wander. I thought of Charlene and wondered whether she would have agreed to go to dinner with me. I thought of my ex and tried to figure out whose fault it was that we broke up. Things weren't so bad. If only she hadn't met that rich banker, maybe we could have worked things out. Damn him! His shoes were always spit-shined. Maybe if I'd met Walter earlier.

Again and again, I tried to free myself from the accursed fitting machine. The realization finally crept into my consciousness that the only way I was going to get out of the situation was if someone came to buy shoes or maybe came looking for Walter or drop off the mail or make a delivery.

~—~

That was four days ago. I sip the last of my warm, flat soda. Between my own excrement and Walter's decaying corpse, the place is starting to smell really bad, even though I've gotten kind of accustomed to it. Watching the picture of the shoes still tumbling and revolving there on the screen right in front of me is driving me crazy. To taunt me even more, my new shoes sit waiting there a few short feet away.

I wonder if a man in a dentist's office somewhere paging through old issues is in need of new shoes and knows a bargain when he sees one.

Was that a car I heard going by? "Help. Help."

Morning In The Country

The sun is yawning as it wakes,
In no rush to show itself
Above the eastern hills.
A gentle breeze moves the blades of grass,
Bright metallic green, in the meadow where I stand
With coffee cup in hand
Rubbing my eyes to clear away the sleep
That held me in its mother's arms
Safe from all the day would bring.

Across the lane
A farmer, head down, Wellies on his feet
Swings wide a wooden gate
Behind which four thin cows with swinging tails
Eagerly wait for milking.

Beyond the cows
Above the field of sorghum and rye
The mist hangs low,
Held by gossamer strands and
Hiding in its blue-gray shroud
Restless deer afraid to venture from their bed.

As the sun finally tells me it is here
Breaking its crystal wand on
A tree at the end of the lane
Splinters of light fall upon the leaves.
I drink the last of the bean,
Impatient, not waiting for the mist to rise,
Turn and trudge slowly up stone steps
Toward the big octagonal barn.

My Wall

For my first six months here, I stared intently at the same white wall every day. It represents to me the seemingly endless time that stretches to the horizon of my existence. The wall is my horizon. When I face the wall, I face west. That makes the wall special to me–since my dog lives in the west. So does my best friend, Celia. That makes the wall seem friendlier. The two of them live together in a house that I have never seen.

I live confined in a room that has no windows. The room started out as all white: white walls, white door, white ceiling and white floor tile with white grout, except for the spare oriental design on the white screen that blocks the sanitary facilities from my view.

I intentionally tried to scuff the tiles and spilled juice on the floor. When I did that, Lucian, my jailer and provider, quickly responded with a bucket and mop and a command that I clean the floor.

Celia visited me once, shortly after I came here. She didn't bring the dog. Lucian wouldn't have let me see him. The dog never liked traveling anyway.

It was a short visit. She told me about her small house and that it was in the west. She mentioned the house; she pointed at the west wall. "It's a long way away from here in that direction," she said. "I'd guess it's about a thousand miles away. Maybe more or maybe less. I don't know. And it has a picket fence." She said that she had a job as a medical assistant and that the job was not difficult and paid well enough for her and the dog to live comfortably.

I asked her to get me out of there. She said not to worry. She said that Lucian told her I would be released soon. That was five years ago.

A short while after Celia left, Lucian suggested to me that if I stared at the wall long enough, my mind might conjure images of her. He was correct. I often saw her playing with the dog, throwing a tennis ball that he retrieved over and over again, neither of them ever tiring of the game.

My furniture consists of a bed, a table, and a chair. The sanitary facilities—commode, sink, and shower—are behind a tall screen that has the oriental design on it. A brush-stroke fish swims in a pool beneath a brush-stroke bamboo tree.

Sometimes I hear what sounds like thunder and then a lightning crack. Sometimes I think I hear a plane flying overhead, and once I'm sure I heard a truck growling through the gears. But mostly it is quiet here, except for me and Lucian.

Recessed ceiling lights provide twenty-four-hour light, but I can use a dimmer switch to darken the room and help me sleep. Lucian doesn't mind me doing that. I also have a small table lamp on the desk. I can turn the lamp off and on.

The western wall used to be white like the other three. That changed when Lucian brought me oil paints, large tubes of zinc white and ivory black, and brushes.

"These belonged to a dear friend of mine who died," he said. Lucian told me that he wanted me to have them. Lucian said that there would be a condition, however. "You may only use them to decorate the wall you stare at for so long each day. The other walls must remain white."

In a floor to ceiling, rectangular space centered on the wall, I completed my first painting: a trompe l'oeil mural of a tall window giving out onto a narrow balcony surrounded by an iron railing. Beyond the balcony are forests and beyond the forests are mountains. Below the balcony, Celia and the dog play in a grassy field.

Since I painted the mural, the wall is even more friendly than before—a welcome break from the pure white, which I must strive every day to ignore lest I go mad. I cannot let the whiteness define me—empty and bland and wholly without character.

Lucian comes in every Christmas with a present for me. That's how I know it's been about six years since I arrived here. Six years. Six presents. This year he brought me a computer, so that I might write stories and set down how I feel about being confined. It is really a tablet, and I have no modem or blue tooth or anything to connect me with the world beyond the walls.

On this Christmas Day, we sang carols and drank egg-nog spiked with rum and watched, on a small portable TV, a Yule log burning. He said that it was a videotape of the fireplace in some governor's mansion somewhere. It repeated every half hour, but who can tell since it is random flames.

Each time Lucian visits me, I say, "Lucian, tell me why I am held here and when I might leave." Each time that I ask him, Lucian shrugs and replies that he is simply an employee hired to care for me.

How did I get here, you might wonder. When Lucian brought me into the room, I was thinking I was coming for a job interview. I ought to have been surprised that the room I entered had no windows. My mind was full of visions of the illustrator's job I hoped to get.

The first few weeks, I ranted and threw one tantrum after another and threatened Lucian with grave bodily harm every time he came into the room.

My room has one door that is always locked. Lucian is, to describe him, a giant. I am five feet seven inches and of slight frame and have never even thought to overwhelm him, my threats being no more than idle gestures born of frustration.

I have considered trying to escape. Lucian described long ago how the outer doors are secured with locks that only he knows how to open. He carries no keys. He has given me no hope of escape. So here I am, six years older, and on the verge of complete madness.

My next painting project is the ceiling. I will not embark on such a project without the permission of my jailer. I've decided to ask Lucian for more paint, blue, and orange, and white. It will be an evening sky with clouds, a rising moon, and stars.

Please do not tell me that you can't see stars during the day. I know that. One corner will begin with a light, cloudy sky. That will gradually get darker and darker until, in the opposite corner, I will be better able to see the individual stars.

I intend to ask Lucian for star charts to give me an idea of what the skies above us look like during the nighttime hours. To enhance the effect, I will turn on the desk lamp nearest the daytime corner.

My major pastime is reading. However, my reading material is limited to novels and magazines available six years ago. I have asked Lucian again and again for some more recent novel. He smiles and agrees to try. Yet he has not brought me anything topical. I'm not asking for news, only for fiction, pure fiction. He contends that even fiction is replete with topical references to new things and new people of which I would be otherwise unaware.

A few weeks ago I pointed to my western wall and said, "If you do not provide me with newer reading material, I will begin to write on my western wall all of the thoughts I have about what the world is like right now and all the changes that have occurred since I was imprisoned here."

He laughed and said, "And if you do so, I will remove everything you might use to write, even your computer."

Despite what he said, my threat must have bothered him because he left abruptly and did not return to my room for more than two weeks, leaving me to subsist on water and the hard crackers that I am given from time to time to eat on other days when he does not appear. On those days, I fear that some catastrophe has befallen him, that I will starve.

On those occasions, I have come to realize any fleeting thoughts of suicide are not to be acted upon. I will myself to survive, to endure, to understand that there is a purpose to my life even if such purpose was not yet apparent to me.

After Lucian returned following his long absence, I told him of my plan to paint the skies. "That is not possible," he said, shaking his head slowly from side to side while he stared up at the white ceiling.

"And why not," I asked.

"Is it not obvious?" he replied. "On your wall, you have already painted a picture of the out-of-doors, of the world beyond the wall. Should you paint stars and clouds on your ceiling, it will be as if you are already outside. In a certain philosophical sense, you will have thus escaped."

"Yes. That's the object of such an endeavor."

"So, since you will be outside, you can understand that on your wall, you will need to paint a different picture, a picture looking in, a picture of you sitting here in your room."

I opened my mouth to argue. He silenced me with a raised hand, spun on his heel, and left the room.

The news that I must choose between my wall and my ceiling has been devastating. Looking at a painting of me sitting here in my windowless room would be depressing in the extreme. That is out of the question.

I wish Celia would visit again. She might be able to persuade Lucian to let me paint both wall and ceiling.

Perhaps if I took a clever tack, I might be convincing; for example, I might point out to him that if I painted support beams, the painting would not put me out of doors but merely under a glass roof supported by the beams.

I resolved then to keep asking Lucian about this. I was certain that in time I might change his mind. I could even talk him into bringing me a tall step ladder. I'd need that. My ceiling is at least nine feet high. And I will have to remind him of the star chart.

The other walls can be transformed, as was my west wall. One shall be a lush garden, one a forest inhabited by creatures that I will dream.

Since I cannot escape physically, I will escape mentally. Using my artistic gifts for which I came here originally to employ, I can bring the outside world into my life. My only limit is my own imagination.

Four days ago, Lucian told me that the dog died. He also said that I was about to be released. He didn't say precisely that. But that is how I chose to interpret his words. His exact statement was, "The dog died. Time in this room is nearly ended."

With mixed emotions, I receive this news. If given the choice, I may stay on long enough to create in the room the world of which I dream. I'll complete the west wall first. My picture of Celia and the dog takes up only a portion of it.

When Lucian returned, I broached the subject of my staying on and painting the room as I see fit. "You are completely mad," he replied. "You have been here six years and have thought of nothing but getting out. Now when the prospect of release is presented to you, you tell me you might wish to remain."

"You so don't understand," I said. "I have become accustomed to my life here with you. I am content here. I now understand the purpose of my existence. The thing missing has been color. With a set of paints, which I assume you will provide to me if I am no longer required to stay, I can create that."

In A Manhattan Walkup Apartment

Catherine's apartment was small,
The front room an activity hub,
Bedroom in back,
Beyond the lion-footed tub.
She worked in a sweatshop
Washed every evening
And ran the clothes on a pulley.
The girls had two outfits each to wear.
Always they
Were clean and neat:
New blouse or skirt
An unaccustomed treat.
Two fire escapes
Their air-conditioned patios,
With happy little plants
To brighten the day.
The suitors would come and
She would have to caution the girls.
With no man around she could
Have been lonely, but I think
She only was for a short time
When her husband slipped away.
Her building sat two blocks from
The subway line and she up

Three flights of stairs.
All the doors on all the floors
Were painted brown.
When I came to visit now and then,
The Murphy bed was opened
In the front room while
The three of them slept in the
Big bed.
The radio played during supper.
They had a Victrola
That they sometimes cranked
For me.

Saturday Friend

~—~

Albert Carnegie pulled from his trouser pocket the watch he had been given at his retirement luncheon. He thought back to the following day when he and his wife, Margaret, had watched the accumulation of a lifetime being stuffed into the end of a moving van for the trip to Tampa.

Albert stood six feet, two inches tall. Years of repairing heavy equipment had made him hard and wiry. His sparse gray hair was neatly barbered. His wide cuffed trousers bore a sharp crease. His black leather shoes carried a high shine. Over his wrinkled dress shirts, he wore a blue hopsack blazer with gold buttons and a Tarpon Springs Yacht Club insignia embroidered on the breast pocket. It was almost new and had been a rare find at the Hospice Thrift Store. For a time, he had taken his shirts out to be starched and ironed but eventually found it not worth the cost or the effort to walk the seven blocks to the cleaners.

He popped the cover of the large, round timepiece and studied the hands for a good ten seconds, wondering as he did so if Sammy would show. Ten thirty. He had been waiting for almost an hour. For the first time during the three years they had been playing chess together in City Park, Sammy was late.

Albert first met Sammy on a crisp December morning with grey clouds overhanging The Park and rain threatening. Sammy had suffered a bent wheel on his bicycle. A spoke snapped, and Albert had offered to help. "I can fix that wheel so you can get home on it; he had offered."

"Wow. Could ya? That'd be great. Name's Sammy."

"No problem, Sammy. You got all the tools I'll need right in that sack tied under your seat."

Sammy, short and pudgy, and wearing a way-too-tight cycling outfit struck Albert as quite the caricature of an athlete. Being a gentleman, he made no comment. He was not one to judge a man by looks alone, knowing that people were often much more than they seemed on the surface.

While they worked on the bent wheel, Albert and Sammy talked, eventually getting around to the subject of chess when Albert likened the manager of the Rays baseball team to Bobby Fischer, his all-time favorite chess master.

Sammy had said, "Tell ya what, Al Baby. How 'bout you and me playin' a game or two one of these days? I'd really like to learn."

"I'd like that too," Albert replied. "We can use my set. Pieces are kind of old, but they're nice and big, and they're heavy too, so if we have any breeze, well, you know, it won't knock them over. I have a gentleman that plays with me sometimes on Saturdays, but he had a stroke."

"Good. Saturday it is then, Al Baby. Saturday at 10:00?"

"Ten is good for me," Albert replied. "Let's make it 10:00."

Albert eventually got the wheel straightened enough for Sammy to ride away.

Albert would normally have bought a bagel and coffee from the vendor in the park and then sat at one of the three public chess boards formed of black and white marble squares embedded in a slab set atop a round concrete pedestal. He knew that one of the other players would most likely want a game with him. If nobody showed by the time he had finished his snack, he would sit and watch the passersby or play both sides of the board, trying to beat himself. "There's always more to learn," he had told one of his former co-workers.

The day he met Sammy, Albert was suddenly seized with a need to hurry to the public library and work through games from a book of famous chess matches. For the next two days, Albert could scarcely contain the excitement he felt over teaching someone to play chess.

On Saturday, two days after he had fixed Sammy's bicycle wheel, Albert rose early and headed for The Park. The shoebox cradled under his arm was repaired with duct tape at all four corners with little of the original cardboard showing. Three heavy rubber bands held it closed. For almost as many years as he had played chess, he had stored his set of carved wooden chess pieces in it. The set had been a birthday present from Margaret.

Albert closed the watch and stuffed it into a pocket. He shuffled toward a vacant chessboard. The mild stroke experienced four years earlier that caused his deliberate shuffling gait had left him partially paralyzed and forced him into early retirement. The board was located under the roof of a pavilion that had roll-down, plastic curtains, so it could be used comfortably on chilly days.

That first day three years ago, Albert had the chess pieces set up when Sammy arrived exactly at 10:00 wearing a tweed sports jacket and carrying a brown paper lunch bag. He reached out a hand. "Al, Baby. Good to see ya. Didn't think youse'd show. Thanks, fer givin' me the white," he said. "Ain't played since I was a kid, but I remember white is better. You'll need to start from scratch with me."

Sammy eventually told Albert that he was a retired college professor from Chicago. Albert was not surprised. Sammy chewed on a pipe, and his tweeds and "chinos" spoke to Albert of an alma-mater and ivy-covered walls.

Though Sammy conversed mostly about his daughter and his grandsons, Albert found him easy to talk to about all sorts of things. He decided that in Sammy, he had found a sympathetic ear, a soul mate, someone who would never laugh at his questions like his former co-workers had done.

"I moved into the condo after Margaret died," he had explained to Sammy before their first chess game. "It's been hard for me to get used to the noisy neighbors in the next unit, and I haven't been able to decide what I ought to be doing about it. They turn the radio up loud every night."

Sammy looked pensively at the sky and stroked his chin for a moment before replying. "There's a number of solutions to yer problem, Al, Baby. For example, ya could talk to 'em, but that wouldn't do no good, or ya could go out for a walk. The best solution is to buy earplugs. They sell 'em at the drug store."

"Never thought of that. Thanks."

At first, Sammy played very poorly, losing two games quickly. When Albert offered a comment on his play, Sammy held up a hand and said, "I ain't a child. I can figure it out by myself. You just make sure you play your best. I'll learn from that. Can't be all that hard."

By the third game, he was doing better, but Albert figured Sammy would have lost again had he not purposely made a series of blunders, which Sammy eventually capitalized on.

The Park Ranger appeared about 11:30 and rolled up the plastic on two sides of the pavilion. At noon, midway through their fourth game, Sammy reached into his lunch bag and pulled out a carrot, munching away as he contemplated his next move. His play had become much more deliberate. Sammy had opened with pawn to King4. Albert had answered with pawn to King4. Sammy played Knight to King's Bishop3. Albert quickly answered with N-QB3. Albert was surprised to see Sam play B-N5, even though Sammy had studied the board for an inordinate length of time before he did so.

To counter the threat to his center, Albert played P-Q3, with Sammy all the while gnawing on his lunch, a satisfied grin on his face.

Albert, weakened by his poor fourth move and a subsequent blunder, had eventually conceded at exactly 12:30. Sammy abruptly stood and announced that he had to go. He thanked Albert for being patient with him and jogged into the grove of trees beyond the pavilion.

Albert put the chess pieces away, wondering if he would ever see Sammy again. He had no idea where the man lived.

On the following Saturday, a drenching rain had greeted Albert. He was having trouble deciding whether to go to the pavilion that he knew would be damp and uncomfortable. Since his alternative was to spend the day alone, he finally decided to go just to see if there was anyone he knew. Not that I think Sammy will be there, he thought. He's not likely to come back. I should have given him more games. He probably is one of those people who need to win all the time.

Albert wrapped the shoebox in cellophane and put on his plastic raincoat. With his large golf umbrella to further protect him and the chess pieces from the rain, he walked the two blocks to the pavilion.

As he was shaking out his raincoat, the deluge stopped abruptly. A few minutes later, precisely at 10:00, Sammy appeared.

Thereafter each Saturday went much the same. Sammy arrived

promptly at 10:00, ate his lunch, and left abruptly at twelve-thirty, no matter at what stage in a game they might be, leaving Albert to remember where the chess pieces were, so they could pick up the game the following week.

On the last Saturday in June, Sammy announced he was headed for his daughter's house in New Jersey. "See ya in October, Al, Baby, yeah, first week in October. Not sure of the date, but check the calendar. First Saturday," he had said. It was the only day through all the many weeks that they played that Sammy mentioned them getting together in the future.

By the end of the second winter, their typical game had been taking two hours. Albert was surprised Sammy didn't seem to improve because he could recall every move of every game they played.

Albert found himself at the library more often studying famous players to improve his play and become a better teacher. He didn't like to intentionally lose games, but it was the only way he could figure out how to teach Sammy, who rejected any overt coaching or advice.

He again checked his watch, wondering where Sammy might be. A short concrete bench stood on either side of the concrete and marble chessboards, each one large enough for one person to sit comfortably. Albert dusted the board with a tissue, placed the shoebox on it, and removed his sport coat, which he turned inside out and folded carefully at one edge of the bench. He always chose the bench facing west to avoid the morning sun. Sammy never challenged him for the bench, but then he couldn't be certain he might do that someday. They had never talked about it.

The October morning was cool, and Albert felt chilled without his blazer. He went to the space heater hung on metal straps from the rafters and placed his hand in front to test for warmth. It was not turned on.

I'll have to talk to the Ranger about this. Sammy doesn't like to be cold. Gets into his bones, he says.

With the roll-up, side curtains down and the heater on, they could use the pavilion very comfortably all through the colder months. They could meet there comfortably regardless of the weather.

In the winter, the pavilion was often quite busy, attracting cyclists and walkers, stopping to rest or eat lunch. Albert seldom talked with any of the younger people, although he liked to have them around because it made him feel more youthful and vigorous. He knew that they could be his friends if he had wanted.

Before returning to the chess table, Albert again took his watch from its pocket and studied the face as if he were seeing it for the first time. He replaced the watch and carefully took the white chess pieces out of the box, setting each in turn on its appointed square. It was Sammy's day to start with white, so he put the white pieces on the west side.

After he had placed all the pieces on the board, Albert breathed a sigh of relief, remembering the time last year they were short a pawn, and he had used one of the gold buttons of his blazer for the missing piece. The button had been about to fall off anyhow. Sammy had been upset when it appeared that they would have to cancel their match but seemed content enough with the replacement pawn. He had left the button on the board until it was captured late in the game.

He and Sammy ordinarily talked for about a quarter-hour and then started playing, but once engaged, each became quietly absorbed in his own game strategy. Sammy usually started out by telling Albert all about the latest events in the life of his daughter, the Medical Doctor, and of his grandson's escapades. From Sammy's asides during these talks, Albert concluded that Sammy played chess only once a week—with him in the pavilion—and never played at his daughter's. Sammy said that he didn't own a chess set.

Once Sammy had told Albert that he was his closest friend. Sammy had hugged him and had held his hand for a long time. "Ya know, Al, Baby; I never had a friend like you. Ya ain't never let me down. Nope, not ever. And I know you never will." Albert thought he saw a tear form on Sammy's cheek and almost broke down himself.

For a third time, Albert studied his watch. Sammy's very late; he thought, probably waited for the rain to stop like I did. Heck, he came the second day. It was raining cats and dogs. Neither of us has missed a day in three years, and he's not about to start today just because of some pesky rain. Maybe he's sick. Maybe he died. Oh, God. And I don't even know his address or how to get hold of him. I don't even know his last name to check the obituaries.

It was the second Saturday in October. They had played chess the previous week, talking for almost an hour with only a brief mention of Sammy's daughter before they started the first game that didn't end until one o'clock. They had never gone that long without Sammy abruptly leaving. But that day, Sammy was interested in talking, talking chess.

As soon as he sat down, he asked Albert about the strategies of Alekhine and Fischer and seemed annoyed that Albert could only recall by memory Alekhine's game in 1922 against Yates. However, he knew many of Bobby Fischer's games. Albert was surprised and somewhat disturbed that the usually quiet Sammy had talked all during the game, commenting at length on each move that Albert made.

Albert sat next to his coat and absently fussed with the chess pieces, taking care to place each in exactly the center of its appointed square. He stared at a bird nest in the rafters. He stared at the couple that had taken a table on the other side of the pavilion. He stared at the chessboard for a long time before he moved the white pawn to King4. He moved his black King's pawn to King4 and then the white pawn to Queen4. As he collected the white pawn, he suddenly realized that Sammy was standing by the other bench.

"Penny fer yer thoughts," Sammy said in a breezy tone. "Like ya to meet Reuben. He's right there behind you," Sammy said, gesturing over Albert's shoulder.

Albert put a hand on the board to steady himself and turned all the way around, so he could see the man.

"Reuben's been teaching me chess. He's good, a Master. He can beat just about everybody who plays around here."

Reuben, a man, looking to be about ten years Albert's junior and sporting a Santa Clause beard, extended his right hand. Albert recalled seeing him from time to time over the years that he had played chess in The Park. Under his left arm, Reuben held a shiny, wooden box with inlays of black chess pieces on the top. "Pleased to meet you, Albert," he said. "I understand that you and Sammy have played chess a few times."

Albert still turned awkwardly on the small bench, gripped the edge of the board as the man pumped his hand vigorously. "A few, yes."

Reuben looked down at the chess pieces and then up at Sammy. "I see what you mean, still pretty basic."

"I was doodling," Albert said. "I know pawn takes pawn is a weak move."

"Whatever," Reuben said. "Hey. If you aren't going to be using the table, you know, just doodling, would you mind if my buddy Sammy and me used it to play a game. It'd be okay if you hang around and watch. Might learn something."

"There's only the two small benches," Albert said.

"What's that you're saying?" Reuben asked quickly while he placed the shiny box on the board and used it to sweep the chess pieces toward Albert.

Albert looked at Sammy, who shrugged but said nothing. Albert picked up the shoebox, pulled off the lid, and carefully gathered his chess pieces into it, replacing the rubber bands to secure the top. He raised himself and looked at Sammy for a long time. He said in a low voice, his eyes moistening, "Sorry, I won't be able to play you next Saturday."

Reuben slapped his knee, let out a horse laugh, and said, "What do you mean? He'll be playing with me."

Albert turned to face Reuben. "Well, I don't know about that. I suppose you like to play with someone that gives you a challenge. You wouldn't play very long with someone who doesn't."

"You got that right, Champ. I've been watching you play the last couple days. You're pretty damn good, good reputation around The Park too. Sammy told me about how many games he's won playing with you."

He looked at Sammy. "How many?" Before Sammy could say anything, Reuben continued. "I'll tell you how many, over 100. He beats you almost all of the time. He'll give me a right smart run for my money while I teach him a few tricks."

Albert laughed so hard he nearly dropped his shoebox. He knew something that just about every player in The Park knew, but Sammy and Reuben did not: Sammy had never won a game unless Albert intentionally let him win.

The following Saturday, when Sammy arrived at The Park, Albert was already well on the way to winning his first match against Reuben. Sammy came up to their table and said, "Hey, fellas. What's goin' on here? Neither man responded, each for his own reason.

Eddie Thurgel's Quandary

The first day of the International Robotics Convention had been upsetting for Eddie Thurgel. It was the anniversary of his wife's death. He had talked to dozens of potential customers without even a single nibble of interest. On top of that, he had been unable to find a manufacturer's rep he was supposed to meet.

Right after the last speaker had finished exactly at 6:00 PM, Eddie headed for the hotel lounge where he sat at the bar quenching his thirst with an ice-cold beer. His finger traced a happy face in the condensation on the side of the mug. Since the death of his wife, Julia, he had been unable to close a single sale for his company. Eddie missed Julia so much.

He spun around on the barstool and stared at the passageway that led to the hotel lobby, trying to will a beautiful woman to come through it, a woman who would immediately see him and engage him in conversation.

"Send me a sign, Julia," he whispered, "a sign that it's all right for me to start dating again."

No one appeared. Eddie turned back to the bar. He held up his empty beer mug and wiggled it to catch the attention of the bartender, a buxom, hard-featured woman. She glanced in his direction.

"That's it for the beers, Gretchen," he said. "I need something a little more substantial. How 'bout a gin and tonic? Put a lime wedge in that, please."

"Know whatcha mean, Sweetie. I have days like that."

She set a tall glass in front of him, filled it two-thirds full with ice and tonic, and then floated in a good measure of gin, completing the process by dumping a lime into the mix and adding a swizzle. She winked at him. "First sip is best. Ya look like ya need a jolt. Seem kinda sad for a conventioneer."

"I got a lot on my mind."

She surveyed the empty bar. "Half hour, this place will be crawlin' with guys. Every one of 'em lookin' to belly up, have a drink, find a nice girl. They'll all be laughin' and carryin' on, makin' fools outta themselves."

"Not everybody."

"Oh yeah. They'll do that 'cause they're away from the wife and the boss. They can relax without somebody all over 'em tellin' them what to do. So, handsome, what's there to be sad about? You're at a convention. There's girls comin' outta the woodwork. Ya must know some of 'em. I'm not talkin' about the working girls."

Eddie shook his head in a slow, metronome sort of way. "Got no wife to tell me what to do. I'm a widower, you see. The boss. Well, he's something else. Has me working a special project on this trip. This is a really important convention for me, not something I can take lightly."

He took a sip of his drink. "My day didn't go so good. Supposed to meet someone, but haven't found him."

Gretchen shrugged and leaned her ample bosom on the bar, outstretched elbows supporting her. "Why don'tcha tell Auntie Gretchen about it, handsome."

Eddie took another sip of his drink and leaned back. "You see, Gretchen, this is the first time the company's sent me to a convention since my wife died. I've been depressed. Can't concentrate on the job. I figure the boss is letting me know the company's been patient long enough. We always write new business at these conventions. Yet while I was manning our booth this morning, not one single person even talked to me."

Gretchen nodded. She pursed her lips, appearing very interested in what Eddie had to say.

"We were only married for three months. I was driving. Happened a year ago today. Lost control. Car spun off the road. Rolled down a hill right into a tree. Her name was Julia."

Eddie picked up his gin and tonic and took a long drink. He stared at Gretchen's large blue eyes for a moment before he said in a monotone, "I've spent the whole year in a funk, a great big pothole in the road of life."

Gretchen nodded and said, "Man like you needs a woman. Ain't no good fer a man to be alone, especially a handsome one like you."

"My co-workers at Jetsun Company, that's where I work, figured the same thing. They fixed me up last week with one of the secretaries: Caitlin Dunning. Told me she was 25. She looks a lot more than 25. The date was a sheer disaster. Caitlin blew her nose the whole evening. When she wasn't blowing, she snorted, barely able to get a sentence out without a snort or two. I can appreciate a good laugh but not a snort."

"Hope that sour date didn't discourage ya."

"Actually, Gretchen, it had the opposite effect. One benefit of the whole shipwreck of a date is that for the first time since Julia's tragic death, I understood that I needed romance back in my life, or at least some healthy action."

"How did that happen?"

"Good question. The evening began well enough with Caitlin walking into the bar wearing a red dress, skin tight, cut down to her navel. The truly awesome sight of all that flesh—well, you ought to know about that sort of thing."

Gretchen glanced down and laughed. "Know all about it, handsome."

"She had a plain face, not pretty, not ugly—just plain. But her figure, now that was good. If it hadn't been for the infernal blowing and snorting, I would have spent the whole night with her. What a turnoff. You can't imagine."

"I hear ya. Ya wanna start datin' again, but ya feel guilty because the crash was yer fault. So there'll always be somethin' about the date that turns ya off."

"I suppose so. Anyhow, seeing Caitlin reminded me that to spend the rest of my life in mourning would be unhealthy. Doing it for myself gets stupefying after a while. Less and less satisfying, you know."

"Whoa, handsome. I'm done around one. If ya want some company, let me know. No need to go it alone. This old gal can still show you a few tricks."

"I appreciate the offer, Gretchen. I really do. I understand I need a woman in my life. I don't want to wind up a bitter old man spending his idle hours all alone."

"No need. Happy to oblige. Just say the word."

Eddie reached across the bar and touched Gretchen's arm. "Thanks, doll. That's probably the best offer I'm going to get tonight."

She patted his hand and said, "Go on with yer story. Sorry I interrupted."

"Well, let's see. Where was I?"

Gretchen turned toward a man about to take a seat. She pushed herself off the bar. "What'll ya have, Charlie?"

The man mumbled something Eddie couldn't understand. But Gretchen did because she pulled a beer out of the refrigerator, popped the cap, and set it down in front of the man.

She turned back to Eddie. "OK, handsome, let's get on with yer story. Ya got me all wonderin' about ya."

"It's my boss. He's new. Normally I could goof off on convention like everybody else, do a lot of drinking, schmooze with the boys about robotics. But no. He gives me this job. Calls it a special assignment to get me back in the thick of things.

"I got to evaluate one of our new products. Supposed to meet a guy from our manufacturing vendor today. I must have looked at my phone a hundred times. Been by the hotel desk at least that many times. No message. Nothing!"

"You got a phone. Why didn'tcha call your office and find out what's up with him?"

"Couldn't do that. Make me look like a fool if he was looking for me too. Just never got together. Maybe he left a note, and the clerk lost it. Who knows? Maybe he's getting in late. Nope. I'll wait 'til tomorrow before I do that."

A loud group entered the bar. Gretchen looked up. "No waitress until later," she hollered way too loud, and then in a more ladylike voice, she said, "Whatcha drinkin', boys?"

With Gretchen busy serving the newcomers, Eddie went back to watching the passageway. Not a minute later, a woman walked into the bar: a beautiful face with a body to match. In her high heels, she stood a few inches shorter than he. She had a thin, straight nose and full red lips and a dimple by her mouth.

Eddie's mind raced, his thoughts tumbling over themselves. Such a figure. I got nothing to compare it to, no actress, no model, not even Julia. So perfect. And her face? Well, her face is beautiful, radiant. That soft alabaster skin is almost golden in this low light.

She looked straight at him and smiled.

Her blue eyes pull me right in. I've never seen a woman with such inviting eyes.

He felt the nascent longing in his body—a lump formed in his throat. His muscles tightened. Eddie felt his heart beating.

The woman said, "You must be Eddie Thurgel. They told me I would find you here."

Eddie nodded. He rubbed his palms on his pants to dry them. The woman that he had been fantasizing stood right there. He was both gratified and afraid.

What've I done that this fantastic creature has come here looking for me? Could it be some sort of telepathic signal I sent out that drew her here to me? Might it be the work of Providence? Or could Julia have sent her to me as a sign?

She moved a hand toward him, palm down, as if to touch him, and then quickly drew it back. "Sorry, I didn't get a message to you earlier. Wall to wall clients. Of course, that is what these things are for. Is it not?" She moved her hand toward him again, this time holding it out for Eddie to shake.

The instant their hands touched, he felt a shiver as if they had kissed for the first time. Her skin was soft and warm but not clammy, her grip firm but still feminine.

"My name is Davie Collins from Smithstone Brothers. You look surprised. Happens all the time. Guys think I'm a man. The name—Davie, short for David."

"I'd never make that mistake."

She smiled and then laughed a short laugh deep in her throat. "Real name's Davina. Mom was a Scott. I was her divine creation. Yada, yada, yada. Should have left you a note and signed it 'Davina' so you'd know. I do that sometimes. You know, sign stuff 'Davina' and then put 'Davie' right next to it in parenthesis. Anyhow, we finally meet."

Eddie breathed deeply and tried to push the tightness from his body.

"What are you drinking?" The words came out sounding as if he sang base instead of tenor.

"Silver Slipper."

"Never heard of it."

"Not many people have. The drink comes out of California, my home base. Oxnard. Used to be all strawberry farms. Now, all built up. Things are always changing. You know how that is."

Eddie called out to Gretchen, "Silver Slipper, Gretchen." The bartender nodded and smiled and gave him a thumbs up.

Davie continued. "And as I was saying, been busy all day. Really sorry, I could not at least get a message to you on your cell. I had neither your cell number nor your e-mail. I did leave a note with the concierge."

Eddie nodded. "My fault. I should have guessed. Never thought to ask the concierge."

"That is perfectly all right. I am a little nervous about this whole thing. My first convention. Been running here, running there. Everybody wanted a couple minutes with me. They wore me out."

"I know how that is."

She sighed. "All is well that ends well. I finally tracked you down. Right, this minute, I am in desperate need of a drink. The one you ordered for me is just a tricky way of saying gin on the rocks. Kind of like a very, dry martini–the ones they make by pouring in a drop or two of vermouth and then emptying that out–but not in that fancy glass, just an old tumbler."

He settled back on the stool and let an unaccustomed calm flow over him like a warm shower. He felt complete. For a moment, the concerns of the day vanished.

I'm beginning to enjoy Davie Collins. She drinks her gin out of a tumbler like the guys I used to work with at the plant when I was younger–before I got into sales. She seems vulnerable: like Julia. Ordinarily, I don't appreciate talkative women. This woman is different. Her non-stop monologue is actually charming.

But Eddie was a conscientious man. Thoughts of his product testing assignment intruded. "Tell me more about the new product, Davie. When can I get hold of it?"

"No rush on that. Tomorrow is tomorrow. Let us savor our drinks tonight and get to know each other. Like you, all I have to go back to is a dreary hotel room with a lumpy bed and poor lighting."

"Not the best hotel I've stayed in either. You probably been on your feet all day. Come sit with me." He motioned to the barstool next to him. "We don't need to talk business if you don't want."

Davie Collins slid onto the bar stool as if she had practiced doing it without having to hike up her tight skirt. "Warm in here," she said after taking a swig of her Silver Slipper and settling against the back of the stool.

"Well, I don't think you need that shawl, or whatever that thing is, you got around you."

"They call it a 'bolero,' and yes, I think I can take it off and be more comfortable." She slipped her arms out of the jacket. He felt his heart beat faster and his throat tighten.

Thank you, God. I don't deserve this. But thanks all the same.

He gulped down the last of his gin and tonic and picked up the one that Gretchen had left in front of him moments ago.

In his mind, he conjured visions of him gently easing the dress off Davie Collins' shoulders. He fought down the images, thinking of his job and remembering that Davie Collins could be passing judgment on him in the morning, maybe even jeopardizing his employment with a bad report.

When she had adjusted her jacket on the back of the barstool, Davie said, "They told me about your wife. I am sorry to be having to meet you on the anniversary of her death. No control over that, though. They run the show, not me."

"It's OK. Really."

"Surely, you think of her all the time and especially today."

"That's right."

"Maybe we can simply talk. I don't mind if you talk about her or about work or about anything you like. Yes. Talk will be good. Tell me anything you want. I'm a really good listener. Everybody tells me that I am. So it is not just me saying it. You can tell me anything. All that we talk about tonight is off the record, strictly off the record. Nothing that happens tonight will exist in the morning. The slate will be wiped clean."

"I would like to know something about the new product. I'll be up all night worrying. I've only been asked to evaluate a new product once before. That time I programmed the robot wrong and ending up welding the doors shut on two cars.

Davie laughed. Eddie stared at her heaving breasts. She seemed not to notice.

"Eddie, that is the funniest story anyone has told me in a long time. Guys in Oxnard are not anyway near as much fun as you. They are all physicist types who stand around and scratch at their beards like they are wondering what the world is all about."

"They most likely were scratching their asses, not their beards."

"Not fair, Eddie. I am one of them. I have a Bachelor's Degree in Mechanical Engineering, a Masters from Stanford, a Doctorate from MIT. I do not have a beard, and I do not scratch my ass."

"There I go screwing things up. I've forgotten how to talk to a lady."

Davie ignored his apology. "We do the work. Your guys call themselves scientists. We are the more practical. They just dream up stuff. It's up to us to build it. I assure you that you will not have any trouble with the new product. Relax. We'll have a sample at breakfast tomorrow. Worry about tomorrow tomorrow. Enjoy the evening. Have another. What are you drinking?"

"Gin and tonic with a lime wedge."

"Have another gin and tonic."

"Only if you join me."

"Why not," she said and drained her glass.

Gretchen produced a second Silver Slipper and another gin and tonic, giving Eddie a surreptitious thumbs up as she walked away. Davie immediately grabbed the glass and gulped down nearly half her drink before she set it on the bar. By this time, Eddie had decided he was going to spend the evening with Davie Collins.

To hell with the boss! So what if I lose my job. At least I'll have had a night with the most beautiful woman I'll ever talk to. No. It's more than that. I'm suddenly and crazily in love. I've found the perfect woman. Thank you, God. Thank you, Julia. I know you're doing your thing up there in heaven. I know this is what you want for me.

He turned to Davie. "How's your Slipper Dipper?"

"How the hell do you think it is? It's gin right out of the bottle. Nothing to mix. A monkey could make it."

What's happening to me? Eddie thought. From any other woman,

I would see that kind of response as a rebuke. From Davie Collins, I see in it a toughness that I can appreciate: a smart, drop-dead gorgeous, hard-drinking woman who can tell it like it is.

"I meant, how are they going down? It seems like you're drinking a lot of booze in a very short time."

She threw back her head and laughed. In an instant, he laughed right along with her, a laughing contagion, laughing so hard that he could barely catch his breath. He had no idea what she found so funny. But he hadn't laughed so hard since Julia was alive.

When she regained her composure, she placed a hand on his arm and said, "I am so sorry. I have never had a man who gave a damn how much I drank. In fact, the guys at Oxnard tried to get me drunk. Gave me four of these one time, one right after the other. Tried to get me blotto. You are worried that I might get drunk. You worry that I have been all day on my feet. It is so sweet of you to be worrying about me."

She leaned toward him and kissed him on the lips–just a peck–and then whispered, "Everything that happens tonight never happened." She winked and slid off the barstool and took Eddie by the hand. "You're going to brighten up my room tonight, Mister Eddie Thurgel. We worry about business in the morning. Nights are made for fun."

Eddie dropped a twenty on the bar and grabbed his drink. They headed for the elevators.

Davie's room turned out to be not so dreary as she had described. In fact, it was a brightly lighted suite with a large sitting room that had a separate wet-bar and a bedroom with a king bed. The bathroom included a Jacuzzi tub.

Following the quick tour of the suite, she pushed him onto the couch. "A girl needs to freshen up. Give me a few minutes."

Eddie at first felt foolish when he glanced at the glass he had carried from the bar to the room. He thought a moment, looked up at the well-stocked bar, and shrugged.

Instead of finishing off the little bit that remained of his drink, he tossed it in the sink and made another in a fresh glass, pouring in the gin first over the ice cubes and then adding just a touch of tonic water. He stirred the concoction with his finger and took a sip.

A broad smile lit up his face. For the first time since the night of the car crash, he felt his life was back together. He closed his eyes.

"Thank you, God, for sending me this sign. And forgive me, Julia," he said softly. "I gave you the whole year. I know you wouldn't want me to suffer any longer. I've done my penance. Right?"

He opened his eyes just as Davie came out of the bedroom dressed in a short teddy cinched loosely at the waist. Smooth, white skin peeked out where the two sides failed to meet. Eddie set down his glass.

"I don't know about this," he said and flicked a bead of sweat from his brow. "You're going to be evaluating me tomorrow. I don't want to have to worry about disappointing you tonight."

Without answering, she came close to him and draped her arms around his shoulder. Her blue eyes locked on his. Her fragrance wafted into his nostrils.

O my God! What is happening to me? What am I doing? I shouldn't be here.

She kissed him softly, running her tongue around his lips. He took a half step back. "Relax," she cooed. "This is not as if we worked in the same office or even for the same company. We can do what we please. What would you like to do?"

Eddie said, "I'd like for us to run away to France, to Paris France, and make love all day. Too bad, we both need to work."

"Great idea. Let's do just that."

You're forgetting that I have a lot to do tomorrow. You remember: the new product?"

"No. No. The product can wait. Let someone else evaluate the damn thing. Let us do just that," she said. "We will run away together. Have you been to Paris?"

"But your job, your career. It's not easy for a woman to get hired in this field."

She frowned. "Those idiots in Oxnard with their stupid beards and their white lab coats think they have me figured out. Truth is, I have them figured out. Don't need them. Can get a job anywhere and likely with better pay."

She touched his arm, moving her fingers gently against his flesh as if she were playing a piano keyboard. He shivered from the touch. She lifted one side of her mouth in a sly grin and winked. "I am my own person. I do what I damn well please."

"You're serious."

"Why not? We're both single. It feels right for me. We shall sit and talk. No need to rush. Think of this evening as a beginning, not as an end."

She undid the belt and let the teddy slip to the floor. He stood motionless, enjoying the nearness of her. They sat on the couch, her leg draped over his lap.

Davie talked and talked with Eddie listening intently, enthralled by her stories about her travels. She told about traveling all over the world, interspersing the travelogue with personal bits and pieces. He hung on her every word and didn't mind at all her constant chatter.

Eddie asked her if they might sleep together. She readily agreed. He felt no remorse. Eddie awoke in the morning to the sound of his alarm clock on the bedside table. Davie Collins was nowhere to be seen. She had left no evidence that she had been there, no note, nothing. But then, he was in his own room, not hers. He wondered if maybe he had dreamed it all. His head ached with a hangover headache like he had not had since his college days.

He combed through his memory, trying to recall exactly what happened. He remembered Davie on the couch, half-naked in her sitting room. He couldn't recall anything after that. He had no idea how he got back to his own room or if they had sex or anything beyond her chattering about her travels.

He phoned down to the front desk to get her room number. He never bothered to notice what room she had been in or even the floor. The hotel operator put him through to the room. "Collins," the man's voice on the other end of the phone line said.

Damn! She swore she was single. Well, maybe she didn't actually swear. But she did say we were both single.

He slammed down the phone. "Should have known," he said to himself. "It was all too good to be true. I got to stop drinking so much. I'm hallucinating."

Eddie showered and dressed and headed to the restaurant for breakfast. He shuffled through the line at the breakfast buffet for attendees of the convention, getting ham and fried eggs and tomato juice and coffee, and sat at an empty table. He had no sooner put the juice glass to his lips than he heard his name. He looked up to see a tall man with a gray Vandyke beard smiling down at him.

"Aren't you going to ask me to join you?"

"Sure, why not. You seem to know me. I'm sorry. I don't recognize you. What can I do for you?"

The man put down his tray and offered Eddie his hand. "I'm David Collins from Smithstone Brothers. Sorry for the bit of subterfuge. Your boss thought that this would be a good assignment for you, what with losing your wife so tragically and all."

"I'm sorry. It's a little early. I had way too much fun last night. Working on a nasty hangover."

"Yes. Yes. I know all about that. So what did you think of her?"

"Your wife?"

The man laughed and then caught himself. "I shouldn't be laughing. There was no way for you to know. Although I only realized after she met you that we hadn't given her a purse. I thought we'd blown it for sure. But you never seemed to notice."

"Don't tell me. You're one of the guys from Oxnard she was talking about."

"Probably."

"You're telling me she's a robot? An android?"

"Yep."

"No way! You're putting me on. Nobody is much beyond levers and gears. I know my field. You're talking way beyond anything known to date in artificial intelligence. We're fifty years away from anything so perfect, maybe even more."

David Collins smiled. "Yes, perfect. I designed her to be every man's dream companion. She is flexible enough to adapt her approach for different situations. Never the same. I've spent my working life perfecting her. Up 'til now, the project's been super cosmic top secret. You can give us your written evaluation when you get back to the office. For now, though, I'd like any off-the-cuff impressions."

Eddie thought back over the prior evening's encounter with Davie. It had been wonderful beyond imagination. He was at once both happy and sad. Happy because the evening had held so much promise, sad that the promise had evaporated like the morning dew.

Enough already for the wool gathering. Time to get back to reality. There's a job to be done.

"Well, she's a little talkative and maybe a bit forward. Aside from that, she's perfect. I'd like to spend more time with her. Is she for sale?"

Collins laughed. "That good, huh?"

"More than good."

"I hope you enjoyed it."

"That I did. The perfect partner."

"Here, she comes now. When you meet her, she'll have no recall of anything that happened between the two of you. It will be like you are a different person. She remembers stuff about Oxnard and traveling different places because that's in her firmware."

"Like Paris," Eddie said.

David Collins nodded. We've been tearing our hair out for the past two years, trying to increase her explicit working memory for new experiences. She doesn't seem to retain things for long enough to store them properly in her long term memory. That's no good. Every two hours or so, she resets.

His thoughts went back to his first meeting with Davie the previous evening. Eddie's felt his heart beating and his body tightening. The morning Davie was even more beautiful than he remembered.

Collins greeted her with a cheery, "Morning." She smiled at him quickly, her lips barely moving. He continued. "Like you to meet a friend of mine, Eddie Thurgel. Eddie, this is Davie."

The robot offered Eddie her hand. He looked into her eyes, trying to find a glint of recognition. He found none. She intoned in a measured cadence, "How do you do? I am very pleased to meet you, Mister Thurgel." When they shook hands, her touch gave him the same thrill as it had the past evening, and he shuddered as if some invisible spirit had passed into his body.

David Collins motioned for her to join them and then proceeded to give his full attention to breakfast. Before sitting, the robot touched Eddie's arm, moving her fingers gently against his flesh as if she were playing a piano keyboard. He shivered from the touch. She lifted one side of her mouth in a sly grin and winked. As she was sitting, she looked up at him and silently mouthed the words, "Paris. Yes?"

Special Delivery

I sat on my front porch nursing a cup of freshly brewed hazelnut coffee with cinnamon sprinkled on top. This was the fateful day. If the check from my last job didn't come soon, my boarders and I would soon be on the street; our butts plopped on the curb with our belongings piled around us. Saw that once when my uncle got evicted.

The mail carrier came at her usual time, driving up in her blue and white truck to open my mailbox and stuff all sorts of junk mail into it. She comes really early on Saturday. She's nice. I always give her a greeting when I'm out. With a wave and a smile, I hollered, "Hi Dianne. Great weather, huh?"

"Good morning to you, Mister K." She called everybody by their first initial. We had two Mister Ks on the street. The other one lived three doors down on the opposite side. He's Kerk, and I'm Kirk. We're both, Walter.

I checked the weather report for the day on my cell phone, sunny and hot. Showers late in the day. Another Florida scorcher. About the time I finished my coffee and walked out to collect the mail, Dianne was coming back, delivering to the other side of the street, the odd numbers, Walter Kerk's side. My flip-flops slapped the concrete driveway, a comforting and familiar sound.

I got to my mailbox about the time she arrived opposite my house. She leaned forward and looked in my direction. "Hey Mister K. You have a letter that was mailed a long, long time ago. It was still in your box this morning. You must have missed it."

"You mean already in the box when you opened it today?"

She nodded. "Yesterday was my day off. My substitute must have delivered it. I put it on top of the pile, so you'd be sure to see it. It only has three cents postage. That was for like a hundred years ago."

Three cents. Wow. "Thanks for telling me, Dianne. Let me take a look right now." I flipped the door down and fished out all the mail. The envelope that Dianne had called my attention to sat atop a pile of bills and catalogs addressed to me and to the other people who lived in the boarding house with me.

I studied the small, straight, cramped, perfectly formed letters. My brother Tommy wrote that way, like the scientist he was. He'd been dead for some five years. My heart rate picked up. A chill breeze came up all of a sudden. An osprey swooped low and wheeled above my head.

I set the other mail down on the driveway and examined the envelope. It felt flimsy and had blue borders. The return address wasn't my brother's address. He never lived in D.C. The letter carried a 3 cent stamp just like Dianne said. The stamp had an eagle on it and said "air mail" across the top, the words separated by a shield. The letter was postmarked, December 7, 1941.

The handwriting: I knew it couldn't be my brother's. He wasn't even born in '41. My dad would've been a young man, but I remember seeing his handwriting. His used big loops to start the sentences and had a slant that Ma said meant he could have been a famous actor if he hadn't been killed in the war. The writing had to be my grandfather's.

My mother's aunt and uncle raised me after mom died in a traffic accident. They never liked my father's side of the family, never told me much about my father or his father except to say that they were rich. I think they became angry when they found out my father left everything to a charity, leaving me with only a small trust that terminated when I reached maturity.

They did tell me that my grandfather was in the navy. Commanded a destroyer, aunt Betsy once told me. His boat sank with all hands when a torpedo hit it amidships, she said. The story never rang true to me.

I realized that the mail truck hadn't moved. Feeling eyes on me, I glanced up. Dianne had come out of her truck and stood watching, a look of anticipation in her face. "It's really old, isn't it," she said.

"Sure is. From my grandfather. Must have fallen behind a desk or something and not got found until they remodeled a post office somewhere. I read about that happening."

"You've only lived at this address for five years. How come it's addressed to you here in Florida?"

"That's a great question, Dianne. Let's see. Hmm. My great uncle's name was Walter. He lived in Florida. Maybe he lived here a long time ago. The place has been in my family for generations. Wasn't always a boarding house. I had to take in boarders because I got laid off. It would be a real coincidence. But who knows?"

"I got to get back on my route," Dianne said. She waved goodbye to me and shouted, "Let me know what it's all about when you figure it out. Might be that someone's playin' tricks on you."

I picked up the bills and the catalogs and shuffled back to the porch, avoiding my usual flapping as if it might be somehow disrespectful of my precious cargo.

Sarah, one of my boarders, had come out and sat in the glider. She was in her mid-60s. Age hadn't erased all of the beauty that made her a successful photography model in her younger years. She had on the blue terry cloth robe that she wore most days over a blouse and skirt. Her short, sturdy body rocked slowly back and forth, making the little squeaks and groans that I had come to associate with the ancient glider. She flashed me a broad toothy smile and said, "You flirtin' with Dianne again, Walter?"

"Got a strange letter." I put the junk and bills on the table next to the glider and waved the letter at her. "From my grandpa, Sedgwick. Dad used to call him Sedgie. Used to be in the navy. I always figured he was a submariner. Nobody knows what happened to him. His boat never came back from a cruise. Most likely got blown up. Maybe it was like in that Clark Gable movie, you know, the Bungo Straits where all our subs got sunk.

"Your grandpa, huh?"

"Yep. Mailed in 1941."

Sarah laughed and slapped her knee. "Man, that mail carrier is slower, 'n I thought. They ain't kiddin' when they call it snail mail now are they?" I sat beside her, my heart still racing and feeling a little giddy, the letter from my grandfather held tight between my fingers like it might be some fragile thing. Sarah stared at me a while before she said, "Well. Ain't ya gonna open it? Find out what it says?"

I examined the envelope. It was one of those old letters that are actually the envelope. You wrote the letter and then folded it up, so it formed the envelope. You wrote the address on the outside. Saved weight for airmail letters. I would need to be careful about opening it. Using my finger as per my usual approach to letter opening, I might tear it. Then it'd be difficult to read without taping it all back together.

I stuffed the letter in my shirt pocket. "Think I'll go in and have some breakfast right now, Sarah. Maybe read it a little later. Been around since '41. Don't suppose a few more minutes will make a difference.'

"Reckon you're right there, Walter. Strikes me it's like a bottle of fine wine. Might could be better to live with the hopin' rather than pop the cork and find the wine's changed."

Inside the house, I joined the three other people who shared the home with Sarah and me. There was Jeb. I liked him the most after Sarah. We called him, Doctor Pepper, 'cause of his unruly mop of pepper and salt hair. Kate and Hector were brother and sister. Neither of them had married. They were younger, in their fifties, nice too.

When I sat down at the table, I tapped my letter and said, "Got a letter here addressed to me that was mailed a long time ago."

"Looks old," Kate said.

"It is old, Kate. Mailed in 19 and 41."

"Doctor Pepper said, "I remember those envelopes. I bet it's got the words "air mail" on it too."

"You'd win that bet," I said.

Doctor Pepper said, "You into collectin' old stamps, Walter?" He craned his neck to get a closer look at the envelope.

Doc chuckled way down in his throat. He said, "Who's it from? What's it say? You read it yet? Must be somethin' important." Then he got a strange look on his face, his lips pursed, and his brows knotted. He made his eyes into slits. "Wait just a darn minute, Walter. You're puttin' us on. No way that letter could be just now delivered. You found it somewhere."

Hector jumped up and hollered, "Read it to us. Read it to us."

In a fit of exasperation, I shouted, "All right. I'll read it." Sarah, who had followed me into the house, produced a letter opener from her robe pocket and handed it to me.

Fixed on her face, the ever present smile that displayed her rows of brown teeth. She had no money for proper dentistry. I'd got my dentist to give her some free work. It wasn't near enough. I swore that if I ever became rich, one thing I'd do first off is get her a new set of teeth so she could be pretty again. Fat chance that. I couldn't even keep the house.

About then, I remembered that I'd forgotten to look for the check. I reached over and tore through the stack of mail that Sarah had dropped on the table. No letter. Only the junk mail. My boarders undoubtedly thought I was crazy. They didn't know they were about to be evicted.

I closed my eyes and took a deep breath. My hands trembled. Could it be that this strange letter might be our salvation? With the greatest care, I gently slid the opener under the flaps and unfolded the envelope until a sheet of creased white paper lay on the table in front of me. My four companions pressed in behind and beside me, bending over, Sarah's sweet breath on my cheek and her ample breasts pressing into my arm, all of them clearly more eager than me to discover the words that lay upon the page.

I read aloud. "Walter, I write to tell you that by the time you receive this, I am on my way to take command of a warship. I do not expect to survive the hostilities. Therefore I want to tell you of the family secret that has been handed down by the men in our family for many generations. The women are never, never, told. Your father's plane was shot down in France. He did not survive the crash, so it falls upon me to be your advisor in these matters. Knowledge of the secret has been the source of our wealth since our forebears stumbled upon it many years ago. I must go now. I promise to post a further letter that will describe for you what you need to know."

The rest of the letter contained impersonal comments on the nature of war and its causes. I quit reading aloud, believing that it was of no interest to anyone present.

Doctor Pepper complained that he couldn't see the writing without his spectacles that were upstairs on his nightstand, and he didn't feel like going all the way up to his room to fetch them what with his bad leg and all. Sarah read it for me.

In very tiny writing along the edge of the letter, granddad had written something illegible with all the words seeming to run together. I could make out only my name.

Kate said, "It must be a pirate's treasure map."

"It's written in invisible ink," Hector declared in a loud voice as if to force us to believe the truth of the statement.

Sarah said, "Nope. Both wrong. That stuff only happens in stories. Might could be a bank account number."

Doc said, "You never told us you was rich, Walter. Just how much money you got?"

"Well, duh! I never got told the family secret, did I, so I never been rich."

"Oh yeah. Right. We'll have to wait 'til he writes you again."

Sarah said, "Then you can let us all live here free 'cause you won't need any more money."

I held up my hands. "Wait a darn minute. This letter is a trillion to one shot, like getting struck by a bolt of lightning when the sky is clear blue. If my grandfather wrote me any more letters, what makes you think lightning could strike again? Don't you all think that would be too much coincidence?"

I realized I had at least one sane person in the group when Sarah said, "Might could be."

When I'd re-folded the letter and put it back in my pocket, Doc pointed at me and waved his finger. "Like to have that stamp for my collection." I gave him my version of a withering stare. "When you're done with it, of course. Didn't mean right this second."

For the rest of the day and all day Sunday, the conversation centered around my letter and whether I might be getting more letters. Speculation on what might be the family secret ran rampant with each outrageous suggestion topped by a still more outrageous possibility. The cook even joined in, "Walter must be related to British royalty. As a 'royal,' he will get a huge pension." Cook hazarded a timid guess that it might be near a million dollars.

I asked, "Is that a million a week, a month, a year, or maybe altogether?" She closed her mouth and dropped her head and quickly left the room. I felt bad for putting her down. But I was darned sick of my assumed wealth being the main topic of conversation.

By Monday morning, things were out of control. I didn't like being treated as a newly minted rich guy, especially since I was still as poor as ever. My fellow boarders began addressing me as Sir Walter and bowing to me when I entered a room. At the table, they passed the food to me first and with exaggerated flourishes.

A guy can dream, even if he thinks the dream will never come true. I was of two minds on the matter and didn't want to let loose of the idea of coming into great wealth. That's probably why I got annoyed at Hector for suggesting that the letter was meant for Walter Kerk, who lived down the street. "That Walter's been in his house since he was born." I told him to just mind his own business. He said, "Yer a dummy of the worst kind."

"And what does that mean, smart guy?"

"Hah! Hah! *El stupido*. Ain't no way ya could be the right guy the letter was sent to. It's fer Walter Kerk, and ya know it. Yer *el stupido*, Walter."

When I picked up a lamp off the side table next to the sofa and pretended I was about to toss it at him, he ran and hid behind his sister, hunkering down and peering out at me from behind her skirts like a little kid. I couldn't stay angry at Hector. But I couldn't let him think he got one over on me either, so I said, "Think what you want, Hector. When I find out the family secret and get rich, there's no way I'm going to share it with you. Everyone else will get some but not you." He made a sad face and tears welled in his eyes. My imagined riches were making me a jerk.

Hector's hectoring got me to thinking. Might be that he was right. Might be that Walter Kerk was the intended recipient of the letter. I looked again at the envelope, studying the address. The "i" could be an "e." I found no dot above what I had taken initially to be the letter "i." The mind can play tricks. After all these years, the dot may have faded.

The Street number was definitely 1974. Dianne had read it that way. But was it? I took it under the lamp and examined it closer. The last number began to look a bit like a European 7 with a cross stroke instead of like a sloppy 4. The numeral 1 had a little flag like the Europeans use sometimes. Walt Kerk's family was originally from Germany. Perhaps it was the Kerk family with a secret that could make Walter Kerk rich. I took out the letter and read it again.

The whole crew was sitting around. Sarah lounged on the sofa reading a new romance novel she'd bought for a dollar in the used book sale at the library. Hector and his sister played a child's board game. Doc sat at the dining table, studying his stamps with a large, round magnifying glass. Sitting there in his tattered and threadbare smoking jacket, he looked like a pathetic Sherlock Holmes down on his luck.

"Hey, Doc. Can I borrow that glass from you a minute?'

He looked up from his work and stared dumbly at me for a while. He chuckled and said, "You want to look at the old stamp, I suppose. Remember, you promised it to me, so don't you go startin' your own collection now."

He wanted me to confirm that the stamp was indeed to be added to his collection. I wasn't in a bantering mood, so I stood across the table from him and locked my gaze on his lidded, rheumy eyes. He held the magnifying glass close for what seemed like five minutes before he held out his hand and let loose of it.

I took the glass, thanked him, and retired to the ottoman where the light was better. By that time, all eyes were staring at me. My fellow boarders knew something was brewing and were eager to know what new and exciting fact I had discovered.

Upon closer scrutiny, I concluded that the tiny writing at the bottom of the letter might be in German. The German's use those great long words. Hmm.

My phone rang its irritating default jingle that I kept meaning to change but never figured out how to keep it from going back to the default ring every time I shut down. I fished it out of my pocket and looked to see who might be calling. I recognized Walter Kerk's number.

"Hey, Walt. So good to hear from you. We haven't run into each other for a while. How are you?"

"Good," Walter replied.

"Happy to hear it. What's up?"

"I hate all this heat, don't you?"

"I get used to it. What's up?"

I have a letter that might be for you. The mail girl delivered it this morning. She doesn't seem to mind the heat. I noticed that she has a big fan mounted on the dashboard of her truck. You know that she gets our mail mixed up sometimes, especially in bad weather. Our names are so much alike, and...."

"Yeah. Yeah. Did you open it?"

"No. Misplaced my spectacles. I'm blind as a bat without them."

"How'd you know it's for me?"

"Must be. Damn. Wish it would rain. We could use some rain."

"We sure could, Walt. Why must it be for me?"

"Only mail I get is advertisements and catalogs. I can tell by the feel of it that it's something personal. You know, like flimsy, like a love letter. It has a colored border sort of." He giggled. "You expecting a love letter Walter?"

"Matter of fact I am expecting just such a letter. Thanks for calling."

"Not surprised. Thought it must be for you. I haven't got a real letter in at least ten years, not even a Christmas card. You remember last Christmas when we thought it might snow, it got so cold? Nearly killed my bougainvillea."

It might not be Christmas for Walter Kerk, but if the missive turned out to be the one I was expecting, it might be Christmas for me. In no mood to make small talk with Walter about the weather, I said, "Be over in a couple minutes to pick it up; thanks," and ended the call.

The instant I returned the phone to my pocket, Sarah, who by then was sitting on the edge of the sofa, the closed book on her lap, said, "He has your letter. The one that tells you how to be rich."

"He has a letter Dianne delivered to him by mistake. It's only a letter. Don't get your hopes up."

I handed Doctor Pepper back his magnifying glass. He took it with a smile and said, "You won't be needin' that stamp now."

His obsession with the stamp was getting on my nerves. But I'm basically an understanding guy. Instead of saying something sarcastic, I shook my head and replied, "Got to see what's in the second letter before I can give it to you. Be patient."

Walter Kerk sat on his front porch in his pajamas, chewing an unlit cigar, the kind you get five in a box at the drug store. No hint of a smile ever dared invade the downturned mouth or wrinkle the corners of his eyes. In his hand, the hand of a working man, large and rough with thick fingers, he held a letter that looked a lot like the one I received on Saturday.

Walter seldom left his house, preferring to have groceries and other necessities delivered. He did spend a lot of time on the porch. On my walks around the neighborhood, I often took a moment to talk to him. He talked but remained cool and aloof. Never did he invite me in or even to have a seat in one of the rusted chairs that stood in a neat row, each exactly the same distance from its nearest mate. I would stand on the sidewalk, and we would talk about the weather, always the weather.

"Another scorcher," he said and fell silent. I thought for a moment he might be referring to the letter he held out in front of him and waved slowly back and forth, as if using it to fan himself.

I approached tentatively, not knowing exactly what he expected of me. At the bottom of the old wooden porch steps, I stopped. He glowered at me. In my best neighborly tone, I said. "Weatherman says it'll cool off this afternoon. He's expecting a front to move through, bring some rain."

He grinned. "Found my specs. It ain't for you. It's for me. So you just go on home."

"Now wait just a darn minute, Walt. I'm expecting a letter just like that one. I know it's for me. Just because you never get any personal mail doesn't give you the right to take mine. You know that taking my letter is a federal offense. You can go to jail."

He grinned, waved a dismissive hand at me, and said, "Get outta here 'fore I call the cops." I figured that he meant it. The old fool was stupid enough to do that.

I decided to retreat. The letter wasn't going anywhere. He probably planned on building a shrine for it with flowers and candles – his first real letter in ten years. In a way, I couldn't blame him for wanting to keep it.

Back at the house, I told my companions what had happened and asked them for ideas on how to retrieve the second letter, the one that held the key to my fortune. Hector's response was immediate and somewhat drastic. "That old fart Walter will be the rich one. That smelly old fart don't scare me. One punch and he's out, and I get your letter."

I appreciated Hector's willingness to go to battle for me. Of course, I couldn't let him pound on Walt. I told him, "We can't go around hitting people, Hector."

Doc said, "How about when he's not home we sneak in and take the letter. We can leave one in its place that looks kind of like it. He won't have new specs for a couple days. With his bad eyesight, he'll never know we switched."

"No good, Doc. He never leaves home, and he found his glasses."

"No problem," Sarah said, "One of us can lure him out of his house. The rest of us go in and get the letter."

"Whom did you have in mind as the lurer?"

Sarah laughed. With a circular motion of her shoulders, she shook off her robe and let it slip to the floor, then unbuttoned the top two buttons of her blouse and pushed out her bosom. She pinched her 64 year old cheeks and shoved her long hair back from her face to tuck it behind each ear. Her skirt she hiked to the knees. The transformation proved to be quite extraordinary.

I said in as soft a tone as I could manage under the circumstances, "Okay. So, Sarah gets the job of lurer. We're a democracy. Anybody opposed?"

A dead silence ensued, during which I am sure we all tried to digest what Sarah had just agreed to as her role in our little caper. Hector broke the silence with a loud "Yeah. Right on." The rest of us joined in with clapping and shouts of encouragement. Doc surprised the hell out of me when he shouted, "Take it off. Take it all off." Sarah advanced toward a red-faced Doctor Pepper with a slow, hip-grinding walk.

I concluded that she was more than up to the task of luring. Old Walt wouldn't know what hit him. His only pleasure for the past how many years most likely consisted of nodding off with Victoria Secret catalogs propped on his pillow. He was a goner for sure.

Cook, whose name was Hanna Heilbronner but who we all called, Cook, and who had entered the room sometime during the conversation, shouted, "Hurray for Sarah." She knew Walter Kerk and sometimes cooked for him. However, I was certain that she had no idea what was going on, so I didn't worry about a security breach.

The rest of the day, we occupied with in-depth discussions of what Sarah might need to offer to lure Walter Kerk away from his home long enough for us to find the letter. Doc surprised me again and again with his lurid instructions on the art of seduction. Hector concentrated on mapping out a plan for the search. He insisted that we begin in the kitchen because that's where his mother opened letters.

The next morning, Sarah came down to breakfast dressed in a red skirt and white blouse with the three top buttons open. The clothing fit tight about her hips and bodice. Hector couldn't take his eyes off her breasts that pressed against the sheer fabric of her tight blouse. "That will do it. That will definitely do it," he repeated again and again.

Sarah had used lipstick and other sorts of makeup. Her eyes were shaded, her eyelashes longer. Her eyes looked bigger and set deeper. She had tied up her hair in a bun, reminding me of the German housekeeper my friend Moises had when we were kids. I had never seen Sarah made up. She looked ten years younger and came across as quite pretty. She would have no trouble seducing Walter Kerk.

"Wish me luck, guys," she said when she began her mission. We followed her out to the porch.

"You go, girl," the usually quiet Kate advised. In silence we watched Sarah saunter down the street. Her ample backside swayed, defying the laws of gravity and questioning the laws of decency. She crossed the road and climbed the steps to Walter Kerk's porch. He sprang from his chair and reached out a hand to greet her.

The plan was for her to convince Walter to take a stroll around the block and join her for breakfast at the local pancake house about a half-mile away. I was glad that she decided to start in the morning because the weatherman had predicted another hot one. Too hot to walk very far in the Florida summer.

Pretending not to be interested in what transpired between Sarah and Walter, we kept a close eye on the proceedings. After sitting for almost a half-hour, the two of them got up and headed arm in arm down the road in the direction of the pancake house.

The game was afoot. The instant the two rounded the corner, Doc said, "Let's roll." He shot down the steps and strode off with a gait that belied his 75 years. The quiet stamp collector had morphed into a leader.

Hector shouted after him, "Wait a minute, Doctor. How do we get in?"

Doctor Pepper froze in mid-stride. He turned and shuffled back to us; his head bowed, his mouth turned down. He seemed to be confused. "What do we do next, Walter," he said, looking up to meet my gaze. So much for our new leader.

"Hector will go in through a basement window. He can go up and open the front door for us."

"No basement," Hector said. "Flood plain. Nearly all of Tarpon Springs's in a flood plain. You got a plan B?"

There was no plan B. There was no plan A either. We never discussed much beyond Sarah getting Walt out of the house. Probably 'cause it was actually Sarah's plan, and she concentrated on the luring part, leaving the other details up to the rest of us. Stalling, I said, "Well, yes, I do, Hector."

Doc spoke up and rescued me. "He uses one of them ventilation screens in the first-floor windows. Hector can just raise up the window and climb in. We boost him up. If he has a nail or somethin' to stop us from openin' the window more, Hector can still fit through."

"That's what Walter was gonna suggest," Hector said. He turned to me, "Wasn't that what ya was gonna tell us, Walter?"

I decided it was time for action. "Show of hands," I said. We go with Doc's plan." Hector raised his beefy hand in a tight-fisted salute. Kate raised her hand. "Doc?" Doctor Pepper raised his. "The motion passes. Let's go then."

Kate opted to stay behind, explaining that any well-planned caper required a lookout. I wondered exactly what a lookout might do under the circumstances but didn't want to get into that with her.

Inside Walter Kerk's house, we found a neat and orderly array of ancient furniture. The place was spotless. Walt must have spent all day cleaning and polishing. Everything had been detailed, from the nooks and crannies of the kitchen to the highly polished floors.

I found the letter on a small table by his front door. With the letter in hand, I joined Hector and Doctor Pepper, who seemed certain that they would find something of interest in the kitchen. "What's that noise?" Doc asked.

"Which noise? Hector said.

"The bell. Sounds like somebody ringin' a school bell."

"Forget it. Let's concentrate on business," I said. "We need to read the letter. We have lots of time. I can take a picture of the letter with my phone if there's anything in it we can use to make a fortune. We'll put it back exactly where I found it. Walt won't suspect anything. We take the letter, and Walt will know he's been had."

"You leave the letter, and he'll know how to get rich too," Doc said.

"True. But we'll know before him."

I took a seat at the little Formica-topped breakfast table on one of the chrome legged chairs. Hector and Doc joined me. "Read it out loud for us," Hector said. Doc nodded in agreement.

I heard talking that seemed to be coming from the back yard. Doc heard it too. "It's Sarah. They're back already. They must have cut through one of the lots. They took a shortcut."

"No way they had breakfast in that short a time," I whispered. "Something went wrong."

I snatched up the letter and made a run for the front hall with Hector behind me pushing and Doc in the rear. I tossed the letter onto the table, and the three of us ran out the front door and all the way back home.

Kate greeted us with the school bell in hand. Cook stood at her side. So much for security.

Kate said, "Told you we needed a lookout. I rang the bell soon as they rounded the corner headed this way. Lucky for you that they went around to the back of the house."

"Thanks, Kate," Doc said between gasps. "You did well."

Soon as I caught my breath, I said, "Sarah was laughing like a schoolgirl. Doc, what do you think happened?"

"No idea. Would of thought she might be a mite tense knowin' we was in the house."

"Know what I think?" Cook said.

"No. What you think, Cook," Doc replied.

"I bet you anything the two of them are over there makin' a good old time right now. You men are all the same. All you can think is how horny the guy will be. You forget that Sarah hasn't had a date in years. She's hornier than that old German ever was. And I should know."

Hector laughed. "Good for Sarah," he shouted.

"If only I had known," Doc said, a note of sadness in his voice. "I spent too much time buried in my stamp collection. Come to think of it, I recall a couple times she came on to me. You remember the mistletoe incident last Christmas?"

I had little interest in discussing Doc's sex life. Guys his age ought not to be preoccupied with it.

Sarah didn't come home until nearly six. She wore a toothy smile so wide that I thought for a moment the ends of her mouth had split.

"I never knew that Walter was such an interesting man," she said. When I heard that as the first words out of her mouth, I knew we were in trouble. "We played checkers and had a couple of drinks. And we talked about all sorts of wonderful places he's been. Wants to take me to the movies tomorrow."

"Why'd ya come back so quick?" Hector asked.

"Oh. That. I'm sorry about that. The pancake place was closed."

"I'm happy that you two hit it off on your first date," I said. "Did he say anything about the letter?"

"Oh. That. He showed it to me. It was from some vacuum salesman. Not a personal letter."

The news made my heart sink way down to my toes. It was as if somebody had dropped me off the side of a tall building, and I was free-falling.

Hector said, "Glad I didn't go out and buy stuff. I'd have to take it all back."

"Sorry, guys. Maybe someday the second letter will come. Let's be optimistic."

I took my letter out of my pocket and handed it to Doctor Pepper. He studied it for a moment and then let out a whoop like a crazed New York Rangers fan.

"What is it, Doc?"

"The stamp. The stamp. The stamp."

"Take a deep breath. You're sounding like Hector. Slow down. Tell us what it is about the stamp that's got you all charged up. Don't want to have to call 911."

"Did your granddaddy ever work in the place where they print stamps?"

"Aunt Betsy said something about him being a printer when he was younger. Maybe she said something about stamps. Don't recall exactly. Why?"

"Well, the six-cent eagle and shield airmail stamps were issued in May of 1938. The one on your letter is in a three-cent denomination and says 'air mall' instead of airmail. It was a mistake, like the old upside-down Curtis Jenny biplane stamp of 1918 designed by Claire Aubry Huston.

"I always thought it was a legend. Not really true. Supposedly all of these, along with the plates, were destroyed. The error was discovered almost immediately. The Jenny is worth nearly a cool million with fewer than 100 in existence. This eagle and shield would be worth more, a lot more than that.

I looked at the faces of my housemates. For the very first time since they moved in, all of them smiled. I'd never felt so good.

"Let me see that, Doc." I took the letter. I studied the stamp. The word "mail" was, in fact, not spelled correctly. I had looked right at it when the letter first arrived and never saw the mistake. With a loud smack, I kissed it and raised it up at arm's length. "We're rich. We're all rich."

Making Up

~ — ~

By the polished apples,
By the mottled grapes,
By the tasseled ears of corn
Near the point of no return.

When I came to love you.
When you came to love me too,
When we vowed a life to share,
Together we'd go everywhere.

If you do stay with me.
If I also stay with you.
If we both make up now
We will have a life to show.

So let us buy the apples
And the mottled grapes.
Let us leave the ears of corn.
We'll fill our basket later on.

Trout Fishing

At a bend in the cool green river
Trout by the fisherman fed
Where the water moves ever so swiftly
To there the doomed swimmers are led.
Years of quick water flowing
Soil below undercutting
A trap by the eddies is made.
Fish that hold to the bank
By colorful insects betrayed.

Bless Me Father

Roger Cantrell blessed himself with holy water from the font near the church door. He walked, quickly–head down and with apparent purpose–toward the confessional box where a line of penitents stood. As he approached, a woman emerged from one side of the confessional. He strode past the waiting people and pushed back the curtain. He dropped to his knees on the hard wooden kneeler. He faced a small rectangular door with a sliding closure. He waited, turning up his nose at the heavy odor of cologne. A few minutes later, the door slid open with a loud snap. Cantrell crossed himself and said, "Bless me, Father. I have sinned."

After a long silence Father Thomas Bergen, the priest hearing confessions that evening, said, "Continue, please. What sins do you want to confess?"

"I did horrible things, Father, things so terrible that I can't bring out the words."

"Maybe you can tell me which commandments you've broken. Maybe you can start that way."

"I don't know the numbers."

"Just say the title, like, 'You shall not covet your neighbor's wife,' or 'You shall not steal.'"

Cantrell remained silent for a moment and then said, "Thou shall not kill or rape or torture. Thou shall not kill a whole family, including the wife and all the children. Thou shall not set fire to their house and watch it burn to the ground with one of them still alive in it and enjoy listening to the little Thompson girl scream."

Father Bergen heard the words but had difficulty absorbing their meaning. Though only a few months out of the seminary and mere weeks into his assignment at Queen of Peace parish, he had heard nearly a hundred confessions. A late in life vocation—before becoming a priest, he had seen bloody combat as a marine and later had worked as a professional wrestler. He considered himself worldly. Yet he had never experienced anything like what the man seeking forgiveness was telling him.

Never had he been asked to forgive any serious transgressions. Mostly the stories were of relatively harmless activities like young children who confessed that they had played pranks on their teachers or teens masturbating or adults missing mass—no murder, no robbery, no theft, not even a wayward husband or wife.

Panic seized him. What could he say to the murderer who knelt only inches from him, maybe armed and ready to do to him what he had done to the family he had killed? And what might he do to people in church praying or waiting for their own confessions to be heard, those souls fearful of losing salvation because they had merely harbored a bad thought or wished ill of their enemies?

Father Bergen breathed deeply. He pressed his palms together. His thoughts turned to his seminary instructions on the sacrament of reconciliation. No matter the gravity of the man's sins, he had a duty. His job was to evaluate the man's confession and, through the power given to him as a priest of Christ, decide if the confession was sincere. If he so decided, then he was required to forgive the sins, conditioned on the penitent doing an appropriate atonement for the sins confessed.

But what ought to be the penance? Surely he must ask the man to give himself up to the police. Was this sin so terrible that if the man declined to accept such atonement Father Bergen himself had an obligation to report him? No. The bond of silence was sacred, a sacred trust. But who was this murderer? Father Bergen thought of peeking out to try and see what the man looked like. Even if he did that, he would have only a fleeting glance at the man's back. What if the man turned around and saw him? Might he draw a gun and kill again to protect his identity, perhaps killing all the people in the church?

"Have you any other sins to confess at this time?"

"I been screwin' my lousy, always-complaining landlord, so I don't have to pay any rent."

"Do you love her?"

"Him. Nope."

"I see."

"Anything else?"

"I haven't been to church in years. You know, I don't go to church on Sunday like I should."

"You haven't murdered any other people, families?"

"Only this one since my last confession."

"When was that?"

"About ten years ago."

"When did you kill the family?"

"Yesterday morning. I really feel bad about it."

"Were there any extenuating circumstances?"

"What do you mean?"

"Were you defending yourself? Were you in a state of temporary insanity or high on drugs or anything like that?"

"Nope. Just pissed off."

"And what got you so angry?"

"The jerk husband tried to be a hero. He should've given me his money, but I got some of that when I used his credit cards. Got my wallet full of his cards, but I promise not to use them. I suppose I should have confessed that too. Don't know if stealin' from a stiff is the same as me stealin' from a live guy. If it's like a separate sin, consider it confessed."

"Promise to destroy them—all of them?"

"Sure."

"To show the Lord you are contrite."

"Sure. Okay."

A freight train of thoughts rushed through Father Bergen's mind. He was certain that he heard a note of aggravation creeping into the man's voice, maybe anger. The more he thought of the situation, the more he mused about a solution to the dilemma the confessed killer presented. He doubted the man's sincerity as well as his regret for the murders, but that judgment he would leave to God. To absolve the man in such circumstances and not see to his arrest was unthinkable. Somehow he had to accomplish both.

Father Bergen breathed deeply and said in as soft a voice as he could manage in the circumstances, “I can forgive you your sins, all of them, but it must be based on some serious form of penance to which you agree before you leave this confessional.”

“I'm not going to the cops if that's what you mean.”

“I will not ask you to do that. I promise.”

“Okay. I'll take whatever you toss at me, but no cops.”

“Do you accept God's wrath for what you have done, His wrath of whatever nature the good Lord might choose and whatever instrumentality our good Lord might use. Do you agree to accept the wrath of God?”

“Except giving myself up?”

“Except giving yourself up.”

“Yeah. Okay. I do.”

“Do you know the prayer we call, The Act of Contrition?”

“I think I remember it.”

“Say a sincere Act of Contrition.”

Cantrell mumbled the prayer. Father Bergen said, “Go and sin no more.” Father Bergen slammed the little door shut. He lifted his six foot five, two hundred and forty-pound frame from his seat. He shoved open the door of the little confessional. The man who had just confessed was pushing back the curtain and stepping out into the church aisle. He was tall like the priest but not nearly as muscular.

Father Bergen's meaty fist caught the man with an uppercut that sent him reeling back into the confessional. With an audible thud that could be heard throughout the church, he landed partially on the floor and partially on the kneeler. He grunted and tried to raise himself on his arms. The priest leaned over him and punched him again. Blood spurted from Cantrell's broken nose.

The other people in the church watched but made no move to stop the beating. A woman gasped. Another woman shouted. “Stop. You'll hurt him.” Still, another woman became hysterical and screamed.

Father Bergen turned toward the screaming woman who shouted, “You are killing him.”

“Nothing I could do to him could be in any way near as painful as the fire of eternal damnation.”

A man waiting said, "Wow. He musta done somethin' bad."

For a while, Father Bergen said nothing. He looked at the man he had just struck and then at the waiting penitents. "Bless you all who came tonight to honestly and humbly confess your sins. As your penance, recite the Lord's Prayer five times, and say a good act of contrition. After you do that, your sins are forgiven." He made the sign of the cross. "Right now, this gentleman and I are going outside for a few minutes to continue our little discussion."

The priest pulled Roger Cantrell to his feet. He pushed Cantrell toward the church door, reached into the man's back pocket and pulled out his wallet. He pulled a pistol from the man's waist and shoved it under his own belt. He forced Cantrell against the emergency bar. The door opened. The two men shuffled awkwardly into the warm summer evening. The door closed behind them. With a sweep of his arm, Father Bergen sent Cantrell to the grass where the confused man lay on his back, staring up at the priest.

Father Bergen said, "Why did you come here this evening?"

Through a bleeding mouth, Cantrell said, "I came for forgiveness."

"And don't you agree that you got what you came for?"

A police car swung into the church parking lot.

Cantrell said, "You promised. No cops."

"I kept my promise. Someone inside must have phoned them. I didn't."

A uniformed policeman, Gerry Perkins, pulled up alongside and stepped out of the patrol car. "Good evening Father Tom. What's going on here? We got a call that you were beating up someone in the church. Something about a penance? Didn't make a lot of sense. Woman was sort of hysterical."

Father Bergen nodded. "That's pretty much the bones of it, Gerry."

The policeman turned toward Cantrell. "What have you got to say?"

"He attacked me. Broke my nose. I can feel it."

"You must have done something to provoke him. I know Father Tom. He doesn't go around fighting with folks, least not since he gave up professional wrestling."

"He broke my fucking nose."

"Most folks use another part of their anatomy for that."

Perkins pointed to the revolver the priest had at his waist. "What's with the artillery, Tom?"

"I took it from a penitent this evening."

Cantrell struggled to his feet. "Okay. Okay. I can see where this is going. No hard feelings. I won't press charges."

Father Bergen opened the wallet and glanced at the driver's license. "Mister Cantrell here made an agreement with the Lord."

"You say, Cantrell. Would that be Roger Cantrell?"

Cantrell nodded.

"We had a complaint today from your landlord that you been making too much noise and disturbing the neighbors."

Father Bergen handed the wallet to Cantrell. "Why don't you give that to Officer Perkins, so he can confirm your identity, and you can be on your way? I'm certain he won't want to arrest you for making too much noise."

"I promise. No more noise. Not a sound."

The priest nodded to the policeman. "You don't want to arrest Mister Cantrell for that crime since he's promised to be quieter."

The policeman laughed a short, humorless laugh. "If Father Tom is willing to vouch for you, that's enough for me—even though he seems right angry at you."

Father Bergen took the gun from his belt, emptied the cylinders and handed it to Cantrell. He dropped the bullets into his pocket. Cantrell took the gun. He frowned but offered his wallet to the policeman.

"Right there on top," Cantrell said, "The license is right there. No need to go looking at my personal stuff."

Perkins studied the license and then looked at Cantrell to compare him to the picture on the driver's license. "Now what about that gun Father Tom just handed you?" he said. "You have a carry permit?"

"Yeah, I do."

"I need to see your permit."

Cantrell looked to the priest and at the policeman. He hesitated, staring at the gun the priest had handed to him. He put his hands in each pocket as if searching, shifting the gun from hand to hand. "I must have left it at home."

"Sorry," Perkins said. "I really would like to oblige you, you being a friend of Father Tom. If I don't see a permit to carry, I can't let you keep a gun on your person."

"I'll put it in the car."

"Sorry, still need to see it before I can let you leave with the gun."

Cantrell thrust the gun at the policeman. "Here you take it. I can come by later with my permit and collect it."

Father Tom said, "Why don't you see if the permit is in his wallet."

"No. No. I'm good. Not in there. Told you it's at home. I left it home. I forgot."

The police officer turned to the priest. "You think I might find it here? He said that he left it home."

"Never know what you might find in a man's wallet."

"You promised," Cantrell said.

"And I have kept my promise."

"What's going on here, Tom? What am I missing?"

The priest stepped to the side, trapping Cantrell between him and the patrol car. "I've said all I can on the subject. I am truly sorry, Gerry."

Perkins looked again at the wallet. He produced a credit card. "Thompson, Roger Thompson? This card belongs to a dead man. He drew his gun. "You have some explaining to do, Mister Cantrell."

Tatha Twinkle's House

Tatha Twinkle lived with Harvey in a small house.
The Twinkle children were Sarah, Tommy, and Bobby Joe.
One day Tatha found a piece of string.
She picked it up and put it in a drawer until another string she found.
Placing that piece with the first, she wound it round and round.
With each bit of string, she spied,
In no time she had tied
A string ball taller than herself.
Tommy Twinkle never met a book he didn't like.
As Tommy grew and grew,
His book collection got bigger and bigger too.
Until his room was filled with rows and rows
Of every kind of poem and prose
To be found in shops or stores.
Sarah liked collecting straws and rubber bands and, of course, her toys,
Even some toys that were made for boys.
Bobby Joe was very neat and didn't like collecting.
But Bobby loved his baseball mitt.
Tatha and Harvey lived in what some might call a little house.
They lived near the water, and on weekends they would sail.
Sailors needed lots of things like anchors and lines to hold the boat.

"You can never have enough line," Harvey liked to say
And bought more and more against the day
When the old line might break.
The twinkles collected so many things that
It wasn't long before their house seemed small
So crammed with things it was, from wall to wall
They moved to a new house that was bigger and taller.
It had ten rooms and an attic and a cellar.
"The attic is great," Tatha exclaimed.
"It has space for the clothes that the children can't wear.
It's a comfort knowing the clothing is up there.
Each year on their birthdays, Bobby and Sarah
Got so many presents that they were confused
And sometimes forgot whose was whose.
Harvey saved the wrappings from the gifts that were sent.
Bobby asked why they had to be saved.
Tatha said, "Never know what we'll need for a special event.
Some of these designs I've never even seen
But they might be good for Chanukah, or Christmas, or maybe Halloween."
Harvey on trash collection days collected furniture
Almost like new:
A chair without a leg or two
And a highboy chest with most of its drawers.
He put them away until he found time
To mend these precious finds.
When the television quit, Harvey stored it in the stove.
"It's old," he said to Tatha, "and has taken much abuse.
But it's like a friend that you cherish and love.
We don't trash friends no longer of use."
Tatha knew the logic was sound.
Sometimes new friends were nowhere to be found.
Though they were young and had no cash
Sarah found no lack of chance to add new toys to her growing stash.
And like her parents, had no plan to rid herself of things
Like toys or clothes or books or even straws or string.

And Bobby Joe had his baseball mitt.
"I want a cat," said Sara Luan when she was just turned six.
So a cat named Lew joined the happy crew.
With Lew came catnip and litter and a scratching post
To sharpen his claws and help him relax when he needed it most.
Lew needed boxes for litter and paper, one for the cellar and one for each floor.
When he went down the cellar, they sometimes shut the door.
There came a time when the attic was full.
There were rooms in the house where no one could go,
Filled with things, there was nowhere to stow.
One day Bobby Joe heard a groan,
Not from his parents and not from a mouse being chased by the cat–no, not that.
The groan he heard had come from the house.
Bobby was frightened and ran to his mom.
"We need to get rid of some things right away.
The house is bulging from us and our stuff."
"Now Bobby Joe you know,
We never keep things that aren't just so.
The clothes in the attic and the toys in the cellar.
Are all things we'll need–whenever, you know."
But Bobby persisted,
"If we keep stashing our stuff, the whole house will blow."
But nothing changed. Harvey brought home in his truck
All sorts of things he found.
Tatha and Sarah were always on the lookout
For clothes and toys and string when she found it about.
The house complained as room after room
Was chocked full of things and never cleaned with a mop or a broom.
Louder and louder sounded the groan.
But only Bobby worried, especially when he was home alone.
All their collecting came to a halt one night after supper.
It was no one's fault. Bobby knew it had to happen sometime.
They were standing in the kitchen washing and drying and put-

ting away.
They couldn't use the washer.
It was filled with old dishes that they no longer used.
Lew was standing atop the fridge surveying the scene,
Wondering why dishes had to be clean.
With a sound like the town had never heard,
They dropped the dishes and raced to the yard.
The house blew into pieces and frightened some birds.
It was suddenly all gone along with their stuff,
Blown to the winds in one giant puff.
Harvey and Tatha looked at each other and then at the kids.
Harvey said, "Everything will be all right.
We've just had the house and all of our things blown to the wind,
But we have each other, and no one's been hurt."
Then Tatha said, "People are much more important than toys or comics or string."
She put her arms around Sara and Bobby. "We'll have to find a new hobby," she said. And they did.

John Sparkle and The Moon Rock

~—~

John Sparkle knelt and dug four small holes. In each, he set a begonia plant he had brought from Earth. He stood and pushed up the wide brim of his straw hat. As if to agree with himself that the plants were all precisely where they ought to be, he nodded in admiration of his handiwork.

Surely they will appreciate my expertise and not ship me off to be a zoo exhibit.

The sparse atmosphere of Farplace, the synthetic, specimen world upon which he stood, offered his fair skin little protection from the sun's penetrating rays. He let the soft breeze cool him for a moment before he mashed the hat back down on his head.

He thought back to his gardening days on Earth, back when people believed theirs was the only inhabited planet, back when gardening pushed out the loneliness that each day gripped his wakening. That was before the aliens, with their round heads set atop long, spaghetti-like necks, kidnapped him. Hundreds of others from all parts of the United States suffered a similar fate.

The spaghetti necks knocked on his front door early one spring morning. He knew what they wanted. The president didn't intervene. A few hundred citizens here and there seemed a small price to pay for not being incinerated by the thin necked intruders.

When John opened his door, he encountered two of the creatures. One of them said, "Come with us, John Sparkle. Join your fortunate neighbors in a new and exciting experience."

They waited while John packed his meager personal belongings. Along with his clothing, razor, toothbrush, four packaged begonias he had recently purchased, and miscellaneous toiletries, he chose the moon rock that his great grandfather, the astronaut, gave to him on his tenth birthday. Since the day he got it, the rock sat atop his chest-of-drawers in a place of honor.

The rock, only the size of a softball, held great personal meaning for John. "This rock," he told his classmates one day in show-and-tell, "is my way of remembering that I am related to a very famous and important person. I plan to be just like him–important and famous."

Save for young Carl Cronk who lived in the house next door; John had no friends. When the time came for him to leave, John knocked on Carl's door. "Carl, I want you to have my compupix phone and everything else you find in my apartment. Weight limits, don't you know." John felt good when the young man's face lit up with wide eyes and a broad smile.

"Have a safe trip, Mister Sparkle," Carl said. "I'll worry about you."

Having a person worry about him made John imagine that in some small way, his life was not a complete failure.

The spaghetti necks took John to a large transport vehicle, which stood hissing and groaning and sending clouds of steam into the morning air. The aliens transported him and the others to a planet that they called Smdfbgcnmkrrd. Finding the name difficult to pronounce the same way twice, John named it Farplace.

John and the other people taken from Earth were put in a compound surrounded by high walls and a tall gate. He was assigned to a tiny room with a cot and a table and lamp. The first thing John did when he unpacked was to put the moon rock in the center of the table. He unscrewed the lamp from its base and, turning it upside down, used the base as a display pedestal for the rock.

His head ached every morning after he breakfasted on the foul tasting garble-seed stew that the spaghetti necks served.

Rather than complain, he resolved to develop a palate for whatever food the aliens made available.

When one of his companions asked, "Why d'ya think they manufactured a planet when there're so many real ones to go around?" John shrugged. Such questions held no intrigue for him. Things were what they were. One person could never change anything.

While his companions plotted escape, he put such thoughts aside. He'd heard stories about people who complained or became unruly, being carted off to spend the rest of their days in a zoo with spaghetti-necked children making fun of them.

Since he had been observed on Earth repairing his bicycle wheel, the Talent Analysis Office set John to work repairing complex machines. The master mechanic told him, "You are not destined for a career in the mechanical arts." He sent John back to the compound.

For three days, John dreamed of what it might be like to be locked in a cage on public display with no privacy. When the master mechanic summoned him, he trembled in fear of a future he could not endure.

"You're being reassigned," the master mechanic said. The words gave voice to his worst fear, and he grabbed the master mechanic's desk to stay on his feet.

"Your companions from Earth told us about your gardening knowledge. You will work on my estate, caring for my daughter's garden."

The master mechanic's estate consisted of a residence, stables for horse-like animals, and a shed, all set on a flat expanse of brown synthetic soil.

John saw the desolate landscape as a blank canvas upon which he might create a masterpiece, the centerpiece of which would be his begonia plants.

"Emiltrude, my love," the master mechanic said by way of introduction, "this be John Sparkle. John, he comes every day. He'll be making your garden special."

Emiltrude approached John while he stood admiring the begonias he had just planted. "What on Smdfbgcnmkrrd be those green things you stare at so intently, John Sparkle?"

"They are begonias, Miss Emiltrude."

"Be you making sport of me? Green be the color of a funeral shroud."

"But, the flowers will be red or white."

"She snorted. You think me a fool? Red be the color of blood, white the color of sickness. Cannot these plants produce a black flower?"

John thought a moment before he replied. "I'm sorry that I don't have any black flowers. Let me sleep on this, figure out what I might do to make your garden special."

Emiltrude whirled on her heel with a grace John thought remarkable for such a large woman. Her waddling figure struck him as somewhat alluring, especially since her thin neck flowed gracefully from side to side to keep her round head centered.

With great reluctance, John pulled out his precious begonias and threw them into a trash can. What a fool I am to have brought them here.

That evening, sitting on a hard bench in the dimly lit communal dining hall, John spoke to Moises, one of his companions, "I don't have any plants with black leaves and black flowers. I'll be sent to live in a cage."

"That won't happen, Moises told him."

"But what can I do?"

"They don't plant flowers or trees here. Nothin' grows in this darn plastic ground here anyhow. Ain't you noticed? They got sculpture gardens."

"Really!"

"Yep."

"I'm no sculptor."

"Ain't no need to be. Just make do outta what's lyin' around. It's called found art."

John smiled a cautious smile. "Found art. Yes, I know very well what that is, skillfully arranged junk. I could change the display every couple of weeks. Keep myself busy but not have to do anything difficult. How can I fail?"

Moises gave John a high five. Pleased with themselves for having gotten the better of their strange captors, they both laughed.

John worked diligently for the next week, rounding up all sorts of odds and ends to place in Emiltrude's garden. She seemed happy when he asked her for one of her cooking pots and elated when he tore the weather vane from atop the stables.

By the week's end, John had assembled household utensils, furniture, old vehicle tires, a tall iron pedestal, the roof from an ancient Volkswagen, and part of the nacelle for a warp-drive outer arm.

When Emiltrude found him resting on her porch, she brought him food and drink. She sat next to him and told him of her youth on a far-away world. She told him that she liked his tall, thin frame and his thick gray hair. Sometimes she put a bulbous arm about his shoulder or leaned her bald head against his.

As the days passed, he grew fond of her and was sad when one day, she said, "John Sparkle, I need travel back to my home world. I be away for many days. I will miss you." She touched her mouth briefly to his. John shivered. The kiss felt good.

Shortly after Emiltrude left, John began to arrange the garden. He draped the newly planted items with bed sheets and table cloths he found in a shed.

John suggested to Emiltrude that she have a garden-unveiling party upon her return, invite her friends and neighbors and make an evening of it.

Directly upon her return from the visit to her home world, she sent out dinner invitations, hired a caterer, and arranged special lighting.

For the big night, John put on his only suit jacket and a necktie. The guests all arrived by the time darkness settled over the estate, and the two moons of Farplace became visible in the night sky.

Emiltrude rang a loud bell to gain the attention of her guests. She thanked everyone for coming and then introduced John as her new gardener.

With one hand on his chest and one behind his back, John bowed deeply. When the polite applause died, John unveiled the first planting. He stripped the coverings off each, one by one. No spontaneous gasps or claps or cheers arose from the assemblage.

John watched Emiltrude's face cloud as if a storm were moving across it. Her eyes became icy and narrow. Her brows wrinkled. Her mouth drew tight. The master mechanic mirrored his daughter's reaction.

John uncovered the last item with a flourish as if sweeping aside a matador's cape. Emiltrude nodded and stood, looking at the garden.

She finally spoke. "That is a very nice garden, John Sparkle. You have created a truly interesting arrangement."

Her words were kind, yet her voice held no hint of approval. John pushed from his mind the vision of him standing in a cage and looking out at a crowd of jeering children.

He raised both hands with his palms toward the guests. He waited until he had their full attention.

"Folks, I have saved the best 'til last. It will be the centerpiece of Miss Emiltrude's garden. It will make it better than any other garden on the whole planet."

He reached into a sack at his feet and slowly pulled out the moon rock his great grandfather had given him. The spaghetti necks became suddenly quiet. They came closer and crowded about him; their thin necks craned in his direction.

Raising the rock high so all could see, John said, "This is part of the moon of Earth. This rock is very old and very rare. This moon piece is an important artifact in the history of my planet. My great grandfather brought it back from a trip he took long ago to our moon."

He placed the rock on top of the tall pedestal he had located in the center of the garden. He stepped back. The guests gasped, cheered, and applauded.

Emiltrude said, "You are remarkable, John Sparkle. You will be the most famous gardener on this entire world." Then she smiled and, turning her head, so that her father could not see the gesture, winked at him. The guests pressed around him, shook his hand, and patted him on the back. Some even hugged him.

One of the spaghetti necks took him aside and said to him. "No zoos for you, John Sparkle. I am the chief administrator. Tomorrow I be appointing you our master gardener. And it be a permanent appointment. You will be one of us now." The chief administrator squeezed John's arm and smiled.

John thought of the day at show-and-tell when, as a ten-year-old boy, he displayed the moon rock to his classmates.

He looked up at the two moons and whispered, "Thanks, grandpa. I've traveled farther into space than you ever could have dreamed. I know you'd like that. And I'm a celebrity just like you."

John looked at Emiltrude and again at the two moons of his new home. He knew that never again would he feel lonely.

The Worker In Clay

The sculptor works in molding clay
Making lifelike forms
In a grandly vibrant way
To my joy and great delight.

I have often seen her warming
Some resisting clay
By pushing, scraping and deforming
Until the graying clay submits.

From the formless clay she massed,
Ever gently now,
When some time has passed
Begins to live what she creates.

A bit of clay goes on a cheek
Being there to
Mark a carefully located peak
As favored characters appear.

Here is taken space to put
Upon the form
Graceful arm or tilted foot
So now it takes its final shape.

The beauty of the molded clay
Does not rely
On any time of day,
But well it shows in any light.

But she does best when she applies
Her gentle way
A task she modestly belies
To make one feel so much alive.

When she sets her love to work
She does not fail,
Goodly massed clay to mark,
To my joy and great delight.

The Sculptor

The sculptor has a barn
Set back from her house at
The end of a stone walk.
She gets up early,
Before the West brightens.

Some days she spins pots.
These are simple shapes,
With a simple design
Of scratched-in lines,
Near the rim.

Sometimes she carves
A bold head, a soldier, a nymph,
Depending on her mood.
On those days she labors long
And as the natural light declines
She lights an oil lamp,
It's flame to dance
Upon the walls where
Shadows play.

When the last of daylight fades
She is wearied by her efforts,
Sad to not complete
That day
A piece she had begun.

Before trudging to her house,
She loads old pieces and fires the kiln.

After dinner and a nap
She takes a book from the shelf.

She reads about great artists
And of their struggles.

Real Zombies

I don't really believe in zombies, but then there are so many stories that a person sometimes has to wonder. My recent experience that began at a local bar has been enough to resolve all but a tiny thread of lingering skepticism.

I'd seen movies of living dead people with their rotted clothes hanging off them, their faces contorted and drooling blood. They sometimes take quick little baby steps. Sometimes they loped along in wide strides like they were stepping over cow patties. Often they had their arms out in front of them as if blind and afraid of bumping into pickup trucks or burning gas pumps.

When they're not tearing their victim's limbs off or eating a face or two, they pick up folks and hurl them across the room. Even zombie women can do that.

Zombies typically are represented as folks who don't like anybody that hasn't died at least once. I don't recall that ever being explained. It strikes me as some type of social bias. They pass up horses and cows and chickens, so it's not the blood and guts alone. There's something more involved.

It all started when I first met Robbie. The day had begun badly for me. I lost a big account. There would be hell to pay when I told the boss. My answer to the feeling of total despair engulfing me was to sashay down to the hotel bar and order up my favorite non-prescription sedative.

I'd just downed my second gin and tonic and was considering if I needed just one more to help me sleep when he settled himself onto the stool next to me. “Hey there, Sport. Name’s Robbie,” he said, sliding his arm across his chest and offering me his hand.

Being a friendly sort and always open to the possibility that somebody will buy me a drink, I shook hands with him. He offered a firm, manly shake.

I turned to him and introduced myself. “I’m Chuck. Real name’s Charles, but mostly they call me Chuck.”

Robbie slammed a ham sized palm on the bar so hard I thought he’d broken his wrist. “Chucker, it is pal.” I smiled and nodded, happy that he hadn’t decided to give me a friendly pat on the back.

Other than an odor about him that reminded me of dead fish, Robbie came across as a cool guy. His bulk told me that he spent a lot of time shoveling in wheat germ and muscle mix if he wasn’t pumping iron. He wore an expensive monogrammed golf shirt and a diamond-studded watch with a gold band, most likely a custom job straight out of some classy Geneva shop—one of those places up the hill from town and so exclusive that you need an appointment to walk through the front door.

“What you drinking, Sport,” he asked.

“Gin and tonic.”

He waved a fifty and hollered, “Barkeep. Another one of those gin and tonics for my friend here—make it strong—and a pitcher of your best brew on tap for me. I got a terrific thirst since I died.”

The bartender chuckled but responded well to the appearance of the fifty dollar bill. He produced our drinks in record time. Mine tasted like straight gin. The guy earned the outrageous tip Robbie gave him.

“Thanks,” I said. “Here’s to good friends and good booze.” Robbie ignored the glass the bartender gave him and took a long swig directly from the pitcher. He raised his pitcher in a salute. I clinked my glass gently against it. “Now tell me what was that crack about you being dead all about?”

“I’m a zombie,” he replied without even a hint that he might be kidding. Of course, I doubted his word on that mostly because he looked so way too healthy. Another persuasive argument was that he didn’t immediately begin to make a meal of me. I’m not a dummy. I know that real zombies quickly turn on everybody they meet—excepting maybe some of the gorgeous women zombies, and I’m not a gorgeous woman.

Even when I wrinkled my brow and smiled out of the corner of my mouth, he persisted. "No, I really am one. I want to get that bit of information out of the way. That's so there are no hard feelings later if I get hungry."

The wisecrack sent a shiver down my spine. I wondered if it might be a good idea for me to clear out just in case. But that would be impolite, what with me letting him pay for my drink.

"Robbie," I said, "you are no more a zombie than I am."

He quickly blurted, "But you have your doubts. I know you do."

"People need to be dead before they can be the living dead."

He waggled a gray finger at me no more than an inch from my face. "And that's something I want to talk to you about. I had a simply wonderful funeral service, a service that you did not attend by the way."

"I didn't know you. How could I know about your funeral?"

I couldn't believe I'd just mouthed those words. It was as if Robbie already convinced me about him being a zombie.

"I don't mean that I believe a word you're saying. I meant to say that there's no reason I might go to your funeral service, assuming you even had one."

"OK, so I didn't have one yet. But if I did, you wouldn't have come, now would you?"

"Nobody goes to the funeral service of someone they don't know."

"You are dead wrong there, Chucker. You know how many people attend memorial services for Elvis every year. And he has been gone for a long time. They could not all have known him."

I emptied what was left of my gin and tonic in one gulp.

Turning to Robbie, I said, "That's because they're famous. People don't know those celebrities personally, but they do know their life story. That makes them feel they actually know them. Or maybe they just want to feel part of a famous person's life."

"What you saying there, Chucker?"

"OK. Tell me what you're famous for."

"I invented the squiggly."

"What the hell is that?"

"You mean, you do not know?"

I nodded like my head was on a bobble doll. He smiled and ordered another round. "The squiggly is that red frog-shaped toy that you toss on a wall, and it sticks and then walks down the wall as if it is alive."

I laughed. "Sort of like a zombie, huh? Not alive but walking."

"Wait a minute. I think I resent your tone, pal. A zombie has to be alive first. The squiggly is a plastic toy. You trying to insult me?"

I'm not at all the shy type. My first reaction was to be confrontational and agree that I meant to do exactly that, even though I hadn't meant to offend anyone. Because I've seen some pretty brutal bar fights, and because Robbie looked mean in a friendly sort of way, I held my tongue.

For at least a half a minute, we both sat there looking directly into each other's eyes. Neither of us said a word.

Eventually, Robbie raised his head and cackled like one of those seagulls they call laughing gulls, short and crisp, and without any hint of humor. His eyes drilled into me. I swear that for an instant, I could feel him eating away at my innards. For a fleeting moment, I thought it might be that he really was a zombie.

"They bury you with the expensive watch and all that bling?" I asked, beginning to be more than a little intrigued by my barroom companion and his bizarre comments."

"Not buried yet."

"I'm sure that's a story in itself," I replied.

I truly don't want to alarm anyone at this point in my story; however, I noticed that Robbie's eyes appeared to be lifeless, like looking at a couple of marbles floating in a bowl of oatmeal. Oh, they were clear and blue enough, but there didn't seem to be much of a pupil. Except for the tiniest pinhead at the center, his eyes were almost all iris, like his camera lens shut down.

The aspect that bothered me was their lack of expression. He had dead eyes. No, no, I don't mean he could shoot well, I mean that his eyes had no depth. They didn't seem to me to be focusing on anything. Of course, the near lack of pupils didn't make the look any more human. OK. I said it. Not human. His eyes were not human.

The oatmeal look bothered me as well. Robbie obviously had spent few of his recent days outdoors. I mean, even if he only walked outside to get the mail, he'd have some color in his face.

The gray complexion, coupled with what I can only describe as a lumpy look, told me that he quickly was going to flab. The face is the first to go.

For some reason I don't understand, I couldn't free myself from his gaze. I found myself forced to stare at him and his unblinking eyes. That's right. He never blinked. His gaze held me like some sort of Vulcan eye lock that Dr. Spock from Star Trek might use. How did his eyes stay lubricated and not dry to a raisin? Hmmm.

After a couple of minutes, Robbie released me from the eye lock. The instant I looked away, he said, "What sort of business you in, Sport."

"Salesman," I replied; still a bit shaken.

"Sales. Yeah. I used to be in that racket when I was alive. Couldn't make any money at my real talent. I am an entertainer. You should hear my Elvis impression. And I play a mean guitar."

Not relishing the thought of my strange new companion breaking into a rendition of "Love Me Tender", I said, "What do you sell?"

"Used cars. Made a pretty good living at it too. Fact is that job is what did me in. Killed me sure as the pile of shit killed the mocking bird."

"The what?"

"You never heard of the mocking bird?"

"Of course, I know what a mocking bird is. It mocks other bird calls."

"Well, then you must know about the farmer who dropped a load of manure on the poor little mocking bird and killed him bigger than shit."

"It's a new one on me."

"Robbie stroked his oatmeal chin for a moment. He asked, "Where you say you come from, Chucker?"

"I didn't say, but I'm from Jersey."

"That explains your ignorance. The thing about the bird is what you might call a regionalism, a regional expression. You being from New Jersey, I would not expect you to be familiar with it or much of anything else for that matter."

I chose to ignore his remark about my home state. "You were killed by a pile of manure."

"See. There you go again being a wise ass, trying to insult me. But I got thick skin. Salesmen need to have thick skins, even dead ones. Maybe even more so when you get to being dead."

"How'd you die?"

He waggled a finger in my face again and said, "Let me answer that. First, I think we both need another round. Barkeep?" Robbie pulled another wrinkled fifty dollar bill out of his pocket and waved it at the bartender.

We sat in silence, staring at our respective images in the mirror behind the bar. The bartender set two drinks in front of each of us. "Third one is on me as well," he said.

Robbie took a swig of his beer. A toothy smile flashed across his face, his one gold filling catching for an instant the light from a sconce lamp.

"You being in the business, you know that sales is a lot like fishing. Had what I thought was a live fish on my line. In the process of setting the hook, I made a small miscalculation.

"Turned out, the customer was very interested in a particular vehicle. Only problem was he had no interest in paying for it."

"Doesn't sound good, Robbie. Doesn't sound good at all."

"No, not good at all. We drove to what he told me was his wife's place of business, so he could show her the car before he made the final decision to buy it, or so he said. What did I know?"

"What happened?"

"He drove to a cold storage warehouse. Invited me in to look at a huge fish he said he caught. Said his wife would be along in a minute. Being a fisherman myself, I was interested. He broke my neck right there in the cold storage room. He grabbed me by the throat and just broke my neck. Never felt a thing. Bam! It was over in a New York second."

Robbie pulled down the collar of his golf shirt and turned his head to give me a good look at his neck. I didn't see any bruise but thought there might be a lump.

"That's terrible," I said.

"Not exactly the way I ever expected to cash out."

"I should think not. When did all this happen?"

"Couple of weeks ago. Got a lift here to the hotel from a kind stranger."

"Just how long were you on ice, so to speak?"

"Good question, Sport. Whole thing is fuzzy. Woke up stiffer than morning wood. I realized I could not move a muscle. I panicked. Let me restate that. I will not call it a panic, more a realization. Zombies have no emotion."

The remark about emotion I couldn't let pass unchallenged or at the very least unremarked. "In the movies, you guys always seem to lust for blood and guts. Isn't that an emotion?"

"Really don't know, Sport. Need to think on it a while."

"Fair enough. Tell me. How come you didn't stay dead?"

"You really know how to hurt a guy, Sport. How the devil should I know? The zombie thing is a new gig for me."

"Sorry. Tell me, if you couldn't move, how'd you get here?"

"Power failure last night."

"Yeah. I remember that, but the lights were only out for about an hour."

"Must of blown a fuse because I started to thaw."

"How come your clothes aren't soaking wet?"

"They dried," he replied and then looked down at the floor. Up to that point, my sixth sense told me that he was telling what he thought was the truth. I can read people pretty well. His last response though, came with a note of deceit. But I didn't want to press the issue at that point in our conversation." He looked up at me. "Dried out pretty quick. Must be a zombie thing."

"Must be."

"I told you all about myself, Sport. How about you? What sort of salesman are you?"

"I handle a line of watches, jewelry, some cosmetics."

"Robbie did another one of his palm slams on the bar. It gave me such a start that I nearly dropped my drink.

"Hey, Sport, I think you and me can do some business. Zombies need things like watches, and what zombie doesn't like jewelry."

Robbie sure wore a beautiful watch. I wondered where he got it on a used car salesman's commissions.

I put my misgivings aside. If zombies needed cosmetics, particularly the women, and perfume too, very strong perfume, I could expand my line.

Excusing myself, I headed for the men's room to take a pee. On the way, I wondered how Robbie had suddenly become such an expert on zombies, him being one for only a short time, leastways one that wasn't frozen solid. In my mind, the frozen hours didn't count in zombie time.

Robbie was beginning to grow on me. I half believed him, and half didn't. At any rate, he held my interest.

My depression needed someone like him to keep my mind occupied and off losing that big account. If he truly became a zombie, then I could learn something new. If not, then I had an entertaining companion who kept me from thinking about my own problems. I've heard a lot of wild stories from fellow barflies. None to match Robbie's—and he told it in such a matter of fact way.

The first thing I said when I got back to the bar was, "Hey, Rob. Do zombies ever—you know—have bodily functions?"

"You mean do we pee and crap?"

"Yeah, that."

"Not sure. I believe it is only if we eat or drink."

Finally, I'd opened up a gaping hole in his account and decided to press my advantage. "You're dead. People eat to stay alive. You don't need to eat. You're not alive."

Robbie didn't miss a beat. "I'm basing my answer on rather slim evidence."

"How so?"

"I woke up in my own crap. Knew that I needed to find a change of clothes if I'm going to be acceptable in polite society."

"Don't tell me. The guy that gave you a lift today."

"Him. Yeah. Fortunately for me, I am about his build. The clothes fit pretty well. Unfortunately for him, I was hungry, it being so long since I had eaten."

"You didn't."

"Could not help it. Anyhow, I got the trots almost as soon as I finished with him. He went right through me faster than grass through a goose."

"You hungry now, Robbie?"

"Nope. Not sure how these things work for somebody like me. I mean someone in my position. Maybe if I drink enough booze, I don't get hungry."

"We've been talking for a while, and you're on your fourth pitcher of beer. You haven't excused yourself once yet to pee."

He laughed. "You really are a funny guy, Sport. Don't you know that alcohol is a preservative? Seems like when you're dead, you absorb anything that might help preserve you. I suppose that it's sort of like a survival instinct for zombies."

"Wouldn't know anything about that. Until I met you, I had never given much thought to people who've passed on other than to maybe offer a prayer for their eternal rest."

"I obviously have not, as you put it, passed on. Maybe passed out but not passed on." He giggled at his little joke. "And I haven't got any rest. Not even the least bit tired, actually."

At that point, Robbie started to wear on me. It didn't help that the unpleasant odor hanging about him seemed to be getting stronger.

A long sip finished off one of the drinks the bartender had set in front of me. I picked up the next one. I glanced about the bar. The place had started to fill.

In the mirror, I spied a young woman walking toward me. I thought she was going to take a seat, but instead, she stopped directly behind me. I spun around on my stool.

"Buy me a drink, handsome?"

A real beauty, fortyish, long black hair, and a figure that would make a preacher blush. Her well-tailored, pinstripe business suit clung to her like plastic wrap. I took her for a working girl until I saw the expensive Hublot Black Caviar watch, the one they call the Bang, the one encrusted with diamonds, the one that costs north of a million dollars.

My ex never looked as good as she looked, even on our wedding night. You never know. This gal might be looking for Mister Right. Forget the age difference. I still am pretty handsome.

Suddenly she seemed to become aware of Robbie who'd not made any comment but had been checking her up and down. When she turned to him, he said, "Hey, young lady." She looked at his face, at his oatmeal complexion and his strange eyes. This ought to be interesting. The woman pushed herself between us and turned her back to me.

Robbie looked at me over her shoulder. He wiggled his eyebrows and winked, reminding me of a bad stand-up comedy act, the kind you might see in a comedy club located in a rundown strip mall.

While Robbie and the girl, who said her name was Susan, made small talk, I tried to figure out why Robbie had come to a bar instead of going to work. Eventually, I figured that he got fired when they decided he wasn't coming back with one of their cars. The cops were probably looking for him at that very moment.

I resisted the urge to pinch Susan in the ample ass that she firmly planted against my bar stool. Man, did she have a figure or what?

I fought back a wave of jealousy. If Robbie really was a zombie, he couldn't perform. What a waste. Will she be surprised if she gets him into bed. Dead guys can't get aroused over a girl. You need blood for that. Judging from the pallor of the oatmeal man, he had not much of anything running through his veins.

The opposite was true for me. With her perfume assailing my nostrils and the womanly scent of her silky hair brushing my face when she threw back her head and laughed at one of Robbie's jokes, I was the one getting aroused. The crease the barstool made in her soft butt encouraged the images flitting through my head to become progressively more risqué.

I was only paying half attention to what Robbie and the girl were saying when I caught the word "hungry." Immediately my full attention focused on their conversation. I totally gleaned that Robbie wanted her to accompany him to a fancy restaurant downtown.

She asked him more about the restaurant without negotiating a price for the evening. I realized for sure that she wasn't a prostitute. But prostitute or no, I couldn't let her go with him, him being a known watch collector and all.

How could I let her suffer the fate of the former owner of Robbie's bling? I truly believed the part about him stealing the man's jewelry and car–zombie or no.

Maybe Robbie wasn't a zombie. Maybe he didn't really have an appetite for flesh. Maybe he just liked to steal watches and jewelry.

I tapped her on the shoulder and whispered, "Susan." She turned an angry face to me and said in a tone that sounded more like a hiss, "What?"

"Let me talk to my friend here a minute before you guys go gallivanting off for the evening. Order a drink on me. Be back in a few."

"That will work," she said and flashed me a wide toothy smile.

I took Robbie out to the street in front of the bar. I pointed. "See that guy there, sitting on the pavement with the bottle of Thunderbird in his lap? The guy next to the shopping cart"

"Yeah. So what?"

"If you're hungry. Take him to dinner, not a beautiful young girl like Susan."

Robbie stared at me with his jaw open. He glanced over at the homeless man sitting on the sidewalk and slid his tongue across his upper lip. To my eternal surprise, he said, "You're right. I should be ashamed of myself."

A zombie showing a conscience of sorts, now that floored me. I thought of the business that I might have done with Robbie and his friends, maybe enough to redeem myself for the lost account. Yet in my heart of hearts, way down deep, I knew that it could never work out. Our partnership would eventually have ended badly. And how could I live with myself knowing that when he wasn't around me, he might be out eating innocent people?

I didn't worry much about the man on the street. His stench and filth surely would make him unpalatable even to the most experienced and determined zombie. He was safe with a newbie like Robbie. I couldn't say the same for the bottle of Thunderbird.

Robbie smiled and nodded. "It has been really nice talking with you, Chucker. I got to go."

"You never told me your last name," I said.

"Higgins, Robbie Higgins." He turned and headed toward the man with the bottle of Thunderbird.

"It's been a pleasure, Robbie Higgins," I said to his back.

The girl sat in Robbie's seat. She made eye contact with me in the mirror and smiled. I smiled back. She winked and blew me a kiss. She still had on the Hublot, and why not?

Before joining her, I fished out of my pocket the cell phone Robbie had left on the bar. I'd grabbed the phone on my way out. I dialed 911 and told the cops where they could find Robbie Higgins, the missing car salesman. I also told them that he'd murdered a man, stolen his car, his jewelry, and his clothes.

On my way to the bar, I smudged off my fingerprints, just in case somebody retrieved it from the trash basket I tossed it into.

While walking the short distance to where my new lady friend sat, I said to myself, "Susan, here comes your Mister Right."

Somehow I knew that we were perfect for each other. But then I hadn't yet considered her gray, oatmeal complexion, well hidden by a thick layer of makeup.

Fall, Upstate New York

Steadfast blue-green pines
Defend the mountains
Against a riot of colors
Painted by the cold night air.

Children limber up the spines
Of new textbooks to begin
Their assault on ignorance
And on the teachers too.

Rows of pumpkins sit
On a roadside stand
With imaginary faces seen
Only by the young at heart.

Scarves and muffs come out
Of summer hiding and hang
From handy hooks
Replacing swimsuits.

Baseball gloves are put away.
Footballs magically appear.
Neglected ice skates honed
For hockey on the lake.

Thoughts of Goblins come to mind,
Scary masks for Halloween
"Trick or treat," the magic words
To fill a sack with candy.

Stores too early filled
With Christmas toys.
Let us have the turkey first.
Let's not skip Thanksgiving.

Billy

My then eleven-year-old brain processed Billy as a sophisticated eighth-grader when first I saw him in the hall with my brother, Charles. Billy had a nonchalant way about him. When I first saw the two of them, he had one arm draped over Charles' shoulder. It was usually the other way around. Billy was tall, and his long blonde hair made him like a god to me, a pudgy god, but a god nevertheless. I could hardly wait until lunchtime when I had a chance to corner Charles in the cafeteria and ask about his new friend.

"Names Billy, Billy Clarke, from Scranton. I'm his mentor," Charles told me. He'd met Billy Clarke that morning in the principal's office. The mentoring program was a program they had to help transfers, you know, meet the other kids, get to know the clubs and the teachers, and that sort of stuff. Billy was 14. He had played baseball in Scranton and would be trying out for the Star Deli Raiders, Charles' team.

"He's a good athlete, and he'll probably play first base. I think he can pitch too," Charles said. "I saw him tossing the ball around yesterday. Boy, can he zing them in there."

I heard all of this as really dull general information. But I got interested when Charles told me that Billy had moved into a house on the street right behind us, the one kitty-cornered from us on the hill where the big rock juts out.

"I've invited him over to watch TV," Charles said, I thought a bit defensively.

Looking back, I don't think Charles had the first clue. He thought my curiosity was my usual baby sister's meddling. I remember him saying, "We'll probably be watching sports or something else that girls aren't interested in, so you'll have to watch in the kitchen or upstairs with Mom."

I remember, too, not wanting to appear over eager. I said my time was already planned out and that I wasn't interested in whatever they would be watching.

That first evening I eavesdropped on them through the kitchen door. They didn't talk much to each other. Mostly they talked to the television like guys do or fussed with their cell phones. Charles came into the kitchen to put some popcorn in the microwave. I had the TV tuned to the same station, hoping that he would invite me into the den to watch with him and Billy. That didn't happen, but he did tell me Billy would be coming over the next night to watch some sort of game. I don't remember exactly. Maybe it was hockey or maybe basketball.

After that first evening, Billy stopped by a lot. Eventually, his visits became a ritual. He and Charles would watch TV for about two hours, finish off a giant bag of microwave popcorn, or sometimes they played video games, and then Billy would leave.

Charles and Billy played football together and baseball too and became best friends though they didn't ever refer to each other like that. Billy double-dated with Charles to the school dances. It was always somebody Charles fixed him up with. Billy never had a real girlfriend.

Billy showed, like, zero interest in me before the first night, I joined them in the den. I was fourteen, and Billy had been around for about three years. It was a snowy evening. A high wind had dropped a big limb off the oak in our front yard. When I answered the front door for Billy that night, he immediately grabbed my arm and pulled me out the door. Breathing hard, he said, "Look at what just happened." He gasped. "That big limb missed me by mere inches. Thought I was a goner for sure."

He was excited and all out of breath, so I knew that what he said was probably true—even though I had come to know how Billy exaggerated.

The falling limb was leaning on our electric line and pulling it down almost to the ground. I was afraid it would snap and maybe come flying at us and electrocute the two of us right there on the porch.

Charles came out. The three of us talked about what might happen if the power went. We couldn't take our eyes off the limb and the power line until the line broke in two and shot out a big spark. We raced back into a darkened living room.

Mom called down from upstairs to see if we were all right. Charles said his usual, "Yeah, Yeah," and the three of us went into the den and sat around and talked until the men came about an hour later to fix the line. Billy seemed interested in me that night, in his excitement at being part of a dangerous adventure—barely escaping certain death. Thinking back, he would have talked to a cheese sandwich if it had been sitting in my chair and had a head to nod once in a while.

After that night, I would join them if there was something on the television that I wanted to watch. They usually tuned in to sports, but sometimes we did the sitcoms. They never played video games once I showed up. No complaint just dropped the games from then on.

Billy wasn't there every night. He never came on the weekends, Friday, Saturday, or Sunday. But Monday through Thursday, he was always there, showing up following dinner right at seven and leaving around nine. He almost never stayed very late because of school the next day. One time when the next day was a teacher's convention or something, we played Monopoly. He didn't leave until nearly midnight. I remember that I had a great time that night. Billy told his crazy stories. I laughed until I had pains.

I never, like, had any real boyfriend while I was in school. Charles would fix me up, but they never called back after the first date. Eventually, he exhausted his inventory of friends, so I mostly stayed home. It's not like I didn't have any friends. I got to know another girl like me. Her name was Jane Dunkins. We were best friends for a while. She came over to the house to do homework together. We would sometimes sit with Charles and Billy for a while before going up to my room to study. Billy was nice when it was only me. When the two of us were there, we might as well have both been invisible.

Sometimes Billy went upstate with his family to a small house they owned on Lake Otsego. I don't remember the name of the town. It was a little bit north of Cooperstown. Charles went there with him a few times. He enjoyed going through the Baseball Hall of Fame.

Once Billy brought me back a Yankee's baseball cap. I was sixteen at the time and a sophomore. He said, "I picked it out, especially for you,

Sally, 'cause you're my special girl."

Right after that, I went out to a movie with Billy and Charles. Charles was dating Margaret by then and thinking about going to college. He and Billy had been working for a man that owned a landscaping business, cutting lawns and trimming bushes. Billy was smart. But he had no interest in college.

Charles announced one night that he was going to be an electronics engineer. Since he was always trying to fix radios and once took an old television apart, we weren't surprised.

He applied to MIT and was accepted. Mom and Billy and I drove up to Cambridge with him. We had a big dinner, stayed at a Motel, and drove back the next day.

Billy couldn't quit talking. He talked about what he liked and disliked. He told us about his early years, you know, before he moved to Van Winkle Street. We stopped for lunch. He came and sat with me in the back seat. Mom didn't seem to mind. She didn't say anything about feeling like a chauffeur as she sometimes did. Billy and I joked and kidded each other there in the back seat. Billy even tickled me. Nobody but Charles had ever done that. It felt different when Billy did it.

I suppose it was after that ride together that I thought Billy was interested in me, you know, like maybe some romance was brewing. I went on a diet for the first time in my life and lost almost ten pounds. I was still on the heavy side but a lot better proportioned. I went to a hairdresser and had my hair cut and styled.

I didn't see Billy the week we got back from taking Charles to college, and then he just showed up right at seven o'clock on Monday, knocking on the door three times and then three times more, a code he had adopted after seeing a spy picture. It gives you a little idea of what he thought was funny. We didn't talk much. I made popcorn in the microwave. We watched sitcoms.

Night after night, Billy came to the house exactly at seven like he had when Charles was home. Some nights we talked about his job, or he would tell me about sports. He really liked baseball. He knew a lot about baseball statistics. He took me on a sort of virtual tour of the Hall of Fame. He must have memorized every inch of the place.

This went on for weeks and then months. I kept waiting for Billy to ask me on a date. I gave him every sort of hint that I could think of but got little response. One night I sat on the arm of his chair and fussed with his hair and rubbed his neck. He smiled, but that was about it.

I graduated and got a job as a legal secretary and had to work a little late some nights. Billy would be there when I got home, in front of the television with his feet on the ottoman eating our popcorn. Mom let him in. We would have fun talking and watching the television.

Then I met a guy at the office. He had a job in the mailroom in my building. He seemed to like me and invited me out. We went to O'Charlie's for dinner. His dad was a stockbroker. He was thinking of going back to college, so he could get a job on Wall Street. Maybe he wasn't the greatest catch. He has that weak chin, and his hair is thin, and he drinks way too much beer. That's why he's so big. Weighs almost two-thirty. He's not as near as good looking as Billy.

The Monday after O'Charlies, I decided about Billy. It was a cool fall evening, and the trees had already turned and were losing their leaves. Billy knocked his special knock. I opened the door. He looked at me in a funny way, like he was puzzled. You know how a dog looks at you sometimes with its head off to one side? I suppose it was the way I looked at him. I didn't ask him in. Said I had brought work home from the office. We talked for a few minutes. I told him he shouldn't come by anymore.

Telling Billy he couldn't come over was the toughest thing I ever had to do. The next night he sauntered by the house. I was watching for him out the front window because I thought he would come like he always had for so many years. He turned, came back, and stopped a moment by the walk that leads up to the porch. He shouted, "You're a real bitch," and tossed pebbles onto the porch. It was the last I ever saw him.

He moved out of his parent's house a few weeks later. His parents told me that he married some rich guy up in Cooperstown. The news made me real happy for him. I'll always love him. Billy was my first true love.

His Autumn

~—~

Brightly colored pages turn
In a lusty breeze that blows
Against his life
And rattles his wits.

On the north side of the man
The frost will creep
Into the spaces between his toes
And up the rattled sapience.

He will fall down and break.
He may be confused for a while.
He will begrudge the ice-blue days.

After that, the snow will come
To place upon him
A blanket
While relatives and friends
Crowd his bed
To say, “Goodbye.”

When at last he breathes no more.
When the Reaper calls his turn
He will then depart for sunny climes.

The Healing Blanket

John Chambers, a tall, muscular man who had recently celebrated his 35th birthday, stretched out a beefy hand and pulled the wool blanket about him. He touched the rusty pin holding it tight around his neck. The blanket was a gift from Jerry Badger, his oncologist. Doctor Jerry had told him that its fibers possessed healing powers. It had been blessed by a holy man, a shaman. All one had to do was wear it day and night and believe in its power. The blanket would do the rest.

In his hiding place beneath the boughs of a giant fir tree, John had no fear of being discovered by his former friend and associate, Arthur Livingstone, a man who had vowed to kill him. The snow upon the lower limbs made him and his companion, Kathleen Crow–his girlfriend of three months–invisible from anyone outside their natural hideaway. It also protected them from the biting wind that brought the chill well below 15 degrees Fahrenheit. To her close friends, Kathleen was known by Namid, a Chippewa name, that she said meant star dancer. John called her Star.

The tree was located in a small grove of evergreens twenty yards in front of John's small, three room cabin to the right of the long dirt road that led from the highway. He had decided to wait under the tree in the freezing cold rather than in the cabin because he wanted to surprise Arthur, to talk him into rethinking his thirst for vengeance, to explain that he understood and did not hold a grudge. Let bygones be bygones. His plan was to wait until Arthur got within range of his shotgun and then confront him. He had not expected Arthur for several more days and had been surprised when Arthur phoned that morning to say he was on his way.

In the glow of a waning moon, the new snow lay like a blue-gray shroud. During the four hours that they had patiently waited under the tree, falling and blowing snow had long since obscured their tracks to the tree from all but a practiced observer. Except for the wind wailing through the forest canopy, the scene was quiet.

John pumped a shell into the chamber of his Remington 870, checked the safety, rested the barrel against one of the tree's lower limbs, and waited.

Star whispered, "We've been here for hours. He's not gonna show."

"Patience, my dear. He will come. Just running a bit late. He will not stop until he kills us both."

John's eyes fixed on movement in the distance where the open field rose up from the highway located a quarter-mile away. He made out a distant figure trudging slowly toward him through the knee-deep snow.

He knew Arthur would come, that he wouldn't leave them alone until he was dead or they were dead. John regretted the fact that Star had become a target. Yet Arthur, when he phoned that morning, had made clear he planned to kill her first. Since the call, John had not permitted Star to stray from his side.

"We should've waited in the cabin," Star chided. "We could see him just as well from the cabin. Be a lot more comfortable too."

"He expects us to be there. We have no way of knowing if he might bring Kevin or some of his other sycophants like that brute, Udo, the one they call 'The Dutchman.'"

"So what are you waitin' for? Shoot him now."

"He's too far away."

Arthur stopped. He looked from right to left several times before resuming his slow progress.

"He sees us," Star said, taking in a gasp.

"He does not see us. He is simply being careful."

"There. Look. He's starin' straight at us. He knows we're here."

Arthur carried a rifle slung on his shoulder and a pistol in a holster high up on his waist. He had a small backpack. He stopped, dropped to one knee, and eased the long gun off his shoulder.

"What's he doing now?" Star said.

"I lost him. Wait. Yes. There. He is looking through the scope. Looking right at the cabin. Being really cautious."

"What's he lookin' for?" Star asked.

John turned to Star and whispered, "He's probably tired. Trying to walk through such deep snow is a tough go without snowshoes."

"Why doesn't he have snowshoes, John, or skis?"

John reached out and touched the snowshoes that Star had set against the tree, so she could sit more comfortably. He smiled. "Arthur is a city boy, Star, from the Deep South. Born and bred in Tampa. Never even went hiking, much less in the snow on a frosty winter night. I think that this might be the first time he ever saw snow in his whole life."

"He could've learned about the outdoors in the scouts–like you did."

"Arthur? No. He thought the boy scouts were a bunch of wusses. I used to sometimes walk by his house in my uniform. He made fun of me. Called me, Weird Jack. Then I'd walk over and punch him really hard, and he would laugh and say, 'That the best you can do?' He was always short and skinny as a kid, just like he is now. I would have squashed him if he ever tried to fight back."

"And he was a friend, right?"

"One of my closest friends back then."

"Guys're weird."

They watched as Arthur rose and headed to his left, away from John and Star. With every plodding step, he glanced toward the cabin where lights were burning, and smoke rising from the chimney was caught by the wind and sent dancing across the wooden shingles. He stopped again and settled himself against a large oak. He stretched out his short legs and laid the gun across his lap.

Speaking in a low whisper, Star said, "Why'd he stop?"

"Not sure. He might have decided to wait 'till we are asleep. Might be waiting for someone. I don't know."

"When this is all over, will you tell me why the hell he's chasing us?"

"Something really awful happened between us. I testified against him. He went to jail. Got a good lawyer. Got out."

"He got out. So there must be somethin' else to make him want to kill us."

"I promise to tell you the whole story, only not right now. I need to focus."

Star nodded and said, "Doesn't look like your city boy's dressed very warm. Goin' down to twenty-five below tonight. If he doesn't get out of the wind, he'll freeze to death in that light jacket."

"Arthur always has a plan. He must be waiting for someone, maybe The Dutchman."

"Isn't he close enough for you to take a shot?"

"He needs to be a lot closer. I figured he would stay on the road. Figured I might get the drop on him as he came up the road. I wanted to confront him and give him a chance to change his mind about killing us. We got to wait and see how this works out."

For another half-hour, they watched and waited. Arthur rubbed his arms every few minutes. Though he had on gloves, he kept shoving his hands into the pockets of his jacket.

Star whispered, "Somebody's comin' up from the road."

Arthur swung around and looked in the direction of the newcomer who moved slowly and with effort through the deep snow. As the man came closer, Arthur raised himself slowly. "Took you long enough," Arthur said in a booming voice."

"It's Kevin. I see him."

Kevin said, "Not my fault. Can't even see the damned road. With all the snow, I lost your tracks. In the snow, everything looks like everything else. Besides, it's dark."

"Next time make it quicker. I'm freezing to death. Aren't you cold?"

Kevin, a grotesquely obese man, patted his stomach and let out a humorless snort. I carry my own insulation."

"What happened to Udo? He's supposed to be with you."

"Said he was goin' back to find somebody his size that had a coat and boots. He ain't never been out in the cold like this. Said he'd meet us."

"We won't wait for him. If he comes okay, if not okay. We don't need him."

Arthur waved a hand in the direction of the cabin. "Go circle round back and see what's going on. I'll wait here."

Arthur sat down again with his back resting against the tree. He waited. John and Star waited. When Kevin returned about fifteen minutes later, Arthur said, "Took you long enough. I could have walked back to town in the time it took you to go a hundred yards."

"Screw you."

"Anything doing in back?"

"The TV's on. Fire in the fireplace. Didn't see no one inside." Kevin snorted again."

"Footprints?"

"Nope. They ain't here. We're wastin' our time. I'm leavin' now."

Arthur brandished the rifle. In an angry tone, he said, "Listen, damn it. I didn't bring you along to hang out and give me a hard time."

"Screw you. I ain't one of your stooges."

"Shut up and listen. Their car is here–fire in the fireplace. They got to be in the cabin."

Kevin snorted again. "He's probably been in there screwin' her brains out all day."

John tapped Star on the shoulder. "Listen to those two arguing about something. It's not going like I expected.

"I thought he'd come right past us, right up to the front porch. If they circle around on the other side, I won't ever have a good shot from here."

"Shit. You're a damn sniper. What about all that talk about hitting a target a mile away? "

"Not with a shotgun. No. We have to get out from under this tree while they're arguing. Be as quiet as you can."

John and Star crawled around until the tree trunk shielded them from the two men. They slipped on their snowshoes and headed toward the cabin. Keeping brush and trees between them and their pursuers, John and Star schussed in a wide arc until they came upon Kevin's footprints at the back of the cabin. John pointed to the tiny guest house located behind the cabin. "Look. The guest house door is open."

Star said, "He sat on the pile of fireplace logs. He sat there to feel the warm air coming' out of the guest house. That's why he took so long."

"Cold is getting to him despite what he says to Arthur."

"We can go in the back door and get them as they come up the front."

"No. No. We need to stay outdoors."

"Why not go inside where it's warm."

"They have the advantage then. There are two of them and another one on the way. We only have my shotgun and my revolver with no extra ammo and that .32 of yours. I know Arthur. If he thinks we are in the cabin, he will not come up the front steps with guns blazing. He will burn us out."

"He wouldn't."

"I bet my life that he has grenades in that bag of his. He would think nothing of setting the place ablaze and shooting us as we came out the door."

"Holy crap!"

"Yep. Best to keep them outside. We have heavy coats, leggings, boots. Like you pointed out, neither of them is dressed for the cold. Kevin's not even wearing gloves. And look at him, a heap of blubber. Plodding after us through deep powder will give him a heart attack. We know the area. They don't. We can last a lot longer than they can."

"Arthur spots us, and we're dead."

"So we don't let him see us. We make it look like we ran out of the cabin. Like we're running. We get them away from the cabin and on up to higher ground where it's colder and windier."

Star stomped around on the fresh snow to make it appear that they came out of the cabin and ran away.

"That's enough," John said. "Let's get going."

They hurried through the trees on a gradual uphill grade, making sure to leave a clear trail for their pursuers to follow. When they reached a large open meadow stretching for more than a quarter mile in front of them and on either side, they stopped.

Star said, "That blanket looks good on you, John. You wear it like a serape. Very fashionable."

"Hey. Knock of the wisecracks. This is a serious situation."

"I understand. Just that I want you to know how happy I am that you're wearin' it."

"It's warm, and you want me to wear it. That's enough for me."

"It will work. I know it will."

"I believe things I can see, like my shotgun, like the lunatic following us, not ghosts or shamans."

"What do we do now?"

"I want to get them as far from the road as possible. We go straight ahead."

"Hold it a minute," Star said, "I got an idea."

"Let's hear it."

"How about I go off at an angle to the left. You go straight. I'll walk for a few minutes and then put on the shoes and catch up with you at the trees. On the other side. It will split them up, maybe slow them down a little."

A muffled explosion echoed against the far hills. John said, "A grenade. Told you he'd try to burn us out. We need to keep moving. But first I want to make certain he knows we're out here. This needs to be finished tonight."

Arthur sent another grenade slamming against the cabin. He turned to Kevin. "You positive they didn't go out the back?"

Kevin, who Arthur sent to watch the rear of the cabin and arrived there after Star and John had gone, said, "Nobody came out."

Arthur stared in silence at the wrecked cabin. He shook his head slowly back and forth again and again. Eventually, he turned to Kevin. "They're around here somewhere."

"Nobody's here. They already lit out. It's colder than a whore's ass. Let's get back to the cars." Kevin pointed at the sky. "Someone's callin' your name. They're saying 'You got to do better than that, Arthur.'" Kevin turned his ear toward the sounds. "Now somebody shootin' a gun. It's a ways off."

Arthur nodded. "I don't hear anyone hollering, but I heard that gunshot. They're here. Bastards. They're taunting me."

Kevin shrugged and followed Arthur around to the rear of what was left of the cabin. Arthur pointed at the snow. "There. You can see their tracks. They lit out into the woods. Can't be much ahead of us. We can catch them."

Kevin said, "Wait a damned minute. Our deal didn't include me havin' to go running 'round in no snowdrifts. I can barely feel my toes already. I need double what we agreed."

"Okay, double. Now quit your complaining, and let's get going."

At the spot where John and Star had split up, Arthur stopped. He studied the two tracks. "The woman went that way." He pointed to the left set of tracks–visible in the moonlight. "John's a lot taller. He didn't disturb the snow so much. You follow the woman. Do what you want with her. Make sure she's dead when you finish with her."

Kevin nodded and broke a smile that nearly reached his red ears already darkened by the cold to match the color of his unruly mop of hair. With his naturally ruddy complexion made redder by the cold wind, Kevin's face looked like it had been sandpapered.

Kevin shook off a feeling of sudden panic and followed Star's track. He muttered curses and complained to himself about the cold and the snow in a singsong beat to match his progress. "Ain't never been this cold before 'cept when I met that Alaskan whore. Ain't never seen so much snow before 'cept when I opened the freezer door. Ain't never been this cold before, 'cept when I went to the ice cream store." The wind had picked up and howled off the hills. New snow was falling.

For the first time in his life, Kevin was afraid. He had never been so cold in his life. But the thought of going back balanced poorly against the extra five thousand Arthur promised him. The money won the argument, so he clomped on. His broad shoulders swayed from side to side as he alternately put his weight on one leg while he lifted the other leg to get it free of the snow. He stopped. He squinted off to his right at the figure of Arthur, already way ahead of him, becoming nearly invisible in the dim light. He looked back toward the cabin and then at the expanse of snow surrounding him. Kevin felt alone. He shivered.

Kevin had taken his hands out of his pockets to help keep his balance while he struggled through the deeper drifts. He curled his fingers into a fist. They felt stiff and sore. He held his closed fists to his mouth and blew into them.

Dropping to his knees, Kevin gasped for breath, his large chest heaving. With difficulty, he stood and continued in pursuit of Star.

Star meanwhile had observed Kevin following her. He was so preoccupied with his struggle through the deep, powdery snow that he never even thought to look up. She decided to step off to the side, hide, and wait for him. Might as well end this here and now, she decided and crouched behind a low bush.

When Kevin stopped about twenty feet from where she waited, she raised herself up and stepped out from behind the bush. "That's as far as you go," she said.

The smile that crossed Kevin's face surprised her. She had expected him to be the one surprised.

"There you are sweet thing," he said. "Now, be a good girl and give me that pea shooter." One hand reached in her direction, the other went to the .45 in his shoulder holster. His cold, stiff fingers managed to clear the gun from the holster but couldn't hang onto it. The gun dropped from his hand.

Star observed a look of panic cross Kevin's face. He pawed frantically at the snow.

"Start walking," Star said.

Kevin stopped searching for the gun and looked up at her. For a long moment, he stared in silence at the Beretta. He reached down and pulled at his pant leg. As he struggled to draw a short-barreled revolver from an ankle holster, Star watched. She didn't fire until the snubby cleared the holster. Her bullet tore the fabric from his jacket and entered his arm just above the elbow. Kevin's arm jerked back from the pain. The revolver fell into the snow.

"You bitch. You shot me. You broke my arm." He stared at the wound.

Star said, "If you have any more surprises, I'll have to kill you."

He took two lunging steps toward her. She tried to step to one side but fell backward. Fortunately for Star, Kevin too fell. Terrified, she watched the big man get up and take first one slow and deliberate step and then a second.

"Stop. I don't want to shoot you."

He kept coming. In a few more steps, he would be on top of her. She fired at him. The shot missed but caused him to hesitate, giving her time to regain her feet. Mumbling profanities and holding his wounded arm, he spun around to his left and headed back in the direction he had come.

Star shouted. "Not that way. Go find your buddy, Arthur."

Kevin swiveled his head to look at her but continued following the path he and Star had made.

She waved her gun in the general direction of where she thought Arthur might be. "He's over that way." The big man kept walking. She fired the Beretta into the snow. He threw up his uninjured arm as if to shield himself from her next shot.

She had read in his face the distress and the fear and wanted to help him. She knew that decision would be suicide, so she said, "I mean it. Walk or die." She closed her mouth and glowered at him through squinting eyes.

Breathing on the one hand that he held close to his mouth, Kevin took baby steps to turn his back to Star. Then he began a slow, labored trek through the deep snow, lifting one foot high, pushing off with the other, shifting his weight to the front foot, and standing erect, before starting the whole process over again—trudging in silence. Star felt giddy. Her hands still trembled from the adrenalin rushing through her body. She incongruously thought of an old Monty Python movie she had seen on late night television where the actors high stepping in an absurd gait, pretended to be riding imaginary horses. She giggled.

She would not have imagined that Arthur, a ways off and in pursuit of John, would find humor in her situation for a different reason—certain that Star had been disposed of by Kevin.

Star watched Kevin move with ever greater difficulty through the deep snow, in places drifted nearly to mid-thigh. He turned to his right and headed back toward the cabin. She fired another shot. He shouted a curse and continued toward the cabin. Star watched until she lost Kevin in the swirling powder mixing with new snow that fell from a dark sky. The wintry landscape that had been fairly bright thirty minutes earlier was now a darkening gray. She slipped her feet into the straps of her snowshoes.

Star joined up with John near the second tree line, he hugged her and said, "Thank God you're not hurt. Those shots sounded like your little Beretta."

"It was Kevin. I had the drop on him, but I couldn't kill him. I felt sorry for him. He seemed scared to death. Imagine, a big oaf like him scared of a little girl like me."

"That's fine. I understand. No problem. What did you do with him?"

"He's headed back in our tracks. He was in a bad way. Panting like a tired hound. Hands so cold and stiff that he dropped his gun, trying to get it out of the holster. Lost it in the snow. He's wearin' street shoes. Toes're frostbitten by now."

John nodded and patted her on the shoulder. "Don't you concern yourself about him. By now he's probably warming up in his car."

"I couldn't kill him, John. I'm not like you."

"I know. Not to worry. You did good." He pushed up the sleeve of his parka and glanced at his watch. "It's been a half-hour since we left the cabin." He looked at the sky. "Those clouds. Heavier snow is coming. We need to keep moving. We can't count on a whiteout protecting us forever. If he has night vision glasses, we could be sitting ducks." Star nodded.

Even with John still walking without his snowshoes, they quickly reached the nearby line of young trees. "We'll make our stand here," John said. "First, we'll go a ways into the wood and then circle back. He's smart. Going to know we can easily flank him. He'll be cautious."

Star wrinkled her brow. "He is an idiot. He's not dressed for this weather. He must understand that."

John shook his head. "You think he cares which one of us dies tonight? He's so filled with hate."

"How can he hate you so much?"

"He holds me responsible for the death of the woman he loved. He and Beth were an item before Beth, and I got married. I suppose he never stopped loving her."

"What happened?"

"I found them together in the cabin. He came uninvited. I spotted his car parked in front. Didn't think anything of it. He had been there sometimes. The minute I came through the front door, Arthur pulled a gun. Beth stepped in front of him. I suppose she was trying to diffuse the situation. His bullet hit her in the chest." John hardly got the words across his lips that he broke down and cried in low, agonized gasps. His body shuddered.

"She was your wife. He had no business loving her. Shouldn't you be the one who hates him?"

"Maybe."

"You testified against him."

"They called it manslaughter. In his warped mind, he convinced himself that he was trying to do us both a favor—putting me out of my misery and taking care of Beth after I was gone. He knew I had the cancer. The whole thing is a tragic mess."

John wiped the tears from his cheeks. He turned his head away and gazed into the darkness. He squinted as if that might help him see through the falling, blowing snow. He turned to Star. "I'm worried that Arthur might not follow our tracks. He might veer off a bit so he can surprise us. He knows the general direction we're headed. He'll know that he can find our tracks easy enough when he reaches these trees."

"What can we do?"

"I'll prop up the blanket like it was me sitting in the snow. The wind will blow the blanket, so it looks like I'm moving around, maybe putting on my snowshoes. He takes his shot. We see where he is."

"No, John. You can't. That blanket is a healing blanket. You know what Uncle Jerry told us. You wear the blanket and believe, and the cancer will leave you."

"Star. It's not magic."

"Yes, it is. It's Native American magic. The blanket lets you commune with the spirit world, especially on a night like this in the snow and the wind and the cold. Can't you feel the spirits floating on the wind? It's like they're speaking to us."

"It's only the wind."

"Exactly! Don't you understand? The spirits gave us the cold and the blowing snow as our very own magic blanket to hide us from our enemies."

"But I can put it back on later."

"No. It wasn't given to you for that reason. It would be like you're disrespecting it. We say that a healing blanket is woven from strands of time and space. You do that, and the healing power will leave it. You'll get worse. I don't want to lose you."

"Very well. We can settle down behind one of the trees and wait."

Star reached out and patted John on the chest. "She whispered, "There he is. I can see him. I don't think he sees us yet."

John put a finger to his lips and whispered, "Keep low and head for that clump of brush next to the big oak."

Star followed him, reaching down and slipping off her snowshoes as she went. They both crouched and waited. Star said, "You were right. He didn't follow your tracks all the way. And he got here really fast. He's in good shape. Tough."

John tossed first one side of the blanket over one shoulder and then the other side over the opposite shoulder. He raised the shotgun and sighted along the barrel.

From his cover, John watched Arthur slip from one tree to the next. Behind each tree, Arthur waited, always looking first at the ground and then at the surroundings, swiveling his head slowly, rifle at the ready, making crunching sounds as he walked.

John felt weak. His hands and arms shook. He let the shotgun rest on his knee. Star put a hand on his forearm. He looked at her. She smiled and wiggled her automatic in front of his face. "Don't worry. I reloaded. I can take him. He's close enough. In a minute, he'll see our tracks. By then it'll be too late."

John shook his head. He tried to will his body to stop shaking. He recalled a cold and snowy night nine years ago when he shot a man from ambush. His hands shook then.

Arthur had stopped for nearly a minute, studying the snow-laden fir trees to their left. He stepped out into the open, for an instant giving John a clear shot. John shouted. "Drop the rifle. Let's talk. We may not be friends anymore, but nobody needs to die over this. I'm ready to let it go. I told you that this morning."

"Up yours," Arthur shouted back. He ducked behind a skinny tree trunk and raised the rifle to his shoulder. He fired.

John waited. Arthur stepped away from the tree and fired again. John stood and fired. He pumped a new cartridge into the magazine but did not fire again. Arthur lurched to his left. His right arm flew up. The rifle he still gripped in his hand. Arthur swayed but didn't fall. Powdered with the snow that John's shot had dislodged from the tree branches, he grinned and said, "Damn buddy. You always did pack a wicked punch. Near took my arm off." He turned sideways to give himself more cover behind the small tree.

"You try to raise that rifle again, and I kill you. It's a standoff. Let's talk."

"I think I'll just wait for my guys to show up, Johnny Boy. They can finish you off. Kevin already extinguished little Kathleen, your dancing star. I'm sure you heard the gunshots a while back."

Star shouted. "You sent a boy to do a man's job."

John noted the look that crossed Arthur's face peering from behind the tree. In it, he read doubt but also anger. He knew that his former friend was assessing his situation, deciding on his next move, wondering what might have happened to his backup.

"Kevin won't miss the second time, little star dancer. And you don't want to know what the Dutchman will do to you. He'll follow you to the very gates of hell."

"Kathleen shouted, "You and your boys are the only ones hereabouts going to hell."

Arthur fell sideways. His knees buckled as he went down.

John slowly walked toward Arthur–keeping the shotgun ready to shoot if Arthur tried to move. He stood for a moment and stared at his former friend. John felt a heavy sadness descend on him. He felt as if it was pushing him down. He imagined his feet being pressed into the frozen earth, his body sinking into the ground.

Arthur turned his face toward John. "You got me fair and square, Johnny Boy," he said in short gasps. Pretty soon, it's your turn. The Dutchman is one of my best. He's out there right now, drawing a bead on your cursed head. He'll blow the brains right out of your skull like it was a ripe watermelon. We got a lot of those in Florida." He coughed. "He'll get that slut of yours too. Best if we're all dead."

~—~

The Dutchman, Udo, had driven back to town and quickly located a man his size. He lured the man into an alley under the pretext that he needed help for his wife, who had fallen and broken her leg. After he had killed the man, he removed the man's heavy down parka and boots from his lifeless body. Udo was pleased to find that the parka fit him perfectly and that the boots were only about a half size too large. He enjoyed killing but had more important things to do than trying to find a pair of his exact size. He decided to take the man's gloves and heavy woolen socks as well. Feeling warm and comfortable in his fresh wardrobe, he drove back to John's cabin.

Moving at a trot through the snow, Udo easily traversed the half-mile from the highway to the cabin. Once there, he quickly figured what had happened and set out on Arthur's trail, his pace nearly double that of Arthur.

Udo heard a gunshot and noted that they came from directly ahead of him. He stopped and studied the trees, trying to make out movement. In his heavy clothing, he was well protected from the biting wind, yet he felt the need to pull tight the straps on the fur-lined hood of his parka. He became aware for the first time of the steam he breathed out into the chill night air. He coughed. He patted his chest to make sure the .45 pistol was in its holster. He caught sight of Arthur moving to a position behind the thin tree trunk. He saw the blast from John's gun and watched Arthur fall. Udo crouched and moved to his left, planning to come up on John from behind. "I got you now," he whispered to himself. "You're a dead man, Chambers."

Udo moved toward the trees, keeping low and continually scanning the scene in front of him for movement. He had not yet seen John or Star. He finally spotted John standing and looking down. He watched John look behind him and speak to someone. He made it to the trees and inched in close to John without hearing any alarm raised about his presence. Udo crouched down and waited, watching.

"He's dead," John said.

Star replied, "At first, I thought you missed him. He just stood there with that strange look on his face. I hope he didn't suffer much."

"If you don't hit the spine or the brain or the heart, they don't always go down. But suffer? No. He didn't suffer. Probably never felt anything more than the initial shock."

Udo unzipped his parka and pulled his pistol from the holster under his arm. The dress gloves he had stolen from the dead man let him keep them on and still manage the trigger guard. He saw John glance in his direction and silently cursed himself for making so much noise getting at the gun. He crouched lower and waited for the person with whom John spoke to appear in his field of vision. He would kill them both.

Kathleen turned toward the sound Udo made. An instant later, she flattened herself on the ground and held her little Beretta in front of her, her elbows resting against a deadfall tree. John dropped to a crouch and whispered, "What is it?"

Star pointed to where she thought the sound had come. She put her finger to her lip and motioned John to get down. He crouched lower and signaled his plan to flank whoever might be hiding.

Every few steps, John stopped and looked intently for some sign of movement. He had no idea how far to go to be behind the person that lay in hiding. He counted his steps, estimating each to be about two feet and stopped at the count of twenty. He dropped to one knee and waited. He looked to his left toward the place where Star was hiding behind the dead tree.

Five minutes ticked by. He heard Star move. A moment later, he heard a shot from directly in front of him. The muzzle blast from Udo's

.45 was easy to see in the dark. A second and then a third round were fired. John put the shotgun to his shoulder and fired. He pumped and fired again. He heard a groan. He dropped to one knee and shoved four shells into the magazine, he pumped and fired a third time. He shouted, “Star, are you all right?” He got no reply. He shouted a second time. Still, no reply.

John stood. He pulled the automatic from his holster and advanced toward Udo’s position. He found Udo and, from the looks of his wounds, assumed he was dead. But he still aimed his pistol and put three shots into the body to relieve the anger he felt. He shoved the automatic back into the holster and ran to check on Star.

John found Star lying on the ground. The Beretta lay near her outstretched hands. He knelt and studied her wound. He found that she had been hit in the head. He pulled out his cell phone to call 911. When the call didn’t go through, he peered at the face of the phone, trying to will even the smallest of the bars to light. After the third try, he gave up and turned his full attention to Star. “Got to get you to a doctor,” he said and picked her up, cradling her in his arms. He took a few steps and realized that he didn’t have on his snowshoes. John set Star down gently, so he could slip into them.

John looked at the girl he loved. He had lost Beth. He would do all in his power to save his star dancer. He opened the large pin that held his blanket around his shoulders and let the blanket fall onto the snow. He picked up Star and laid her on the blanket, wrapped it about her, and fastened it with the large pin. He kissed her and again cradled her in his arms. With grim determination, he headed back the way he had come.

The snowshoes allowed him to move much faster than he had been able to walk through the deep drifts. John was happy the wind had changed. It seemed to be embracing him, propelling him. He felt they were gliding across the frozen landscape.

As he neared the cabin, John found Kevin lying face up, staring at the sky, the snow around him flecked with red. John stopped and nudged Kevin with his foot. He noted the blue skin and the empty holster and the arm wound. “This was definitely not your best night, big guy,” he said to the lifeless body.

At what was left of the cabin, John again tried his cell phone. He was able to reach the 911 dispatcher, who called for an ambulance. John described the wound and mentioned Star's name. The dispatcher promised to alert the hospital to have the neurosurgeon on call available when they arrived. John then told the dispatcher there had been a shooting and that two people were dead.

First, one siren broke the silence, then a second and a third. Within minutes it seemed to John that the air was alive with sirens.

With a bit of zigging and zagging, John's four-wheel-drive vehicle had no problem plowing a path to the main road where the ambulance sat waiting alongside cars from the Sheriff's Office and the local police. The EMTs took charge of Star.

A deputy who knew John from his work with the Cops and Kids program, asked, "The call said there were multiple casualties. Is Miss Crow the only victim?" John shook his head. "What's the situation?" the deputy asked.

"Three dead. Arthur Livingstone. A man named Udo. A young man named Kevin. Two are up there by the second tree line, way up on the hill. Kevin is lying in the snow somewhere not too far from the cabin."

~—~

Four days later, Star awoke with John sitting on a chair by her hospital bed. She touched her hair and tried to smooth it. "I must look a mess," she said, the words not more than a whisper.

"You look beautiful to me. Thought you were a goner. Your neurosurgeon said you will be fine, except for some nasty scars they can work on later when you feel better. He told me it is a miracle you are alive. You had a close call."

She smiled. "You're here, so I guess we got the bad guys."

"That we did. The two of us. I explained everything to the Sheriff. They found Kevin in the morning–frozen stiff. The autopsy said he died of a heart attack. I may be in some hot water, though. The shots I pumped into Udo's carcass have the police thinking execution. Fortunately for me, he has a rap sheet. He's wanted for three murders. They suspect him on at least a dozen more. Besides, your uncle talked to them. I think it will be good."

Star gasped. "John. I just realized. You're not wearing the blanket. Go get it right this minute and put it back on."

"It got lost. I tried to find it, but nobody even remembers seeing it. It was sort of confused at the cabin what with all the cops and the EMTs. A doctor even showed up."

"What do you mean?"

"I wrapped the blanket around you while I carried you back to the road. Figured it might work some of its healing powers on you."

"But you didn't believe it. I had to threaten you with all sorts of things to get you to keep it on."

"I believe now."

Star tried to push herself up on her elbows but fell back. She stammered, "No. No. It was not for me. It was for you. You shouldn't have taken it off. Now you've gone and ruined everything." A torrent of tears ran down her face.

He took her hand in his. "You don't understand. I went to see your uncle. Remember? I had an appointment with Doctor Jerry on Thursday. It seems that blanket worked more than one miracle. The scan was clear. Nothing. My cancer is in full remission."

Big Charlie And Little Charlie

Charlie Budnose lived with his mother, Jane Budnose, in a little house on Elm Street. He had been using a walker since the age of three when he fell down the stairs and hit his head on the concrete sidewalk. Charlie underwent a series of surgeries. Each operation brought him closer to full recovery.

In the meantime, because he had trouble with his balance, the doctors recommended that he use a walker. Since no walker could be purchased off the shelf for such a little body, his uncle, the machinist, built his first walker. It was truly a custom job, unlike any other. The first surgery did not heal him; over the next seven years, he required many more.

Charlie remembers little of his early childhood, and his mother will not speak of it. The doctor died, and the hospital burned to the ground, along with all its records. It was in a time before clouds and digital files and backups. So the exact issue that the operations addressed is lost in the mists of bygone years. That doesn't bother Charlie. Long ago, he reconciled himself to a life that included some type of contraption to lean against for support and to push in front of him.

He recalls having a series of new walkers as he grew and matured. Each one, his uncle styled in special ways. Each arrived carefully geared to Charlie's activities by the inclusion of such things as a tiny fold-down seat, a steering arrangement, and all-terrain wheels. The uncle also festooned the contraption with accouterments: a rearview mirror, a built-in iPod complete with speaker, headlamps, and mittens for the cold weather.

The last surgery occurred the day before Charlie turned 10. After the last surgery, the doctors declared him cured. He no longer needed a walker for support or even a cane.

But by that point, he was addicted to his walker, which he called "Little Charlie," addressing it often by name. He could not give it up. Each time he tried to walk without his walker, he fell to the floor. "Charlie," Jane scolded. "There is nothing wrong with your legs or any other part of you now. You are completely cured. You don't need the walker. Say goodbye to Little Charlie."

"But ma," he replied. "You don't understand. I'm trying as hard as I can. I am sick and tired of pushing this metal monster around. Trouble is that my legs don't want to hold me up unless I have Little Charlie to hold on to. I let go of Little Charlie; the room starts to spin. I get light-headed. My legs just crumple, and down I go."

Jane let him have his way for the rest of the day. That night, hiked up on the tips of her toes, she sneaked into his room and quietly removed the walker from his bedside. She left a silver dollar under his pillow. She hid Little Charlie in the barn under a pile of hay.

The next morning, when Charlie awoke and noticed his beloved walker gone, he became agitated, at first screaming and crying and then demanding its swift return. But Jane held steadfast in her resolve and told Charlie that the walker fairy had come in the night because he no longer needed it. She told him that the fairy took his walker because some unfortunate boy needed it more than he.

Charlie was not moved by the emotional aspects of the story. He cursed that other boy. Soon he became so distraught that Jane summoned a medical doctor. When the doctor told Charlie to sit up on the edge of the bed, Charlie discovered that he could not move his legs. The doctor borrowed a hat pin from Jane. Again and again, he drove the needle into the flesh of Charlie's lower extremities, eliciting no response whatsoever.

Jane, observing the procedure with an increasing alarm, eventually shouted, "No. No. This can't be."

When the doctor looked up at her, locked her in his gaze, and shook his head in measured beat, Jane dropped to her knees. She beseeched the Almighty to forgive her for doubting her son. Being ever a prudent woman, she said nothing of the visit by the walker fairy or of the purloined walker.

The following morning Jane peeked in on Charlie when she heard his alarm clock ringing. She had set the alarm the previous evening, so that she might observe Charlie's wakening.

The moment he spied his walker leaning against the wall by his bed, he reached for it and drew it to him. "Thank you, good fairy," he shouted. "Thank you for returning Little Charlie to me. I missed him so."

With no effort apparent to Jane standing by his door, Charlie sprang out of bed and stood. Rolling the walker about the room, he hopped from foot to foot. He danced a little two-step as if Little Charlie were his partner. Tears welled in Jane's eyes. So what if her son wanted to have his walker with him. He'd grow out of it eventually. She thought of the Charlie Brown cartoon and of Linus and the security blanket he carried everywhere. "How different is it really," she whispered in thankful prayer.

The next year, when Charlie turned 11, he graduated to middle school, where sports became more important to the students. The principal of the middle school recommended to Jane that Charlie try out for the swim team. Perhaps because of physical therapy at the pool in his younger years, Charlie took to swimming immediately. Although Little Charlie was never farther away than the edge of the pool, he didn't need Little Charlie to help him swim. He easily made the swim team, the members of which elected him captain.

All was well with Charlie until the day he happened by the ball field and stopped to watch his classmates playing baseball. The next day he went to the coach and asked if he could try out for the team. The coach looked at Charlie and Little Charlie and said, "Why don't we make you an equipment helper. That way, you can be with the team. You can't expect to play with a walker."

The coach's answer did not dissuade Charlie. He and Little Charlie headed straight for the office of the Principal, Mister Blindspot, where Charlie eloquently pleaded his case. When Mister Blindspot snickered, Charlie let drop that he had recently been reading the Americans with Disabilities Act. He explained that the school had an obligation to make the playing field disability-friendly. Charlie went on to describe such a field, with its moving walkway connecting the bases, a swivel chair at the pitcher's mound, and a special bar at home plate for Charlie to lean on when he hit.

Faced with Charlie's obviously superior knowledge of federal laws, and the expense the Charlie's proposed redesign of the playing field, not to mention the turmoil, Mister Blindspot picked up his telephone and called the baseball coach. When he put down the phone, a smile lit his usually dour countenance. "Charlie," he said through smiling lips, "Coach has considered your earnest desire to take part in the Great American Sport and wants me to tell you that you are on the team. Please report to the field tomorrow."

The other boys on the team laughed when Charlie and Little Charlie rolled up to the plate. Charlie casually knocked the clay from his cleats, locked Little Charlie's brake, and leaned over the plate. With his teammates booing him with gusto, he took two called strikes before he hit one onto the roof of the administration building. His slow but triumphant trip around the bases drew cheers from his former tormentors.

The coach put Charlie in right field where he managed to catch not a single ball; not even a high fly ball hit deep. Every opposing batter tried to hit the ball to Charlie. Though his team won few games, due partially to his poor fielding, he came to love baseball even more than he loved swimming because baseball did not separate him and his best friend, Little Charlie.

Charlie wore out a series of walkers, and sometimes they lasted only a matter of weeks, so rough was he on them. Jane seldom challenged him, though she supposed he could do just as well without the support of the long ago superfluous device.

Jane tried to find for Charlie a group similar to Alcoholics Anonymous or Narcotics Anonymous. None could she find that specialized in walker therapy. One group, designed as a catch-all for addictive personalities, rejected Charlie. Although the group included people with what Jane considered to be very odd compulsions and strange fetishes, Charlie's addiction was considered too bizarre.

The day Charlie turned 16, Jane took him to see a psychologist named Dr. Heliotrope Brainspooler, a woman experienced in working with a wide variety of addictions. Heliotrope had never heard of anyone being addicted to a walker, yet her mind stood open to the new challenge.

Jane inquired about the cost of the therapy sessions. Dr. Heliotrope replied, "If you give me permission to write about your son's case, I will give you a special rate. I can write about it in a learned paper and receive the adulation of my colleagues, for never has the world seen such an addiction." Jane readily agreed. It would be nice to have her son be a celebrity, no matter the manner of that celebrity. Perhaps she also might be mentioned in the paper.

To rid Charlie of his love affair with the walker, Heliotrope Brainspooler applied every technique she knew, even including a very aggressive and painful aversion therapy. Many sessions later and nearly at her wit's end, Dr. Brainspooler turned to virtual reality therapy.

During the second session with the virtual reality headgear, Charlie danced and cavorted about the office while Little Charlie stood alone in a corner awaiting his master's attention. VR appeared to be a particularly promising way to cure Charlie of his walker addiction. That promise obtained until Heliotrope said, "Now you understand you don't need your walker anymore. Let me take off the headgear. Close your eyes. Don't open them until I tell you." She removed the virtual reality headset and set it aside.

"Can I open my eyes yet?" Charlie asked.

"Not yet. I will count to twenty slowly, and you will count along with me. Then you'll open your eyes. When you open them, you will be able to walk alone." Counting slowly, she hid Little Charlie behind her desk. At the count of ten, she said, "OK. Now open."

Charlie opened his eyes. He looked about the room for Little Charlie. His knees buckled, and he promptly collapsed to the floor. Dr. Heliotrope Brainspooler's dreams of professional glory fell with him. Successful in addictions from sin to gin, she met her match in Charlie Budnose.

Jane gave up after the failed therapy sessions and resigned herself to seeing her son go through life hampered by his addiction to a walker he no longer needed. He worked a series of jobs, but only where there existed no need for him to stand or to move about. Charlie became familiar with computers and found that his quick mind adapted readily to programming. He often went to the gun range and became a marksman of some notoriety with the pistol his uncle had fitted atop Little Charlie's frame. One evening he broke up an attempted burglary and became a sort of local hero for a few days.

Charlie's greatest challenge came just before his 20th birthday when he met Faith, a girl his age with large blue eyes, dimples at the edges of her full pouting mouth, and long red hair. For Faith, her feelings for Charlie sprouted forth upon first setting eyes upon him. Being a practical girl, she understood that to win Charlie, she needed to wean him from his irrational attention to the walker–to Little Charlie.

For their first date, Faith chose a low cut bodice and a very short skirt. She wanted to make sure Charlie had every opportunity to appreciate her bulbous breasts, her tight bubble butt, and her well-shaped thighs. At 5:30, Faith took up station by the front door of her house with her hand on the doorknob, anxiously awaiting Charlie's arrival.

Being nothing if not punctual, Charlie, with Little Charlie leading the way, appeared on her door stoop at exactly 6:00 PM and rang the bell.

Not wishing Charlie to see her as anxious, Faith took a deep breath. She turned the knob. She opened the door with a slow and deliberate motion intended to kindle in Charlie an expectation of the pleasures that awaited him. "Why Charlie," Faith gushed, trying very hard to use her most sincere tone. "It's so good to see you." She knew by reputation that Charlie's experiences with the fairer sex were far from pleasant.

Faith had learned through the local grapevine that he attended every high school dance without a date. No girl wanted to go to a dance with someone who had to shove a walker around. It was not so much they harbored prejudice against physically challenged persons. With a walker between them and their partner and barely within an arm's reach, being close enough to enflame sexual passions became impossible.

Charlie, with his athletic build, his ready laughter, his curly hair, and his handsome face marked by deep-set eyes, a strong chin, and a perpetual smile, attracted many eager young girls. Predictably, each time, the relationship soon withered, for Charlie had a terrible addiction. He even had taken to bringing Little Charlie to bed, folding him with a gentleness that ought to have been reserved for lady friends and pets and laying the walker beside him on the bed.

Faith had one more bit of information about Charlie that she thought important. She knew that a considerable inheritance awaited him when he turned 21. That gave her not only an incentive but also a year to spin her web and capture him. It also gave her a year to wean him away from

Little Charlie. She felt confident that her objective was obtainable and approached it with a firm resolve.

One evening, after they had been dating for a time, Faith put her plan into effect. Charlie knocked on her door. Faith opened the door slowly. "You can leave Little Charlie here on the stoop," she said. "I'll hide the walker behind the porch swing, so it won't get stolen." She threw one arm around Charlie. With her other arm the amply endowed Faith swept the walker to one side. She drew Charlie against her heaving bosom. Even in his buskined shoes, Charlie stood a good foot shorter than Faith with the result that his nose burrowed into her cleavage. "My love," she whispered in his ear.

His beloved walker was, for the moment, forgotten. Charlie breathed in the fragrance of the well-chosen scent that enlivened his pheromones to a near toxic degree. He gasped. Faith held him close to her a long moment. She released him, and, in a single fluid motion, flung an arm about his waist.

With Faith supporting him, Charlie stepped over the threshold into her apartment, into a new world where Faith ruled. At that moment, he half turned and scarce audibly breathed the words, "Forgive me Little Charlie Budnose. I will be back for you."

Bumps formed on Faith's flesh. A shock raced from the top of her head to the toes of her feet. Icy fingers gripped her heart. She twirled Charlie around and again pulled him to her.

Stoked by her fear of losing Charlie to the walker, as had so many of his earlier female friends, a new thought burst forth in her frontal lobes. With Charlie's face nestled in her bosom, in a tone soft and comforting, she said, "What is there for me to forgive, Big Charlie? I am always with you."

Upon hearing these words, and in a rush of wisdom that comes only with the adult years, Charlie understood it was time he got a different kind of walker. From that day on, Big Charlie affectionately referred to Faith as his Little Charley Budnose.

Little Charlie, the metal walker, never again left the front porch where Faith had hidden it, forgotten, rusting away until eventually being thrown out with the trash.

The Soldier In The Park

The metal statue stands
Neglected in the city park
Upon a marble base.
And on the base a list is
Carved of the town's fallen:
Heroes of a long-forgotten war.
A crown of thorns
Grows up
To lay upon the helmet
That sits atop his head.
When some people stop and look,
A loved one can be seen
In the rain-smeared face,
Where thorny boughs blossom
In colors of life.
He is always there, steadfast,
In the shadow of the trees
Where happy children play.
They do not know
From whence the soldier came
Nor do the young ones care.
Yet they are his spirit.
In their innocence
They do not understand that
He was once like them.

Summer Morning

Out through the door
Push the wood-framed screen
Bellied by my hands, broken
By my foot,
Patched enough
To discourage flies and moths
On active summer days.

Squeaking and creaking
As it always did,
Protesting, swinging back
With porch shaking
House shaking bang.

Earthbounders detour while
Birds glide on summer air.
If only I could fly
Over Mrs. Carrol's garden

Run as fast as you can,
Catch me if you can,
Throw up your arms.
Skip, and jump, and whirl.

Through the garage,
Out to the alley,
Draw with a stick
In gravel and ashes
Pictures to last forever
Or until the next car comes by.

Dementia

He lives with us now
Beyond a far shore.
He walked down slowly to the dock
One evening and set sail
Just before the dark.
There was room in his boat
For none but him.
Slowly he untied the lines
And pushed away
From the grasp of cogent reasoning.
He looked back as he departed,
Eyes waving to me a last good-bye.
I think he knew.
Before that
He would take little trips on which
He would be gone for a while
And then
Show up for a while
And then
Go out again
To a place about which he could not tell.
We did not sail with him on those trips,
Though we might have liked.
And when he came back, he did not

Share with us the travels he had taken.
I cannot see his boat now,
Maybe drifting on the sea,
Maybe anchored on a far shore
Only God knows where.
We cannot go to him
Because we do not have a compass
That would show us the way.
If there dwelt a waterman to guide us
We would sail to him, but
Even if we found him,
That would do no good.
Even if I called out to him,
He would not reply.
I do not know his name now
Or the language
Which he speaks.
He does not remember mine.
With his presence all about us
We struggle with the knowledge
That he will not return.

William

William woke one morning from a deep and troubling sleep.
Overtaken by a fever, he was sick and weak.
He was very restless and wanted something new to do.
His agitated state increased when he thought about the coming day.
He resolved to settle down and look at the world in some different way.
William found his ladder, set it up against a cloud, and began to climb.
He climbed until he could see beyond the present date and time,
But the weather there was hazy, so he could not see infinity.
When William looked upon the world, reaching then a middle rung,
He thought he glimpsed his future in shapes of clouds that overhung.
But he would know his own life soon enough.
What he wanted now and what thrilled him most of all was the thought
Of knowing what the world would be after he had died.
So William climbed some more and reached a higher place from which
He spied a thing beyond his life and was so overwhelmed, he wept.

He could not keep his eyes upon that vision lest he miss his step,
For his knees were trembling uncontrolled from the emotion that he felt.
William turned his head so he could see what was behind him.
When he looked back from there, he saw familiar things,
The stories he was told in youth of palaces and kings.
But they were not the only things to see from his ladder perch.
Many times and tribulations swam before his view in rivers of remorse.
But of course, he could do nothing now, for it was too late to repent.
The ladder he was climbing reached far above the farthest star.

Partners In Crime

The Molotov cocktail lit the cold night air in a fiery, smoky display of flying glass and burning gasoline. "Damn," Coggie Dawkins said. He jumped back to avoid the flames. "That's some tough glass for a bodega window. Thought that bomb would do the job easy."

His companion, Moe Amehu, laughed. "Tole ya it wouldn't work," he said. "Them is for makin' people catch on fire, you know, the burning gas sticks like glue. Not for breaking glass. Needs more like a real bomb, you know, the one made out of some kind of cook pot–a thing like those boys in Boston used."

"You idiot. That was a smoker. They use them to roast pigs and stuff. A cooking pot wouldn't be big enough."

"No. No. A smoker would be too big. Couldn't carry it in a backpack. It's what you cook whole hogs and stuff like that with."

"It was a small one. Anyhow, who's the expert here?"

Amehu only stared at Dawkins, making no effort to respond to the rhetorical question, though he didn't know it was rhetorical, only that he didn't feel like answering it since he had nothing new to suggest. He would let Dawkins do the brain work. He was happy to be the muscle, though he was beginning to wonder if Dawkins had any brains to work.

"That's the last time I take a suggestion you make, Moe. Molotov cocktail. Yeah, right. I should have known that glass won't break glass."

Moe knew that the gasoline had been Dawkins' idea, not his. He decided to let the matter go and not argue the point. He would focus on the job at hand.

"Look for a brick or something, Moe. Look for a really big brick."

"A big brick?"

"Biggest one you can find."

"I think they're all kind of, like, all around the same size. Don't think I've ever come across a big brick. Nope. More I think on it, don't believe there is any such thing. Can you imagine a wall made with all different sized bricks? Really would look funny. Be hard to make too."

"There's all kinds of bricks. You know, like the kinds they make brick streets with are lots bigger—and stronger too, I might add for your edification."

Moe shot him a look, dropping the ends of his mouth and wrinkling his brow. "Them are cobblestones, not bricks," he muttered.

Dawkins peered up and down the dark road lit only by a single, dim street light at the corner, getting no help from a moonless black sky. He tilted his head like a dog might—as if listening to some far off sound adrift on the cold night air. "You hear that, Moe?"

"Don't hear nothin'. Hell, it's one in the morning. Anybody with any sense is in bed."

Dawkins shrugged. "What was I talking about?"

"Bricks. You wanted me to find a big brick."

"Oh, yeah. Start looking."

"I am. Don't see no bricks. Nobody's gonna leave bricks on the sidewalk. Somebody would trip over them."

"That vacant lot way down near the corner." Dawkins pointed. "Try there. If you can't find a big brick, look for a really big rock or something to toss at this window."

Moe waited for a pickup truck to pass. The truck had a string of various colored bulbs along the edges of the bed. They blinked, giving the vehicle a holiday air. Moe was happy that the driver had taken the time to brighten the night. He stepped into the street, taking his time to cross, in a shuffling J-walk, the short distance to the lot where he stood for a moment before glancing back at Dawkins. His partner in crime had settled himself onto the sidewalk with his back against the knee wall of the bodega. He sat, head down, punching at his cell phone.

Moe had to admit that the Molotov cocktail was not one of his partner's better ideas, yet in his defense, it had not been the first suggestion as to how they might break into the store. Dawkins had first wanted to bring a sledgehammer. Dawkins, who considered himself the brains of the caper from the beginning, had eventually nixed that because a sledge laying in the bed of the truck might have seemed suspicious if they'd been stopped for some moving infraction–like speeding. From riding around town earlier with Dawkins, Moe knew that Dawkins had a lead foot. Dawkins admitted to having experienced numerous short periods of time that his license had been suspended for speeding, so maybe he had a point. In any event, Moe had acquiesced to the cocktail when Dawkins nixed the idea of using his truck to simply knock down the door.

Moe had met Dawkins in a bar when he stopped off to grab a brew before buying a Christmas tree. He hadn't been doing so well on the job front. In fact, he'd waited until Christmas Eve to look for a tree because the prices were a lot lower. The last chance for a sale looming made the tree sellers eager to move their inventory at any price. He eventually scored a really full six footer for five dollars. His mother loved it. He told her it cost forty dollars.

When she had said, "You really must love your old mama to pay all that much for a Christmas tree," Moe had nodded and given her a hug. He did love his mama and took care that she had available to her, not only the necessities of life but, also, that she experienced from time to time some small luxury–like the fur coat he had brought home for her the previous Christmas.

Dawkins settled his ample backside onto the barstool next to Moe. Moe mentioned about waiting to buy the tree at the last minute to save money. Dawkins immediately began to lay out a plan for a smash and grab. He made it sound easy. Said he needed some muscle to help him scoop up the loot. Said he was willing to do an even split. Moe came up with the bodega suggestion to which Dawkins readily agreed. It was a good location because there were no outside cameras anywhere in the block, and it was really close to his mama's house. Moe knew that the owners kept cash in a desk drawer with a false bottom. They ran all sorts of illegal activity from that location.

They shook hands and resolved to meet back at the bar later that afternoon. Moe hadn't really liked Dawkins, mostly because he made a couple smart-assed remarks about folks of color, but the thought of a quick and easy score with a guy who wouldn't hang around to give him trouble—Dawkins being from out of town and all—was something he found impossible to resist.

Construction debris lay scattered across the open space between a hardware store and a jewelers. None of the debris included a brick of any size.

Moe shook off thoughts of the misgivings he had about his partner in crime. Intent on getting on with the job at hand, he concentrated his thinking on the extra money he would have for the Christmas holidays.

Dismissing numerous bits and pieces of wood and concrete as unsuitable for the intended purpose, Moe chose a concrete block and carried it back to Dawkins, who still sat fiddling with his cell phone. Moe set the block down in front of Dawkins.

"Too big," Dawkins said, stifling a yawn.

"You didn't even look at it."

A car passed, its bright lights making Moe feel exposed. He controlled the urge to check to see if the driver gave them any notice.

"Saw you carrying it. Knew it was too big the moment you started across with it."

Moe frowned. He picked up the block and backed into the street until he was about halfway across. He waited until Dawkins rose and stepped to one side. Moe pulled the heavy block against his chest and ran toward the bodega. When he got to the curb, he took one last step—more of a leap than a step—onto the sidewalk and shoved the block forward. It fell short and broke into chunks as it hit the pavement. Shards of concrete flew in every direction.

"Way to go, Moe. Just about the right size now."

"I was tryin' to break the window, not break the block."

"Whatever. You did okay. Toss one of those big pieces. Ought to do the trick."

Appearing a bit like a shot putter, Moe picked up the largest piece of block in one hand and heaved it at the store window. The chunk of concrete hit the window and bounced off. Dawkins had to do some fancy footwork to avoid being hit when the concrete ricocheted in his direction. Again, bits of concrete flew in all directions.

In an angry voice, Dawkins shouted, "Damn it to hell, Moe. Let me show you how it's done." He bent over and lifted the biggest chunk of the block left intact. He held it away from his body and moved it up and down as if to judge its weight. “Here goes,” he said and twirled around with the concrete held at the end of his outstretched arm. He let go. The block sailed toward the store. The glass held. The concrete again fell to the sidewalk.

Moe laughed.

“You laugh at me, but you didn’t do any better. Dumb ass!”

Moe nodded. “This glass is too hard. Used to be a bank at this address. We lived a couple blocks from here. I walked by every day on my way to school. Probably used some sort of ballistic glass ‘cause it used to be a bank. I bet we couldn’t have busted it even with the sledge.” Let’s do a drive-through.

“You mean, drive the truck through it?”

“Yeah.”

“Another one of your bad ideas. I told you. That might work if we could hit it head-on. The street is really narrow here. We could start way down the block and get up speed, but there’s no way to hit it other than a glancing blow. Damn stuff is so tough; even the pickup might not bust in the door if we can’t hit it head-on. Anyhow, I don’t want to damage my truck by jumping that curb and slamming into stuff. Nope. Think of something else.”

“I got a couple sticks of dynamite in my garage.”

With the heel of his hand, Dawkins whacked Moe on the side of the head. Headlights appeared at the end of the street as a vehicle turned the corner. Moe and Dawkins stared at the slow moving car. Despite the frosty air, the driver’s side window was rolled down. “You fellas okay?” the driver asked.

Moe replied, “Yeah. Me and Coggie was just goofin’. We was takin’ a walk and saw this crap all over the sidewalk. Looks like some concrete rolled off a truck or sumpthin’.”

Dawkins shook his head as if to indicate that his friend was really dumb. “My friend wanted us to try and clean it up. It was a stupid idea. That’s why I swatted him.”

The driver said, “No. No, that was a noble idea. However, be assured that the owner will take care of it after Christmas. Don’t worry. Enjoy your walk. If you hang around in this spot, somebody might think you’re trying to break the window.” He chuckled a sort of back of the throat chortle. “Now, if I found you two in front of the little jewelry store across the street, that is exactly what I might have concluded." He chuckled again, gunned his engine, and was showing his tail lights before Moe could think of anything to say. Moe smiled and waved.

Dawkins stared at the departing car. "You know that was a city vehicle, don't you?"

"How do you know–from the tags?"

"When we met in the bar, I didn't take you for the idiot you turned out to be. He has hub caps. Nobody buys a car with hub caps anymore. Might even been a policeman. Like what he said about the jewelry store. Something a cop might find funny."

Moe said. "So, let's go knock off the jewelry store across the street. They took stuff outta the window, but I looked in. Saw a lot of stuff still in the cases. Didn't used to be a bank neither. And they got lots more concrete blocks in the vacant lot too."

"A great partner I have. You got me trying to rob a bodega while right across the street is a jewelry store with stuff just asking to be robbed."

"Wait a minute, Coggie! I know the guy who owns the place. He keeps lots of money in a secret drawer in his big desk. And he never cleans out the cash drawer except for what he needs to maybe buy something on his way home. It was a sure thing. Easy money like you said you wanted. No need to fence anything. Cold, hard cash."

"The jewelry store. We do the jewelry store."

"I dunno. On second thought, it's getting' late, and I'm freezin'. Got to be near fifteen degrees. It was near twenty when I left the house. My mama's gonna be wonderin' what the hell I'm doin' out all night on Christmas Eve. Let's do it another night. What's the rush?"

"It's Christmas. That's why nobody is around. What! One, maybe two, cars come by all the time you've been goofing around here."

Moe had grown to dislike his partner to the point of nearly just walking away. He didn't trust him either and wanted to worry him, play with his head a little. "The cop might be more suspicious than he was lettin' on," Moe said. "Probably remember you. You look pretty dopey with that cowboy hat and those boots you got your pants stuffed into."

"He wasn't suspicious. Most likely has the two of us pegged as environmentally sensitive citizens, you know, worrying about crap on the sidewalk and all."

"He could come back from wherever he was drivin' to."

"Not likely, you dumb ass fart. This is a one-way street. He has to take a different way to come back. If he does come, he'll be somewhere else. He won't be seeing us. Now get your stupid butt over to that lot and pick out a nice big brick. I'll move the truck, so it sort of blocks the front of the window. We ought to have done that here. Just didn't think of it. Anybody driving by will think we're a couple workmen fixing something."

Moe turned up the collar of his light jacket and tugged at the zipper to make sure it was as tight against his neck as it would go. He blew into his hands that had begun to get stiff from the cold. He hadn't felt the night chill while he was involved with breaking into the bodega. With nothing to think of but the criticism his new partner heaped on him, he began to concentrate on the cold.

By the time Dawkins pulled his pickup to the curb in front of the jewelry store, Moe had already broken the glass on the door. He was savoring the warmth of the store and filling his pockets with jewelry. Dawkins joined him, stuffing jewelry into his pockets. When their pockets were full, they unzipped their jackets, unbuttoned their shirts and stuffed jewelry under their shirts. The two robbers soon had the place cleaned out of everything in the displays.

"I see a small safe in the backroom," Moe said. "Let's try to do something with that. I bet with the two of us hauling, we can lift it into the truck."

"Moe. That is the first good idea you've had all night. Let's do it."

Dawkins left Moe to wrestle with the safe while he turned the truck around and backed it up over the curb and stopped close to the broken door. They unlocked the door from the inside. With strength bred of necessity, they managed to slide the heavy safe to the truck, lift it onto the tailgate of the pickup, and shove it into the truck bed.

As he fastened the tailgate, Dawkins smiled broadly at Moe, who stood in the street nodding and otherwise looking satisfied. "Nice job, partner. Couldn't have done it without you. Stand there a minute while I get the truck away from this mess and back onto the street. We'll have to go somewhere we can open the safe. No telling what's in it. Most likely, it's the really expensive stuff they didn't want to leave in the display cabinets, things people left off for repairs too—really valuable stuff."

Moe was sure Dawkins planned to drive off and leave him standing there in the street. He hurried around to the passenger side. Before he reached the door handle, the truck bumped off the curb and moved onto the roadway. Dawkins steered his truck to the opposite curb where he parked and got out, leaving the motor running. He motioned Moe to join him.

Moe was relieved that his partner was not abandoning him. He had made a point to get Dawkins' cell number, but he didn't relish the thought of tracking the guy down later. "Shouldn't we be haulin' ass outta here?" Moe said.

"Right. In a minute. I think my tail light might be out. Don't want some cop pulling us over for a bad tail light, not with that safe in the back. Mind standing behind me and letting me know what you see. I'll work the turn signals. Might be stopped for that too."

Moe nodded and walked behind the truck, leaving about six feet between himself and the rear of the vehicle. He wasn't surprised when he saw the white backup lights or that Dawkins gunned the engine. He learned a long time ago to be really careful around white folks who made jokes at the expense of people like him. As the truck cab came abreast of where he had jumped to be out of the way, he shot Dawkins dead with the nine millimeter he carried in his coat pocket. He opened his mouth wide and shook his head to quiet the ringing in his ears. It didn't help. He resolved to find someone who could get him a suppressor. The gun was just too damned loud.

The truck continued down the street in reverse. Moe never even looked at the pickup receding toward the nearby cross street, but he hoped no one would collide with it at the intersection. It was after midnight. It was Christmas. He didn't want some innocent driver hurt. He jogged to the back of the vacant lot and through the narrow alleyway between the buildings on the next street.

Moe was careful not to drop any of the loot he had tucked into his clothing. He wasn't worried about the guy who'd stopped to talk. His car had Colorado plates, and he was clearly in no shape to be behind the wheel of a moving vehicle. Unlikely the stranger would ever come forward with information, even if he did chance to read about it in the newspaper or maybe hear about it in the remote event it made the TV.

Moe was nearly at his mama's house when he heard the sirens.

Mama Amehu would be happy that he had been able to pick up some really nice pieces. It wouldn't be the first time her son had brought home jewelry for her to fence. A black man without an education and burdened with more and more frequent seizures was not about to be hired by anyone. He rationalized his occasional thefts by convincing himself that he was doing it for his mother. As for Dawkins, well, that was no more than self-defense. What was he supposed to do, let the guy run him over with that big, ego-tripping truck of his?

He didn't mind the cold. It felt warm and fuzzy, comfortable. Moe looked forward to downing a beer before turning in for the night. He had to be up early on Christmas to sing in the church choir.

It's All In The Planning

Larry, my partner for the past six years, spent fifteen minutes describing to me all of the great gadgets in his new car. He proudly declared, "It even turns on from inside the house."

I immediately recognized that he had provided me the perfect way to get rid of him. In addition, I could collect on the insurance policy he had taken out years ago with me as the beneficiary. To show that I cared as much about him as he did for me, I took one out for a similar amount, $3,000,000, with Larry as the beneficiary.

In the past couple of years, Larry has developed a disturbing behavioral problem. He drinks vodka tonics for lunch. By evening he has a buzz that makes his eyes bloodshot and his speech fuzzy. That's when he grabs a brew and sets himself down to watch the 6:00 news. Now don't get the wrong idea. Larry is a swell guy. They say that about people in the old black and white movies they show on the TV really late at night.

That's what Larry is, a black and white movie. He has no range of emotion. He's never happy. He's never sad. He's always incredibly bitchy but never truly angry at anything. To him, everything is funny or completely screwed up. There is no in-between with him. That's most likely why he does so well drawing his comic strip—despite his drinking.

He has the personality of a crocodile. He'll sit as if he's asleep, but he sees everything, and he takes advantage of every situation. Like the crocodile, each evening, Larry gets hungry and starts looking for something to eat. He raids the refrigerator and makes these enormous sandwiches. I feel the need to warn guests that he might eat them if he gets hungry enough. They laugh at what they think in my double entendre and don't take me seriously. Should he actually turn cannibal some evening, I will have done my best to warn them. My conscience is clear.

I shout, "Larry, turn the television down, will you? I'm trying to write."

He shouts back even louder, "If I turn the TV any lower, I won't be able to hear."

"Larry!"

"Okay, okay, but you know my hearing's going."

See. That's what I'm talking about. He's glued to the television set, which is a flat screen, 4K ULTRA HD Smart LED HDR set with high fidelity wireless ear phones–which he never uses. It hides our new wall air conditioner duct. Larry is the most inconsiderate man I have ever known. We've been together for six long years. I don't even know what I ever saw in him in the first place. But who can explain love? It's like poop. It happens.

"There's nothing wrong with your hearing, Larry."

"Well, the surround sound doesn't work unless the gain is way up. Woofer doesn't woof right. And some of the more subtle overtones–you know, the higher frequencies–they're lost."

"Larry, you know that's a load of bull."

"Is not."

"Is too."

"Not."

I take a deep breath and count to ten.

"Larry, why don't you go and work on the strip."

"It's all done. Besides, I get a lot of my best ideas for Carrot from the TV."

"You told me that you get most of your ideas for your character's antics from your readers."

"Yeah. That also. But I got to keep up with all the latest political stuff going on. Most of my readers rely on me to tell them what their politicos are getting their pimply asses mixed up in."

"Well, go draw some pimply asses. I got to work too. If I don't crank out stories, I won't be able to keep up with my share of the expenses."

"Like you've contributed anything for the past two years."

"Larry, please!"

The TV goes silent. I get back to work.

As I was telling you, Larry has given me the perfect way to dispose of him and keep myself out of jail. I originally had thought to poison him. The problem with poison is that I know zip about chemistry. The only chemical I know to try is rat poison. I don't even know if an autopsy might find it. How much is needed to kill a person? I remember the rat that we tried to get rid of lived for days after he ate the poison we set out for him. I had to forget the rat poison.

Larry worked as a movie stunt man before he started drawing his comic strip. That eliminated the usual putting stuff on the stairs, so he trips and breaks his neck in the fall.

One sunny October afternoon, I tossed the football onto the roof during a game of catch. Larry knew I tossed the ball up there because I was tired and wanted to quit. He didn't get angry. He simply laughed and said, "You'll never make the pros with that chicken arm of yours."

I'm thinking that maybe he'd tumble off the roof trying to retrieve it. I watched in dismay as he cheerfully scampered up the tree that has a big limb overhanging the roof, Larry all the while laughing and thanking me for giving him an idea for his next comic strip. "Carrot will try this and fall on his big ass to show what happens to folks who make fun of Democrats."

Watching Larry climb down with the ball in one hand and the other hand confidently grabbing at tree limbs, I concluded that electricity might well be my best bet to get rid of him and collect on the insurance.

I went to the library and began to research stories about electrocutions. I didn't want to leave a trail of searches on my own computer. The government records everything you do on a computer. Electricity presented a fertile range of possibilities which I vowed to pursue.

Then he bought the new ride.

The car has a neat feature that lets you start it remotely. It works off a satellite, so theoretically, you can be anywhere in the world and call your car engine and tell it to start. My problem was to get Larry in a situation where I would remotely start the engine and, in turn, let the exhaust fumes asphyxiate him. I could be miles away. I might even be able to trick him into writing a suicide note. It would be the perfect crime. No more of Larry's bitchiness, and me a lot richer. All I needed to do was to work out the details.

To make the plan work, three items required my attention. The garage needed to be sealed, so that once in, he couldn't get out. In order that the cops won't bother to investigate, he needed to leave a suicide note. Thirdly, I had to take his cell phone to prevent him from calling for help.

The sealing of garage exits was a no-brainer. The garage has no windows except for a couple of small eyebrows up way too high for anyone to reach without a ladder. The door from the house is on an electronic key. So is the overhead door. A bit of electronic tinkering takes care of them both. The garage is built really high for my big SUV. Five feet four, Larry can't reach the emergency rope. To be sure, I'd take it off and hide it.

Our house is in the middle of a fourteen-acre property. There are no nosey neighbors nearby.

I can take his phone and hide it easily enough. He's all the time losing it for days on end. It turns up only when I eventually go looking for it to stop him bitching like a girl about losing it.

The suicide note was more of a challenge, but I had an idea of how to get him to write one.

My planned timing had me arriving at the house four or five hours after Larry was already negotiating with the angels for syndication of a comic strip about life in heaven—or hell. All I had to do was get home, plant the cell phone and the suicide note, and call the police.

Larry is a man of inflexible habits. He takes a bottle of Blue Lagoon beer from the second refrigerator in the garage at exactly 5:55 every afternoon. He sits in the all-purpose room, watching the 6:00 news and nursing the beer.

My plan was foolproof. How could it miss?"

I'd run a little home security business. I quit to become a writer. Making the doors inoperable by phoning into our home security system was easy. Even the manual override won't function.

My next issue was the suicide note. I cornered Larry in the kitchen moments after he had constructed a ham and cheese sandwich of enormous proportions as his late-night snack.

"Hey, Larry. Got a minute?"

"I don't know. You know I hate it when you wear that awful orange tee-shirt. Makes you look like a fruit."

"Very funny. Can you help me?"

"Not really. I'm kinda buzzy–busy–right now."

"Only take a minute."

He stared at the sandwich for a long time before he said, "Okay. Just for a minute."

I pulled out the chair and sat down across from him. He narrowed his eyes and looked askance at the writing pad and pencil I plopped on the table along with my proposed suicide note. I pushed the sandwich plate to one side and shoved my note and the pad and pencil over to him. A confused look crossed his face. He let loose a loud guffaw. "What is this? You were planning to end it all?"

"It's not for me. I'm trying to create a suicide note for one of my story characters, but it really doesn't work. I can't seem to make it real."

"Boy. That's for sure," says Larry. "Look. You started it with 'to whom it may concern.' That's no way to write a suicide note. They need to be addressed to some person; preferably some loved one."

"I told you it's no good."

"And why do you say, 'Goodbye cruel world. I need to end it all.' That sucks. I suppose somebody might write something like that, but it sure isn't up to your writing abilities."

"Please, Larry. Help me out on this."

"You're stuck, and you want me to write something for you."

"Yep. I've been trying to write a convincing suicide note for the past two days. The words aren't coming. Can you give it a spin?"

He eyed the sandwich again for a moment before he nodded and picked up the pen. "Guy or gal?"

"Guy."

"Why's he want to kill himself? His boyfriend give 'im the old red ass?"

"No. He's fed up with life. Nothing special. A little depressed and fed up with living."

"Who's the character's best friend?"

"He doesn't have any friends. He wants the world to know that he's been treated badly."

"Sweet. What happened to 'im to feel that way?"

"That's a little complicated," I replied. I hadn't expected so many questions from Larry. All I needed was a plain-vanilla suicide note in his handwriting.

Larry said, "I need to know. Folks always have a reason for suicide. They don't wake up one morning and tell themselves they want to end it all."

"Okay, Larry. Let's try a different approach. Pretend it's you writing the note. Short and to the point. How would you word it? I can adapt what you write to fit my character or change his situation to fit your note. The note is my hang up. Simply can't find the words."

He narrowed his eyes. A grin crept across his lips. He tossed the fake note that I had written in the trash can and began to write on the pad. When Larry finished, he pushed the pad across to me. "That ought to help you with the story," he said. "You don't have to worry about changin' anything. This is a very effective, one-size-fits-all, suicide note."

I glanced at what he had written. "That's great," I said. "Well done. Thanks, Larry. I knew you'd come through."

Part two of my plan was in place. Larry even signed the note. Perfect.

The next day, Tuesday, I flew to Philly to meet an agent, taking with me Larry's spare car key fob and the note. I left the cell phone because I didn't want anyone tracking it to Philadelphia.

My flight back was scheduled to land at 6:56. Completing my meeting with the agent by two o'clock, I arrived early at Philly International and chatted extensively with everybody I came across. I wanted to make sure they remembered me.

My jawing with the bartender caused me to miss the announcement that the plane was delayed. At the gate, I discovered that we weren't scheduled to board until 6:00. At 5:50, I sent a text to my home security system to set up the locks, so Larry couldn't get out of the garage once he went in for his nightly beer. At 5:56, I started the car's engine.

The instant I did that, I had a pang of deep remorse. Yet as quickly as I was remorseful, I was deliriously happy. Not only would I not have to put up with Larry's peccadilloes any longer, but I would be three big ones richer. And, being he left everything he had to me, I could run his old cartoons and make another bundle. I was on the cusp of committing the perfect murder, a murder that I knew people would marvel over, reading my diary after I'm dead and gone.

The flight was bumpy, one air pocket after another. My seatmate was a talkative guy who looked as if he'd slept in his suit. He had insisted on talking to me in the waiting area and insisted we sit together. His white shirt sported a big tomato stain. Said he sold computer systems. Said he had six kids, five girls—until finally a boy. I just knew that everything he said was a lie.

He introduced himself as Woody Williamson. I feigned interest and asked for his business card. He said he was fresh out of them but did give me his office phone number in Manhattan. You can never have too many alibi witnesses. During the flight, he was a nonstop talker. He seemed way too inquisitive for someone I just met. Figured he was a sales type. At least I had a good witness.

We circled White Plains for thirty minutes. The pilot came on and told us we were diverting to LaGuardia. I began to sweat. The diversion would add hours. What would Larry be doing? Might he be screaming and clawing at the walls? What if one of our friends decided to visit? I felt nauseous.

"You don't look good," Woody said and handed me a flask from his breast pocket. I gratefully took a couple of long swigs of some of the best whiskey I ever tasted. I didn't even ask how he got it through security.

"Good stuff," I said. He gestured, twirling his index finger. I took a couple of gulps before handing it back to him.

Woody smiled and said, "Glad I had it with me. Airline lost my suitcase yesterday. Been wearing the same clothes for two days."

"Yuck."

"I'll have a limo waiting for me at LaGuardia. How about I give you a ride to White Plains? You can pick up your car. We can maybe stop off for dinner somewhere. Not every day, I get to meet a professional writer."

I asked Woody how he could have a limousine waiting when he was scheduled to land in a different airport. He explained that his driver kept track of his flight and would hustle over to LaGuardia when the new destination airport was announced.

I saw Woody in a completely different light. Maybe some of his talk was true.

Though I repeatedly declined his offer, he kept insisting. Finally, I relented. What were a couple more hours? Larry was already singing with the choir of angels, so to speak. Poor guy. If only he'd been able to control his boozing, maybe I could have tolerated his incessant bitching. What a kvetch.

Woody and I stopped off at a little café near the airport. Woody liked to talk and drink. By around 11:00, I was in no shape to drive. Our conversation ranged over a variety of subjects, though he was most inquisitive about my writing—explaining to me that his real dream was to publish a full-length novel about his life.

Woody cheerfully paid the bill, left an overgenerous tip, and said, "Can't let you drive in your condition. You live sort of on the way to my place. It's not a problem. Never forgive myself if you got into an accident."

"I'm good, Woody. I'll wait a while before I start home."

"I insist."

"I appreciate your thoughtfulness, but it really doesn't help. I have to get my car home sometime. I'll sleep it off before I get on the road."

"Nonsense. One of my people will deliver your car round to your house tomorrow morning."

"Your people?"

"Actually, I own the company. Remember to give me the keys and the ticket."

Things were looking up for me. Larry would have been dead for, like, six hours by the time we got to my place. Cops wouldn't suspect me when they determined the time of death. Woody was not the slob salesman I had figured him to be. The respected owner of a technology company dressed in a new suit and a shirt without a tomato stain made a perfect alibi witness.

By the time we got to my place, it would be midnight, too late for him to be asking to meet Larry. I happily handed over my car keys and the parking lot ticket.

Woody was the inquisitive sort. He'd been in the army intelligence and knew how to pry out of a drunk all sorts of stuff I really ought not to be telling him. By the time we got to my house, I'd managed to tell him that Larry had been getting on my nerves the past couple of years. I wondered if he might remember what I said when the police questioned him.

We turned into our long driveway. Woody pointed at the house and said, "Your lights are on. It looks as if your partner is still up. I'd really like to meet him. You've told me about him and his comic strip."

"Probably left them on for me."

"I know it's late. I'd really like to tell him how much I like Carrot."

"Yeah. Carrot is everyone's favorite."

"You know, now that I think of it, Carrot looks a lot like you. I bet your partner Larry did that on purpose. Right? Right?" Woody punched me on the arm way too hard. "I have to meet him. I won't take 'no' for an answer."

Suddenly the porch lights went out. I froze. The hair on my head felt like it was standing straight up in a Goth or maybe a Steam Punk hairdo. I knew it wasn't, but it felt that way. The lights began to blink on and off. My stomach felt like it was down in my shoes.

Woody shouted. "It's code. The lights are blinking an SOS. It's erratic, but you can make out the dot, dot, dot, dash, dash, more dots. Your friend's in trouble."

Woody was out of the car and bounding up our front steps before I managed to slide across the seat and follow him. He was fumbling with the lock when I reached him. For a moment, I wondered how he got my key chain and then remembered giving it to him along with my parking stub. I hadn't even separated the car fob from the house key.

"Let me do it," I said and elbowed him off to the side. My heart was pounding. My brain was confused. I felt light headed, ready to faint. I opened the front door and made a show of running through the rooms shouting, "Larry, Larry, where are you? Where are you?" Since I thought him long dead, I really didn't expect him to reply. I made the show anyhow.

It took me a while to realize that Larry was answering me, hollering, "In the garage. I'm in the garage."

I ran to the garage door and flung it open, managing to hit Larry so hard that it knocked him to the floor where fortunately we had a thick rug that I had put there to catch oil drips from my car. Unlike Larry, who could happily live in squalor, I hated to see oil drips on the garage floor. I prided myself on the fact that the garage held nothing but the two vehicles. No tools, no garden stuff, no junk, just the rug.

Woody was right behind me, pushing me. I nearly joined Larry on the floor. I turned and glared at him. He backed off. The door to the main electrical panel was open. Obviously, Larry had been using it to signal.

Larry groaned and raised himself to his elbows. A wide grin spread across his face. He giggled and said, "You nevers gonna dream wha' happen' ta me."

About that time, I noticed the pile of empty beer cans in the corner. There must have been at least twelve. Larry was very, very inebriated. The smell of urine didn't surprise me.

I needed to continue the charade. "Larry. Why are you in the garage trying to make the Guinness book of records for most beers consumed in an evening?"

Larry belched, drew a deep breath, and responded. "Well. It wuzzzz like this. The car turned on when I came out to get my beeer. Somethin's wrong with the doooors. I couldn't get back in the house. Been stuck here since six. Goood thing I had the fridge full. Had a real fright but then remembered the motor turns off in a couple minutes if nobody opens the car door."

"Everyone knows that," I said, attempting to throw the bloodhounds off my scent."

Larry looked up at me with wide eyes. "What the hell happened to the garage door? Why zit it locked?"

Listening to Larry, I realized that on my second try, I would need to plan better. How could I have missed the obvious safety feature that automatically turned off the engine if nobody got into the car? I tried the knob on the garage side of the door. The lock was still on. Fortunately, Woody had stayed in the doorway and kept it open. Next time I tried to kill somebody, I would need to keep a clear head and not go out drinking.

Crocodilian Larry seemed oblivious to my attempt on his life. Yet I could not believe he hadn't figured it out. He doesn't miss much. That's why his comic strip is so popular. I wonder, is he waiting for his chance? I'd need to work fast. Maybe go to plan B. Wait a minute. I had no plan B. Damn.

We helped Larry to his feet. He wobbled a moment and then regained his footing. Larry smiled as if he had just planted a flag on the top of Mount Everest. We helped him up the three steps to the house and steered him to a chair in the all-purpose room.

Woody held out a hand to Larry and said, "I'm Woody Williamson. I'm a real fan of your comic strip. I like the Carrot character. You make him out to be a real bastard." He glanced over at me.

Larry ignored the comment and asked Woody to join him in a tall gin and tonic. I excused myself and went to bed, leaving an animated Woody and a regenerated Larry chatting cheerfully as if it wasn't nearly 1:00 in the morning.

I woke around nine, put on my robe and slippers, and padded down to the kitchen to brew some coffee. Larry was in the guest bedroom sleeping off the previous night's carousing.

I expected to find my briefcase and my kit bag by the front door. When I didn't find them after a quick check of the closets, I looked out the window to see if the limo was still there. It was gone.

Thinking my things were probably in the garage, I went to check there. I saw that my belongings were not in the garage. I was annoyed but not particularly concerned. They would turn up when Woody's people brought my car around. My wallet and cell phone and Larry's fake suicide note were all in the briefcase.

Suddenly I found myself wondering if Woody was what he claimed to be. I had a growing sense of uneasiness about him, nothing I could pin down, just something not genuine about him. And how did he and Larry suddenly become such good buddies?

Seeing that I had closed the door behind me and remembering that the door from the garage to the house was still locked, I went over to the emergency rope to open the overhead door. The rope was gone. I tried to recall if I had taken it off the latch that was way too high for me to reach without a ladder. Due to my fastidious nature, no ladder or anything else was in the garage, except the rug and Larry's car.

Resigning to being trapped until Larry freed me, I opened a cold beer and sat on the step to the house.

The car's engine started. I figured that Larry was up and heading out to meet his cronies at the local fast food joint. In a minute, he would come through the door. I relaxed–until I spotted on the car's dashboard the fake suicide note I had written to trick Larry into writing one of his own. I imagined my dead face on the garage rug, my lifeless eyes looking skyward. I was in a panic. I decided to break into the car and use it as a battering ram to knock out the overhead door. Larry would have thought of that but would have died before he put a scratch on his new ride.

The car's engine stopped. I relaxed.

The engine started again. I yelled. I banged on the door to the house. I thought to kick out one of the car windows, but how could I manage that? If I tried that, I would simply fall down. The car was still locked. I decided to break the car window with my elbow like they do in the movies. The glass held. My arm broke. The pain was excruciating. I was trapped. The engine stopped. I relaxed.

The engine started a third time.

Seasons Of Life

~—~

My seasons I have woven
Into a cloak of days:
Green leaves of spring,
Warm summer taupe,
Red leaves of fall
Cool winter teal.
I cannot fashion now another
To drape upon your form
For I in winter's
Icy grip am held.
Seasons new, I will not weave.
Still, the cold is near upon us.
You have no coat to wear
To stand away October winds
That chill in time your bones.
Take this colorful cloak
To put about you.
On it, I will sew
For the days we share
A clasp of pure gold,
So when winter comes
This cloak will stay about us
And we will both be warm.

The Offer

The offer that Waldo Wallbender spied in the glossy color insert of his Sunday newspaper seemed too good to be true. "Do only five simple good deeds and receive a reward of $10,000. Phone now to be sure and not lose out. A limited number of slots are still available in our good-deed program, but they are going fast." A phone number was included for those who might want more information.

Waldo typically spent his days creating and installing computer software for the telephone company. His evenings were devoted to hacking into all sorts of networks. He considered it a hobby and a way to hone his skills for his day job. He figured that it gave him some insight into the outcomes he bet on with his favorite bookie though he usually lost and had run up a considerable debt.

I can easily do five good deeds, he mused. With that kind of money, I can pay what I owe my bookie and have cash left over to keep playing the ponies.

He decided to telephone for more information. A recorded male voice thanked him for calling and told him that someone would call back later in the day. About fifteen minutes later, the phone rang. A woman's voice said in a perky lilt. "Congratulations on your initiative. By calling this number, you have shown yourself to be a person of amazing prescience."

Waldo was immediately enthralled by the voice, husky, yet at the same time silky. "What is your name, Sir?"

"Waldo, Waldo Wallbender."

Well, Mister Wallbender, you are indeed a lucky man. You have called just in time. We have only one spot unfilled. Should you agree to the terms, you will be in the program. How does that sound?"

"Sounds pretty good to me. What program exactly will I be in?"

The voice laughed. "And you have a keen sense of humor, Mister Wallbender. That is very good. You will do well. With your obvious high intelligence and that crazy sense of the absurd, you may even become eligible for our 'double points' drawing."

"I sure hope so," Waldo replied, his skepticism evaporating in a sense of well-being. The voice had quickly recognized him to have prescience. Though he had no idea what the word meant, he knew by the tone of the voice that it was a good thing to have.

"Count you in then?"

"Sure."

"Outstanding! Your first assignment, to be completed before midnight next Friday, is to help an elderly person get his or her groceries from the store checkout to their car. Simply obtain a short note to that effect from the person you help, copy the note to your computer, and attach the copy to an email that you will send to helpingpeoplesweepstakes at makelifeseasy.com.

"Once you have shown your good faith by finishing the first assignment, we will mail you a contract. You need to write in your full name and current address, sign, and mail the completed document back to us. Be sure to also include your check made out to us in the amount of one thousand dollars. That is what we call earnest money. You get it back along with your prize money when you successfully complete the program. Upon receipt of the signed contract, you will be fully enrolled. If you wish to continue, you will telephone me for your next assignment."

"I can do that."

"Excellent."

"By the way," Waldo asked, "what's your name?"

"My name is Linda. That means beautiful. When you call me, the answering machine will first ask you for your case number, which is 53644433. The 536 is the prefix for all the people working on this project. The number 444 is me. You can call me 444 if you wish. Or you can call me, Linda. Write it down: 53644433."

"OK. Linda, it is. Has anyone ever told you that you have a sexy voice?"

"Linda giggled. No one until now. May I call you, Waldo?"

"Of course, beautiful."

"Waldo, there is one other very important aspect of the sweepstakes we haven't discussed."

Waldo let out a long sigh. "Here's the catch. I knew it."

Linda said quickly, "No. Not a catch. Nothing like that. However, should you accept any assignment and then fail to complete it in the time allotted, you will lose the earnest money deposit."

"That's a bummer."

"It's not all that bad, Waldo. You can quit at any time."

"If I quit, will I get back my grand?

"Unless you fail an assignment that you may have already accepted."

"That doesn't seem fair."

"I am surprised to hear you say that, Waldo. Here I'm thinking that you're a betting man. You know, a real sporting guy. Anyhow, to make the game legal, there needs to be some significant risk. Otherwise, it is a lottery, and the State will shut us down. You understand"

"Maybe. Will I know the assignment in advance?"

"Of course. Always. You may reject any assignment when I describe it to you. However, if you decline any assignment, you are out of the game and receive nothing for your troubles. We, of course, must retain a portion, one percent, of the deposit to cover our expenses.

"Sounds fair to me. Anything else I need to know?" Waldo asked.

"Not right now. Do you have any questions before I ring off?"

"I do. Who's behind this? It seems to me that someone is terribly generous."

"Someone is. I work for a foundation set up by a rich billionaire. He wishes to remain anonymous. However, he is intensely interested in what you might refer to as pay it forward. In other words, he believes that if he can get a few people doing good deeds, the idea will catch on. First thing you know, everyone will be helping everyone else."

"That is truly a generous person, Linda. One more question."

"Anything for you, Waldo."

"Will it really be you that I speak to during the contest, or are all the operators named Linda 444?"

"Please remember, Waldo, this is an important social program and not a contest. And, yes, I will always be your contact. The number 444 is my number and mine alone. Has been for over three years. Feel free to telephone me at this number if you have something about the program on your mind—any clarification, any question, anything. If you forget the case number, you know my extension, simply dial extension 444.

Waldo held his phone to his ear until he was certain the line was dead. He even asked a couple of times if Linda were still on there before he stuffed his phone in his pocket and went about his chores. All Waldo wanted to think about was someday meeting Linda. He imagined her to be a shapely young blonde with a beautiful face.

On Monday, an eager Waldo hurried to his local grocery store right after he left work. He waited for an elderly lady to emerge with a cart full of groceries. No people he considered elderly came out of the store for the first half-hour. Waldo decided that he needed to broaden his concept of the elderly and immediately chose a very thin fiftyish lady with a slight limp.

He stepped in front of the cart, tipped his cap, and said, "Good evening, madam. I would like to help you with your groceries."

The lady scowled at him. She waved her arm as if to brush him aside and said, "Get out of my way, you pervert, or I'll call the cops."

Waldo hesitated a moment, contemplating the terrible things he might do to punish her for her insolence, but he stepped aside and watched the woman push the cart to a nearby car. She popped the trunk lid and hauled the grocery bags one at a time into the trunk, glancing in his direction after loading each bag.

Waldo collected himself and chose as his second victim, a white-haired grandmotherly type who was breathing hard and using the grocery cart for support.

"Good morning, miss. My name is Waldo, parking lot security. We had a purse snatching last week. A lady was knocked down and suffered severe injuries. I will walk along with you and help you push, and when we get to your vehicle, I will even help you load your groceries."

"Why, thank you, sir. I hadn't heard about that. But a lady can't be too careful. You never know about people these days, do you?"

Waldo shook his head. "For sure."

The two of them walked slowly to her car, where Waldo unloaded the groceries according to her instructions. When that was finished, he shoved a pad and pen at her and asked her to write a short note that he had been courteous and helped her with her groceries. "It's part of a survey they're doing," he said.

"I understand completely, young man," she replied. She smiled a grandmotherly smile and wrote the note.

That evening Waldo dutifully sent a copy of the note off in an email to helping people. In response, he received an email reciting his case number and reminding him to phone the following week if he wished to remain in the program.

On Tuesday, Walter dialed the helping people number and punched in his assigned case code.

"Well, hello there, Waldo, Darling. I see that you have completed your first good deed. I knew the first time I heard your voice that you were a man of high caliber."

Walter felt his face flush and was glad that Linda could not see his embarrassment. "I guess I did do pretty good, didn't I?"

"You certainly did. Just because I like you so much, Waldo, I am going to give you an easy second assignment."

"You mean you can decide what jobs I get?"

"They are not jobs, darling. They are assignments that encourage you to do good deeds. But, Yes. I have a great deal of leeway in the selection of assignments."

Waldo felt a thrill. "What's my next assignment?"

"I have picked a very easy one for you. For your second assignment, all you need to do is assist a blind person to cross a road and obtain from that person the usual note of confirmation."

"I'll do it. I accept." Waldo waited for a response. After a few moments, he decided that he had lost the connection. As he was looking up the helping people number, the phone rang. It was Linda.

"I am sorry, Waldo. We must have lost the connection. Let me say I am happy you have accepted the assignment. That is just wonderful. Simply respond by next Friday, midnight."

"That's not this coming Friday, but the following Friday."

"Correct. Since you have acted quickly to complete your first assignment, you have nearly two weeks to finish this second assignment. And

Waldo, honey."

"Yes?"

"Good luck."

Waldo noticed that the number showing on his caller ID was different when Linda phoned him back. It was not the helping people number. In fact, there was no number at all. It said "restricted" on his phone. Waldo thought the number might be Lind's home phone. At work, he did some checking. Using software he had developed, he found the restricted number. Thinking he might ask Linda for a date, he entered the number on his speed dial.

To Waldo, the second assignment seemed like a no brainer, and he quickly set about trying to formulate a plan. On Friday morning, Waldo received in the mail the contract from helping people. He signed it and returned it that afternoon with his check for one thousand dollars.

By the following Monday morning, Waldo had decided on a course of action. He rose early and stationed himself at the busy corner in front of the building where the blind people came to make brooms. The weather was warm. Waldo would have worn short pants but decided shorts would not give him the professional look he wanted to display. One person stepped off the bus, a man wearing dark glasses and carrying a tin cup. He brandished a red and white cane. Waldo sprang into action.

"Good morning, sir?" Waldo said in his most gracious tone.

The man looked directly at Waldo and scowled. "What you want, buddy?"

"I want to help you across the road."

"I ain't goin' across the road. This right here is my corner, so piss off."

"You're not blind, are you?" Waldo said.

"Shut up, fool. Somebody might hear you."

"Okay. I'm looking for a blind man, but you'll have to do. Look. Let me take you by the arm and walk you across the street. After that, I'm out of here, and I don't give a damn what you do. You can turn around and come right back here if you want. But wait till I leave before you do that."

The man smacked Waldo on the leg with his red and white cane. "Get the hell off my corner. I ain't gonna tell you again."

Waldo pulled out a wad of bills from his hip pocket. He stuffed two ones into the cup. "Now, may I help you across the street?"

"Cheapskate," the man said.

Waldo peeled off a five and stuffed it into the cup. "Now, can I help you cross?"

The man smiled and said, "I'll need to consult with Andrew Jackson afore I decide."

Waldo shoved a twenty into the cup and took the man by the arm. Negotiating the crossing without incident, Waldo said, "I need you to write a short note saying that you are blind and that I helped you across the street. You need to include your name. My name is Waldo."

"That'll cost you another Jackson, Waldo."

Waldo scowled at the fake blind man. "How about a Hamilton for writing the note, and I don't get the cops onto your little street performance?"

The man nodded. Waldo handed him the pad and pen. The man jotted down a note stating that he was blind and that Waldo had helped him cross the street. He handed the pad back to Waldo, who handed him another ten, thanked him, and strode off. Waldo felt elated. Thirty-seven bucks to collect ten grand. That's a pretty good investment, old boy; you are on a roll.

On Tuesday, Waldo sent off his email with a copy of the note confirming the completion of his second assignment. On Wednesday, Waldo called the helping people number. When he punched in his case number, a man's voice answered. "Where's Linda," he asked.

"She called in sick. Is this Waldo?"

"Yes."

"I have a message here for you from Linda. She says that your assignment for next week is to go down to the homeless shelter and serve soup to the homeless people. Do you accept the assignment?"

"Yes. I accept. Tell Linda that I hope she makes a complete recovery."

"I will tell her. One question Waldo."

"What?"

"That man you helped cross the street. Was he really blind?"

"He had a cane and dark glasses and got off the bus in front of the blind-broom factory."

"If you run into him again, please congratulate him on his excellent penmanship."

Waldo's day at the soup kitchen passed without incident. Waldo enjoyed his third assignment better than the first two because the people running the shelter were all grateful for his assistance, as were the homeless people he served. He silently offered a prayer of thanks for such an easy assignment and added a request that Linda have a speedy recovery.

After his time at the homeless shelter, Waldo emailed a copy of the note confirming that he had helped at the soup kitchen.

Waldo found himself thinking more and more about Linda. But because he was busy at work, he didn't find time to phone Linda until the following Monday. He punched in his case number. "Linda?" he said when he heard a clicking sound.

"Yes, it is me, Waldo. I missed you last week."

"I missed you too."

"That is sweet of you, dear."

"How are you feeling? All over your cold or whatever kept you out?"

"Why yes, darling, and thank you for your concern."

"What have you in store for me this week? I bet it's a real challenge. I only got two more assignments."

"Bet that you can already smell the green ink on those bills you will get when you cash your big check. Am I right, honey?"

Waldo could just see in his mind's eye, Linda winking at him. To him, she obviously was giving him easy assignments because she had fallen in love with him. That had never happened to Waldo, even in person much less over a phone. "I really would like to meet you, Linda," he said rather tentatively and added, "but that's never going to happen, is it?"

"Waldo, my dear one, this is truly your lucky day. I see from your address that you live right near the city. In fact, you live less than five miles from my house."

"I didn't know. That's good. Right?"

"Of course, my darling. It means that we can finally meet. I have a neighbor on a nearby street that needs his grass mowed. He was in a car accident a couple of weeks ago and can't get around well enough to push his mower. His grass is really tall. Some of the other neighbors are complaining. If it gets much higher, the city will surely cite the poor man. You know how those bureaucrats can be."

"I'll mow it for him."

"Of course you will, dear one. See how getting in the habit of doing good deeds makes you want to help people? Let us make this your next good deed. Good deed number four."

"I accept. I accept. How difficult can it be?"

"I don't wish to mislead you, my darling. This neighbor can be a real pain at times. In fact, he is not really a very nice man. He is big and tough and very angry. He is not going to want any help from you."

"That's OK. I'll figure something out. I've dealt with folks that were not very nice. I want to do it."

"The man has been arrested for assault at least six times, spent time in prison, and he carries a gun."

"Wait a darn minute. Are you trying to talk me out of the program, so I don't get the prize?"

"Why dearest. I am hurt by that. And after all, we've meant to each other, are you accusing me of wanting you to fail? Do you know that I get extra bonus points every time you successfully complete an assignment?"

The words made Waldo feel bad. He wanted to apologize, so he said, "I didn't know that. I'm sorry, Linda. I wasn't thinking. So many people are scam artists these days. A guy gets to be cynical."

"Of course, Wally. May I call you Wally? Waldo seems so, so unromantic, so formal."

"I'd like that. Nobody ever called me Wally. It'll be our special thing."

"Wally and Linda's special thing. I like that."

"I want to do the mowing when you're around. You know, so we can meet."

"Of course, my dearest. I want that too. You can't imagine."

"How about Wednesday? Around five. It's still light. That good for you?"

"Perfect. Bring your mower. His may not work or may need gas or something like that. I will email you the address."

"OK. Six then. On Wednesday."

"Until then, darling." Wally thought he heard Linda making a kissing sound. The goosebumps rose on his arms again.

A half-hour later, Linda emailed him the address, 76 Liberty Street, in Saint Pete. He didn't bother to check out the location on a map, choosing to let his GPS do the work of finding the place on Wednesday.

Waldo left work early on Wednesday and headed to the address Linda had given him, his lawnmower in the back of his battered pickup. He turned down Liberty Street. It was a short street ending in a cul-de-sac. On each side of the street were two abandoned houses, and at the end stood a single dilapidated house surrounded by a ten-foot-high chain-link fence topped with razor wire–number 76. The fence was festooned with no trespassing signs and violation notices from the city health department and the code enforcement department. One sign promised that trespassers were to be shot on sight.

High grass and weeds filled the front yard strewn with old cars and miscellaneous junk. Two large pit bulls roamed the perimeter barking at him each time he approached the fence.

Linda was nowhere in sight. Waldo wasn't worried. He figured she would show before he was finished with the fourth task.

From his truck bed, Waldo took a pair of bolt cutters, which he used to cut the lock on the front gate. He returned the bolt cutters and removed a shotgun from behind the front seat. He loaded five shells and racked the slide. He swung open the gate and stepped inside the cluttered front yard of number 76 Liberty Street.

The two barking dogs that ran toward him, he shot dead. He waited for someone else to appear. Walter waited a full five minutes before he slung the gun over his shoulder and unloaded the mower. He cut what grass he could find and loaded the mower back in his truck. Though Waldo waited for nearly an hour, no woman appeared.

Waldo fished his cell phone out of his pocket and dialed the helping people number. When prompted, he punched in his case number. A recorded voice came on the line. It sounded like the recorded voice he heard when he first inquired about the contest.

"Please note that our records indicate you have undertaken an assignment that you were not able to complete. We regret to inform you that your $1000 earnest money payment has been forfeited as per the contract. Have a pleasant day."

An unhappy Waldo tapped an alphanumeric code into his phone. A street address and home phone number appeared, along with the number he had entered for Linda. He tapped the green phone icon at the bottom of the screen and put the phone to his ear.

"Hello, Linda. This is Waldo."

A surprised Linda said, "Waldo? How did you get this number?"

"I want my money back."

"Screw you," she responded angrily. Don't you ever phone me again."

"But Linda, I thought we had something, you know, you and me."

"Screw you."

Waldo again asked for his money. When he realized he was speaking into a dead line, he got back in his truck and entered the street address for Linda into his GPS. He reloaded the shotgun and headed for the address on the GPS screen.

Paul

My friend Paul is what you might call, socially intrusive—never wants to stay in his own lane. Has to jump right into the middle of things. I say to him, "Just walk away." But he never does. His response is always a big, "YOLO."

Last Friday, Paul and I sat at the bar in Fitzgerald's Pub nursing beers and lookin' over the crowd. I like Fitzgerald's because it has a horseshoe bar. Rather than havin' to sit and stare at myself in a mirror, I can sit on the end and look at the people on either side. That night the place was really crowded, with people two and three deep. Folks not tweeting or texting were elbowing each other and hollerin' for the bartenders' attention. The noise made it hard to carry on a conversation.

Just before finishin' off his third pint of beer, Paul declared, "See that damsel, the one sitting next to the tall guy with the long hair?"

"What about her?"

"That girl needs somebody to speak up for her."

"Why?" I asked.

"Because the fool she is with is polluting my favorite watering hole on this vast, arid plane."

"This what?"

"You know what I mean, Jimmie. It's a literary reference."

"I don't know what you mean, Paul. You're just bein' your pretentious self again."

"Pretentious. Now that is a good word. Up yours is a good word too."

I could see that Paul was starting to get really agitated about what he thought he saw. Paul is the opposite of most people. The only time Paul is not angry is when he's completely cashed. Getting him that way takes a truly awesome amount of alcohol. I think that maybe his time in the army helped him get a little too friendly with a lot of different brews.

Paul only weighs in at about 160 soaking wet. He wears metal-rimmed spectacles and at 35 still has a jet black mane that he parts in the middle. He usually wears tan chinos with a white dress shirt. And Paul uses a plastic pocket protector with at least three pens lined up in it. All very retro. Classic modern. Yes. That's what Paul is—classic modern.

He never starts a fight. I mean, he never throws the first punch. He just drives asshole types crazy until they eventually take a swing at him. Paul's problem is that he wants to change the world one incident at a time. All he has to show for his troubles are mended fractures and arthritis in his hands.

Paul turned to me and said, "Go find Harry and tell him to turn to some better music."

"Find him yourself. I like this stuff."

Paul is into country and bluegrass. He likes Rascal Flatts and Kenny Chesney. He loves Reba. I prefer Lady Gaga and Lil Wayne—the good stuff. I suppose that Paul and I are not really much alike, but somehow we seem to have something like I imagine brothers might have. Not really sure about that since I don't have a brother.

He's thirteen years older than me. Could be my older brother—sort of. We met in a lit class that was as far from underwater basket weaving as you can get. And the teacher was a bear. Assignments were death traps. Paul saved my grade point average by helpin' me understand what the guy wanted in an essay.

Paul likes attention. One evening a couple of weeks ago, after downing the equivalent of a dozen bottles of beer, he walked all the way home from Fitzgerald's on his hands. It's only about a quarter-mile from the dorm, but it still is so totally awesome—the stuff of legends. He had somebody filming it for YouTube all the way. For a few days it was trending on twitter. Showoff, Paul.

Paul pointed. "That guy next to her is really angry. Looks like he's mad at her."

"A lover's quarrel."

"He keeps grabbing her arm."

"Maybe somebody needs to give that guy a lesson on how to treat women. But it doesn't have to be you. Finish your beer. Wait and see what happens. In the meantime, finish up what you have in front of you."

"I will have to give that waffle-head some lessons in respect," Paul said. "You only live once."

I knew that if I waited long enough, he'd be barely able to stand. All I had to do was keep him focused on his beer and not on the dark skinned girl sitting across the bar from us.

"Paul. Let's try some of that heavy stuff, the lager I think they call it."

"Why not? The darker, the better." He gazed across the bar at the girl, still arguing with what I assumed was her bully of a boyfriend. "She's beautiful," Paul said. "No dairy queen there. That cluster she's with doesn't even see it. Hey, if she gives you any attention at all, like, you know, like winks at you or something, ask her to come up to your room and look at your etchings."

"Etchings? You know I don't have any etchings."

"It is only an expression, a euphemism for sex. You know euphemisms. We talked about them in class."

Paul half stood and mimicked having sex, wildly rocking his pelvis. "Hey, I can just picture you having sex with her."

"Stop that, damn it! Everyone's lookin'. Anyhow, that's a disgusting visual."

Paul stopped his gyrations and said, "Hey, my folks would like for you to come home with me at the break."

"Can't."

"Come on. Don't be a barracks rat. You cannot spend the whole vacation sitting around like moss on a log."

"Won't. Got to fly to Ireland with my folks. One of the rich uncles left us property. My father wants to check it out. The only time he can get away from work for a week is right around Christmas."

"Forget it then. Hey, I need one of those dark lagers."

I swigged the last of my pint and ordered two lagers. I don't know enough about beer to order a particular brand. Neither does Paul. You totally don't need to know the history of what you're drinkin' to enjoy it.

Paul's not Greek material–too old–but he does like his foam parties. Gets invited to a lot of the fraternity bashes. I think he's an alcoholic, but I seldom raise that topic with him because he shuts down and won't talk about it—except to tell me I have no idea what an alcoholic really is. Maybe he's right. Who knows?

Took Paul about half a minute to drain the glass and set it down hard on the bar. I have no idea how he can hold that much beer.

Paul tilted his head back and closed his eyes for a moment. Then he looked me square in the face and said, "At's a mellow brew, my good man. Believe I'll have another 'fore I go over and whack the crap out of that bully. Man, is that girl totally awesome or what? I could go for her."

"Yeah. Right. You know, Paul, sometimes you are such a crock of shit that figurin' you out is hopeless. Anyhow, the guy is way bigger than you. And he seems to have a friend with him. In fact, I think the guy next to him is encouraging him."

Paul squinted and craned his neck as if to see better in the dim light.

"You talking 'bout the squirt in the Hawaii shirt."

"That guy. Yes. Take a good look at him. He may be short, but he obviously works out. Looks like a short version of Arnold Schwarzenegger in his Terminator days."

"Looks to me more like Arnie Bruschetta from school."

"Why? The man boobs?"

"Screw you, Jimmie."

I signaled the bartender to pour another lager for Paul.

"I can take them both," Paul said.

"You're not a fighter. You're a lover. Just leave it alone."

"Look at her."

"You can't hear what they're sayin', so you got no idea what the argument is all about. Besides, they're only talkin'."

Paul has no clue how to speak nicely to people he sees as wrongdoers. If he does eventually confront the guy with the dark skinned girl, he won't talk politely.

I know that from experience. Paul will probably ignore the guy and say to the girl, "If you want to dump this gumball, come on over to meet my friend, Jimmie." Then he'll point to me, and the bully and his little friend will look daggers at me—even though I've done absolutely nothing.

Just lookin' at Paul, you can see that he's not athletic. But he does have brass cojones.

Unlike Paul, I look as if I can handle myself in a fight. Being six-four and weighin' in soaking wet at around 260 creates a certain Hulk Hogan impression with people who don't know my sweeter side. My tats do nothing to change that impression. The two guys will excuse Paul because he's such a twerp. They'll decide I'm the worthier opponent. And that's alright because I do feel protective of Paul. He's already fought enough battles. I can fight a few for him. And so it goes.

Paul took a sip of his fourth beer of the night. He showed few signs of insobriety when he slid easily off his stool and headed for the men's room with only a hint of wobble. I watched the folks across the bar still arguing. I probably ought to have gone with Paul, but I knew someone would grab our stools if I did, so I sat and sipped my beer and studied the swirls in the top of the bar where somebody had started to scratch initials.

While Paul was taking a piss, I looked around at all the different people. A kid that looked to me to be underage was arguin' loudly with a bartender about his ID. The bartender thought it was a fake. The kid didn't look more than sixteen. An old guy with a long white beard was slammin' down shots that the bartender had set in a row in front of him. He has to be running away from something.

When the girl swam back into my consciousness, she was still there nursing some kind of girly blue drink in a martini glass. The diminutive Terminator type was hunched over the bar sippin' a brew. The guy with the long hair that Paul had been workin' himself up to take on was nowhere to be seen.

I waited and waited. Paul didn't show. The girl continued to sip her blue martini. I felt sorry for her but not enough sorry that I felt like givin' up our stools to go over and comfort her. After about fifteen minutes, I was sure Paul had encountered the bully and that the two of them had confronted each other and taken the fight outside.

I was about ready to go lookin' for Paul when he came toward me. The long-haired character was with him. They walked toward me side by side—difficult to do in a crowded barroom. As they made their way easily through the crowd, neither showed any evidence that they'd fought. In fact, Paul was grinning.

"Jimmie, I want you to meet my new friend, Greg, from Chicago."

Greg held out his hand. I glanced at Paul. His smile could've given Lewis Carroll ideas. He gave me a quick nod. I offered Greg my hand.

As we shook hands, he said, "Hi. How yuz doin'?"

Paul said, "Jimmie. You know the girl you were talking about. Well, she is Greg's sister. She is really angry because he came out. Afraid the guys at work will give him a hard time. He'll be working on the docks. You know how things are on the docks."

Not knowin' how things are on the docks, yet knowing exactly what Paul was talkin' about, all I could do was stand there with a blank look. He would have had the same comment wherever the guy worked.

Paul waited a moment for me to comment before he continued. "Greg is new around here. Just moved to town. Staying with his sister until he can get settled."

Paul tossed a twenty on the bar. "Him and me are gonna go over to Manny's. I wanna introduce him around. Can you take his sister home?"

"You mean, "He and I?"

Paul tilted his head, narrowed his eyes. He shrugged, but he didn't reply to my taunt.

"Sure," I said. "And what about the other guy?"

"Forget him," Paul said. He winked. "Or not."

"Screw you," I said.

One thing more, Jimmie."

"What?"

"Greg's sister's name is Kiesha. He just texted her that you'll be driving her home. Greg doesn't know the guy with the Hawaiian shirt that she's been talking to, but the guy thinks she's going home with him. No worry. You can take him."

"He looks like the Terminator–short version."

"She's waving at you. Smile."

Leaving The Hills

So long my hills, my home.
I am sad to see you grayed
By clouds so quickly moving,
Clouds so long delayed.

The sky, magnesium blue,
Held the sun from falling down
But not from baking land
Or turning grasses brown

When winter wrapped the hills in snow,
Cold winds swept me down the path
To crackling wood,
A dry martini and
A steaming bath.

Bones are getting brittle now.
Eyes are not so keen and sharp.
The hills are not so friendly.
Finally, it is time to part.

As I turn so not to weep,
Lightning rips the fabric
Of the gloom.

Left to right a jagged tear
Framing hills for those like me
Who see them from so far away.
My hills echo their last goodbye
When thunder rolls
Across the void.
I voice in sadness my own
"So long, my friends, so long."

Heart Of Gold

I found the young woman huddled behind the band shell in Craig Park. She wore a long tan raincoat and a floppy hat that she had pulled down over her ears. Her long blond hair poked out from under the hat to hang in wet clumps. "What happened, Miss?" I asked.

She looked up. "Get away from me," she replied in a low, husky voice which would have sounded sultry under different circumstances.

"I won't hurt you, Miss. My name is Harry Alderman. I work for the City. I was out and about, taking one last look for anything that might become a hazard, if the hurricane hits."

"Go away," she said

When I left work, the TV was predicting that the worst winds would hit Tarpon Springs sometime near dawn. Gusts already exceeded 60 miles per hour, bending palm trees, and skating trash cans and debris across lawns. It was only a matter of time before downed power lines cut off electric service.

She pushed at me. "I am okay. Leave me alone."

"You can't stay here. We need to get you out of the weather. It's going to get a lot worse. Might be the most destructive hurricane we've ever had, even worse than the storm of '21 that turned buildings on the barrier islands into match sticks.

"Don't you try anything," she said.

"I won't. What's your name?"

She stood slowly, smoothing her coat as she rose. "My name is Penny, Penny Wilst. I came to Tarpon Springs to bury my mother and see to her property. Her home is near the high school, on the water."

"I know the house. I'll drive you."

Penny Wilst nodded, "Alright," she said.

I headed for my car with head down, shoulders bent against the wind and the slashing rain. She followed a half step behind.

In the car, I again asked what happened. She stared at my face, seeming to study my every feature.

"I was having dinner in the restaurant at the end of the sponge docks. A strange-looking man sat down at my table."

"Strange? How so?"

"He was old, like, maybe in his fifties. All kind of bent over. He, like, had a Quasimodo hump in his back. He wore a black suit. And his eyes." She stopped and gazed at the rain pounding against the windshield

"What about his eyes?"

"It was like he only had eye sockets with two black orbs glinting way back under his protruding brow. I suppose he really did have eyes. But the restaurant booth was dark. My overall impression was an old face with two black holes in the skull and two gray floating orbs where the eyes should be."

"That sure sounds scary. But how did you end up the park? Did he abduct you from the restaurant?"

"Soon as he seated himself, I felt a wave of dizziness and became disoriented. At first, I didn't connect the way I felt with the stranger sitting across from me. He smiled and said that my mother could not rest in peace as long as I was in the house. He told me I must leave because it was not safe for me to be there. He shook his finger at me. 'I'm warning you,' he said. Then he said, 'My dear, you have a heart of gold, but you are foolish and impetuous. Do not sell the house before you think well on it.'"

"That is strange."

"Sure is. I asked him what the blazes he meant. Without answering, he got up and walked out. There was something vaguely familiar about him. Could not for the life of me figure out what. I decided to follow him. The rain had only just started to sprinkle. I took a taxi to the restaurant. Thought I could duck in somewhere and call a taxi to take me home. Anyhow, he walked for nearly twenty minutes until I lost him in the park, Craig Park. It was dark. The black sky. The failing light. The rain was coming in torrents by that time."

"Followed him, huh? Probably not a good decision."

"I know that now. But at the time, I was more curious than afraid. In the park, I remember a noise behind me, like a whine. For a moment, I thought it was a cat. You know how cats whine. They sometimes sound like a child crying."

I nodded.

She continued her story. "When I turned around, I saw him shuffling toward me."

"You saw the old man in the undertaker's suit."

"Yes."

"And he was whining?"

"He made that strange, whine-like crying sound. He reached out with both hands as if he was trying to grab me by the throat. I remember his eyes, those dark holes, and the orbs where his eyes should have been. I pushed his arms up like they taught me in the self-defense class. I kicked him in the crotch and stomped on his instep."

"Like they taught you in self-defense class."

She nodded. "I was scared right out of my wits. I ran and hid behind the band shell where you found me."

"He must have lost sight of you in the dark and all this rain."

"Probably," she said.

I slowed down to make the turn into her deceased mother's driveway. Margaret Wilst had been a fixture in Tarpon springs for years, a reclusive widow rumored to be fabulously wealthy.

She lived simply in the large house that stood behind a high wrought-iron fence lined with tall bougainvillea and oleanders. Turning into the open gate, I continued down the long, winding driveway to the house—near enough to the water that even in the failing light, I could make out the white caps. It was a tall Victorian-style structure, painted dull gray, with an ornate front door and slate tiles on the steeply slanting roof. Peeling paint, a missing windowpane in the cupola, and missing chunks of the gingerbread trim that framed the wraparound porch gave the place a sinister look.

A huge live oak with long tufts of Spanish moss hanging from nearly every limb grew in the front yard. One of its long limbs arched menacingly close to the house. On what was once a manicured lawn or perhaps a beautiful Victorian garden, only scattered stands of high weeds and grass with expanses of dirt remained.

"Please come in with me," she said.

"Got to be getting home myself," I replied. "Need to feed the cat and take in the loose stuff around the yard."

"Please. Just a few minutes. I'm afraid he might be in the house. Anyway, the least I can do is offer you a cup of coffee for rescuing me."

Although I hadn't had a date in months, and she was a beautiful young woman around my own age, my first reaction was to decline the invitation. She reached out a hand and placed it on my arm. She was trembling.

More words of invitation come tumbling out in rapid-fire delivery. "I really would like to show you I appreciate you rescuing me. Coffee only takes a moment to brew up. I have one of those new makers. Please!" Her voice wasn't sexy anymore but was coming from way down in her throat as if her vocal cords were tight. She wasn't merely afraid. She was terrified.

"OK, but only for a while. I really should be going."

She thanked me, opened the car door, and was out before I could get around to escort her. I gave up on trying to be chivalrous and followed her to the house. Penny fumbled with the ring of keys she had taken from her purse, trying one and then another in the lock.

Before she could find the right key, a tall, thin man opened the door. He faced us in the doorway dressed in a top hat and a formal shirt and waistcoat with black cargo shorts. He had flip-flops on his bare feet.

Penny stepped back. For a long moment, she stared at the apparition in the doorway. Regaining her composure, she said, "Who are you, and what are you doing in my mother's house?"

The man in the doorway stepped aside as he opened the door all the way. "Come out of the weather," he said and waved us in with a flutter of his hands as if shooing flies.

Penny charged past him and turned to face me. "At least stay until I can find out what is going on here. I'll fix us some coffee."

I brushed my elbow against my side to assure myself that the pistol I carried under my rain jacket was there if I needed it. With a last glance at the debris swirling about in the heightening gale, I stepped inside.

The man in the top hat closed the door behind us. "I have coffee made," he said in a matter of fact tone, delivered as if he might have been the butler awaiting our arrival.

"Who are you?" I asked, hoping that the same question coming from a man might elicit an answer.

"Mistress Penny summoned me," he said. "I am here at her request."

"I did no such thing. Tell us who you are and why you are in my mother's house, or leave right now."

"I am known as Tiny Timothy. I was your sainted mother, Margaret's, spiritual guide. I have a key. I am here to minister to her spiritual needs. I stay in the guest room."

"Penny scowled. What sort of clergyman dresses like that. You look like some nightmare juju man straight off the boat from Jamaica."

"Not from Jamaica. From Nigeria."

"Great! My mother never spoke of you."

"Margaret spoke of you–often. I promised her that if you ever called me, I would come."

"Called you? I never called you. How did I call you?"

"Your sainted mother is a telepathic as am I and as are you. When you were in the park, I heard you speaking to Margaret's spirit. You were asking for help. I am on the same telepathic frequency, the same telephone line, so to speak."

Penny scowled again and said, "That's nuts." Timothy shrugged.

She abruptly turned and headed for the back of the house. I followed. In the kitchen, Penny doffed her hat, slid off her dripping raincoat, and threw both on a kitchen chair. She poured us each a mug of coffee. "I suppose you drink it black," she said.

All I could do was smile, thinking that her telepathic powers were working fine.

When she took a seat at the old Formica top kitchen table, I joined her.

She had on jeans and a work shirt and looked very beautiful. Hoping to get her mind off the encounter with the man in the park, I said, "Tell me about your mother."

Penny sipped her coffee for a moment. She said, "Soon after we moved to Tarpon, my father died. I was in kindergarten. Mother sent me away to boarding school until I was ready for college. I was away at college and then went on to take my Master's studies in Washington—at Georgetown."

"You never saw Tiny Tim?"

She chuckled. "I was not here much, but I am not surprised at him being here, now that I know who he is. Margaret was a strange woman. Always interested in the occult, calling up spirits from the afterlife, predicting things to come. I found it unnerving, yet she was nearly always right in her predictions, and her knowledge of past events was broad and deep—personal things that she never experienced and had no way of knowing unless she communed with the dead."

"That certainly would unnerve me. Where did Timothy disappear to?"

She smiled and shrugged her shoulders. "I have no idea. I suppose he is still around here somewhere."

We both called out his name. He didn't respond. "We ought to look for him," Penny said.

I said, "Let's go together. I don't trust the guy."

We went around the house looking for him. We searched every room and opened every armoire. The only evidence of Timothy was a small valise on the guest room bed. Back in the kitchen, Penny refilled our coffee cups. We retired to the library to settle into the two overstuffed wing chairs in front of the fireplace.

"He seems to have gone," she said.

"If it's okay with you, I can ask my neighbor to feed the cat, check the yard. You're not very high here. Might have to get to higher ground if the water starts to rise. In this weather, you'll need some help to do that. I can stay if you want."

"Could you? Even if Timothy shows up later, I'm not so sure I want to be alone with him, especially on a night like this. Do we need to, like, do anything to protect the house from the hurricane?"

"We don't have to board up your windows. When we were looking for Timothy, I noticed that the place has new windows. They look pretty sturdy. The glazing strips are fake. The windows are all heavy frame, one pane, except I can't figure out why she didn't replace that broken one in the cupola."

"Margaret had the place upgraded a few years ago. That broken glass is on my to-do list for when I put the place up for sale."

"Good. I'll look around outside. Maybe there's pots or furniture that need to be put undercover."

I texted my neighbor that I wouldn't be home and retrieved my little flashlight from the car before circling the building looking for possible problems. The house was built on a rise at least four or five feet higher than the surrounding yard. The foundation added a good eighteen inches to the first-floor level.

The house might be high and dry, but if the yard flooded, my car would be ruined. The detached garage sat on the same little hill as the house. The door wasn't locked. I drove my car in and left it next to a new Mercedes AMG, all $100,000 of it. Be a crime if water got to that. I made a mental note to move both cars before the flooding got too bad.

A blood curdling scream from the house brought me charging up the porch steps and through the front door. I found Penny in the library, pointing at the open French doors. "He went out that way," she said, gasping to catch her breath.

I ran to the open door. The porch was empty. I poked my head under the mahogany desk that stood across from the fireplace. "Don't see anybody."

"It was the man who tried to choke me," Penny said. "I heard a commotion. I came in here to find out what was going on. I felt dizzy, disoriented. For an instant, I thought I was hallucinating. He was tossing books on the floor."

"Did your mother collect rare books?"

"He didn't seem to be interested in the books. He appeared to be taking the books out so he could pull and push on the wall. It was weird as if he was trying to find a lever to open a secret passage. I saw that in an old horror movie a couple of nights ago."

I tapped on the wall. It did sound hollow. Could there be a hidden room? I turned to face Penny. "Rumor has it that your mother was very rich. Maybe she had a hidden room for her money. Maybe she had a safe room?"

Penny shook her head. "I doubt it. No money in stocks or bonds that I know of. No sign of any bank savings or brokerage accounts, only one checking account with a modest balance at the branch in Tarpon Springs.

"Her accountant wrote to me that she lived frugally. If she wanted to give to some charity, she wrote a check on that account. He had no idea where the money came from. She never filed a tax return. She kept him on retainer even though she never used his services for much of anything. Once a month, he visited her for tea. She must have kept him on just to have someone come to the house to talk to her."

"I bet your guy in the black suit was looking for a secret hiding place. He might have been blackmailing her. With her dead, he needed to find out where she hid her money."

"No. He talked about me leaving my mother in peace. Maybe he is, like, a ghost or something."

"Explains why she summoned the juju man."

The thought of the old Victorian being haunted gave me chills. I checked again to make sure that my pistol lay close at hand. But what good was a gun against a ghost?

The wind had picked up. I closed the French doors and secured them top and bottom. One of the shutters banged on the clapboard. I made a mental note to secure it before the storm got much worse.

I asked, "Why does a ghost search for money or valuables? You can't spend money when you're dead."

"It has to be something really sinister. Like, if I sell the house, he won't have any place to haunt."

"Let's take a step back. Are you certain he was trying to choke you? Might he have been attempting to communicate something to you?"

"What are you trying to say?"

"Think back. Did he say anything?"

Penny pulled at her chin and knotted her brows. "He may have been mumbling, 'You whore, you.'"

"Could he have been gesturing as if he was holding something? Could he have been saying, "You. For you?"

"I suppose." Penny wrapped her arms around her and rubbed her shoulders. "It's cooling off. Can you make a fire—or two or three? We sure have enough fireplaces in this old Victorian, one in every room, even the bedrooms."

Using the dry firewood that had been stacked neatly on the raised library hearth, I soon had a crackling fire burning in the old Rumford firebox. While not really being cold, I had to admit that the fire felt good. The shallow design was letting the fire quickly radiate into the room. I untucked my shirt to hide my pistol and took off my jacket.

Penny said, "I hope that's not all you're going to take off."

"The fire will really heat up the room. I was already roasting in that raincoat."

Penny laughed. "Only joking. Get as comfortable as you want. Looks like a long night. Nobody will get much sleep."

"You know, Penny, I believe you have this ghost guy all wrong. I think he's trying to tell you something. Let's take a few more books off the shelves. Look for a lever or something that might be a handle."

"You mean that maybe something is hidden in this house, something valuable?"

"Exactly. What was the last time you saw your father?"

"I was about seven years old."

"Do you recall anything about him?"

"Not much. My mother never showed me a picture of him. Said memories hurt too much. She did say that he had a heart of gold, that he would give anybody the shirt off his back."

"Was he tall, short?"

"I remember him as being stout. I was a little girl. He was always leaning over to talk to me."

"Did he wear black suits?"

In an obvious moment of inspired thought, Penny shouted, "Mother summoned Father's ghost! Let's find that lever." She reached out, and we exchanged high fives.

A few minutes later, we discovered that the entire bookcase moved on hinges to reveal a passageway between walls. The big old house hid a warren of passages. From the back, the entry doors were obvious. Stairs led to the second floor. Every room had a hidden entrance.

At one end, a ladder led up toward the attic. My flashlight was dimming. We decided to leave further searching until the storm blew over.

I helped Penny stack the scattered books in neat piles on the desk. She joined me on one of the Wingback Chairs, sipping coffee and listening to the wind and the rain.

Penny turned on the TV above the fireplace mantel. We watched the Weather Channel. The announcer was saying that Tarpon Springs had run out of luck. Saint Nicholas, protector of the town from storms since the big Cathedral had been erected downtown in his honor, had abandoned us. Ninety miles an hour, gusts were pounding the town. Sustained wind at that speed produced a category one hurricane.

Our inspection of the space between the walls had not revealed any hidden treasure. Yet, I was certain that somewhere in that house, a fortune was stashed. Every few minutes, I rose and walked to the fireplace. Each time, I stoked the fire or put on another log. I found the fire-tending routine comforting as well as warming. On one such foray, I looked up from the fire to see Timothy standing near the doorway. The lights blinked off for a few seconds and then came back on.

"Timothy," Penny said. "We totally looked all over for you. Next time you go out, please let me know, so I don't worry. Where have you been?"

"I went to see how the water is holding. The boat was swinging wild on the davits. I drove it to the little cove and beached it. Pulled it to high ground and secured it to a sapling. On my walk back here, I saw a big limb across the road. We are trapped here until the storm is over, and the tree can be removed."

"Timothy, did you ever see a photograph of my father?"

He shook his head. "When Margaret was alive, we never discussed personal matters. We only spoke of spiritual things: healing and redemption. Since her spirit passed to the new realm she has expressed to me concern for your wellbeing. She wants you to be financially independent."

"She never spoke of my father?"

"Oh, yes. She often told me that he was a wonderful man that he had a heart of gold. She said that you inherited his heart of gold. She loved you both very much."

"She used to tell me that also."

"Such a tribute. Perhaps that is your true inheritance."

To me, the reference to finances seemed out of place. Finances didn't seem like what a dead woman talks about to her spiritual advisor. I decided to press the point. "Penny's mom left her with nothing but this house. Did Margaret discuss exactly how her daughter might be made financially independent? The house is worth something, but not near enough to make her independently wealthy."

"Right after her spirit passed to the new realm, I did search the house. Searched it top to bottom, even the little cellar beneath the kitchen. I found no money or jewelry save for the pieces that are still in the jewel box in her bedroom."

"Did you search the hidden passages?"

Timothy started to say something and stopped. He seemed confused. He looked from me to Penny and back to me. He said, "I know of no such passages."

"Did my mother have a boyfriend, a little fat man that dressed in black?"

"There, indeed, was such an individual. But he was her accountant. They had tea each Wednesday in the library. She called him, Penn. A disagreeable sycophant at best. She did most of the talking. All he ever did was mumble. 'Yes. Yes. I see. Yes. Yes.' Sometimes she handed him a small package. Sometimes he handed her a wad of cash."

The lights blinked off. The flames dancing in the fireplace cast eerie shadows, a larger than life shadow of Timothy and then another shadow, shorter and stouter. The lights came on again. Penny shrieked. "He has a gun."

The short, stout man in the black suit holding the 40 caliber automatic said, "Sit down–all three of you. Don't make me use this." He waved the gun. "I will if I have to. Now sit!"

Penny sat on the couch. Timothy and I ignored the command. "What do you want from us?" I asked the man with the gun.

"I want to know where Margaret hid her gold."

"We do too," I replied.

"Don't play dumb. Every room has an intercom. I've been listening from the attic. I can listen in to everything that's said in the whole house."

Timothy said, "If you have been listening, you know that what the Master said is true." To my surprise, the two of them began a back and forth discussion of possible hiding places for Margaret's gold. I got the impression that they had discussed the matter.

The lights blinked off. I lunged at the short man. Before I knocked the gun from his hand, he got off one shot that missed me but hit Timothy. The gun dropped to the floor. I was on the floor too. Timothy picked it up and fired again and again into the intruder. Seeing the number of holes in the man's chest and head, I didn't even check to see if he was dead.

I immediately tried to phone the police, but my cell wasn't connecting. Penny's phone had the same problem. Timothy said he didn't use cell phones, calling them the work of the bad spirits. He must have relied on telepathy. The house had no landline.

Timothy shoved the little man's Smith & Wesson into his pant pocket. "That man was a very bad person," he said. "We must be certain that the spirit arising from his dead body does not contaminate us all." He reached under his shirt and pulled out a small bag that hung on a leather thong around his neck. He opened it and sprinkled some of the contents onto the dead man. He began a slow chant in a language that I didn't understand. The howling wind and the patter of rain on the tin roof of the garage lent a haunting background to the chant. Despite the warmth of the room, I felt goosebumps rise on my arms.

Bent at the waist and with head lowered, Timothy straddled the body, all the while continuing the chant, repeating the same sounds over and over, and sprinkling dust from the little bag.

He stopped, straightened. "It is done," he declared and shoved the bag back under his shirt. "The spirit can no longer harm us. The evil has been purged from this man. He is now good."

"Good and dead," Penny said.

Timothy wrestled the pistol from his pocket and aimed it at Penny. "Now it is time for one of you to tell me about dear Mistress Margaret's gold or whatever she had. We know she was rich. Penn knew she never used banks because she gave him gold bars to cash when she needed money. We know she hid it somewhere in this very house. Neither of us was successful in getting the information out of her. In the end, the poor tormented soul died rather than tell us."

Penny shouted, "You killed my mother? You bastard. I suppose that creep on the floor you killed, so you don't have to share with him."

Penny was cut off by a heavy branch from the old oak that came crashing through the front window, knocking Timothy to the floor. An instant later, the room was plunged into darkness.

I took hold of Penny's arm and propelled her toward the bookshelves. I pulled the way I had done earlier. In a second we were through the portal and had it closed behind us. We heard nothing from Timothy.

I said, "We need to get away from here. He might figure out how we disappeared and decide to shoot through the wall."

The two of us scurried to the narrow stairs and ran up to the second floor. I said, "Might as well finish our search. That ladder must lead to the attic." I went first. At the top of the ladder I pushed up on the ceiling and was surprised to find myself in the cupola with the broken window. "Come on up, Penny. The view is great."

Penny joined me in the small space. Broken glass crunched underfoot. Wind and rain blew in through the broken pane. Penny pointed. "Look. There's Timothy, heading for the garage. If I had a gun, I would shoot him dead."

"He won't go far in the car," I said. "Seems he forgot the downed tree he told us about. And look at his leg. He's bleeding badly. I think Penn hit the femoral artery. If I'm right, Timothy's done."

We watched an unsteady Timothy limp to the garage and swing open the door. A few minutes later, the Mercedes pulled out and sped toward the street. It crashed into the wrought iron fence.

Penny pointed again. "Over there by the old oak. A man is looking up and waving to us."

"He looks like your description of the man at the restaurant."

"I am sure it is him, and the same person I saw in the library tossing the books."

The storm blew a large branch back and forth in front of the figure. Suddenly he wasn't there anymore. I wondered if he had existed only in our overactive imagination.

Stairs led down from the cupola into an attic space. With my flashlight, I guided us through the attic to another set of stairs. Penny said, "This is amazing. I haven't been here. It was another thing on my to-do list, to figure out how I get up here."

A small trunk blocked the stairs. With my foot, I slid it aside.

"Let's take it down with us," Penny said, "The power is out, and the cell phones are not working. We are going to need something to take our mind off this storm."

I nodded and grabbed the little trunk in one hand as we navigated the stairs. As I suspected, the door opened easily from the attic side. We found ourselves in a closet with rows and rows of old clothing hanging on racks. During our search for Timothy, neither of us had seen the attic door. The closet served the master bedroom.

I handed Penny the flashlight. "Pretty sure I know where your mother hid her gold."

Penny let out a very unladylike, "No shit!"

"Yes. The clue was your mother's reference to your father's heart of gold. When I heard you say it, it sounded to me like you were saying, 'hearth of gold' I expect we will find it in one or more of these fireplace hearths—a fortune in gold."

I set the trunk aside, knelt and studied the raised hearth in the master bedroom. "Hold the light closer, Penny. That's right, shine it on the space under the overhanging bricks."

It took me only a moment to find the latch and slide the top of the hearth aside. As I had suspected, it was filled with gold bars.

"You have a fortune here, and we most likely will find money and more gold under the other hearths. You are a very rich young woman, Penny. I'll let you decide what to tell the taxman. In the meantime, I can help you sort this whole thing out and get your gold safely stored in a more appropriate place."

Penny hugged me and kissed me until I had to push her away. She repeated over and over, "Thank you. Thank you."

I found Timothy dead behind the wheel of the Mercedes and decided to leave him there for the police. I hauled Penn into the guest bathroom. I knew I shouldn't disturb a crime scene. But I had no idea when we might be making contact with the police. He died right in the doorway, and I had no intention of stepping over him every time we walked in or out of the library.

Fortified by coffee mugs filled with a lot of gin and a little bit of vermouth, Penny and I watched the Weather Channel describe how the storm had made an abrupt turn to the north and spared Tarpon Springs the worst winds. Saint Nicholas had again saved the town.

We opened the little chest. It was filled with family pictures of Margaret; and of Penny as a young child; and of a short, stout man with deep-set eyes and a Quasimodo-like hump on his back.

A New Reality

The mood was somber. The eclectic mix of souls that stood, sat, and paced about the small anteroom appeared to me to be zombie-like with their pasty faces and hunched shoulders. The wall calendar was turned to December 1990, nearly a year earlier, about the time our family realized it had a serious problem.

The warm room should have felt cozy considering the season, but the low recessed lighting in the ceiling barely penetrated the smoky haze and made the place feel spooky and uninviting.

The absence of chairs and occasional pieces and the people sitting on the floor enhanced my feeling of being superior to these unfortunates. How did people have so little self-respect? I have nothing in common with these folks.

Before moving to the low table festooned with half-empty donut boxes and a large coffee Thermos, I turned my head toward the open door behind me. A breath, deep and desperate, fed my lungs with the clear night air. Once the door closed, my breath became shallow in my hope that the second hand smoke would somehow spend itself on my donors and would not blacken and clog the narrow filaments upon which my life depended.

Fortified with a full Styrofoam cup of black coffee and a selection from one of the donut boxes, I felt less out of place. At least it was something to do with my hands. I have a pretty good sense of myself, and usually, when walking into a roomful of people, I have a sense of belonging.

Being with folks who seem like me—PLMs—is comforting. Sometimes it's their clothes. Sometimes it's their age or the way they move about or their speech, maybe their choice of words or subject matter in conversation.

In this room, I was isolated from those who milled about me. No one had taken any note of me. A smile, no matter how fleeting or insincere, would have helped. In such a densely packed room, in the ordinary course, someone would have nudged me or brushed against me. Here there seemed to be an invisible shield around my person, like a force-field repelling anyone that might venture too near.

With my full cup and my donut, I sidled to a vacant spot along the wall and took a sip of the coffee. It was hot and felt good going down. The donut was fresh and sweet.

A woman about my age stood next to me. Her long face was sallow and drawn, her hair well-coiffed, her clothes expensive looking—the kind of outfit I might have seen at Nordstrom's. She had her own cup of coffee, which she sipped as she looked at me over the top of her steel-rimmed glasses. When I caught her eye, she broke the force field with a smile and said, "Hi. Cold, huh?"

For an instant, I thought she was referring to the people around us and was about to give her a social commentary on rudeness. Then, realizing that she was talking about the weather, I nodded and replied, "Sure is."

The use of the word "cold" was an understatement. As soon as the sun set, the thermometer had dropped into the teens. The snow crunched underfoot, and the wind out of the Northeast had a particularly annoying way of making the air seem a lot colder. I wondered if my car would start when the meeting was over. I'd had a devil of a time starting it earlier in the day.

The woman continued in her effort to make conversation. "Haven't seen you here. You with someone?" I nodded. "Me too," she said with more life than I had expected. "Son's havin' all sorts of trouble. Been at my wit's end for the past year. He went out for baseball. I thought everything was goin' to be all right. Thank God for these programs."

"How 'bout you?"

"Well, I don't think I'm at my wit's end. At least not yet."

She chuckled. A man in his shirtsleeves moved close to her and spoke to her—said something in German I didn't catch, diverting her attention from me.

I took the opportunity to break off the conversation and look about me. More people had entered. The smoke appeared to be thicker. Too bad there wasn't some way I could hold my breath until the whole thing was over.

I unzipped my parka against the warmth of the room. A few minutes before, I was freezing and now felt sweat on my neck and under my arms. With the back of the donut hand, I wiped my brow and felt the moisture that had accumulated there in tiny beads. The last piece of the donut got stuffed into my mouth and washed down with the rest of the coffee.

The crowd had representatives from all age groups—an elderly lady with snow-white hair to a youth who couldn't have been more than a teenager. The majority of the people in the room were younger on average. One of the men had a thick beard. A young woman sporting purple hair talked to a man who also had purple hair. She slowly waved her donut as if she was conducting an orchestra of bakers playing a dirge. The uniform of the day was blue denim of various designs, bulky jackets, and heavy shoes and boots.

No one else seemed to be affected by the heat in the crowded space. The heavy jackets were mostly still zipped, some still all the way up to the throat.

I glanced at my watch. The meeting was scheduled to start in five minutes. Karen hadn't arrived yet. She was usually late to things; though I had expected her to be on time for the first meeting we would be attending together. The gaunt woman walked up to me and laid a hand on my arm. "Don't worry yourself," she said. "He'll be here."

Her presumed familiarity annoyed me. I wasn't there for her or her son or anyone of the others.

"I'm waiting for my daughter," I replied, keeping my eyes on the outside door.

"My son's not coming," she said, ignoring my response. "The director just told me a few minutes ago. Wants me to stay for the meeting anyhow. Says it's as much for the co-dependent as for the addict."

I turned to her. "I wouldn't know." She stood inches from me, staring into my face, looking for something that wasn't there. Her large, blue eyes were moist with the tears welling along the lower lids. Though her coffee was gone, she still gripped her Styrofoam cup. She kneaded it with her fingers, picked at the rim, and dropped the little pieces into the empty cup.

"Mind if I sit next to you?" she said.

My only reply was a shrug of the shoulders. "Thank you," she said in response to the shoulder shrug as if it meant that I had agreed.

"I think they want me to sit next to my daughter," I said. "You know how that is."

"Probably. I'll sit on the other side. My name's Bunny, by the way."

"Hi, Dad," a familiar voice said, as it had so many times. I'd been so absorbed with the Bunny woman that I had failed to notice Karen's arrival.

With a parting smile to Bunny, I moved with Karen toward the door that had opened at the far end of the room. The man with his shirt-sleeves rolled up was calling for everyone in the anteroom to lose their cigarettes and coffee and come into the meeting. He spoke with an accent that I couldn't place. I supposed it was eastern European, though I don't know much about languages. I knew that it wasn't Spanish or German. I'd studied both of these, though far from proficient in either. He greeted Karen by name and told us to take a seat anywhere.

About twenty metal folding chairs had been arranged in two rows in a large semicircle with one lone chair at the open end, which I assumed was for whoever would be running the meeting.

"Is there some special place you want to sit?" I asked Karen. She shook her head. I sat in the end chair near the door. Karen sat next to me. Bunny was on her own.

The large meeting room, ice-cold and brightly lighted, was a refreshing change. The windows were all cracked open. The bearded man was in the process of cranking them closed.

My attention turned to the people from the foyer filing into the meeting room. The zombies had been replaced by a rather lively group. The man and woman with the purple hair, to my surprise, sat apart with an older man—distinguished, in shirt and tie and pin-striped suit—between them. I had assumed that one of the young people was the co-dependent, but it seemed maybe that they both were addicts, perhaps sharing a family member.

The man with the beard finished closing the windows and took the chair farthest from ours. Next to Karen sat an unshaven and overweight young man wearing a pair of jeans with both knees worn through. The man seemed to be missing a co-dependent. He exchanged pleasantries with Karen and bent over and gave her a hug–a far more intimate hug than I would have liked to see. I took an immediate dislike to him.

Bunny was one of the last people to enter. She took the lone chair from the front and slid it next to mine.

"Who's your friend?" Karen whispered. I shook my head. "Looks like she's just off a pretty big howl." I laughed, and Karen seemed satisfied that I agreed with her evaluation of Bunny. No one appeared to notice our little exchange–nobody but Bunny. Bunny leaned forward and looked across me at Karen. "I'm here fer my son, Jack," she said. "You know Jack from the college." I could tell by the instant look of horror on Karen's face that she indeed knew Jack. Karen nodded and made a kind of half smile, half frown. She immediately turned her attention to the leader who had found a chair to replace the one Bunny had swiped and was calling for everyone to quiet down, so the meeting could begin.

One-by-one, the attendees stood and introduced themselves. Then it was Karen's turn. "Hi, my name is Karen, and I'm an alcoholic." She sat down. When I didn't rise, she turned and stared daggers at me. With more reluctance than I ever could recall in anything I ever did, I stood to introduce myself to the group of strangers. I said, "Hello, everybody. My name is Jerry, and I'm a, and I'm a co-dependent."

The Artist In The Square

~—~

We sometimes idealize a person upon seeing them from a distance without knowing anything about them. It is what some say is love at first sight. Sometimes the person becomes an obsession. Yet we dare not make contact or perhaps cannot do so. So it is with the artist in the square and her admirer.

Through many days
He watched,
Always from afar,
The artist drawing
In the square.

To speak her name
He would not dare
Nor wish her well
In evening cool
While she gathered
Charcoal sticks
And shouldered the strap
Of her canvas stool.

One sunny day
She did not come
To deftly move

Her charcoal sticks,
To create art
He could admire.

He mingled in the square
And sought in vain
The woman he had come
To love.

He inquired of the strollers
Where the artist
Might be found.

Met by shrugs or
Vacant stares
He went to
Other city squares.
But artists there
He did not love.

Clarence, Hans And Der Teufel

Clarence came to know the Jolicky dragon by a series of rather different circumstances. The first such occurred when Mr. Bachman decided to keep his new breeding bull, a monster of an animal with long, sharp horns, in the meadow next to Clarence's house.

Mr. Bachman bought the bull one fall day, right before Clarence's school started for the fall semester. Mr. Bachman told Clarence that the animal, named, Der Teufel, which means, devil, could be dangerous and that he ought not to go wandering in the creature's pasture. "Der Teufel *speight feuer*," he said. Clarence thought that a silly thing to say because only dragons spit fire.

The second circumstance occurred when Clarence decided to skip the school bus, so he and his friend Punky could walk home and catch up on what had happened during the summer. Punky spent the summer at his grandfather's house in Florida and had many stories of his exciting vacation.

He and Punky walked as far as Punky's house. Punky's house sat on the other side of the pasture where Der Teufel lived. Clarence and Punky drank sodas and played catch. They talked about a new girl in class who Clarence thought had nice legs and Punky thought had a pretty face.

At dusk, when Clarence was due home for dinner, he took his usual shortcut home from Punky's through the pasture where Der Teufel roamed. However, the reaction of the animal, which before had only glanced in his direction, was different. The bull appeared to be agitated at the intrusion.

Clarence knew that if he ran, the bull would chase him. He quickened his step moving toward the nearest fence line, all the while keeping an eye on the bull. Der Teufel pawed the ground, threw its large head from side to side, and snorted.

Clarence reached the fence and slipped through the rails He glanced about looking for something that might have been disturbing the beast. Seeing nothing, he went on his way.

That night the third circumstance occurred. Clarence dreamed of a monster with great large teeth and long horns, horns way longer than those that sat atop the head of Der Teufel. The creature, a dragon the likes of which Clarence had never seen even in books, breathed fire a couple of times before he spoke, not a lot of fire, not enough to singe Clarence's hair, for example, but probably enough to cook an omelet. Anyhow it was only a dream, and dragons don't breathe hot fire in dreams.

The dragon told Clarence that he lived in a cave on Mr. Bachman's property, way up on the mountain where the snow first falls and last thaws. The dragon told Clarence that he was a Jolicky dragon and that his name was Hans. He had flown from his home in Germany and was attracted to the farm because he had known Mr. Bachman's half-brother, Odo, back in Germany. He was the only dragon in all of Europe and was very lonely.

Hans had hoped to find others of his kind in America because he had heard from Odo that his brother in America kept a fire-breathing animal.

Thinking that such an animal must be a sort of dragon, Hans decided to emigrate. The flight over the ocean had been exhausting.

After much searching and many wrong turns, he reached the Bachman farm. Hans looked immediately for Der Teufel. It happened that Mr. Bachman had taken the animal out of the pasture to show him at the county fair.

"Each day for a week," he said to Clarence, "I came down into the pasture from the cave on the mountain looking for Der Teufel."

"He probably smelled you. That's probably why he was agitated today."

"That is possible. I tried to inquire of Mrs. Bachman about the other dragon that spits fire. Upon seeing me, she chased me up the mountain, even firing her shotgun at me. From that time on, I dared not venture far from the cave. Mrs. Bachmann is one terrible sight when she is angry."

On the verge of starvation after two weeks living in the cave and not having found Der Teufel or any other dragons, Hans felt alone and desperate. To make matters worse, the weather had been cold and rainy—not one day without rain. European weather was no better, but everything in America seemed to Hans to be troubling. Most likely, that was due to his weakened physical condition and to his emotional desperation.

Normally, he told Clarence, he could outrun a human or simply fly away. The trip and lack of food had kept him so weary that he barely outran the overweight and out of shape Mrs. Bachman, who spent most of her time in the kitchen cooking for an equally overweight Mr. Bachman.

The dragon was reluctant to eat any of Mr. Bachman's animals for fear of offending one that might be a friend of the fire breathing bull. Odo had told him that in America, it was frowned upon for a dragon to eat a human. He had become friends with several humans and considered Odo a particularly good friend. In any event, the one time he had eaten a human—by mistake—he had found the taste bitter and the meat tough. Hans simply stayed in the cave, getting weaker and weaker.

"I spied you walking with your friend. I decided to visit you in a dream."

"Me? Why not, Punky?"

"Good question. Well. You see. Your friend is too tasty a morsel for a starving dragon, tough or not. You, on the other hand, are skinny and have little meat hanging on your thin bones."

In the dream, Hans asked Clarence to find Der Teufel and tell him that Clarence was looking for him. Clarence advised Hans that humans can't talk to breeding bulls the way they can talk to dragons.

Clarence thought the request to be rather curious. He had seen the animal as late as that very day on his way home from school. Hans neglected to tell Clarence that he had shut himself in the cave and had not come down off the mountain looking for the dragon for several days.

Clarence, nevertheless, agreed to try and find out why Hans had not found the bull.

Hans thanked Clarence for visiting with him in the dream and asked Clarence if he might come by and visit sometime again. Clarence readily agreed.

As far as Clarence was concerned, a deal is a deal. No matter that it is made in a dream, which ought to make it rescindable. And no matter that he was sure he would find the bull standing in plain sight in the middle of the pasture.

The next day after school, instead of playing with his friend, Clarence took the school bus to his house and immediately strode off toward Mr. Bachman's pasture. He was determined to face Der Teufel and somehow communicate to him that a dragon wished to make his acquaintance.

Clarence checked behind every tree in the pasture for the bull. At first, he thought the field empty. When he got to the top of the hill that rose behind his own house, he spotted something in the tall grass. A green dragon lay crumpled on the ground, his long spiked tail still, and his eyes barely open. He knew immediately it must be his new dragon friend.

Clarence had never seen a live dragon up close. He expected the dragon to be bigger. Hans measured a mere eight feet from the top of his head to tip of his tail.

Clarence asked, "What's the matter?"

The dragon opened his eyes and looked up at Clarence. He groaned and belched a great long belch. No fire came out, only a fetid odor that caused Hans to choke.

"Oh. It's you, Clarence. Hello. I don't feel so good."

"Where is Der Teufel."

"And who might that be?"

"Mr. Bachman's prize breeding bull, the one you asked me to search-for."

A strange look crossed Hans' face. The dragon version of a sheepish grin appeared at the corners of his mouth.

Clarence stomped his foot. "You ate Der Teufel, and you got indigestion. Serves you right. Being hungry is one matter, but eating Der Teufel is quite another matter. You probably hiccupped and drew in some of that fire you spit. I'll bet you did just that. Didn't you?"

The dragon raised his head just enough to nod once, slowly, in a great up and down dragon nod before it dropped into the grass and lay still, breathing deeply. "Clarence, you need to learn to look at the bright side of things. The glass of life is half full, not half empty. I gathered all of my strength for one last trip to the pasture to look for the fire breathing, prize bull. The good news is that I found him."

"Well, the bad news is that you ate him. We can't let Mr. Bachmann know you ate his prized breeding bull. He paid a lot of money for the animal and was depending on him to keep his farm going. Without the money from breeding the bull, his family will starve."

"Perhaps there is some way I can pay him for the loss. Certainly, I don't want him or his family to starve."

"You should be sorry. You have been very bad, and after I was so nice to you in the dream."

"I am sorry, so sorry, so very sorry. I didn't know. He charged at me. I had to roast him in self-defense. I figured that since he was already cooked, I might as well go ahead and eat him. I told you I was hungry."

"I never knew dragons cooked their food."

"Oh, yes. We never eat anything raw. Why do you think we breathe fire?"

"I never really gave that much thought. I suppose I figured you spit fire because you needed that to defend yourself.

"You should have eaten one of the heifers or one of the milk cows. That would not have been as bad."

"Sorry."

"You have to get out of here now."

Hans rose to his four legs. He took a few wobbly steps and collapsed.

"What's the matter?"

"Beasts like me need to sleep after they eat. You see, we don't eat very often. When we do eat, we gorge ourselves. We have to sleep for a couple of days while the meal digests." Hans spit out part of a long sharp horn that Clarence recognized as belonging to the late Der Teufel.

He said, "We need to disguise you. I will place tree brush upon you to hide you during your sleep. I need a long-range plan for your safety. Wait here."

"I don't have much choice but to wait. I will lie here very still until

I fall fast asleep." Hans could barely get the words out before he was snoring.

Clarence had no idea if Mr. Bachman might come looking for Der Teufel. He was desperate to talk to someone about the dragon and his problem. His parents did not believe in dragons and would have made fun of his story. He decided Punky could help. He ran to Punky's house and told him all about the dragon and the untimely demise of the prized bull. Punky always got better grades in school than Clarence did, so he relied on his friend for advice when a problem had him stumped.

Punky thought on the matter a while. He said, "We cannot get a new bull for Mr. Bachman. Much too expensive. He is bound to eventually find the dragon and put the two items together. He will conclude that the dragon ate his bull. He will be angry. His wife will be angry too and shoot the dragon dead."

"What are we to do, Punk?"

"I'm thinking."

After a very long time pondering the problem, Punky smiled and said, "The solution is clear. The money that Mr. Bachman got for stud fees must be made up in some way by the hungry dragon. What can dragons do to make money?"

Clarence said, "Punky, you are the cleverest. That is exactly what Hans said."

Punky continued, "I have just the thing. The Bachmans are getting old. Very soon, they will not be able to care for themselves. They will need help. Hans is all alone. There are no other dragons hereabouts. For his own food, he can catch mice and rats and all sorts of creatures that invade a farm, such as wolves and foxes. By eating the right diet, he can earn his keep and keep his belly full at the same time. So simple."

Clarence nodded. "He will need to learn to eat more regularly. No more stuffing himself full and then sleeping off the big meal."

The next day after school, Clarence went to check on Hans. He still lay sleeping under the limbs and leaves that Clarence had placed over him. He slept for three more days. Mr. Bachmann had been scouring the countryside looking for his prize bull, so he had not come into the pasture where the satisfied dragon slept. On his way to school the fourth day, Clarence checked on Hans and found him just rising from his lengthy post-dinner nap.

Clarence did not give the dragon a chance to say a word. “Hans,” he said, “My friend, Punky and I have a solution to your problem. Henceforth you will help the Bachmans. They will allow you to live in the cave. Mrs. Bachmann will not shoot you.”

Hans tried to speak, but Clarence continued. “You will cook for them every day. You will eat any pests—no people, of course—that you find about their farm. There are many odd jobs you can do as well, like cutting down trees and planting seeds and herding the cows and heifers. For a suitable fee, which you will share with the Bachmans, you can help the other farmers as well. For Christmas, they might even give you a cow or a pig to eat if you have been good all year.”

Hans nodded. “It seems to me that from what I saw of his wife, the family eats a lot of food. I can certainly cook for them. That will save them the cost of firewood for the cook stove. With my sharp tail, I can chop carrots and potatoes and all sorts of things. I can fly around on all kinds of errands—save lots of time. Yes, Clarence. That will be a very satisfactory arrangement.”

Clarence and Punky told Mr. and Mrs. Bachman what had happened to their prized bull. The Bachmans were very upset. When they eventually calmed down, the boys laid out their plan for Hans to make up for depriving the couple of a major source of income. Reluctantly, they agreed. What else could they do? Once they met Hans, they felt much better about the arrangement. Over time they grew fond of the dragon who was very helpful and always very courteous. So, Hans found a new home and new friends and lived happily ever after.

About the Author

~—~

Robert J. Dockery is an engineer and attorney who graduated from Georgetown Law School and practiced business and patent law for many years in the Greater New York-New Jersey area before retiring to Florida where he now lives with his wife, Sheila.

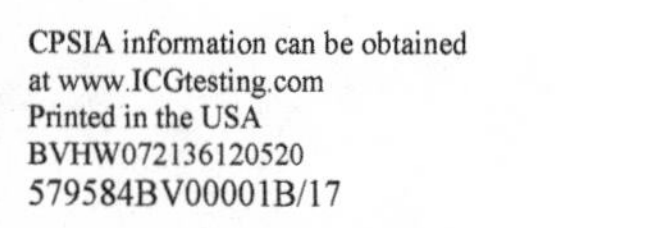

CPSIA information can be obtained
at www.ICGtesting.com
Printed in the USA
BVHW072136120520
579584BV00001B/17